**HE WAS THE WRONG MAN IN THE
WRONG PLACE. AND SHE COULDN'T
RESIST HIM . . .**

"We got nothing to talk about, Mrs. Alexander,
except maybe you've got change coming on your
fifty dollars. Tell me, just how much do you ladies
of refinement and breeding charge for an evening's
diversion?"

Bree gasped and stumbled as though he had hit her.
The gold piece dropped out of her hand and into
the dust. She turned to leave, but Jemson grabbed
her arm and yanked her brutally toward him. His
head lowered and his breath was harsh and warm
against her ear.

"On second thought," he whispered wrathfully, "I'm
not being paid half enough for all the slaving and
mooning around I did. I want more."

His free arm shot out and closed around Bree's
waist, even as his mouth came down on her
searching, demanding . . .

Also by Susanna Howe
from Jove

FEVER MOON

SNOW FLAME

SUSANNA HOWE

A JOVE BOOK

Requests for permission to make copies of any part
of the work should be mailed to: Permissions,
Jove Publications, Inc.: 200 Madison Avenue,
New York, NY 10016

First Jove edition published September 1981

First printing

Printed in the United States of America

Jove books are published by Jove Publications, Inc.,
200 Madison Avenue, New York, NY 10016

This book is dedicated to
Ellin, Connie W., and, in
loving memory, Bruce C.
Massey. And, as always,
to H. H.

PROLOGUE

Georgia
November 1864

Twenty miles to the east of Crosshaven plantation, in the early morning hours, the city of Atlanta sparked and exploded, spewing flame and ash into a chilling wind that licked and fanned its destruction. The fire spread quickly, its ravenous appetite devouring everything in its path. Railroads, mills, and factories went up; Five Points burned, the center of commerce where the city's five main avenues joined. The brick structure of City Hall scorched and baked its insides like biscuits in an oven. Carefully tended homes in the garden district and the lush plantations that bordered what had once been the supply depot for the Confederate army felt the flame's greedy embrace. Late-blooming gardens, the pride of every Southern gentlewoman, withered and died in the intense heat. Hickory, birch, and oak trees were laid bare, stripped of their bark and left smoldering. Nothing was spared of the city. All of Atlanta lay victim to the Union General Sherman's fierce, blazing march to Savannah and the sea.

In the twilight hours, a hazy orange skyline glowed for a hundred miles, visible to anyone who still had the stomach to watch what signified the end of the South, its economy and way of life. Most of those who had fled the burning city for the safety of their friends' and family's homes chose not to view the reality of what had happened to them and their property.

Bree Alexander stood on the third-floor veranda outside her room at Crosshaven and watched the annihilation with dry, resigned eyes. She supposed she should be crying, following the example of her mother, who sat locked away in her room howling and rocking herself in terror and despair. But only twice in her life had Bree allowed herself the weakness of tears, and now it didn't seem to be the time or place for unleashing that particular demon. Even as a child, she withheld her tears during a whipping or when she didn't receive what she felt was her due. Bree's father, a man of indomitable power and opinion, had named her aptly—Bryna, for strength. Even though her mammy, Lucinda, had quickly shortened Bryna to Bree and everyone had taken to using the nickname, it didn't change a lifetime of lessons she had learned from her father.

A fat lot of good Mama's river of tears is doin' us now, Bree thought angrily. She should be preparing for what was to come instead of cowering and moaning across the hall in her bedroom. Her penchant for tears and fainting— that bag of feminine tricks designed to cover up mistakes or finagle from a man what he won't freely give—wasn't going to save them at Crosshaven.

Still, a small part of Bree's heart, something that lay silently buried away, demanded she feel a glimmer of emotion at the panoramic scene of disaster that stretched out before her. Brief flashes of memory coursed through her brain. The Soldiers Relief Society, where she met with other wives and daughters during the first days of the war to sew underclothes and coats for the men. The lead pipes they had collected to make the bullets the Confederacy would use to repel the enemy. The day she helped Sharon E'Bacher hide ammunition in the basement corners of Sharon's townhouse. That was surely one of the explosions that had erupted from the bowels of the dying city. And the three days she had gone without sleep in a musty, stale room at the Atlanta Medical College, holding Neal Petrie's body in her arms and feeling the life slip away from him a little at a time. Was he really the same gentle man she had promised to marry the night before he'd gone

4

cheerfully off to war shouting his assurances that it would all be over in a matter of weeks?

Not even that memory brought scalding tears to Bree's face. It was all part of the past now, burned and charred like the ruins of Atlanta. Everything she loved or cared about was a part of some vague, scarcely remembered yesterday. Once, the South and its people were what she naively considered to be her future. Now Bree accepted the absence of any future, the futility of dreaming, needing, and wanting.

The past four years, she realized dully, had never been in her control. Another force, more powerful and unyielding than she was able to comprehend, drove her mercilessly toward a destiny she had not chosen for herself. She could fight it, deny it, and turn away from it, but still it pursued her like an unrelenting phantom. Why else would she have felt compelled to travel blindly across the country, Georgia to Colorado and back again, only to find what had been lost and then to lose it again?

Riddles! Her whole life was turning into an enormous joke and she had yet to find the key and solve the riddle.

Bree turned away from the veranda and started for her room, feeling herself losing control and cursing her frailty. She raised her fists to her mouth, suppressing the silent scream of hopelessness that rose in her throat, the despair that always accompanied the memory of the joy and pain she had learned to feel, the intense peaks and valleys of emotion.

No! Bree's mind commanded, not now! Don't think about it! She crossed the room to the four-poster that had been her bed since childhood and ran her fingers absently over its silky coverlet. Suddenly, resisting an impulse to strip the worn quilt from her bed, Bree uttered a slightly hysterical laugh at the futility of the gesture. With all the valuable treasures housed within the walls of Crosshaven, her latest incoherent thought had been to save a silly frayed coverlet. It was truly the least of her worries. What

5

was left of her jewels, though meager, had already been sewn into the lining of an old ballgown and packed in the large carpet bag at the foot of her bed.

The heavy crystal chandelier that dominated the front foyer and all the furniture her parents had imported from Europe were lost to them. Family heirlooms, if they were too large to be tucked into the corners of the few bags they would carry with them, would be lost too. Most of their clothing would have to be left behind, along with the silver and china. All of it, everything her mother and father had worked for, would either be stolen or burned when Sherman's troops came to destroy Crosshaven.

Being a Union Captain's mistress the past months had cost her dearly. She was worse than a traitor in the eyes of her friends and family, less than the worst of women who sold their favors on streetcorners. But the shame and humiliation, the contempt they were unwilling to hide— it was worth all she had suffered. Bravery and resistance Bree would leave to the families huddled in the rooms below her. They had not been too proud to seek shelter with the Captain's whore or to eat the food he had provided her family. And *he* had given her something their patriotism could not! A warning, the knowledge that her home would be set ablaze. And time, time to gather what she could before Crosshaven was reduced to ash.

Bree sank to the floor next to her bed and buried her face in the familiar smell of the silk coverlet Lucinda had labored so hard to make for her. She felt the tears creep slowly down her cheeks but made no effort to stop them. She was frightened, truly frightened for the first time in her life. Her mother was useless and her brother too young to shoulder the burden of responsibility. Papa had been buried at Shiloh two years before and even his wisdom and strength couldn't transcend the grave. She was alone, as never before. The war would soon be over and the Confederacy would lose. Because of her liaison with the Captain there was no place in Georgia for her family, no place they could walk with pride. The same people who ac-

6

cepted her hospitality and protection now would be the first to reject them when the Union troops were gone.

Bree swallowed and breathed deeply, refusing to give in to the feeling of total desperation. She brushed the tears from her face and got up, her back rigid with purpose. There was still the wagon to load and food stuffs to be gathered. She walked from her bedroom and down the hall, pausing before her younger brother's bedroom. Opening the door a crack, she saw his prone shape on the bed and smiled. That boy could sleep through anything. Well, there was time enough to force him into early manhood. For now, she would let him dream the dreams of youth.

She tiptoed quietly to the staircase and started to descend, her hand trailing lightly along the highly polished rail. As she passed the second floor, Bree could hear the hum of voices behind closed doors. Her reluctant houseguests. Just then a door opened and a man who had known her since childhood looked out. Seeing Bree standing on the stairs, the older man lowered his eyes and turned away without a word of acknowledgment.

Hypocrite! Bree's fist clenched tightly. A few hours ago that man and his fat wife and sniveling children were begging for shelter. He would have kissed the hem of her gown had she demanded it of him.

As quickly as it had come, her anger drained away. What good would it do? She knew what the man was feeling. In his desperation he would humble himself, lie, cheat—anything to save himself and his family. But he was the male of the species and his actions would later be overlooked, excused as his duty to those who depended upon him. Bree knew forgiveness and understanding would be withheld from her. She had committed the sin of fraternizing with the enemy at a time when the war's outcome was uncertain. She had willingly entered into an affair with the Captain without apology. Poverty, displacement, hunger—none of these things threatened her and the family she had been forced to head since her father's death.

Her motives Bree had kept to herself, a secret she

shared with no one as she watched her mother's eyes grow cold with contempt and her brother's eyes fill with confusion. Even she found it difficult to identify the flighty, gay young girl she had once been and the closed, almost furtive woman she had become.

Bree reached the first floor and stood in the foyer, unsure of what it was she expected to find. The gas lights were out and the moon cast strange shafts of light through the shuttered windows. With easy familiarity she groped in the drawer of the sideboard and found a candle. She lit it and held it high over her head, feeling better for the soft, gentle warmth of its flame.

Without conscious movement, Bree found herself standing in front of the massive oak doors that led to the main ballroom. She swung open the doors and placed the candle in a sconce hanging on the wall. Turning, Bree surveyed the room with sadness. The beautiful gilt chairs and polished tables were gone. Dust had gathered on the floor from months of neglect. The glow from the candle shone only on a small corner of the huge room.

Bree hummed softly and absently lifted her skirt, gracefully turning in circles to the remembered tune. The ballroom suddenly came alive as memories of happy times engulfed her. Oh, the wonderful parties this room had been host to—the dancing and flirting it had seen. And the beauty! Soft-eyed women dressed in yards of fine silk and chiffon, their lace fans snapping as they laughed and whispered with their beaus. And the men, dashing and handsome in formal dress, their courtesy and charm practiced with great flair. The smell of magnolia and jasmine wafting on the breeze through the open doors.

Bree stopped abruptly, depression almost crushing her. Lord, had she ever really been that young and frivolous? The uncrowned princess of Atlanta, sought after, admired, pampered. She smiled without humor, barely recognizing the girl this ballroom knew intimately. There was little left of the coquettish, spoiled girl who had ruled the elite of Atlanta society with a dazzling smile. Small vestige of the selfish, headstrong woman-child who was so sure of the world and her place in it.

Where did she go? I miss that child and her silly vanity, Bree thought sadly, her eyes filling with tears for the second time that night. How did that girl slip away without my even knowin' it?

However, even as she asked herself the question, Bree knew the answer, and the very thing she had been steeling herself against began to slip into her mind and heart. She felt the memory of it lift her from the confines of the ballroom and Crosshaven and carry her over the years back to the time it began.

BOOK ONE

BOOK ONE

CHAPTER ONE

Kansas City, Missouri
June 19, 1860

An early morning stagecoach roared through the outskirts of town, its thick wooden wheels spitting out mud and debris impatiently in its wake. Whirlwinds of dust danced around the wide dirt road, leaving a fine, gritty deposit on storefronts and windows as it passed, stirring up the smell of cattle and hay in the air. The threat of fierce heat from a summer not yet born closed in on the town, and its people moved slowly and talked in hushed tones as if to dispel the elements from gathering strength by setting a quiet, lethargic example.

Heads turned sharply, all eyes glaring reproachfully at the thunderous intrusion of the stagecoach. Wooden sidewalks creaked under the weight of sturdy boots and thin leather slippers. Crowds wandered restlessly along the streets, walking five abreast, turning and squeezing through the steady flow of others walking toward them.

Kansas City was filled to capacity with travelers from nearly every state east of Missouri, all coverging to join a massive wagon train that would take them away from a multitude of problems. Away from dying farm lands, religious persecution, or the black cloud of a civil war between the states to a land that lay gleaming with promise to the west.

The stagecoach careened precariously down the main street, the sound of the driver's whip slicing through the stillness of the morning, and skidded to a noisy, shuddering halt in front of the depot. The driver, sweat-stained and beaten from twenty years on the plains, leaped down from his high perch, anxious to offer his hand in assistance to the beautiful female passenger he had carefully seated next to the door at the last waystation.

She's a looker, that one, he thought happily, and a fine lady to boot! Not many like her came the way of his old coach. Not one before her, if the truth were known, but then he'd had no way of knowin' just how downright plain most women were until now. This one was somethin' to tell the boys about, all right! Flaming red curls goin' every which way and a waist so tiny he'd swear he could span the width of it with his hands and still have fingers to spare.

He pulled open the door, shaking with a lustful reverence, and thrust his whole arm forward so that she could not possibly avoid the gesture. A small, gloved hand moved slowly, hesitating a moment before accepting, then falteringly clasped the driver's rough, callused fist.

Bree stepped from the coach reluctantly, a scented handkerchief held to her face, a futile attempt to stay the gagging, unfamiliar smells around her. A brief, incredulous shake of her small head sent a bouncing cascade of red hair across her face and shoulders. Her flaming mane might have been a point of interest with the driver, but, at that moment, if a pair of scissors had been handy she would have readily cut off every damp, clinging curl.

"Lucinda," she muttered through the handkerchief, pointedly withdrawing her hand from the driver's and dismissing him without another glance. "Lucinda, get on down here and ask this man where we can find decent accommodations. With a bath!" she added irritably. "Lordy! I declare I'll never see another clean day as long as I live!"

"Comin', Miss Bree." Lucinda's smiling ebony face emerged from the darkness of the coach. A striking woman of indeterminate age, she stepped down and stood next to Bree. She was dressed simply in a light linen dress and suffered none of the discomfort Bree's velvet traveling suit had given her.

"Don't you get bossy with me, Missy," Lucinda whispered firmly. "I ain't your nigger, child. I's your companion! Wasn't me what begged ole Lucy to leave home and go followin' that no-account Mr. Phillip and him not even sendin' for you." Lucinda was a woman of stature, nearly six feet tall, and she towered over Bree. Most of the time her large presence was a comfort, but right now it was an immovable menace.

"I'm sorry, Lucy." Bree's bristling retort faded with the stifling heat even before it had a chance to blossom. "You're right, I'm actin' like a spoiled child. But it's this place, this horrible place! I don't know what I was expectin' but it surely wasn't this. How do people live in all this filth and emptiness?" Bree sighed and leaned against the taller woman's shoulder. She still kept the handkerchief pressed to her nose and closed her eyes as if in defense of what they were viewing. Bree thought of the home she had left, the lush green of Georgia, the peace and tranquillity of Crosshaven and the love of her parents. Her clenched eyes filled with tears and she allowed herself a moment of reveling in self-pity. Then, as quickly as they had come, the tears dried and she tightened her mouth with determination.

"Lucy, dear," Bree drawled with exaggerated courtesy, "if it wouldn't be too much trouble, I'd appreciate it greatly if you be so kind as to ask our driver where we can find a room with a bath." She grinned impishly as Lucy turned away to hide her smile and speak to the driver.

They wove their way toward the hotel through curious onlookers, more curious about Lucy than the small woman at her side. For some, it was their first sight of a person whose skin was different from their own but, for others, the hard, questioning glances wondered why a slave dared to walk with her mistress as an equal.

Lucinda was painfully familiar with that particular kind of stare. The South, her home and her father's before her, was riddled with faces that bore just that same expression when looking at her. It was because of those faces that she had agreed to leave the security of Crosshaven and follow Miss Bree across the country. Lucy hoped that the farther they got from the South and its beliefs, the less she would see the look of contempt and superiority. So far, she decided, we just ain't gone far enough.

The gentle brush of Bree's arm against her filled Lucy with warmth and an almost protective maternal tenderness. Poor little Missy. A woman grown and married but hardly bigger than when she was a girl of fourteen. No one knew Bree better than Lucy. Bree's slight frame was deceiving. She appeared to be a tiny Dresden doll, but Lucy knew Bree to have the stubbornness of a donkey, the temper of her Irish ancestry, and a backbone of solid oak. If Lucy hadn't agreed to accompany her, Bree would have started out on her own, safety and propriety be damned!

Lucy cursed under her breath. All that wasted on a fool weakling like Phillip Alexander! Whatever had possessed Bree to marry the man entirely escaped Lucy's thinking.

Later, when they'd found a room and bath and Bree was soaking lazily in a tub of hot, soapy water Lucy broached the much-argued topic again.

"You sure you want to keep on, child? We can turn back and no shame." Luch sponged Bree's back absent-mindedly.

"Shame's got nothin' to do with it, Lucy. My place is with my husband." Bree said each word slowly, clearly, knowing Lucy didn't understand her desire to be with Phillip. "You don't think much of Phillip, I know, but I'll thank you to stop badmouthin' him every chance you get. You'll see . . . when we get to Black Hawk, you'll see how dependable he's become. We'll have a successful store and a nice, little house waitin' for us. I read you his letters; it's all there in the letters." Bree's voice rose slightly, almost desperately.

"Miss Bree, you ain't had a letter from that man in over six months," Lucy reminded her brusquely. "And before that, only two letters in goin' on a year. Tsk!" Lucy muttered under her breath. "No good man! What kind of a man leaves his woman behind all that time with that skimpy kinda letter writin'?"

"What are you mumblin' about, Lucy? Turn around here so I can hear what you're sayin'." Bree demanded suspiciously but got no response. "Well, stop goin' on and shuck off those clothes. You need a bath worse than I do." Bree stood up, the bubbles and water running down her body as she reached for the towel Lucy held out to her. For all her fragile size, Bree's body was without angles or protruding bones. She had a slim, tapering neck and delicate shoulders, made more so by large, rounded breasts and a tiny waist. Her legs were long and curved from hip to ankle. She reminded Lucy of the grecian statues that stood in the gardens at Crosshaven. More for looking at and admiring than for the lusty pleasures of the marriage bed. And, from the casual talks the two women had had since Bree's marriage to Phillip, Lucy guessed that Bree's husband felt looking and admiring were enough to satisfy the needs of a Southern lady. Just another reason Lucy thought him to be a fool. From her own experience, Lucy knew what bodies were for and it sure wasn't lookin'!

Bree dried quickly and threw on a soft wrapper, her mind already spinning with a mental list of things she had to accomplish before the day was out. She listened contentedly to the sound of Lucy's humming and ticked them off, one by one, in her brain. First there were the supplies Phillip had mentioned in his last letter, then the arrangements for a wagon and supplies, and, last, signing on with the wagon train.

She dressed with care, finally discarding the fashion of the day in favor of comfort. Velvets and satins were all very fine during the cooler months in Georgia but in the plains heat, Bree decided, it was very much like purgatory might be. Instead, and happy her mother wasn't there to disapprove, Bree chose to wear one of her "house" dresses, a simple sheer gown designed for comfort and usually worn only in the privacy of the home. She discarded the confines of a corset and the layers of petticoats she would normally have worn, deciding those encumbrances would only defeat the purpose of lighter clothing, and chose only a lace chemise and single petticoat. Secretly, and without really admitting it to herself, Bree was proud of the way her breasts pointed upward without the help of corsets and the way her waist dipped in without assistance.

She picked out a pale yellow dress and pulled it on over her underclothes, delighting in the sense of freedom she felt. Lucy had finished her bath and dressed quickly, reaching out to help Bree with the tiny buttons that ran down the back of her gown. They stood in front of a full-length mirror, and although the glass was cloudy and spotted, it was easy to see why the two of them were such objects of curiosity. Lucy stood at least ten inches taller than Bree, her black skin the color of highly polished mahogany, a shocking contrast to Bree's milk and honey complexion. Their eyes met in the mirror and they began to giggle childishly.

"Lawd, ain't we a sight, Missy?" Lucy howled. "Appears the milk you suckled from me when you was a babe didn't do nuthin' to darken up your skin none."

Bree hugged Lucy impulsively, remembering how well she had been cared for by the large black woman. Lucy had lavished affection, discipline, and understanding more generously than any mother; in fact, Lucy had given her all the things Bree's own mother had neither the time nor the inclination to bestow.

"Well now, Miss Lucy," Bree dropped her arms, ashamed of the bitterness she was feeling. "We'd best get to seein' about our duties." She turned abruptly and began rummaging through her trunk. She found what she was looking for and slipped the copy of Dewar's *Guide to the West* into her purse. Inside the book she had purchased before leaving Georgia was what she unquestionably assumed was the knowledge she would need to continue her journey. Bree smiled at Lucy and beckoned her through the door of the room.

"You take this list of provisions I've written down and

give it to the man at the counter in every general store in this town. Tell them to deliver the canned goods to our rooms and don't let them sell you anything that isn't on this list. Phillip says the demand for these goods will make his fortune. I'll see to the wagons and teams we'll need. Go on, now, I'll be just fine. We'll meet back here in two hours.''

Bree watched as Lucy stomped off down the hall, muttering as she went.

"Phillip says! Phillip says! What's that fool man know, anyhow?''

"Keep a civil tongue in your head, Lucy,'' Bree called after her, without much reprimand in her tone. Lucy was seldom wrong in her instincts. It made Bree sick in her heart to think Lucy was right about Phillip. She shook her head stubbornly, refusing to give in to the doubts, but her thoughts persisted. The marriage was a disaster; something she couldn't exactly put her finger on was wrong and somehow Phillip had managed to make her feel that she was to blame. She had failed him in ways that stood, unspoken, between them. Without knowing why, she felt ashamed and guilty.

As she had a hundred times before, Bree reluctantly allowed her thoughts to drift back in time, searching vainly for answers. Even in the privacy of a rented room in this dust-blown city, Bree's face reddened at the memory of her wedding night and the painful lessons she had learned. During their courtship, Phillip had refrained, he said, from improper advances out of a deep and loving respect. But on that jasmine-scented night two years ago, she realized she had married a man who viewed physical pleasure as unclean, an act to be performed only in the hope of procreating a line of strong sons and genteel daughters.

Bree trembled and leaned against the door for support. A natural sensuality and intense curiosity had prompted her to look forward happily to the first tentative kiss Phillip had pressed against her eager mouth. She responded, surprising herself with the enthusiasm she was ready to give over without question, but even more surprising was the look of astonishment and disgust on Phillip's face. His forceful admonishment still rang clearly in her ears.

Women of breeding, he informed her tersely through clenched teeth, didn't really enjoy their wifely duties. Phillip's face paled, beads of perspiration formed on his aristocratic brow. Certain women, he continued, women of low character, might revel in sinful response but he, Phillip Jerome Alexander, expected his wife to remain a lady at all times.

Chastised and confused, Bree followed Phillip's precise instructions and lay motionless on her marriage bed. She lifted the hem of her nightgown, gathering the voluminous silk around her breasts, and turned her face away as Phillip mounted her silently and entered her tender flesh without endearment or preamble. There was a sharp pain as he moved quickly above her, a burning sensation while he muttered vicious obscenities. It was over. He left her to clean herself and their bedding. When he returned, Phillip kissed her forehead and fell immediately into a deep slumber.

Hours later Bree was still awake and watching her husband's sleeping form, stung with humiliation and despair. Although she was innocent in the ways of lovemaking, she had been kissed before her engagement to Phillip. There had been sweet, stolen kisses on the veranda at Crosshaven and the feeling had been pleasurable. She had watched with envy as other couples held hands and wandered slowly through the garden, losing themselves in the darkness. Whispered voices, soft laughter, and gentle moans had filled the evening air. The veiled comments of married women had led her to believe the delights of the marriage bed were something of wonder and mutual enjoyment.

She adored Phillip, marrying him despite the fact that his father had gambled away the property and house that should have been passed on to his oldest son. She had settled for living with Phillip in her own parents' house at Crosshaven while he learned the workings of the large plantation.

In her heart, Bree knew what had happened between them was wrong. Why, even the infrequent trips her father made to Mama's room resulted in a soft glow on their faces the next morning, and they had been married for twenty-three years. The only excuse her young mind could grasp was self-blame. Phillip, with his gentlemanly manner and keen mind, could not possibly be at fault. He was the personification of Southern gentility—handsome, kind, soft-spoken. Therefore, the weakness lay with her.

Bree fell into exhausted sleep that night planning all she would do to prove herself worthy of Phillip's love and passion. The delicacy and embarrassment of her situation prevented Bree from turning to her parents. She hinted at it briefly when talking to Lucinda, but the intuitive black woman had quickly seen through her light banter and forthrightly asked if the newlyweds were having troubles in their bed. Bree had laughed blithely and retreated, more ashamed than ever.

And, although Bree did everything she could think of to please Phillip during the daylight hours, their nights together remained the same. Phillip occupied her bed but rarely made a move to claim his marital privileges. When he did, the nightmare of their first evening together was repeated.

As the months passed, Bree became tense and uncertain, a crushing feeling of sadness closing around her heart like a fist. There were so many things buried there, secret things she longed to share—laughter, good times, tenderness. But the brooding look of anger on Phillip's face kept her at a distance. The gifts she yearned to lavish upon her husband died of neglect.

Philip's unexpected announcement that he intended to leave the security of Crosshaven to make his own fortune in the gold fields of Colorado was met with incredulous disbelief by Bree's parents. Yet with his smooth, easy way with words, he soon persuaded them to see the advantage of his plans. A few years catering to the needs of the miners and he would return with enough money to buy back the plantation that should have been his by right of birth. His honor, Phillip nobly entreated, his ancestral home would be restored through hard work and perseverance. Of course, the hardships for Bree were unthinkable and she would stay behind at Crosshaven. An absence of a few years between husband and wife was not unheard of, and she would be left in comfort. Bree allowed her parents to believe her husband had discussed his plans with her before telling them. She was too ashamed that he held her opinion in so little regard.

She met the news with mixed emotion. She was relieved that the charade was almost over and she would no longer have to pretend she was a contented wife, but she was saddened because she knew Phillip was leaving to escape the questioning bewilderment he saw in her eyes.

Fortified with her parents' good wishes and the three thousand dollars given "strictly as a loan," Phillip started out a week after his startling revelation. It was months before Bree felt the true depth of the guilt she had struggled so hard to keep beneath the surface of her daily existence.

What a failure she had been! As a wife, she had been found desperately lacking. Something in her character, her needs, was so repulsive that her husband had found it necessary to flee her presence. The more she brooded about it the more determined she became. She would not stay behind at Crosshaven like a snug parasite. No, this was the perfect opportunity to prove her worth. Phillip would see her not as the helpless hothouse flower he imagined ladies to be but as a strong, self-reliant woman. In her mind, Bree could envision the look on Phillip's face when she joined him, unannounced, in Colorado. His eyes would widen with surprise, his jaw slacken as his mouth fell open. Then, when he realized it was really Bree standing in front of him, Phillip's eyes would twinkle with delight. He would reach for her happily, eagerly. Black Hawk Point, Colorado. Even the name of the town was romantic.

After he had been gone six months, Phillip's first letter arrived, and though sadly lacking in endearment for his estranged wife, he was filled with praise for the majestic beauty of the territory. The second letter, eleven months later, was a narrative of bursting confidence. Phillip described the large wood building he had purchased months earlier and renovated before stocking it with foods and dry goods. Unfortunately, he complained, there were never enough canned peaches to soothe the sweet tooth of a miner, and the haul into Denver for supplies was too costly. All prices were tripled in the gold fields because the miners were willing to let themselves be charged outrageous prices for the things they wanted. Phillip related in detail the hanging of the sign "Alexander Mercantile" on the first day of business, the pride he felt evident even on paper. The nights, he added, were long, cold, and lonely. This last Bree took to be his way of saying he missed her.

It was then she decided to journey to Colorado. Bree approached her parents, turning a deaf ear to their protests and threatening to sell her jewelry, anything of value, if they chose not to help her. In the end, as in all things, they indulged their spoiled daughter, insisting only that she travel in the company of her mammy, Lucinda.

And now, Kansas City. Where was the beauty Phillip had extolled—green trees reaching up to touch the stars, fields of yellow flowers swaying in the wind? Dust! Dust and mud!

Bree tossed her head, the past slipping away as she surveyed the dingy hall before her with distaste. She reached into her bag and withdrew a linen handkerchief, dabbing it carefully at her neck and temples. Then, straightening the folds of her dress and tilting her chin proudly, Bree shrugged and started off to make the final arrangements for her new life with Phillip.

CHAPTER TWO

Harald and Sons General Mercantile rose three stories high, a drab whitewashed building dulled alternately by months of burning heat and biting cold. Bree stood angrily in front of the structure, hands on hips, her foot unconsciously tapping in tune with the litany of curses that played through her mind.

Why, that smitty at the livery was no better than a common thief. Conestoga wagons, indeed! Highway robbery was more like it! Imagine, charging her five hundred dollars for two silly-looking, delapidated old wagons and the teams to pull them. They were roomy, granted, capable of storing all the canned goods she planned to give Phillip as a peace offering for disobeying his wishes, but still . . . She understood the principle of supply and demand and she had paid the money the smitty asked, but only after doing her best to let him know she was aware he was cheating her.

Bree marched inside the mercantile and looked around, her lip curled in a faint gesture of contempt. The stores of Atlanta boasted delicate chandeliers, polished mahogany floors, and pastel curtains. Here on the plains the best they could offer was wooden shelves, cast-iron kettles hanging from beams on the ceiling, and bolts of tacky gingham on rough-hewn tables. Summoning her haughtiest demeanor, Bree approached a clerk who was her age or older.

"Young man," she sniffed delicately to make sure he knew the hickory-cured smell of the store displeased her.

"Young man, I will require complete provisions for two. Write this down and, mind you, I'll check to see I'm not cheated." Bree waited impatiently while the clerk gathered pen and paper before drawing the *Guide to the West* from her purse. "Two hundred pounds each of flour and sugar, one hundred pounds sugar," she recited slowly. "Forty pounds coffee, ten . . ."

Excuse me, ma'am," the clerk stammered nervously, overwhelmed by the lady's beauty and condescending attitude. "Did you say two people? You won't be needing that many supplies if it's the wagon train to Colorado you're signing up for. I . . ."

"Young man," Bree's voice rose indignantly, her green eyes flashing and making it clear she was not used to being contradicted. "Are you refusing to sell me provisions in the amount I've requested?" Her slim finger tapped briskly on the book she held. "Dewar's *Guide to the West* specifically indicates the volume of supplies I need. And," she continued, her tone dropping to a hiss, "I will assume a man who has been the length of this country knows more about such matters than a backwoods clerk! Shall we continue?"

"You read that book again, ma'am, and you'll find the fella wrote it for folks back east. You got six months of trail in front of you, it's fine, but you only got about six weeks." The clerk noted with satisfaction that Bree's color had heightened. She knew she was in the wrong but, by God if she'd ever admit it.

Bree's tirade hadn't gone unnoticed by others in the store. Behind her, she heard a muffled snort of laughter. She whirled around to face the upstart and found herself looking at a dusty shirtfront. Her eyes traveled upward, widening with surprise at the largeness of the man. He stood over six feet, looming above her, and he was covered with the same grimy film that obliterated everything else on the plains. A sweat-stained hat was pulled low over his forehead, shielding his eyes from Bree's lacerating glare. A full beard, made grayish in color by the dust that coated it, fanned out from a strong jaw. He grinned and snickered again, flashing straight, white teeth.

Bree grimaced and turned away. Bumpkin, her expression seemed to accuse, another example of western manhood!

Her attention now fully returned to the clerk, Bree leveled her gaze and spoke in a tone that left little room for argument.

"I've underlined the supplies I require. Kindly, gather them together—you can read, can't you?" she asked caustically, unable to stop herself from lashing out at the helpless clerk. "Now, do you think you can tell me where I can sign up for the wagon train?"

"Certainly, ma'am." The clerk grinned back smugly. "Just outside our front door under the banner that reads 'Dunsfield wagon train, sign up'—that's where you'll find it." The flush of embarrassment that crept up Bree's neck was repayment enough for the sharp manner she had taken with him.

Again Bree heard the giant behind her chuckle, but this time she kept her face carefully averted. Stiffening her back, she turned slowly and walked past the stranger and out the door.

Bree took a place behind a line of six or seven men, none of whom seemed willing to step aside for her. She waited impatiently, sighing with exasperation until she finally stood in front of the man whose authoritative attitude made it clear he was the master of the wagon train.

"I'd like passage for myself and my maid, Mr. Dunsfield." Bree's irritation quickly vanished, overcome by the excitement of finalizing the last leg of her journey. "We have all the necessary provisions and two wagons. How much . . ."

"Where's your man?" the wagonmaster cut her off without even looking up.

"My what?" Bree sputtered, caught off guard.

"No lone females," he answered abruptly. "Too much trouble. Stirs up the young bucks. No exceptions." He spat each word sharply, making it quite clear that no amount of persuasion would move him. He looked up, seeing her for the first time. A momentary glance of appraisal, admiration, and then his eyes hardened again. "No exceptions."

"But I've come all the way from Georgia. How am I to reach Colorado if not on your wagon train?" Bree was stunned, her mind racing. Without knowing why, she impulsively decided against revealing Phillip's presence at Black Hawk Point.

"Shoulda took that to account before you left Georgia, miss." Abel Dunsfield looked critically at the beauty standing before him and knew his long-standing policy was wise. A woman looks like this one and there's bound to be trouble, he mused. The bucks'd be killin' each other to get to her. Still, she looked so small and stricken, it was hard not to feel sorry for her.

Bree's shoulders sagged but she held her ground, still frantically seeking a way out of this latest problem.

"Am I to understand, Mr. Dunsfield, that the only way I can obtain passage is to have a man, a husband, escort me?" Bree kept her left hand, with its lovely ruby wedding ring, hidden in the folds of her gown.

"That's right, lady!" Abel retorted defensively. "You show me a man, and," he added suspiciously, "a proper marriage paper and I'll sign you on."

"What about my maid? Does she have to have a husband too?"

"She's a nigra, ain't she?" Abel dismissed the thought of Lucy with a flick of his gnarled hand. "No decent man's gonna bother with a nigra."

Bree gasped, barely able to resist the urge to beat the man's face with her fists. Behind her, men were clearing their throats and shuffling restlessly, anxious to have her move away. Bree sidestepped and frowned, forcing herself to remain calm. She hadn't come all this way to turn back now. Already a plan was formulating in the back of her mind. It was scandalous, unthinkable, but still . . .

27

"Excuse me, Mr. Dunsfield," Bree interrupted the business he was conducting. "When does the wagon train leave for Colorado?"

"Tomorrow, first light." He seemed surprised to find Bree still there.

"Thank you, suh," Bree whispered coquettishly, her brightest smile in evidence as she turned and reentered the mercantile.

She approached the clerk a second time, the forced smile still across her face, hoping a friendly grin and sparkling eyes were enough to persuade him to overlook her shabby treatment of him earlier.

"May I borrow pen and paper?" She inquired softly, using every ounce of Southern guile she could muster.

The clerk hesitated, but then let himself be charmed by Bree's loveliness. His hand lingered on the pen as he passed it to her. When she had finished writing, Bree handed the paper back to him.

"Would you kindly place this ad in a prominent position and inform anyone who inquires that it must be answered today?" She smiled again, catching her bottom lip between her teeth just at the corner, a gesture the clerk found devastating.

He hurried over to a board filled with other notices and attached Bree's ad with a nail in the center of "for sale" notices and messages to relatives. After it was up, he paused to read it, his eyes bulging with surprise.

Any man wishing to make $100.00, the purpose of matrimony, apply Charleston House, Miss Bryna Alexander.

The clerk cursed his rotten timing. Three months earlier before greed and ambition had tempted him in the form of his boss's plump, eager daughter, he'd have, by God, answered the ad himself. Hell, it might even be worth it to chuck everything and take a chance. The lady was so beautiful it gave him a terrible ache, but she had a mouth on her too. She could cut a man to ribbons with that sharp tongue of hers. No, he was probably better off trying to lift Lorrie's petticoats and settling down to run the store. He shrugged and turned away, almost knocking Bree over as she scrambled behind him to stand in front of the board and critically view her handiwork. Was a hundred dollars enough? Should she have been more specific, explaining the delicacy of her situation? She felt more than heard a presence behind her. The hair at the nape of her neck ruffled like the instinctive warnings of a cat.

"I'd be pleased to take you on, ma'am." His voice rumbled over her. "Name's Jemson Tyler."

Bree turned, once again awed by the sheer size of the man who had only a few minutes ago thought her behavior something of a joke. Of course, almost everyone over the age of thirteen was larger in stature than she, but it wasn't only the man's height. Everything about him was big—expansive, rock-hard shoulders, hands the size of pie pans. His sheer size, especially when contrasted to her petiteness, was intimidating.

"I don't have the time to be choosy, suh," Bree snapped, not knowing why she chose to be so disagreeable. "And you look like a man who is in need of money. If you're runnin' from the law, we can terminate this conversation right now."

"Lady, I never run from anything in my life," he growled slowly. "I'm going to Colorado myself with Dunsfield, heard your talk with him outside, and thought I could help you out. You don't want my help, that's fine."

"No, wait!" Bree almost shouted in panic. What if no one else came along who was willing to be of service? "Lordy! Nothin' has gone the way it was supposed to today. My nerves are played raw—I didn't really mean to take it out on you." It was the closest she would come to offering an apology. "I do need your help and I'm sure I can trust you to be a, ah, gentleman."

"I strive to be courtly, ma'am," he answered drily, tipping his hat in an exaggerated show of politeness, aware of Bree's surprise that he slipped easily from the rough language of an ordinary cowboy to that of a gentleman. Surprisingly, he found himself enjoying her confusion and discomfort.

"*If* you'll allow me to explain my predicament, I'll continue." Bree frowned, her face drawing into a childish pout. A warning bell went off in her brain but, single-mindedly, she swept the feeling aside. "First, I've traveled a great distance only to find that my maid, Lucy, and I can't join the wagon train without the company of a man, a husband. Second, I *am* a married woman." Bree lifted her hand as if the ring gave credence to her statement. "But my husband is waiting for me in Colorado so he's little comfort to me now. What I need Mr., ah, Taylor, was it? Well, no matter. What I need is a gentleman to go through the ceremony—a *mock* ceremony—so I can show proof of a marriage and continue my journey."

"That's bigamy in most states, ma'am." Jemson's voice was laced with ill-disguised sarcasm. "And the name's Tyler, not Taylor."

"I'm aware what the word bigamy means, Mr. *Tyler*," Bree sputtered, nervously looking around to see if anyone had overheard his accusation. Satisfied, she returned her attention to Jemson. Her neck was beginning to ache from the angle she was forced to maintain in order to keep eye contact with the man, though somehow his sky-blue eyes drew hers. Giving up, she found herself addressing the black buttons that ran down the length of his shirt. "The marriage, if there is to be one, will be on paper only. Paper, Mr. Tyler, is easily destroyed." Now her head was beginning to throb. "I'll pay you handsomely for a few weeks of your time. If one hundred dollars isn't enough, name your price, within reason. When we reach Colorado, it's understood we'll go separate ways. No one need be the wiser."

"What about your husband?" Jemson drawled lazily. "What will he think of his wife traveling with another man?"

"My husband, Mr. Tyler, trusts me completely. Why,

he'll be so happy to see me he won't even give the circumstances by which I've reached him a second thought." Bree spoke with more confidence than she felt. "That's a perfect example of the differences between Yankees and Southerners. The basis of our society is trust and good manners."

"Appears to me, your men don't put a high enough value on their women," Jemson retorted teasingly. "You don't have much of a drawl for being a Southerner, Mrs. Alexander; why is that?"

"What?" Bree was totally unbalanced by the swiftness with which he changed the subject after so obviously insulting her. "Really, Mr. Tyler, I fail to see . . ."

"Now, don't take offense." He backed away in mock horror. "I think it's charming the way the drawl pops up now and again. I was just wondering."

"*Very well*, Mr. Tyler, I'll satisfy your curiosity if it will help you get back on the subject we were discussin'." Bree sighed. Really, the man was too exasperating! "My pa sent me north, to New York, when I was twelve. I lived with my aunt and took my schoolin' for five years." Bree shook her head. "Mr. Tyler, I don't believe this is going to work. Clearly, we can't remain civil long enough to pass the time gettin' to Colorado." She made a movement to leave.

"Hold on now, Mrs. Alexander." Jemson raised his hands as if in defense, laughter in his voice. "Don't get riled. Look, you called it right. I need the money and you need a temporary husband. We can accommodate each other." Jemson paused. Then, seeing Bree's raised brow and skeptical look, he hurried on. "We'll manage to steer clear of each other most of the time and when we hit Denver, like you said, we'll go separate ways."

There was something about the smoothness of the words that unsettled Bree. Something about the man she neither liked nor trusted. Still, misgivings aside, it was true she could not afford to take the risk of losing this last chance of getting to Phillip. Suppose no one else came along? The

Dunsfield train was the last scheduled to depart without taking the risk of being stranded by an early winter. What choices did she have? It could be worse. Although scruffy and badly dressed, Jemson Tyler seemed a simple sort. The farmer type. A little charm and he would be easy to handle. It was probable that the most important thing on his mind was getting to the gold fields and making enough money to return to his home, wherever that was, and marry a plump, pink-cheeked farm girl, to raise a whole passel of noisy, ill-mannered children. Surely he saw the differences between them and wouldn't even think of bridging the gap that separated them. Bree's objective, her only concern, was to reach Phillip even if it meant going through the pretense of marriage with a great, lumbering oaf like Jemson Tyler.

"Very well, Mr. Tyler," Bree declared. "We have a deal! You'll receive one half of your money after the ceremony, the final payment when we reach Denver. Agreed?" She waited until he nodded his consent before continuing. "Good. Now, if you'll come to the Carleston House in two hours' time, I'll make the necessary arrangements for a Justice of the Peace. We'll have plenty of time to return here and sign up with the wagon train. Good day, Mr. Tyler."

Bree felt confident again, in control of the events that had so recently closed in on her. Although she wanted no physical contact with him at all, Bree reluctantly reached out her hand to seal the bargain. She stiffened and recoiled from the feel of Jemson's callused hand as it engulfed her own. Bree pulled away but he held on and drew her closer, seeming to enjoy the shock in her eyes.

"In view of the circumstances," he whispered, "don't you think folks will find it a mite queer us calling each other Mr. Tyler and Mrs. Alexander? Why don't you just roll Jemson around for a while and see how you like it."

Bree frowned, realizing that two months spent in this man's company was going to prove even more tiresome than she had imagined.

"The ad says Bryna Alexander," Jemson continued affably, paying no attention to her smoldering rage. "Nice name, Bryna."

"Thank you, Mr. Tay-, Jemson. My pa will be pleased to know you approve." Bree removed her hand forcibly, eyes blazing. The man simply didn't know when he was being dismissed. "If you'll excuse me, I have a great many things to do in a short time." Bree rushed the words together in her haste to get away from him.

"Before you go, Bryna." Jemson refused to be hurried. "Mind telling me just how you planned to get *two* wagons to Colorado?"

"Why, Lucinda will take one and I would have taken the reins on the other, of course."

"You ever handled a wagon before?" he asked impudently, his voice ringing with doubt and smirking arrogance.

"No, but there isn't anythin' I can't do once I set my mind to it." As she turned and walked confidently through the door, the sun hit her full in the face, making her squint. They were unattractive, but Bree made a mental note to purchase a calico sun bonnet before morning. It wouldn't do to have skin like dried leather when she fell into Phillip's arms.

Two hours later Bree stood before a Justice of the Peace and exchanged promises with Jemson Tyler. She was hopping mad. Aside from beating off some of the dust from his clothes and beard, the imbecile hadn't even bothered to make himself presentable. It was downright insulting. Getting gussied up would have given the ceremony more importance than she would have allowed, but cleanliness— well, his appearance was just a slap in the face, that's all. And Lucy wasn't making it any easier. Her initial reaction to the solution Bree had come up with was not shock or dismay as Bree had anticipated. No, instead Lucy had mumbled something about hoping Bree made a better choice now than she had the first time.

After the certificate was signed and witnessed and the

33

Justice thanked and sent on his way, Jemson turned to Bree with a wicked smile on his lips.

"Can't really call this a proper wedding without kissing the bride, can we, darlin'," he said slyly, his eyes full of mischief. He stunned Bree by reaching for her with a swiftness she would not have thought him capable of possessing. His arm hooked around her back and drew her close. She had just enough time to clamp her mouth shut before his lips claimed her. Still, he managed to force open her lips and run his tongue along her teeth before she pushed away. Lucy's raucous giggle filled the room.

Bree's hand sprang up and she put all her strength behind a resounding slap across Jemson's face.

"How . . . how dare you!" She sputtered, whirling angrily to face Lucy. "You stop that snickerin' or I'll sell you to the first buffalo hunter we see, you hear!" She felt trapped between the two of them—Lucy's earthy approval and the devilish, teasing look in Jemson's eyes.

"Don't worry, girl, it won't happen again," he assured Bree insolently. "Just proving to myself what I'm *not* missing."

Suddenly his hand was at her arm and he was steering her toward the door.

"We got just enough time to sign up with Dunsfield, darlin'." His voice was firm, as though taking seriously his role as husband.

"No!" Bree screamed and pulled away. "And quit callin' me darlin'."

"Sorry, just trying to make it look real." The tone was apologetic, but there seemed little remorse in the smirk that dominated his face.

"Mr. Tyler, I won't stand for any foolishness, you hear!"

"We back to Mr. Tyler again? Look, I was just having a little fun. Don't let it ruffle your feathers." He was more serious now, the merriment and teasing gone out of his attitude. "The truth is, you don't have anything to worry about with me. I like my women to behave like women, not little tyrants. You don't have a sense of humor, that's your problem. I'll keep my distance.''

"*That* would suit me fine, Mr. T-, Jemson,'' Bree retorted, spitting out his name as though it were a foul taste. She grabbed at Lucy and huffed out the door to the room, leaving Jemson to follow. When they were out of earshot, Bree leaned toward Lucinda and whispered pee-vishly, ''What does a big oaf like that know about humor? I have an excellent sense of humor, don't I, Lucy?'' Lucinda walked silently beside her.

Jemson paused in the doorway and watched the two women as they proceeded down the hall. Little lady, he mused thoughtfully, you serve a purpose right now and I'll put up with your high-toned ways for as long as you do. But there will come a time when you and I are gonna get together. And I'm a lot bigger than you. I'll have my way, and you'll love it.

CHAPTER THREE

Morning came too quickly, much too early for Bree's patrician tastes. As the distant sound of muffled activity hummed outside the window, she grumbled and shrugged off Lucy's prodding, insistent fingers. She opened one eye, peering warily at the dark room. A single gas lamp glowed in the furthest corner.

"It's not even light outside, Lucy," she wheedled drowsily. "Let me sleep a few hours more."

"Nothin' doin', Miss Bree. Man said first light, he means first light." Lucy scolded in a whisper. "You get on up now. I put away some vittles from dinner last night. Least we don't have to start no journey with an empty belly. Come on now, Missy, do as I says."

Bree groaned and rolled her legs over the side of the bed. Her small feet touched the floor and recoiled. The wood had a cold, damp feel. She was tempted to bundle back up in bed and start again later. Would Mr. Dunsfield hold up the departure of the train until it suited Bree's convenience? No, she was forced to conclude. Since yesterday she'd learned some hard truths. Contrary to what she'd believed when she left Georgia, her lovely face and haughty attitude weren't helping her reach Phillip. She had secretly expected her beauty to work as an asset for her, prompting others to fetch and carry and defer to her in all things. To her chagrin, she had discovered that quite the opposite was true. She was stared at, admired, and then dismissed as being a useless decoration. This was a land where the women were expected to be hardy, to pull their own weight and share in the arduous chores of the journey. The way that Dunsfield had looked at her made it clear he thought she would be unable to contribute anything of value.

Bree yawned and stretched her arms high over her head. Her feet found slippers and wiggled into them. As she shuffled sleepily over to the washbasin, a thought suddenly struck her as terribly amusing. Thinking of how she could contribute on the trek farther west, she made a mental list of the things she was trained to do best. What she came up with made her giggle out loud.

Embroidery, petit point, watercolors? She could read and converse in two languages. Did any of the farmers and miners, shopkeepers and cowboys have need for a French interpreter? No? Well, what about the social graces? She could dance, floating like a cloud to the Saturday-night strains of orchestras on the plantation, or sing in a clear, bell-like voice.

The more she thought about her accomplishments, the more she wanted to laugh. She really did have little to recommend in the way of handy, stalwart contributions. Ah well, the end of her journey was in sight and Lucy could be called upon to help in any endeavor Mr. Dunsfield might ask Bree to perform.

"Lucy honey," she mused without much interest, "maybe you better go on down the hall and make sure *that* person hasn't run off with the money I've already paid him."

"You talkin' 'bout yore husband, Miss Bree; *that* man ain't goin' nowhere 'ceptin' with you." Lucy chuckled knowingly. "That man don't rightly know it yet but he gots eyes fo' you, darlin'."

"Don't be disgustin', Lucy. Why, just the thought of Jemson Tyler raises goosebumps on my arms. See?" Bree stuck her arm under Lucy's nose and waited for a confirming nod. "I never in my life met such an impudent lout. And, if you ever refer to *him* as my husband again in that sneaky manner, I'll thrash you."

"Honey, you ain't big 'nuf to thrash nobody, so stop yore hootin'. 'Sides, I was just funnin' with you, so be a good girl an' git yoreself cleaned up afore they leave us behind." Lucy scolded her gently, holding up one of the cotton dresses Bree had purchased at the mercantile the night before. A faded blue in color with an enormous waist and bell-shaped skirt, it was hideous. The bodice was a bit snug but Bree had been forced to buy the size a growing girl must purchase. The women's sizes swallowed her small frame completely and were too long by at least six inches. Bree grimaced when Lucy beckoned her to put it on. It was true that the taffetas and velvets she had packed were unsuitable for traveling, but Bree had seen herself in the mirror at the mercantile and knew she looked ridiculous. There wasn't enough time now, but she was sure Lucy could find the time to alter the dresses once their journey was underway. After all, there were weeks of boring, empty evenings ahead of them and she was certain Lucy would be happy with something to busy her hands.

Bree had just slipped into the offending garment and was wiggling impatiently while Lucy brushed her hair when a soft tapping sounded at the door. Without waiting for an invitation, Jemson strode into the room, his immense bulk dwarfing the tattered brocade settee Bree was perched on. The way he seemed to constantly stress his superior size and strength again irritated her. She'd known him for less than twenty-four hours and he was literally a pain in the neck. Evidence of the bath he'd just taken glistened on his beard and his hair hung in damp ringlets around his neck. What could be seen of his face under all that hair was scrubbed an angry red. Bree felt irrational anger rise in her throat. Why hadn't he felt it necessary to bathe one day earlier, in time for the wedding ceremony they had participated in instead of shaming her by showing up looking like a dirt farmer just out of the fields?

"Where you come from, Jemson, is a closed door simply an object to be beaten down? Or perhaps they don't even have doors in the North?" Bree lectured ungraciously. "In Georgia, a closed door indicates the person on the other side requires privacy and it's considered common courtesy to wait until you're invited to come in before pushin' your way in."

"You done now?" He glowered quietly, his gaze moving over Bree with obvious dislike. He didn't even have the grace to appear chastised or embarrassed. "I've just left Dunsfield. He's ready to move out. If you want to get to Colorado, you've got twenty minutes to plant your backside atop the wagon."

"I'm not accustomed to bein' hurried, Jemson," Bree snapped back stubbornly, more out of habit than anything else. The supplies she'd purchased had been loaded on the wagon late the night before, and all that was left to do was carrying her bags down. Still, it gave her satisfaction to think Jemson was squirming with anxiety.

"Sure, take your time," he answered, shrugging offhandedly. "Maybe I'll see you in Denver." The last of his words were said as he walked toward the door, showing Bree his back.

Lucy snickered, amused by the way their confrontation was going. Lawd, you give that man two weeks and he'd have Missy crawlin' on all fours and howlin' at the moon. He could sure rile her!

"Our bags, Jemson," Bree reminded him stonily, the order unspoken but clear.

"Right," he said, without turning back toward her. "You better get them in the wagon or you'll be wearing that sack all the way to Denver." He looked back at her, his mouth turned up in a half smile, letting Bree know her appearance hadn't gone unnoticed. Then he strode through the doorway and down the hall, his back rigid and unyielding.

Bree sucked in her breath and clamped her lips together. The impulse to scream and hurl the obscenities she'd heard the foreman at Crosshaven use was overwhelming. She was shaking, frustrated and unsure what to do.

"Miss Bree," Lucy tried to soothe her bruised ego.

"Calm down now. Ain't worth it, gettin' so fearsome. You cain't handle a man like Mister Jemson actin' so uppity and fine."

"I couldn't care less, I assure you. The man's not worth . . ." Bree protested weakly.

"Then why is you always tryin' to get one up on him?" Lucy interrupted sagely. "You want that man ta heel, you change yore ways, I'm tellin' you! Some honey drippin' outta that pretty pink mouth of yores instead of vinegar and you see how fast he come around."

Lucy put her arm around Bree's shoulders and gave her a quick, reassuring hug before going to gather the last of their possessions. Bree hardly seemed to feel it. Her delicate brows were twisted into a thoughtful frown, teeth worrying her full bottom lip.

Lucy was right, of course. If Bree pretended tolerance, even a small degree of affection, any normal male would respond in kind. Yet Bree somehow knew Jemson Tyler wasn't the sort of man she could identify and put in a neat class. Gentleman, scoundrel, weak, strong; he just didn't fit. Something within the depths of Jemson's flashing, brilliant blue eyes warned Bree a woman would be a fool to trifle and try to play games with this mountain of a man. Dangerous was a strong, slightly melodramatic word to use but it was the one that sprang to mind. Bree shuddered, her imagination running wild. He probably grew that awful beard to hide his face and obscure the scars he'd gotten in a desperate, vicious fight. Why, a man like that didn't give a second thought to killing another man over a woman or a glass of whiskey. Bree's mind could almost conjure up the image of Jemson stalking his hapless prey. She wondered briefly what it would be like to stand against him, then pushed the thoughts out of her head, angry that she had wasted even a moment's time on the unruly oaf. He was big and powerful, she told herself, but ignorant and harsh like everything else in the West. He wasn't fit to be in the same room with a gentleman like Phillip Alexander and she didn't care what it cost—under no circumstances would she be charming and pleasant with the brute. If the whole trip had to be spent in stony silence, so be it! She would start by riding with Lucy and let Jemson take the other wagon by himself. *That* would put him in his proper place and tell him better than any words just how she felt about him.

Grim in her determination, Bree set her shoulders squarely, took a final look around the sparse, shabby room she had come to think was the best the West had to offer, and, gathering the drab folds of her skirt, swept from the room.

"I'm not going to argue with you," Jemson growled, his fingers biting into the soft flesh of Bree's arm. "Get your butt atop this wagon and stop making a scene. This whole company thinks you're my wife and, by God, you're going to act the part." His arms crushed her, practically throwing her on the wagon.

Bree landed with a thud, her pride stinging worse than her body. So, he was bigger, stronger, and he could dominate her physically, but he couldn't use brute strength to make her speak. At least she had found a flaw in his character. Excessive pride. He couldn't stand to be made the fool in front of others. Bree glared down at Jemson as he walked around the horses checking the gear. Someday, she vowed, she'd use his pride against him and he'd wish he'd never bullied her. Just wait and see, Mister Jemson high-and-mighty-Tyler!

Behind them, Lucy held the reins of the second wagon and grinned. No one had ever treated Miss Bree with the easy roughness Jemson wore like a second skin. Lord, how she wished Missy wasn't meetin' up with that no-account Phillip Alexander. Jemson Tyler was all man, man enough to tame Missy and show her what livin' and lovin' was all about. But she knew that he wouldn't get the chance if Miss Bree set herself against him, savin' it all for Mister Phillip. And, Lawd, she could be stubborn and single-minded. Still, there was lots of time—long, hard days and lonely nights—ahead of them. She would steer clear of Missy and wait to see what happened.

Every bone and muscle in her body throbbed and ached. The dust parched her throat and coated her hair and clothing. The wagon jerked from side to side, missing not a single hole along the trail. Bree would have collapsed in tears except the hot, dry air had dried up every pore in her skin, including her tear ducts. Her hands were raw under the gloves Jemson had silently given her when he'd turned over the reins two days back. Bree wanted nothing more than to turn around and head for Kansas City and admit she'd made a mistake. But there was no one to say the words to—the days since they left Kansas City were spent in silence with Jemson, and at night she sat by the fire, mute with fatigue while Lucy prepared supper. Darkness meant the only rest of the day, when she crawled, bone tired, into the wagon and the makeshift bed Jemson had set up their first night out.

Bree shifted uncomfortably on the bench of the wagon, squinting through the yellow glare of the dust ahead, a voluminous cloud that obscured everything in front of their wagon. She had no one but herself to blame for this. Jemson had warned her that they had to hurry that first morning to get a front place in line or they'd be eating the dirt of fifty wagons all the way to Denver. But, no, she had stood there arguing like an idiot about which wagon she was going to sit on, and now they were positioned toward the back of the wagon train and suffering the truth of Jemson's words every day. It wasn't at all what she had expected, either. Somehow, Bree had thought traveling on the wagon train would be like an enjoyable little outing, only with the added advantage of having a small moving house. She should have let Lucy arrange for the wagons. It had never occurred to Bree that the wagon wouldn't be equipped with the beds and storage trunks they would need for the long journey ahead. Once again, Jemson had taken the situation in hand and forced the mercantile owner to open his store and sell them what Jemson felt they would require. When he had returned with a rocking chair, of all things, Bree had felt it impossible to curb the sarcasm she felt. Now she was glad she had held her tongue. That rocking chair was a blessed haven in the evening around the fire.

Bree sighed and shifted agin. She hadn't said a word to Jemson in three days, and it irked her to be sitting and waiting anxiously for him to ride back and relieve her. Actually, the time she spent walking beside the wagon was something she looked forward to—although the only reason she was set down was so the team didn't pull any more weight than was necessary. Secretly, she suspected, because her weight was so minimal, it was Jemson's way of torturing her and she would never tell him it had quite the opposite effect. She welcomed the opportunity to stretch her legs and feel solid earth under her feet, the freedom to duck behind a bush and relieve herself if she felt the need. That practice had taken some getting used to and it was uncanny how Jemson always seemed to turn his head and smirk just as she came running, out of breath, to catch up with the wagon. He was crafty, that one. Giving her the rocker, and the gloves to protect her hands from the roughness of the reins, making up a bed in the wagon were all designed, no doubt, to break down her resistence and force her to speak. But she hadn't given him the satisfaction of hearing her weaken, although she did feel a little guilty for not thanking him, not even once. Still, what did she have to thank him for? He was just doing the things any "husband" was expected to do for his "wife." The thought struck her as funny and she giggled out loud.

Lost in thought, she didn't hear Jemson ride up beside her. He tied the palomino to the side of the wagon and hoisted himself up beside her without a word of greeting. Bree eyed him warily and prepared to climb down the other side.

"No need." Jemson reached over and laid his hand

gently on her shoulder. His fingers tugged at the brim of her bonnet and exposed her face, reddened and beginning to freckle in spite of the bonnets protection. "You look beat. Go on in back and take a nap. I'll wake you in an hour or so."

Bree sagged, hating herself for the surge of gratitude she felt but unable to refuse the kindness he offered. She looked him full in the face for the first time in three days and whispered her thanks.

"Nothing to thank me for," he muttered harshly. "You sit up here laughing like a loon, next thing I know you'll be talking to yourself. You're no good to me sick."

Bree was too tired and shocked to retort, but the coldness that flooded her eyes was filled with meaning as she pulled away from his hand and disappeared through the flap in the canvas.

Now, what in the world had forced him to say that? Jemson mused, irritated at his roughness. He'd felt sorry for her, for the dark circles that had begun to round her eyes, the grimy lines of dust etching her face. And she was trying to do what she could. Why had he felt compelled to make a simple act of decency seem only a practical device to keep her on her feet and contributing the small amount she was capable of giving. The truth was that she unnerved him, stirring him up like no other woman had ever done, dirty, sullen face and all. When he first saw her in the mercantile, giving what for to that clerk, he had liked her fire. A little too bossy for his tastes but still, she went after what she wanted and Lord help anything that got in her way. And he liked the way her hair wouldn't stay tucked into the chignon at the back of her neck but kept pulling loose in little wisps around her face, the way her pale skin ran like cream from her cheek to the soft curve of her neck and the way the filmy yellow dress she wore that day dipped and clung to her body. It had seemed a lark, going through the phony marriage and getting paid for it. He had plans for the dark, empty nights between Kansas City and Denver. So far, nothing had worked out the way he thought it might. She fell into exhausted sleep evéry night in the wagon and he bunked under the stars. The mumbled "thanks" he'd just heard was the first civil word that had passed her lips. She had grit, that was sure, and he felt the first bloom of a grudging respect for her.

Jemson Tyler had never known a woman he could honestly say he liked. Loved, lusted after, that was something else. But he'd never known a woman he wanted to talk to after the loving was over. Bree's stony silence was a challenge he had never faced and couldn't seem to resist. He found himself really wanting to know what she was thinking, what she wanted. But her actions infuriated him at the same time. He wasn't a man for parlor games. If a thing needed doing, do it and be done! He was confused and set apart from women's intrigues. Small and stubborn as she was, she had a positive gift for setting his teeth on edge.

Bree slept peacefully through the afternoon, waking suddenly when the rocking motion of the wagon stopped as it was drawn into a close-knit circle with ten others. She felt heavy lidded and numb, as though she could easily sleep the rest of the night away. Forcing herself to move, Bree grabbed a basin and started to step out of the back flap; she nearly put her foot on Jemson's arm as he rounded the rear of the wagon, a bundle of kindling for the evening fire pressed against his chest. They froze as their eyes met. Bree dropped hers first, unable to meet the fierce, unbending hardness on Jemson's face. He dropped the wood, then returned to Bree and reached for the basin. She held on to it for a moment out of habit, refusing to give anything over to Jemson, her suspicion and fear prompting her to play a silly game of tug-of-war with the basin. He pulled it easily from her hands and walked to the water barrel strapped to the side of the wagon. After filling it halfway he returned it to Bree, watching her with silent insolence as she grudgingly nodded and disappeared back into the wagon.

She carried the basin to the center of the wagon, her

hands shaking so hard that the basin wobbled and sloshed water over the sides. Unfastening the buttons down the front of her dress, Bree peeled the garment off her shoulders. It fell to her waist, exposing the trim and pink rosebuds of her chemise. She picked up a cloth and dipped it in the sun-heated water and ran it over skin, between the valley of her rising breasts, under her arms and around the nape of her neck. Rinsing it out, she started again, this time scrubbing her face until it was shiny and pink from the effort. The feeling of at least being clean on the surface made her sigh with delight. On impulse, Bree decided to change her dress. She didn't know how it was managed, but between driving a team, preparing meals, and cleaning up after them, Lucy had found time to alter the four cotton dresses Bree had purchased in Kansas City—at night, Bree suddenly realized with a pang of guilt, while she herself had been sleeping like a baby. Although it wasn't deliberate, Bree had hardly found the time to sit and talk with Lucy, let alone show her how much she appreciated everything Lucy did to make the journey more comfortable.

Bree struggled into the dress, a pale yellow flower print that reminded her that she looked like every other woman on the wagon train, knowledge that went against the grain like nothing else. She reached for her brush, and pulled it angrily through her hair until the tangles gave up the battle and her hair fell gently over her shoulders. Twisting the red curls into a rope, Bree wound it around her fingers and fastened it with pins to the back of her neck. She picked up a hand mirror and looked at her reflection. The sun was almost gone and the image she saw frightened her. A pale, gray, ghostly woman with enormous colorless eyes looked back at Bree, drab and accusing. She thrust the mirror aside, filled with foreboding. In her mind she knew it was a trick of lighting, but in her heart Bree felt she knew the gray-toned woman of the mirror intimately. It was not something she wanted to admit, but every day of her marriage to Phillip Alexander had drained her of color, spirit, life itself. Still, she hung on stubbornly, tenaciously, to the hope that the new life in Colorado would some-how be different, a promise of love and laughter. Through her own strength of will, she would *make* it different. Nothing, nothing could stand in her way! And if it was difficult to call up an image of his face after a separation of a year and a half, what did that mean when compared to her determination?

Bree left the question unanswered. She turned and stepped down from the back of the wagon. Lucy had turned over a large washtub behind the wagon to make the descent easier, knowing it was a long way down for a person of Bree's small size. Lucy thought of everything. Bree spotted her bending over a pot of prairie stew. Another pot of flour biscuits browned near the embers. Bree came up quietly behind Lucy and wrapped her arms around her, planting a noisy kiss on Lucy's cheek.

"Here, let me take that." Bree reached out for the spoon and took it from Lucy's hand. "You sit back and have some coffee. I guess I can stir a pot as good as anybody else."

Lucy hid her surprise and loved Bree more at that moment than at any other time in her life. She stood up, stretching and looking down at Bree's child-like figure. It was amazing, but this was the first time she had ever seen Bree do any of the things Lucy took as her mission in life. The closest she had come to the kitchens at Crosshaven had been as a child, slipping a dirty hand up over the table and snatching fresh-baked cookies. Lucy's instinct was to resume her position by the fire and do what she had been trained all her life to do—see to Miss Bree's comfort. But the picture of Missy stirring that pot as though she were churning butter filled her heart with warmth. Besides, maybe Miss Bree didn't realize it yet but there would be no one to help her once they reached Black Hawk Point. No army of slaves to wash and clean and cook. Maybe it was time for Missy to spread her wings. There was hard, thankless work ahead and Miss Bree would have no choice but to do her share. Stirring a pot, though it was a small enough task, was a step in the right direction. At least the willingness was there.

Later, Jemson returned with more firewood and they sat close to the fire and ate Lucy's stew and biscuits with relish. A slab of bacon had been added to the carrots and potatoes, giving the mixture substance, but it was Lucy's secret pouch of herbs and spices, brought from Crosshaven, that filled the air with an inviting aroma. Bree gathered the tin plates and spoons before Lucy could object and carried them to the tub, where she scrubbed them with sand and rinsed them until everything shone clear in the water.

She had just wiped her hands dry when a small group of fellow passengers joined them at the fire. It was the first time anyone had felt even the smallest remnant of energy at the end of the day, enough to mingle and begin to know their neighbors. Netta and Will George came, a couple who looked to be in their forties, and their four children— it was physically tiring to see how much spunk the children still had left at the end of the day. They hooted and ran unchecked around the campsite playing tag. Jemson's face lit up with pleasure as he watched their foolishness.

The smile froze, however, with the next introduction. Robb Andrews was a lone traveler from Georgia, looking cool and arrogant, as impeccably dressed as if he were in the drawing rooms of Atlanta. Bree also felt a momentary flash of irritation—how did he manage to look as though he had just stepped fresh from a bath?—but her smile was genuine and warm when he moved to take the seat next to her. At first, they had looked an amusing group, trudging over with their chairs tucked awkwardly under their arms, but now they were all as snug as could be, sitting in a small circle around the fire. Bree cast a sidelong glance at Robb Andrews. Now here was someone she could talk to, she thought in relief, one of her own kind. Her eyes flicked over and ignored the open look of contempt on Jemson's face. Soon, everyone was laughing and telling stories. It was the most fun Bree had had since leaving Georgia. Although her guests stayed less than an hour,

Bree felt refreshed and happy as they walked off to their own wagons. She called after them to return the following night and set about humming while she picked up coffee mugs and the plates Lucy had served apple Betty on.

"You flirt like that with every man on the train and no one's going to believe you're my wife." Jemson came up behind Bree, his mouth sullen, his voice hard. He stood inches away from her and glared accusingly.

"My behavior was *friendly*, Jemson, merely that," she snapped haughtily. "Just because you don't know the meanin' of the word doesn't make it improper."

"I'll tell you this just once, Bryna, so listen good. You start acting like a fifty-cent Abilene whore and I'll ride off. I won't be shamed in front of the others, you understand?"

"Whore?" Bree gasped. "Why you stupid . . ." She sputtered and swung the plate in her hand, aiming at Jemson's head. The blow missed its mark and landed squarely on his shoulder. He didn't move, hardly seemed to feel the impact. His hand shot out and grabbed Bree's neck, tightening under her jaw, holding her like a vise.

"Maybe in the South a woman can swing on a man any time she likes but, as you're fond of saying, where I come from she'll land on her ass every time." His voice was scarcely audible and filled with threat. "Don't ever raise a hand to me again, understand? And behave yourself; act like the lady you're always putting on to be or I'll leave and Dunsfield won't take you a step farther than the next town." He let her go so abruptly she almost lost her balance and stomped off into the darkness outside the circle of wagons.

Bree rubbed her aching jaw tentatively, sure the pressure of his grip had dislocated something. What right had he to get so all-fired angry, anyway? Whore? Her behavior really had been above reproach. She hadn't behaved like any such thing. Yes, she'd laughed and talked with Robb Andrews, but there was nothing to it, just polite conversation. Robb was an interesting, well-bred gentleman, a man who was familiar with all the things she knew so well. The slopes and pine trees of the Blue Ridge, the waterfalls and rapids of the coastal plains, the excitement of Atlanta during the theater season. Besides, she had spent just as much time talking with Netta George, a task not as easy as it seemed. The shock of learning that Netta was only five years older than she instead of being her mother's age, as Bree had first thought, had surprised her so much she was almost speechless. She had felt compelled to search every corner of Netta's face to find some vestige of youth. Netta's hair was pale, the color of wheat, drawn into a tight coil at the back of her neck. She was thin, too thin, and the bones of her hands protruded through delicate, almost transparent skin. It wasn't so much that she was lined or wrinkled, although her skin had a rough, leathery texture Bree had come to know was caused by months and years of laboring under a meciless sun and drying wind— no, it was the colorless quality that hung around Netta like a shroud. She had the same grayness that had frightened Bree earlier in the darkened wagon; only Netta's was real and not a trick of lighting. This hard life had done that to Netta. Moving from one dirt farm to the next trying to scrape a living out of the land, having a baby for every year of marriage to mark its passing. The only life Netta would ever know had wrung the juices out of her and left her empty and hollow.

The worst thing, though, Bree thought, was that Netta either didn't know or didn't care what life had dealt her. She clucked over her children and doted on Will shamelessly. Her pale smile and soft, shimmering voice echoed the pride she felt in her family. And Will George also appeared to be older than his years. He was six feet tall but his shoulders were stooped from years under the yoke. Like Jemson's, Will's skin was tanned golden by the sun, but the elements had burned deep lines into Will's face, obscuring the good looks that must have once attracted Netta and prompted her to follow him at the cost of her youth and beauty.

Men! Bree thought, suddenly vicious. They were all

strange, demanding creatures. Selfish! Her flow of anger settled on Jemson. He was the worst of a bad lot. All he cared for was his precious pride. It wouldn't have bothered him if she had crawled off to the bushes with Robb Andrews. What mattered was that others had been witness to his idea of "unladylike behavior." A man as sour as Jemson thought anything more than downcast eyes and a curt nod was flirtatious. What right did he have to make demands and set standards! He was hired help and that was all!

Exasperated, Bree dropped the cups she still held, unconcerned that they landed in the dirt in a messy pile. Lucy's silhouette could be seen behind the canvas cover of the other wagon. Without bothering to call goodnight, Bree lifted her skirts and climbed sulkily into her wagon, suddenly tired enough to sleep again.

From the shadows Jemson watched the scene with grim, sardonic amusement. Even while he was bawling her out, Jemson knew he was being unfair. And he couldn't, for the life of him, figure out why the sight of a woman he barely knew and really didn't even like very much had fired him up so. After all, she was just a woman. Prettier than most, more spoiled than most, but still just a woman. Jemson liked his women married, committed to someone else. Fewer problems that way. When it was over, the woman was glad she hadn't been caught, and there were never more than a few courtesy tears, a wistful wish of "if things had been different," and a satisfying leavetaking. As far as he knew, Jemson had never left a woman sadder for having known him.

He had similar plans for this skinny little redhead, but they weren't working out. Of course, the guise of the shabby, red-neck drifter he'd purposely taken wasn't helping any. This one liked her men pretty, with perfect parlor manners. And, if it came right down to choosing between compromising his future or getting a shot at the snotty little bitch, Jemson guessed he'd have to spend a lot of lonely nights on his bedroll. As disagreeable and tense as she was he probably wasn't missing much, anyway. Underneath that blazing red hair and those smoldering green eyes, encased in that round, delicious body that had been the subject of his fantasies since first laying eyes on her, Jemson was fairly certain there beat a heart as cold and frigid as the snow on the peaks of the Rocky Mountains.

CHAPTER FOUR

Grueling, monotonous days passed without event into nights of restless, aching slumber that, in turn, blended into forgotten weeks. The dust of Missouri gave way to mud-encased thickets and swollen, flooded creeks the farther west they traveled. Wagons were constantly being pulled and pried out of the sucking earth. Every day three or four broke down and had to be repaired. But the hunting was good and the travelers were feasting on venison and beaver the hunting party brought in each day. Bree had become adept at handling the team but was still irked each morning when Jemson rode off with his new-found friends to spend the morning hunting and enjoying the freedom of moving about. Finally the land became hilly and gradually rose and flattened out into an enormous plateau of short grass. Dunsfield sent out orders that they would rest for three days while the animals grazed and grew plump and hardy again. But the abundant food supply of fresh game was behind them now and the men would be gone longer, backtracking to the woody riverbeds east of the wagon train.

That suited her fine, Bree thought the first morning of their forced reprieve from the steady, bone-weary push to Colorado. The less she saw of Jemson Tyler, the happier she'd be.

She hadn't said more than fifty words to him since the night of meeting the Georges and Robb Andrews and then it was only to issue sharp, humorless orders and observations of the land he so obviously loved and admired. Will George had gone off with Jemson and the rest of the hunters, so Netta was free to join Bree for a morning of delightful laziness. It tickled Bree to see how easily Netta had been persuaded to forgo the tub of clothes she was going to scrub. Netta had her boys, Ben and Andy, carry her rocker to Bree's campsite and had settled in with coffee and a contented sigh.

"I swear, this feels good, Bree," Netta giggled. "Almost sinful. There's so much to do and here I sit, lollin' around like a queen."

"Good Lawd, don't go feelin' guilty," Bree admonished playfully, turning toward the fire where Lucy was putting the finishing touches on a secret concoction of flour, pecans, and dried apples she'd been hoarding since Kansas City. "Lucy, you drop what you're doin' and come over here. *Nobody* does a stick of work today! You rest along with us."

"Thass fool talkin', Miss Bree." Lucy shook her head, refusing to be caught up in the giddy irresponsibility Bree was proposing. "Who's gonna have vittles for Mr. Jemson when he gits back iffen I sits around doin' nothin' all the day?"

"Let him fend for himself, is what I say, Lucy," Bree retorted with an airy wave of her hand. "Besides, the man may not even be back today. We'll worry about it later."

"You worry it later, Missy; *I'll* do it now!" Lucy walked over and slammed the pan of cake down in front of the two women, her set expression making it quite clear what she thought of Bree's callousness.

"It must be nice to have a slave taking care of your needs, Bree," Netta whispered shyly when Lucy was again out of earshot. "Will speaks against slavery but I sure do envy you sometimes."

"Oh, Lucy's not a slave," Bree dismissed the notion casually. "She's a freewoman. Lots of Crosshaven people are free and Papa pays them a yearly wage, so they stay because they want to. When my papa buys a slave at auction, he looks on it like indentured service. When the slave has worked off what Papa thinks is his debt, he gets his papers of freedom. Lucy's been a freewoman of color for, oh, goin' on five years now, I guess." Once she was started on the subject, it seemed easy to find the words to explain Crosshaven policy, even defend it, to Netta. Bree knew that as Northerners, Netta and Will had preconceived notions about the South and she felt it necessary to vindicate her home. "Crosshaven is unique in all the South. My Papa came over from Ireland during the famine and worked hard and saved his money while he was stayin' with his sister, my Aunt Maggie, in New York. He went south to Georgia 'cause the land there was cheap, and he bought three thousand acres of the prettiest green, rollin' hills you'd ever want to see. Then he bought a colored man and his wife for fifty dollars at an auction and just the three of them began to clear the land and plant, oh, cotton and vegetables, even a little tobacco. By the time five years passed, Lucius and Maddy had their papers of freedom and Papa had ten more coloreds working for him and he started building the main house. That's when he sent for my mama. I was born after that, then my brother, Carlin—we call him Kirk—and in fifteen years Papa had forty workers, most of them free, I might add, and Crosshaven was payin' for itself."

"But I thought all Southerners had slaves, I mean, *real* slaves that they owned and even bred to produce a stronger line," Netta stammered, confused by the contradiction of what Bree was saying and what she had been told all her life.

"That's true, mostly, Bree admitted reluctantly. "The plantations are so big and bustin' with cotton and crops, the owners couldn't afford to hire white men. If they didn't have slaves, I suppose the South would, well, stop bein' the South. But my papa," Bree went on hastily, bewildered by the shame she was feeling, "My papa doesn't think a man *can* truly own another man. He's had some trouble with our neighbors but we pretty much leave one another alone. Crosshaven raises its own cattle and hogs, and we even weave our own wool from the sheep. And everyone has a special duty—carpentry, ginnin', tannin', millin' flour, makin' brick. We don't ask many favors of our neighbors, so it works out fine. Matter of fact, our neighbors usually come to us for one thing and another.''

"How come your papa calls it Crosshaven?" Netta strove to change the subject, aware that Bree was uneasy. She was relieved to see that her question made Bree laugh, when just a moment before she had been so intensely defending the policy of her people.

"Well, my mama doesn't like it much but he named it for a town in Ireland." Bree relaxed, her voice suddenly warm and full of tender memory. She was obviously telling a favorite story. "Papa—his name is Liam McCarty—was born on a poor farm in Killarney and quite a rabble-rouser he was, too. Always doin' what people thought he had no right to do, just for devilish mischief, you know. When he was a young man he fell in love with a girl from a fishing village near Kinsale—Papa's fond of sayin' she had hair like coal and eyes the color of mountain heather. But she was an O'Bannion and their two families had a blood feud goin' for years so she up and married another man and went to live in a village called Crosshaven. Papa says her people had turned her bitter against him and the last thing she ever said to him was that he'd never amount to anything more than a potato farmer. That's when he left Ireland. Papa laughs about it now, but I suspect he spends a fair amount of time thinkin' about that girl and her pale lavender eyes.''

"How romantic!" Netta clapped her hands in a girlish gesture that surprised Bree. "Tell me more about Crosshaven. Did you have many parties?''

Bree smiled happily, eager to share the enjoyment and excitement of Crosshaven with her new friend. She rambled on and on, weaving Netta into a magical web of honeysuckle and jasmine-scented nights, lavish dinners laid out to accommodate a hundred guests, and the sounds of a waltz drifting through a cool, dark evening under the brilliance of a full moon. At one point she caught herself on the verge of relating how she'd met Phillip and been courted by him but stopped herself in time. No, that wouldn't do. Then she would have to explain Jemson's presence, and even if Netta accepted the reasoning behind the plan she had been forced to hastily formulate, would she as easily believe the arrangement between Jemson and Bree was purely a monetary agreement? Then, of course, Netta would almost certainly tell Will, and who could trust a man to keep his mouth shut?

After Netta had left in the late afternoon to feed her children—they were like little birds, their mouths always open, either squawking for attention or food—and Lucy was off buying milk from the Dutchman with two cows, Bree sat by herself and thought about the problem of Jemson Tyler.

She really had gotten herself into a terrible mess. Repeatedly over the last weeks Bree would have given anything to be free of his abhorrent presence. Aside from the unkempt appearance he stubbornly wore like a badge of defiance, the man was incorrigibly sullen and increasingly rude to the small group—with the exception of Will and Netta—that gathered around their fire each evening. Just the other night Bree had been delighted to learn that Robb Andrews was entering into partnership in a business venture with his brother, who waited for him in Colorado, and not chasing the elusive lure of gold like most of the fool men traveling with the train.

"Scrapin' in the rocks and riverbeds ain't the only way a man can find his future," Robb had stated confidently, echoing Phillip's written words almost exactly. "You offah a simple man somethin' he's pinin' for and he'll pay any price."

Bree had agreed enthusiastically but Jemson had been moved from his stony silence, blue eyes clouded with contempt, his voice laced with sarcasm.

"And there'll always be men like you, Andrews, standing around like vultures ready to pick the pockets of the miners."

It took every ounce of Bree's self-control not to lash out at Jemson, as much for Phillip as for Robb. But Robb had lightened the tense moment with a mirthless laugh, treating the insult as a joke.

"How dare you talk to my friends in that manner!" Bree confronted Jemson after the others had gone. "You're extremely lucky, you know. Robb chose to overlook your remarks for my sake."

"Your sake?" Jemson laughed unpleasantly. "That coward would have 'overlooked' it if I'd poured hot coffee down his drawers."

"I don't expect a man like you to understand the way a gentleman behaves. All *you* know are fists and guns and laboring from sunup to sundown," Bree retorted, teeth clenched and shaking with rage. "What do you know of refinement and good breedin'? I . . ."

Jemson stopped her tirade by abruptly grabbing both of Bree's flailing hands and pinning them behind her back, drawing her up and within inches of his chest.

"You're a beauty standing there with your eyes blazing, I'll give you that, but I'm not going to argue with you on a way of life you don't know the first thing about." With that, Jemson released one of her arms and landed a playful slap on Bree's backside. She was left openmouthed with indignation as he dropped her other arm and walked out into the darkness on the edge of camp to see to the teams. Even now, Bree bristled with the indignity of his treatment of her. How dare he put his hand to her in such a familiar fashion? She had half a mind to report his impertinence to Phillip when they reached Colorado. Why, Phillip would take a bullwhip to Jemson and open his back proper, that's all. A moment of hesitation invaded Bree's daydream. The truth was, Jemson was vastly bigger and stronger then Phillip and could, most likely, take the whip out of his hands like a bully taking a licorice whip from a child. The thought sapped Bree's anger and dreams for revenge.

Jemson had more than one insulting episode to answer for, although Bree had to admit Robb was at least partly to blame. She had little patience for Southerners who extolled the virtues and problems of owning slaves to a group of people who knew little or nothing about the economic necessities and viewed slavery as a mortal sin. It was a little like pitting David against four Goliaths and giving him a broken slingshot.

"If all the nigras in Georgia were set free tomorrah, they'd die off like turkeys in a shoot." Robb had rambled on during one of their evening gatherings, oblivious to the cold stares his litany was receiving. "They's helpless, I tell you. Cain't read nor write. It's the nature of a nigra, bein' stupid and that's true. Why, it's a fact, ain't no one but it's mastah can understan what the pore devil's saying'."

"I've traveled in the South, Mr. Andrews," Jemson interjected lazily, a slight, humorless smile playing across his mouth. "And it's been my experience that the reason most slaves speak so poorly and are sadly illiterate is because they take their lessons from the men who own them and force them into bondage. Your slaves, Mr. Andrews, speak two languages—their native tongue and the English of their captors. Surely that indicates an intelligence at least as great as that of your Creole aristocracy?"

"You can learn a bird to mimic words, Tyler, when it already knows how to sing. That don't make a bird intelligent, does it?" Robb answered weakly, knowing he had lost the argument but unable to stop his childish retort. He knew that Jemson had made him appear foolish in front of the others and Bree had seen by the depth of rage in Robb's eyes that he would somehow repay the humiliation tenfold.

But, Bree mused, there were many ways, though not entirely honorable, to exact punishment. Jemson Tyler was an enigma, one moment using the lingo of a field hand, the next, speaking like an educated Yankee. He spent long, hard hours in the saddle and, instead of falling into slumber like the rest of them, prowled the night like a man with a purpose, a man with thoughts weighing heavily on his mind. More and more, Bree had come to realize he was a man with a secret.

The thunderous revelation washed over Bree, leaving her cold. That must be it! Jemson Tyler was perhaps wanted by the law. He was probably a murderer—at the very least, a robber.

Between talking with Netta and thinking about Jemson, the day had slipped away. The sky blazed with the pink and orange hues of sunset. Bree looked guiltily around the campsite, already deciding what she would do. Lucy was nowhere to be seen, probably off bargaining for the food stuffs that added a special touch to the meals she prepared. Bree sighed with relief and peered cautiously toward the wagons. A dark shadow obliterated the underside of the Conestoga where Jemson kept his bedroll and the few things he'd brought with him on the journey.

Glancing once more over her shoulder to make sure she wasn't being observed, Bree made for the wagon and slipped under the wooden planks, her fingers already busy with the task of untying the leather thongs that held Jemson's bedroll secure. A momentary pang of shame washed over her. Reduced to sneaking about like a common thief—it was demeaning! Suddenly she hit on an idea that lessened her sense of humiliation. The marriage certificate Jemson had been sorely pressed to turn over, despite Bree's demands. Why, she had every right to search for it. It belonged to her as well as to Jemson. And if that search took her to a darkened corner under an absurdly shaped pile of wood and nails, that too was her right. And when she found the marriage certificate and whatever else might be hidden in Jemson's horde, she would burn the odious document.

Working quickly, she unrolled the woolen blanket and nudged its contents to the far side of the wagon, away from prying eyes and toward the failing light of dusk. The inventory yielded nothing suspicious—two pair of pants, two flannel shirts, an extra pair of boots, an overcoat, woolen drawers, shaving razor, a bar of soap, a Bible . . .

Bree's hand stopped short. A Bible. Jemson hadn't struck her as the sort of man to carry a Bible. It was new; its leather cover, held tightly with a leather band, was unmarred and shiny. She gazed at it for a few seconds, then loosened the strap and parted the pages. Inside, the Bible had been hollowed out to accommodate a doeskin pouch. Bree's fingers trembled as she haltingly plucked the pouch from its hiding place. She knew instinctively that the pouch held the keys to unlocking the grip Jemson held on her life—the marriage certificate, a wanted poster, a newspaper clipping documenting the horrible deeds he had performed.

Bree sucked in her breath, strangely hesitant to delve into the pouch. Did she really want to know whatever private sins Jemson carried with him? Did she want to be privy to the secrets of his life? What if he really were a murderer—what would she do? Expose him to Abel Dunsfield and pay the consequences of her own part in the deception? Yes, her mind screamed, you would turn him in without a second thought! Still, her hand wavered and she felt weak and uncertain. Phillip, her brain blazed, Phillip! Everything you do is for Phillip. Determined and fired with righteous purpose, Bree pulled at the tie and dumped the contents of the pouch onto her billowing skirt. The first thing that caught her eye was a folded wad of hundred dollar notes. Puzzled, she set them aside and picked up several pieces of heavy paper, thinking one of them must be the coveted certificate that bound her, bigamously, to Jemson. She was disappointed to see that none of the documents mentioned Bryna Alexander. Printed on the heavy parchment were the names of Jemson and Matthew Tyler. As she read the words, Bree's head clouded with mindless, consuming anger. Bank drafts! Made out to Jemson in the accumulated amounts of five thousand dollars, drawn on the account of Tyler and Sons Mining

Company of Monaca, Pennsylvania. Bree grabbed savagely at the wad of bills she'd discarded earlier. Six hundred dollars. It took a few moments to clear her head and think with anything more than directionless rage. He was pretending to be a saddle tramp to protect the money he was carrying, that much was clear. He had even gone so far as to accept her offer in Missouri to further his charade of the gold-seeking, dirt-poor farmer. Who would suspect a shabbily dressed cowboy traveling in the company of his wife of possessing the money she now held in her hands? To further the illusion, Bree had reluctantly packed away her fine dresses in favor of the uglier but cooler cottons that were more comfortable on the trail.

Bree looked down at her hands, red and callused from driving the wagon even though she'd taken the precaution of wearing gloves. *She* certainly had helped Jemson play his game, turning more each day into a typical, tired, dull-witted woman of the plains. From the first night the Georges and Robb Andrews had gathered by their campsite, Bree had unknowingly, yet steadily, let herself slip into a routine that had, no doubt, suited Jemson immensely. She no longer bothered with her clothing or her hair, preferring to pile her flaming red locks on her head and stuff the thick, unruly mess under a bonnet. She had stopped using touches of rouge to her cheeks and mouth, stopped putting cream on her face to make it soft and alluring, because the morning hours left only enough time to eat and ready the team and wagons for the day's travel.

And all the time she had been conveniently turning into the tired hag Jemson needed to carry out his masquerade, that devil had been sitting on five thousand dollars, as sly as you please. She wouldn't even attempt to guess what the money was for—it didn't matter. What *did* matter was that she had been truthful with him, pouring out her troubles, and he had deceived her, pretending to do her a service for one hundred dollars. And, holding it over her head, threatening to expose her if she got out of line. The nerve of him!

Bree stuffed the money and bank drafts back into the pouch and returned it to its place inside the Bible. How like Jemson Tyler to desecrate a Bible! She gathered up the rest of his belongings and carefully arranged them in the blanket before rolling it back up and securing it with the leather ties. Crawling out from under the wagon, she smoothed her skirt and flicked off the dirt, her fingers tapping in steady rhythm as she decided what she would do with the new-found knowledge she possessed. She was surprised to find she was rather disappointed that Jemson was not the desperado she'd imagined. The huge amount of money was bewildering but apparently legal. And just where was the elusive marriage certificate if not with Jemson's other belongings? Surely he didn't carry it on his person—what value could it hold to be guarded so closely? Again, Bree's head was buzzing with more questions about Jemson than she could find answers for. Again, thoughts of him confused her and kept her slightly off center.

A full moon shone over the campsite and a warm summer breeze rustled gently in the air. I wish, Bree thought fervently, I wish I was sharin' this night in Phillip's arms instead of bein' stuck here with a pack of strangers and liars! Lord, it's a lonely place.

From far off, the sound of horses thundering across the plains, the sound of the men returning from hunting, echoed through the night, the ground vibrating beneath her. Bree's heart thumped painfully in her chest and she felt her throat dry up and tighten with excitement. The arid taste of victory rolled deliciously around in her mouth.

A half hour later, when the game had been distributed and the men went wearily back to their wagons, Bree stood like an unmovable pillar in front of Jemson, blocking his way.

"I went through your bedroll this afternoon, lookin' for my marriage paper," she informed him bluntly, a brightness glowing behind her green eyes.

"Too bad you didn't find it," Jemson answered lightly, seemingly unconcerned.

"No, but I did find a very interestin' Bible." Bree could hardly keep from laughing. "Why Jemson, I had no idea the Holy Word meant so much to you."

"So you found the money—so what? Did you hope I'd fall to my knees and beg you not to tell anyone?" He watched her carefully, surprise turning to cold, hard anger. His voice was low and challenging. He moved closer and glared down at her with casual disdain.

"*I* would expect you to be ashamed of deceivin' me, you dirty clodhopper!" Bree shouted angrily. "Pretendin' to be some kind of white trash farmer, wearin' shabby clothes and shamin' me 'cause I'm supposed to be your wife." Bree doubled up her fist and slammed it into Jemson's belly with a force that immediately made her hand throb and ache. She grasped the wounded hand and recoiled. It had been like ramming a wall of solid oak. He didn't even have the grace to wince.

Jemson sighed, tired and suddenly bored with the constant battle of wills Bree forced him into.

"Don't try to hold the money over my head, Bryna," he warned her quietly. "We both have secrets we don't want anyone else to know. It's a standoff. Accept it." He started past Bree and turned his head to see Lucy watching them. She acknowledged him with a quick nod of satisfied approval and smiled. "Lucy, can you hold off that good-smelling stew for an hour or so? I'm bone tired but I've got to take the time to wash this trail dust off."

"Sure thing, Mr. Jemson," Lucy called out happily, refusing to back down from Bree's wilting stare. "You take yore time, we jist be waitin' on you." She chuckled and turned back to tend the simmering stew.

Jemson grinned and stretched his arms in a gesture that made the muscles in his back ripple through the dusty flannel shirt he wore. Unstrapping his gun and dropping the belt under the wagon, he snatched up his bedroll and sauntered off toward the Georges' wagon.

"Dish me up a plate of that stew, Lucinda." Bree advanced menacingly. "Now!"

An hour later Jemson returned to find the campsite quiet and abandoned. The fire flickered unattended, threatening to go out all together. He crossed over to Lucy's wagon and raised the flap, seeing her sleeping form.

"Where's Bryna?" Jemson whispered through the darkness. Lucy snapped to a sitting position and shook her head drowsily.

"She say she tends to fixin' up yore supper, Mister Jemson." Lucy yawned and fell back on the covers. "Miss Bree, sweet chile, she tell Lucy to git my sleep."

Jemson whispered his thanks and replaced the flap. He glanced over at the dim fire and made out the shape of the pot, overturned, its contents spilled out into the dirt.

It took him three minutes to find her. Bree was sitting beside Robb Andrews's fire, laughing and sipping hot, spiced coffee. Without a word, Jemson grabbed her arm and lifted her bodily, flinging her over his hip in a most unladylike fashion. The coffee cup went flying, hitting the side of Robb's wagon with a thud. Jemson lugged Bree unceremoniously to their camp and deposited her rudely in the rocking chair. The wicker creaked and rebelled under the force of his thrust. A low growl began in Bree's throat, threatening to burst forward in a full-fledged bellow of indignation.

"Shut up!" Jemson ordered, his jaw clenched. "I warned you about trailing off after that spineless pantywaist." He threw some wood on the fire and hunkered over to stoke the flames, his back toward Bree. "You're the one always so worried about shame and saving your face . . ."

"Don't you lecture me, Jemson Tyler," Bree gasped. "You're hired trash, that's all. I don't care how much money you've got hidden away or what it's for! You're still nothing but hired help." She got up from the rocker and walked shakily toward him. "I paid you one hundred dollars to be my husband for two months. I will *not* be treated like a possession, a piece of baggage. Our agreement doesn't give you the right to treat me as though I really am your wife. And don't try to threaten me about exposin' me to Mr. Dunsfield. He might make me leave the train but he wouldn't take you with him either, and I have a feelin' you're as anxious as I am to make Colorado before the snows." She was directly behind him now and, for the first time since knowing him, didn't feel dwarfed by his presence. "You were right, we're at a standoff. I suggest we just stay out of each other's way so we can go about our business in peace. As for my friends, *I'll* choose them myself, without any help or guidance from you. And don't ever try draggin' me off again, you hear?"

Jemson turned his face away from the fire and looked up at Bree before standing and drawing himself up to his full height. Anything else Bree might have wanted to say died on her lips. Eyes widening with surprise and shock, Bree studied the man who stood before her. Jemson had shaved off his beard and mustache. His sun-streaked brown hair fell in wayward curls around his neck and the fire lit golden sparks deep in his blue eyes. The removal of facial hair emphasized a strong jaw and a straight, slightly flared nose.

Bree felt as if something hard and cold were gripping her chest. She found it difficult to breathe, so intense was the reaction she felt. She realized with a start that Jemson was handsome under all that hair and dust, the most masculinely handsome man she had ever seen. Not appealing in the way Phillip's beautiful, aristocratic features and bearing had stirred her senses but in a pure, animal aura of attraction. He was smooth, brown granite, a hard, muscled rock of a man.

Jemson seemed to sense her confusion and conflicting emotions. The moment he smiled, sure of himself, Bree reacted and took the offensive.

"Get this straight, once and for all, Jemson," she spat viciously. "Washing up and changing your shirt doesn't make you something you can never be and won't help you get anything that doesn't belong to you. *Nothing* has changed! I want that marriage paper and I want it now!''

''What you want and what you're likely to get are two separate things, my dear wife.'' Jemson shrugged casually. ''I'll make some excuse for you and eat my supper with Will and Netta, if they'll have me. *You* better clean up this mess you've made and get some sleep. See you in the morning.''

He turned and walked off in the direction of the Georges' campsite, leaving Bree trembling with hatred, her fists pressed tightly to her sides. She hated him for his arrogance, his uncouth manner, his way of treating her as though she were a worthless brat, and for being able to bring out all the worst instincts in her character. And she hated him for the feeling that ached in the pit of her stomach, the breathless tightness in her throat, and the sudden unexplainable yearning she was unable to identify.

CHAPTER FIVE

Just past the Cimarron Crossing, more than halfway to their destination, Bree pulled up the team and sagged with relief. Another day had passed, another day closer. She raised a gloved hand and kneaded the tight muscles at the base of her neck, then lowered her arm and slipped off the gloves and critically examined her hands. She had taken to applying cream to her hands before starting the day's travel and it was working wonders. Bree shivered with anticipation. The sun had not completed its descent into darkness and they were stopped for the day to give the women time enough to feed their families and prepare for the party. A party! It seemed like years since Bree had last heard the laughter and music of a party.

She stepped gingerly from the bench of the wagon and landed carefully on the ground, thinking it would be just her luck to slip and break an ankle. Lifting her face toward the warmth of the setting sun, Bree whipped off her bonnet and turned in circles, hugging herself. The party was something they had all been looking forward to for over a week.

She skipped back toward Lucy's wagon and hurried her off it with joyous, silent beckoning of her waving hands, then grabbed her and nearly crushed the shocked woman in a bear hug. Without being asked, Bree pitched in to help with the fire and preparing the meal.

Sweet babe, Lucy smiled slightly, you don't rightly

know it yore own self but you is comin' into a fine woman.

It was true. Without conscious effort or planning, each day taught Bree the lessons she would one day hold invaluable. She could not have pinpointed the exact time it had struck her that Lucy was just as tired as she after a day of driving the teams but, nonetheless, she had begun to join in the work that started when the sun was setting and they were all aching for good food and hot coffee. She wasn't sure when Netta's children had ceased to remind her of wild animals and had instead become objects of delight. Somehow she found the time to show the girls the fine art of petit point and help the boys with the perplexing problem of book reading. And, miraculously, the days seemed shorter now, the work less grueling. The only difference Bree had deliberately sought was in her appearance. Jemson had changed, overnight, into something of a dandy, fanatically clean shaven and fresh after the end of each day on the trail. And she'd be damned if she'd ever hear anyone clucking and saying what a shame it was that poor Missus Tyler let herself go so badly, married to such a fine-looking man. Instead of tucking her hair up under the ever-present bonnet, Bree brushed her red curls each morning until they glistened and gathered the tresses at the nape of her neck with a brightly colored ribbon. The new ritual continued with gobs of cream on her face and hands, followed by just a touch, since there was no need to shock the farmers' wives, of rouge to her cheeks and mouth. Getting up a half hour earlier than the others all these weeks had paid off handsomely. The image she saw in her mirror was greatly pleasing. Her mood was improved, knowing the face that peeked out from under the bonnet was that of Bree Alexander of Crosshaven plantation.

She would never get used to being called Missus Tyler. Even now, the other passengers sometimes had to repeat the name to get her attention. Lucy certainly got a giggle out of calling her Missus Tyler any time she got the chance.

69

Bree knelt and fanned the budding fire, her thoughts focusing on Jemson. Since the night, weeks ago, of their big argument they had both tried to be civil and pleasant while in the company of others. But it irked her so to hear the accolades of praise heaped on him by the other travelers. Will George was sure no one could hunt or ride as well as her husband. No one could find game, Mr. Dunsfield proudly announced, with as much ease as Jemson Tyler could. And, among his own circle of friends, Jemson was considered to be a great hand at poker and the telling of tall tales. In the evenings he would usually leave in the company of Will George and Abel Dunsfield while Bree and Netta enjoyed the wit and social charms of Robb Andrews. It had proved a generally acceptable agreement. If Jemson elected to stay around the fire, Robb would leave after paying his respects. It annoyed Bree to admit it, but she was sure she had seen a flicker of fear in Robb's eyes whenever Jemson was about.

All right, so Robb wasn't a brave man. Still, he amused Bree and, most of all, Netta. At the end of a long day Netta was thirsty for talk and she enjoyed Robb's detailed reminiscences of Georgia and a more genteel way of life. Bree felt her relationship with this woman was vitally special and important. It was the first time she had experienced friendship without the taint of rivalry. Each accepted the other for what she was, drawing from the other's strengths and fortifying the weaknesses.

"Miss Bree!" Lucy's voice broke into her fond reverie. "I done laid out yore purty green dress for the party so's to drop out the wrinkles from it bein' packed away so long. Now you move on over and let me set this here pot to boilin' so's we gits our vittles when Mister Jemson rides in."

Jemson, Bree thought in a rush of irritation. How like him to stay out huntin' and lolly-gaggin' around. He still strove to irritate her at every turn, but in small ways so that no one would be the wiser. No one but Bree. It made her want to scream the way he insisted upon calling her

Bryna when he knew she preferred the shorter, friendlier Bree. He had a way of making Bryna sound like a cuss word. Yes, it would be just like him to stay out all evening just to make her suffer. It wouldn't be proper for her to attend the party unescorted by her "husband." The thought nearly froze her feet to the ground. Would he be so mean? Would he deprive her of the enjoyment of the party just because they didn't like each other? If he did that . . .

Her questions were answered by his slow approach on horseback. He nodded silently, then dismounted and began to unhitch the teams and move them off toward the rotunda.

Bree exhaled with relief, a feeling akin to gratitude for Jemson rushing over her. Now, if they could only be civil long enough to make it through the evening. She supposed she would have to dance with him, if only for appearance's sake. Well, that was the price she was willing to pay for an evening's entertainment. It shouldn't be too difficult to slip away and dance with others once their social duties were seen to. Robb had mentioned a new dance from France she was anxious to have him teach her. Surely Jemson wouldn't make a scene over something as innocent as that. Still, there had been times over the last three weeks when the look she had seen in his eyes had both frightened and fascinated her.

They were camped alongside a stream, swollen with the winter's thaw. After a hasty meal, Bree left the camp with Netta and several other women to bathe. When she returned, her dress clinging wetly to the contours of her body, Bree rushed past Jemson as he was gathering his clothes and shaving equipment and hopped into the wagon to avoid the searching heat of his gaze.

She dallied shamelessly, picking up each piece of jewelry in her case before choosing tiny emerald earrings bordered with small pearls. She had naturally curly hair, and as it dried it fell in cascades down her back. Instead of pinning her hair on top of her head, Bree brushed it and let it fall free over her shoulders. Clad only in a molded chemise, she picked up the corset she would normally

71

have worn and shuddered. It was always so hard to breathe in the damn things. Tossing it aside, she decided any woman fortunate enough to have a seventeen-inch waist didn't need a corset anyway.

Lucy called softly and opened the flap of the wagon. Bree had been so engrossed in the preparation of dressing that she hadn't noticed the sun was almost down. She grinned broadly and took the lantern Lucy offered, setting it on the wooden floor of the wagon. She was only vaguely conscious of Lucy speaking to someone else after reclosing the flap. Bree was too excited about the prospect of feeling the silky texture of the emerald green ballgown against her skin to notice anything else. It had been so long since she'd dressed in her fine clothes.

Outside the wagon, Jemson gratefully accepted the cup of coffee Lucy handed him and settled down next to the fire to wait until Bree was finished dressing. He was pleasantly surprised to find the coffee was heavily laced with whiskey and was about to question Lucy on the whereabouts of the bottle when he realized she had disappeared from sight. He shrugged and looked toward Bree's wagon. The lantern she had placed on the floorboards was behind her and cast a clear silhouette onto the canvas covering the wagon. She was larger than life, as vividly defined as a painting, her small, round body brilliantly outlined above him. Jemson stared as though hypnotized, unable to tear his gaze away as she reached for a jar of scent and spread the oil over her arms and across her breasts. She knelt on the floor of the wagon and leaned forward to peer into the small mirror she had placed on top of a trunk and adjusted the earrings she'd chosen. Using both hands, Bree lifted her hair away from her ears and examined the handiwork. When she stood up again, she bent slightly to brush off her knees, then straightened and began to tuck in the bodice of her chemise. Looking at the dress hanging nearby, she judged the chemise too high in front and unbuttoned it before casting it aside and moving to her trunk to retrieve another, more daring chemise.

Lady, Jemson thought tightly, if you knew fifty men were out here watching you, you couldn't put on a more effective striptease. Damn! He didn't like her much, but he was sure as hell then that he wanted her. He didn't respect her, but he'd like a chance at trying to thaw that mound of snow she called a heart.

The changes that had taken place in Bree hadn't gone unnoticed by Jemson, either. But he didn't give them much credence. He felt that any animal could adjust to a foreign environment, but once back in their natural state, they easily shifted around again.

The minute that woman lays eyes on her gentleman, Jemson mused bitterly, she'll be shouting orders and expecting everyone to wait on her agin. The South bred their women weak and selfish. A lifetime of example couldn't be changed by two months on the trail. Ah, Jemson thought, his eyelids closing slightly, but I sure like the way you hold your head high. I like your fire. Things being different, we could have spent these long nights a comfort to each other.

Damn woman, he cursed silently, I can see it in your gem-colored eyes when you catch me looking at you. It's taking you a mighty long time to understand what all that heat is about. What kind of a man is your husband? If I had you to my bed for a week, you'd sure as hell be able to read the want in a man's eyes quick enough.

Bree heard the whining scream of a fiddle being tuned, the plunking scale of a guitar warming up, the escalating hum of human voices. She reached quickly for her gown and pulled it over her head and then fluffed her hair and attached the buttons at the back of her dress. They were tiny, silk-covered, slippery things, and she was only able to maneuver them halfway up her back. She stomped her small foot and shook her head, knowing she would have to call on Lucy to complete the task. Taking a last look around and satisfied that everything was in order, Bree shut off the kerosene to the lantern and tried to exit through the back flap. Her foot got tangled up in the yards of silk of her skirt and she swore under her breath.

"*Most* unladylike, Missus Tyler," Jemson admonished her playfully. "What would your good neighbors think if they heard you cussing like that?"

"Where is Lucy?" Bree ignored his comments, wondering what he was doing standing there in the dark. "I need her help. Go and get her, would you . . . *please*?"

"I have no idea where Lucy went off to. She left right after I got back for the stream. Maybe she's got a secret admirer."

"A beau? More likely she's washing up!" Bree snapped, refusing to acknowledge Jemson's light-hearted mood and barely able to contain her irritation.

"I'll help you down. Come on, don't be so damned stubborn or you'll miss the party. No telling when Lucy will be back."

Bree hesitated, strangely reluctant to allow Jemson's hands on her. Her breath caught in her throat, that unpleasant churning feeling she had fought so hard to suppress returning, making her dizzy. Still, Jemson's arms were outstretched and waiting. If she wanted to get to the party she would either have to accept the gesture or be rude and chance another argument. She choose the easier of the two options and locked hands with Jemson, but as he helped her down his hands slipped along her arms and caught her at the waist. Bree was about to protest when she realized he was lifting her in order to remove a part of her skirt that had caught on a nail protruding from the wagon. One arm circled her waist and drew her to his chest as his free hand worked to unwrap the stubborn silk from its captor. Bree could feel Jemson's heart pounding against her breast. She was at a loss as to where her own hands should go. She felt like a fool leaning against him with her arms fluttering, like a wounded bird. Finally, she tried to relax and draped her hands carefully around his neck just as he freed her skirt. His eyes had been averted while at the task but now they locked with hers and Bree felt a warmth that staggered her. The position in which he

74

held her forced her mouth only fractions of an inch away from his. The look of hunger plainly visible on his face mesmerized and weakened her. She gasped, sucking in air, realizing that she hadn't been breathing in the seconds that had passed.

Jemson set her gently on the ground, the spell broken, and stepped back, a pained expression leaping into then disappearing from his eyes.

"I, ah, need Lucy," Bree stammered insistently, her heart pounding so loud it rang through her head. "My buttons, I couldn't fasten them all."

"Then around. I'll do it." Jemson's tone was bleak as he nudged her toward the light of the fire. He was angrier than necessary, angrier than he could explain when he tackled the first few buttons. His large fingers fumbled with the dainty, slippery little fastenings and he cursed softly and let his arms drop to his side, defeated by the simple task.

"Try again, Jemson," Bree pleaded. "I can't go to the party with my dress undone. I should have thought you were one man with a great deal of experience with the buttons on a lady's dress." Bree was uncomfortably aware of the darkness outside the circle of light from the fire, painfully conscious of being alone in Jemson's presence and anxious to hurry away. She would be safe—but safe from what—if she could escape the dominance of the feeling that was engulfing her, if she could only get away and join the others at the party. The feel of Jemson's fingers on her bare skin as he began to work the buttons again nearly sent her reeling. As he neared the top of her gown the sensation that had been rolling through her loins, burning and tormenting, burst forward and spread along her body. Her thighs ached and grew rigid, her breasts and nipples strained against the confines of her gown. Dreamlike, she wanted nothing more than to turn to Jemson and have him crush her in his arms and feel the moistness of his mouth against her lips.

Bree choked and blushed with shame. Her mind's eye

could see Phillip clearly glaring at her with the familiar look of disgust and reproach.

"Thank God, that's done." Jemson patted the last button and waited for Bree to turn around. When she didn't move of her own accord, he put his hands on her shoulders and turned her forcibly. "What the hell is wrong now?" he growled, bewildered by her downcast eyes, realizing suddenly he could stand almost anything from this woman except the crushing look of distress that now seemed to overwhelm her. Her anger and intolerance, the spoiled demands were preferable to this wilting behavior.

"Thinking of your precious Phillip? Wishing it was him walking you over to the party?" Jemson's voice was deliberately cruel, hoping she would rise to the bait. "You're paying a hundred dollars for this walk, lady. Let's go." He reached for Bree's arm.

"You've pawed me more than enough for one evening, Jemson." Bree's eyes flashed, the liquid green fire returning. "Keep your hands where they belong." She tossed her head and watched him warily. Any yearning she had fallen victim to disappeared in a flood of rage at his callous reference to Phillip and the money. But in her anger, she noticed for the first time that he was dressed differently. The faded denim had been replaced by soft, form-fitting doeskin trousers. They were tucked smoothly into the fancy dress boots she'd seen when going through his bedroll. He wore a dark blue muslin shirt, open at the neck and pulled snugly over massive shoulders.

"You know, Jemson," Bree observed coldly, hoping to offend and humiliate him, "your homespun, woodsy looks might appeal to a certain type of woman. Perhaps you'll find some unattached female tonight who is well suited to appreciate your charms."

"Wouldn't do me much good, now would it, Bryna? Not with my loving wife in tow." To her chagrin, he seemed more amused than hurt. "Now, are we going to the party or do you want to stand here all night trading insults?"

CHAPTER SIX

Bree stood on the outside of the music and laughter, stubbornly refusing to join in. She knew she was over-dressed, looking more like an indulgent queen granting the childish whims of her subjects than a member of the wagon train eager to lose herself in the shared enjoyment of a party. An hour ago she had rushed from Jemson's side to acknowledge the flowery compliments of Robb Andrews and bask in the unabashed stares of envy from the other, plainly dressed, women. Then the music had begun in earnest and her glorious entrance was forgotten. The evening suddenly came alive with the colors of the women's billowing gowns—blue, yellow, green, red. Singly, the gowns seemed drab and simple, yet as a group they combined in a smiling, lively rainbow. Pink sprang to the cheeks of even the palest of complexions; eyes flashed and sparkled. Bree felt a pang of impotent jealousy. The homeliest woman was as beautiful as she herself when laughing and dancing with a man who loved her.

Bree and Robb stared in disbelief as the dancers formed small boxes and hooted and stomped their feet in time with the high-spirited music, the spectacle staged by a man calling out instructions to the partners.

What they called a square dance, Robb informed Bree drily, something people with little grace and no social gifts called dancing. He, for one, would stay where he was until something that resembled a waltz or quadrille was played. Bree had no choice but to half-heartedly agree and take a position next to him. After abandoning Jemson, there was nothing else she could do without looking the fool. For his part, Jemson had shrugged and taken Bree's advice, grabbing up an unattached woman and joining Netta and Will. So far, there had been three different females; Bree was finding it increasingly harder to follow Robb's conversation. A full moon shone down with the light of a hundred lanterns and the warm night breeze, rich with the smell of the earth and grass, filled her nostrils with its heady scent. A torrent of conflicting emotions boiled inside Bree's veins. She wanted to march over to Jemson, slap him soundly, scratch out his eyes, put her arms around him and kiss away the pain she caused.

Damn him to hell! What about the pain *she* was enduring? It struck Bree what an object of pity she must now seem to the others, dressed in all her finery and standing on the sidelines with a pompous boor while her "husband" flirted and danced with every other woman in attendance.

"Ah say, Miz Bree," Robb repeated insistently, "Ah cain't tell you how much the company of a fine, genteel lady like yourself means to me in the midst of all this. Why, these Yankees don't conduct themselves any bettah than a bunch of nigras."

Bree murmured absently, reluctant to tear her gaze from the spectacle of Jemson and his newest partner. He was deliberately humiliating her! "Well, it certainly isn't Crosshaven." She turned her back on the party, giving full attention to Robb.

"Ah fear you'll find Black Hawk Point isn't Crosshaven, either, Miz Bree. There won't be any of the gracious, elegant surroundings yore used to at this journey's end." Robb moved closer, his sweet-smelling cologne suddenly overwhelming and repugnant.

"My husband," Bree blurted defensively, "is more than capable of attending to my comfort, thank you. Phillip's sensitivities are my own." She rushed on without thinking. "I trust his judgment without question."

"Phillip?" Robb smiled thinly, shrewdly watching Bree gasp and redden. "Ah was sure Mister Tyler's name was Jemson." He snickered as though savoring her discomfort and then hastened to dull the shock. "Don't concern yoreself, Miz Bree. I've known all along that Jemson Tyler wasn't yore husband. Bein' from Georgia myself, I'd heard of Phillip Alexander's extreme good fortune in winnin' the most beautiful girl in Atlanta for his bride, a Miss Bryna McCarty of Crosshaven plantation, Ah believe." Robb reached out and took Bree's hand, patting it clumsily. "You need a friend you can trust. Why don't you tell me what circumstances forced you to tie in with an unsavory character like Tyler."

Bree winced inwardly at the look of condescending distaste on Robb's face. Somehow, it unnerved her to hear someone else speak poorly of Jemson. It was perfectly all right for Bree to dislike and ridicule him, but she suddenly found she wasn't pleased to hear anyone else, especially a weakling like Robb Andrews, find fault with Jemson. Nonetheless, he knew the truth and she found herself telling Robb haltingly about the obstacles she'd faced trying to join the wagon train in Kansas City, of hiring Jemson to play the part of her husband, of going through with a marriage ceremony in order to obtain the certificate a suspicious Abel Dunsfield insisted on seeing himself.

"You mean you married Jemson Tyler in a legal ceremony?" Robb whispered incredulously, his brown eyes widening with stunned surprise.

"Of course it's not legal!" Bree protested impatiently. "I'm already married to Phillip. It was just a matter of necessity."

"Necessity!" Robb erupted, astonished by her naiveté. "More like bigamy!" He echoed the words Jemson had used weeks before. "Do you have the paper? Have you destroyed it?" He seemed almost as anxious as she to erase the evidence.

"No, but I will." Bree spoke with more certainty than

she felt. "Jemson likes to think he can keep me in line if he has the silly thing hidden away. But now," she continued with a note of triumph in her voice, "I know somethin' about him he'd rather not have spread around so I'll get the paper eventually."

"What? What do you know?" Robb pressed cagily. He had moved closer and Bree felt the whiskey-laced heat of his breath on her cheek.

She stared silently, assessing the urgency behind his questions and then moved away, sullen and close-mouthed, realizing she had no reason to trust this man with his fancy clothes and perfumed hair. Shocked, she felt as though she were seeing him for the first time. He seemed anxious and furtive, the furrow in his brow distorting his skin into a pasty softness. He must have taken great pains to stay out of the sun, Bree thought scornfully, because his coloring was white and sickly when compared to the golden brown of Jemson's face. And above his pale face, Robb's black hair was pomaded, and the scented salve trapped and slicked curly locks to his head instead of letting them blow free in the breeze.

Was this how Phillip would appear to her? Bree was filled with horror and revulsion. She had grown used to the healthy, masculine look of Jemson and Will George. Would Phillip resemble more the foppish prig standing before her now? She shuddered, and Robb took the gesture to mean the secrets she had discovered about Jemson Tyler were too horrible to voice.

"Don't distress yoreself, Bree." Robb again reached out and touched her arm consolingly. "You can depend on my discretion." He was breathing heavily, his fingers playing along the softness of Bree's arm. "Ah *want* to take care of you, protect you from the realities of life. Let me see you back home to Crosshaven. There's nothin' but sorrow waitin' for you in Black Hawk Point. Ah can spare you that. Ah . . ."

Bree was so involved in her own thoughts that the words

Robb was whispering and the feel of his cold hand on her arm were like a delayed reaction. When it all set in, she recoiled, removing herself from his touch and the intimacy of his soft voice.

"This conversation, Mr. Andrews," she replied slowly, with false strength, "has gone as far as I wish it to go. *All* I require of you is that you keep my confidence. I'm sure my husband will be sufficiently grateful when I reach Colorado and receive you as a friend. Until then, I am quite able to handle my own affairs." Bree left little room for argument and turned back to view the dancing, unaware of the icy glint that had steeled Robb's eyes at her rebuff.

An instant later, she had made another decision. No matter the cost to her pride, she was leaving the party and retreating to the privacy and comfort of her wagon. It really made little difference. She could stand alone and continue watching everyone, including Jemson, having a wonderful time or she could withdraw like a chastised schoolgirl. Either way, her vanity had been delivered a fatal blow. Stiffening her back, Bree prepared to leave with as much dignity as she could muster.

"Bree?" Netta, dressed in a pale yellow calico, touched her hand softly. She looked lovely and pale. A silk ribbon, caught under her hair at the nape of her neck, adorned her cornsilk hair. "I feel just terrible. Honestly, Bree, it never occurred to me until just now, when Jemson said you don't do the same dances we do. I thought you two were having a little spat." Netta's laughter tinkled gently. "Anyway, I'm just ashamed! Isn't it lucky Mr. Strautsman is from somewhere in Europe? He knows all sorts of tunes for that fiddle of his, only he calls it a violin. Jemson got Feeney to take a rest and Mr. Strautsman is going to play a waltz, just for you." She leaned forward, blue eyes twinkling. "Really though, I could use something a little less rowdy. My dress is wringing wet."

As Netta spoke, the warm night was suddenly filled

with the haunting strains of a Strauss waltz. Will George came up behind his wife and took her hand to lead her out among the other couples. Netta sighed and curtsied.

Bree smiled fondly as she watched her two new friends playfully frolic to the music. Anger drained away, and she felt a rush of expectancy descend around her heart. Jemson's doing! He had arranged a change in the dancing. The thought—I suppose he thinks he has punished me enough—flitted through her mind but, pushing it away, Bree relaxed and waited. She could sense that Robb was on the verge of asking her to dance. Closing her eyes, she tried to halt the black feeling of his desire and hummed softly, slightly off tune, along with the vibrating tones that Mr. Strautsman drew on his violin, creating a fantasy world of music.

Bree could hear the intrusion of Robb moving in front of her. His hands were on her arms and she opened her eyes reluctantly, ready to turn him down. The refusal died on her lips. Jemson drew her closer, one hand edging down the length of her arm to clasp a hand and the other gathering her small waist in his embrace. He moved faultlessly to the music, standing over Bree like a protective shield, blanking out the night, the other dancers, and the uncomfortable memory of the past hour. Instinctively, mindlessly, she leaned closer to the glow that burned from Jemson's body, warming her. Bree forgot everything else—the distressing conversation with Robb Andrews, her faltering loyalty to Phillip, the people surrounding them, the obligatory distance of the waltz between their bodies; all was dismissed as she was pulled toward the fire that was Jemson. Even his words, whispered in her hair—isn't this better than fighting?—didn't faze her. Bree melted forward until her cheek rested on his chest and she could hear the erratic beat of his heart. The sound of it thrilled her, filling her with an almost forgotten sense of power, knowing it was her nearness that caused his blood to pound. She wondered briefly if Jemson could feel the answering thud of her own heart. Every fiber of her being was aching and tormented, wanting to be petted and caressed. Her nipples strained against the confines of silk, her thighs throbbed, and the dizzying, teasing sensation she had fought so long begged to be gratified.

The music stopped and she felt Jemson's grasp at her waist relax. Disappointment flooded over her like a night of rolling clouds. Bree opened her eyes and felt like crying. Then the violin began its magical web of dreams and she felt herself floating once again. Jemson was leading her toward a dim, private place and she shut her eyes again, knowing she needed and wanted what would soon take place. Pressing herself against him, fearful of losing the painful delight she felt, Bree was only vaguely aware that Jemson had stopped dancing. He moved his hand to cup her chin. Now, she thought lazily, now I'll be safe and warm.

Jemson's lips brushed her brow and closed eyelids tentatively and played slowly across her cheek. His hand caressed the curve of her neck and she felt the dam of her emotions break and flood in a wild surge of need. Bree twined both arms around Jemson's neck and forced his mouth to hers, pressing hard until she felt the dull ache of her teeth biting into the tender flesh inside her lips.

"It won't hurt so much if you open your mouth a bit, honey," Jemson instructed softly, a hint of amusement in his voice. "I guess you really are a tenderfoot in a lot of ways." It was said lightly, teasingly, but he regretted the words the moment they were said. Bree stiffened with embarrassment and the soft glaze began to shift behind her eyes. Jemson could feel her slipping, physically, away from him.

Well, he thought morosely, his daddy always said to strike while the iron was hot or, in this case, the lady was hot and he wanted very much for her to stay that way, at least until they reached their destination. Jemson cursed himself for a blundering fool and set about bringing the dreamlike look of desire back to Bree's face. His fingers stroked her neck lightly and he bent to kiss her again. He was surprised to find her mouth slightly parted, a shy concession. His tongue traced the outline of her lips, finding it shamefully soft and pliant. She was like a stubborn child—curious yet loath to follow instructions without getting her own licks in. Although her mouth was yielding, Jemson could still feel the rebellious tension in Bree's body. He wanted to crush her in his arms and ravish her with his tongue and hands but instinct told him to go slow.

She's like a high-spirited filly, he mused silently. She's been rode but she's never been bridled and broke.

From far away, he heard a building crescendo of voices, worried, panic-stricken voices—a woman's piercing cry, a man's shout. He looked at the clearing, where only moments ago the travelers had been laughing and dancing. Now they were gathered in a circle, almost as if they were guarding something at their core. More than anything else, he wanted to take Bree and lead her back to the wagon, lie with her on the softness of blankets, remove the silk trappings that held her body and mind prisoner, fondle the breasts that no cotton sack could hide, and run his hands over the smooth texture of her skin.

But someone called his name, and it set off an ingrained reaction. He dropped his arms from around Bree and looked at her ruefully, as if saying another time, promise me there'll be another time. Her expression of sad frustration told him the moment had been lost to him. He stood uncertain, then heard the voice again, Abel Dunsfield's, louder, more anxious. Jemson let out a long sigh and took Bree's hand, leading her toward the circle of passengers. She followed obediently, shaken and afraid to speak, afraid her voice would betray the weakness she had felt in his arms. Besides, he had made an obvious choice. It was all right to trifle with her in the shadows of a deserted wagon, but when his friends, the people he really cared for, called him, he left her without a second thought.

The crowd parted as they approached and then closed again, swallowing Jemson and Bree, the air thick with fear.

Feeney, the fiddler, lay on the ground, his hands clutching his abdomen. He was flushed, his face contorted with pain. His body jerked spasmodically as his wife sought to touch and comfort him. Abel Dunsfield reached out and pulled Jemson near, his voice urgent, trying to keep what he had to say low.

"Feeney went into Ludlow this morning for a string for that damn fiddle of his! Doc here says he thinks the old fool was exposed to something while he was there, might even be cholera. Can't be sure for a while, though, so better not to start a panic until we know definite. I'll settle the people down. Think you'd be wantin' to ride over to Ludlow and talk to the doctor there?"

Cholera. The word was pushed back and forth, and the circle widened as the partygoers moved back grimly from the writhing Feeney. Some bolted and ran, others stood docilely, awaiting orders.

"Sure," Jemson answered quickly, unconsciously stepping in front of Bree. "Just let me see my wife safe and I'll saddle up."

They walked swiftly to the wagon, Bree's hand still safely encased in Jemson's strong, sure grip.

"Be careful," she said finally, stunned by the desperation she felt as she watched Jemson strap on his gun and pick up the saddle. He turned and headed for the line where his horse was tethered. "Don't do anythin' stupid. If anything happens to you . . ." She stopped short, hopelessly searching for a way to salvage the memory of who she was and what waited for her in Colorado. "If anythin' happens to you, Jemson, it would make it difficult for me to reach Black Hawk Point."

CHAPTER SEVEN

Feeney died and his wife and children were taken ill hours before Jemson returned with the confirmation that the townspeople of Ludlow were waging a losing battle with cholera.

"The whole town's under quarantine now," he told Abel Dunsfield, "but it's a mite late for us, I'm afraid. All we can do is separate the healthy from the sick and bury our dead when we have to."

The first day was a nightmare of crying and fear-pinched faces as the disease struck indiscriminately. A lone camp was set up five hundred yards behind the last wagon of the train. Mothers nursed their stricken children and husbands. Children whose parents were both ill were taken, reluctantly, by other families. Friendly faces grew tight with suspicion as everyone waited to see who would fall victim next. At the end of the first day, twelve people died, and the night was filled with the sounds of moaning and terror from those who were sick and awaited death.

Bree sat by the campfire and listened to the muffled sobs of widowed spouses and orphaned children. She was devastated by death on such a grand scale. Oh, she'd heard of the terrible scourges of yellow fever in the South but she had never suffered a personal lose. Right now, she felt terribly alone and useless. Lucy had joined the doctor in nursing the ill, and Jemson had formed a burial party to take care of the last, grisly detail. Bree was too frightened to step across the quarantine line and too delicate to take up a shovel. Flinching, she thought of how she had tried to stop Lucy from going, citing the reasons she should stay, the dangers she would face.

"The Lord knows my time, Missy," Lucy had replied, her dark eyes calm and unafraid. Although she had not meant the words to sound cruel, they still cut through Bree like a knife. "Hidin' in the wagon ain't gonna stay His judgment or keep me to earth if He calls me to glory."

I'm such a coward, Bree admitted, hating herself for the weakness. Jemson was right about her—she was selfish and stupid and spoiled! I don't care who's sick and dyin' as long as it isn't me, she thought. I'm not capable of a decent emotion toward anyone. Lord, if only I could sleep.

Jemson returned, dirty and weary from digging graves. His handsome, tanned face was pale from exhaustion. Bree's heart nearly stopped with the sudden fear that he might be stricken by the cholera. She handed him a cup of coffee and watched as he sagged to the ground, his back supported by the wagon wheel. Bree eyed him wordlessly, ashamed to speak. Why, why had she been so stubborn last night—"Be careful, Jemson, you're no good to me dead"—why had those spiteful words slipped from her mouth when what she really wanted to say was that his living had meaning for her, that she cared about his well-being. She was afraid to put the sum of her feelings into a single word—love?—and that fear made her say hateful, thoughtless things.

"Feeling bad, are you?" Jemson seemed to read Bree's mind. "Don't. There's nothing you can do anyhow. Just wait, like the rest of us." He reached out his hand and beckoned her closer, too considerate to mention that while the rest of them waited they also pitched in and did what had to be done.

Bree sighed, sinking gratefully to the ground next to him and resting her head on his chest.

"You aren't any stronger than a little girl, Bryna. Wouldn't do to see you take sick." Jemson patted and stroked her head absently, his voice slow and tired.

•   •

The next morning Bree woke sore and stiff from having spent the night in the crook of Jemson's arm. She smiled to see him there with her and then slipped away to check the fire. It had burned out during the night. Dumping out the old grounds, Bree went to the water barrel and started to prepare a fresh pot of coffee. When she turned around again, Jemson was already fanning a newly lit fire. That man moves like a giant cat, she thought gaily. I never hear him until he's ready to pounce.

Their yes met, and Bree felt her knees buckle. A month ago she had wrinkled up her nose with distaste at the sight of this grimy, disheveled man bending over the firepit with the morning sun streaking across his face. Now he seemed infinitely strong and lovely to her. Her breath caught with surprise when she realized the most she would ask of this day was to cross over to him and put her hands on his face. She could almost hear herself telling him the sweet, secret things she was longing to let loose.

"Nothing more than coffee for me this morning," Jemson grumbled and turned away from Bree's naked, trusting face with a pang of self-hatred. Why did she have to look at him that way and complicate things, when all he ever wanted was a simple toss in the wagon? He resented the way she had of appearing all soft and frail and making a man want to shelter her from harm. By God, it was easier to feel lecherous, honest lust when a woman kept her fire. Now he felt guilt. Last night, at the party, he would have taken her and thanks, but then, when he'd kissed her, it was as though she were offering up the whole of her being into his safe keeping. And, dammit, he didn't want that! What he wanted was an occasional toss with a beautiful woman, preferably Bree, *and* his freedom. What he just saw on her face made him realize that, with a woman like Bryna Alexander, nothing was casual. She withheld totally or she gave, wholly. There could never be anything in between for her.

Jemson's back was turned, so he didn't see the sinking

look of embarrassment and despair cloud Bree's face. Her cheeks flamed and she choked on an angry cry of resentment. What did he want from her? Hadn't he, all along, been trying to get closer and, now, when she was ready, eager to welcome him, Jemson backed away. Men! When a woman changed her mind or dallied about, she was berated as being wishy-washy and feather-brained. What did you call a man that swung back and forth like a pendulum? A man of many moods—a free spirit, that's what! It just wasn't fair.

"You won't get much done with coffee sloshin' around in your stomach," Bree observed drily, all the softness gone out of her. She wasn't a moonstruck schoolgirl, after all, to go begging after a man's favor. Besides, she was gamey and her dress stuck under her arms and there was a bad taste in her mouth. Irritable and dirty, she was tired of playing games when she wasn't sure what the rules were.

"There'll be more graves needed," Jemson answered defeatedly, "more belongings to burn, more . . ."

He was interrupted by the sudden, noisy arrival of Will George and his children, their eyes filled with horror and disbelief. In his arms, Will cradled Netta's limp body, a telltale flush of fever blotching her pale skin.

Bree cried out and rushed forward, but Jemson grabbed and held her back.

"She's bad sick, Jem," Will said, tears brimming his eyes. "I can't leave my younguns. You think Lucy would tend to Netta?"

"Lucy has more than she can handle now," Bree answered before Jemson could speak. "I'll go across the line with Netta until she's better."

"No!" Jemson shouted angrily, fear starting deep in the pit of his belly. His grip on Bree tightened painfully.

"Let go of me, Jemson," Bree ordered softly but firmly. "Netta is my friend and I won't see her die because Lucy is too busy to nurse her properly."

"No, don't go," Jemson pleaded desperately, drawing Bree closer to whisper. "Lucy and the doctor are safe from it. They've been with the sick all this time and aren't showing any symptoms. You haven't been exposed. You can't know what to expect."

"Lucy and the doctor are only two people, Jemson. There are twenty patients with them now and more to come," Bree whispered back insistently. "What if Netta woke up and needed somethin' and no one was there to hear? Now, you let me go, I mean it!"

Jemson dropped his arm, beaten by the determination he felt pulsing through her body. He watched in misery as Bree marched off with Will toward the quarantine line. You don't have to prove anything, he longed to call after her. Hearing Bree call Lucy's name, Jemson's optimism rose when he saw the large, black woman wave Bree back, her arms raised in protest. Lucy's will would keep Bree out of the quarantine area.

Just as Lucy was about to bear down on Bree and force her to retreat, Bree sidestepped and ran past her toward the cholera-infested wagons. Lucy moved quickly but not quickly enough. Shaking her head, she took Netta's slight body from Will's grasp and went to join Bree and the doctor, who had just stepped from a wagon to see what all the shouting and commotion was about. Jemson watched dejectedly as Bree disappeared and Lucy lifted Netta into waiting arms. Bree looked so small, like a girl skipping off to play. Jemson's heart felt swollen with pride and a sense of loss as he turned away.

The air smelled of death. It was a sweet, thick musty scent that hovered over the small encampment like a fog. In addition to caring for Netta, Bree found herself given the charge of five other hapless victims, all of them squeezed uncomfortably into one wagon. They thrashed and cried out in delirium, soiled themselves, their sweat soaking through the blankets. Bree administered to each of them with the same dedication and concern she showed Netta— changing the clothing when needed, sponging their bodies with cool water, forcing warm herb tea through clenched teeth. A child, a boy who had played regularly with Andy George, died without a whimper—so quietly Bree wasn't even sure of his passing until she moved away from Netta, her attention riveted to the small, jerking chest.

Bree's weary heart ticked away the seconds, and the hours stretched unnoticed through the morning. Netta moaned softly as if to cause as little trouble as possible. Speaking tirelessly, Bree whispered words of encouragement, hoping the sound of her voice would shake Netta from the grips of coma.

"We'll have such times, Netta, when we're all settled in Colorado. Maybe Will won't want to pan for gold after all, and Phillip can hire him on at the mercantile and you and I and Lucy can pass our days just talkin' and sewin' and playin' with the children. Would that suit you, Netta? Would it? Netta?"

Sometime after nightfall, in the pressing silence of the dark, stale wagon, Netta stirred and, for the first time, spoke coherently. She thought Bree was Will and, grasping her friend's hand, pleaded that he take good care of the children and mind their Bible studies. And, oh, how she loved them and him and the years they had been so good.

Taking Netta in her arms, Bree rocked and comforted her. Netta's body was aflame with fever, and the heat seared Bree's skin.

During the night, Bree fell asleep holding Netta and murmuring what small words of encouragement she could command. When she woke in the morning, Netta lay still and pale in her arms, eternally peaceful. Bree's first thought was one of self-recrimination. She should have stayed awake! Did Netta die because she didn't stay awake?

Choking on tears, Bree finally let loose and felt them coursing down her face. Her sobs brought Lucy on the run. One look and Lucy took the situation in hand, prying Netta from Bree's arms and wrapping her in a tattered blanket.

"You don't look spritely, chile." Lucy touched Bree's bowed head tenderly. "You done all you could for Miss

Netta. She's happy with the Lord now. You go on back to Mister Jemson 'fore you takes sick and breaks my heart. Do as I say, Missy, go on!''

Nodding mutely, Bree stepped from the wagon and swayed on her feet. She felt light-headed and sick to her stomach. Staggering with emotional and physical fatigue, Bree pointed her body toward the safe wagons and pushed herself forward. Every step was agony—the pounding in her head heightened each time she moved.

Jemson stood in the center of their campsite like a welcoming beacon of light, unable to conceal the happiness he felt at seeing her alive and on her feet. He enveloped Bree in his arms and waited patiently while she cried, the ordeal with Netta tearing from her throat in ragged gasps.

"Lucy's right, you know," Jemson agreed gently, his voice husky. "You've got to take care of yourself now." Bree buried her face in the familiar male scent of his shirt. Jemson smelled clean, the odor of soap and hickery-smoked wood. She felt that if she never traveled another step, she had reached her destination. "It's time you let someone take care of you, Bryna. You look off your feed, girl, and that's the truth." Scolding her without anger, Jemson began leading Bree toward her wagon. "After I've seen to you, I'll talk to Will." Bree shuddered and pressed closer to him.

When he lifted Bree to set her in the wagon, it seemed to Jemson she had lost weight in the twenty-four hours she had been gone from him. Climbing in after her, Jemson propelled her gently to the bed of blankets. She stood obediently by the bed and waited. God, she looked so tiny and childlike. He felt more like a doting parent than a man anxious to lie in that bed with her. Hands trembling least his large fingers probe and hurt her, Jemson began to unbutton the clasps of her gown. Bree offered no resistance. She was so bone weary that she seemed hardly aware of what he was doing. When she was undressed to a chemise and petticoat, Jemson put his hands on her shoulders and forced her to a seated position. She went limp under the pressure and sagged back into the blankets, her eyes closing immediately, her knees drawn up to her chest. Reaching for the basin of water by the bed, Jemson wrung out the excess moisture in the cloth and patted her cheeks and brow. She seemed unusually warm to the touch and he began to worry all over again. She still wasn't safe from the killer cholera. Indeed, she had exposed herself dangerously. Although flushed, she wasn't exhibiting any of the other symptoms. More like shock—nothing in her life had prepared her for what she was going through. Jemson bathed her carefully, more than a little surprised at the lack of his sexual urge toward her. She lay asleep and helpless beneath his hands, her pale, creamy breasts barely concealed by a lacy, almost transparent chemise. Yet he felt no surge of lust, only concern, gut-wrenching concern.

Six more people, mostly children, had died during the night. He and the others had their work cut out for them today. Even though he doubted Bree was physically in danger he would have one of the other women check on her from time to time. They would know where to find him if Bree took sick. Chances were she would sleep through the day. It was the odd chance that she might be stricken, that she might be gone from him forever, that tore at his soul.

"All right, I'll say it!" He whispered fiercely to Bree's sleeping form. "I . . . I love you. You're a contrary woman, a Southern hothouse flower—spoiled and arrogant—but I have feelings so strong for you, it must be love. There's nothing for it because your heart wants one thing and your mind wants another. It can't ever come to pass, but I do love you. I'll give you over to that husband of yours without any more trouble from me, I swear! Just don't take sick. Be here smiling and healthy when I get back."

Damn woman, he cursed silently, if she could hear me sitting here mooning over her, she'd get the cholera just to spite me!

Jemson finished and pulled the edges of the blanket up over Bree to cover her. He stood, hunched over in the cramped wagon, and took one last look before leaving.

Bree did sleep through the day and, like a stone, through the entire night. She awoke the next morning groggy from so much sleep. Even in the wagon, she could smell the strong, bitter aroma of coffee and hear the sounds of Jemson moving around outside. Her empty stomach rumbled and complained. As she rinsed out her mouth with water from the basin, Bree had a vague recollection of Jemson seeing her to bed the day before. Strange, but it didn't bother her. It seemed natural somehow. She changed clothes quickly, making a mental note that she would have to scrub and wash her clothes. Lucy would be too busy to bother with such trifles. Lucy. It was time Lucy came back over the quarantine line. Even Lucy could go only so long without sleep.

"Mornin', Jemson," Bree called, poking her head out of the flap. "Would you give me a hand? La, I've had so much sleep, I'm a little shaky."

Jemson was on his feet and offering his arm before she could finish speaking. He averted his eyes while helping Bree down, afraid she would be able to read the depth of his feelings in a single glance.

"Oh, that coffee smells good." She laughed cheerfully. "I could drink the whole pot, I swear!" Once seated, the cup warming her hands and the aroma filling her nostrils, Bree's attitude sobered and she grew pensive. "How is Will? And the children? Oh, Jemson, how will they grow up without their mother?" Bree seemed on the verge of tears again, her brow s drawn.

"Netta bred those children hardy," Jemson answered gruffly, hoping to waylay her tears. "They'll be fine."

Bree grew silent and stared out toward the quarantined area. Minutes passed before she spoke.

"Jemson, all of us who aren't sick, does that mean we won't ever get sick? What I mean is, is Lucy safe?"

"I think so, Bryna. She's been in there awhile and I

guess if it was going to happen, she'd be sick by now. But I don't know about the rest. We could still get cholera if we were infected by someone in the early stages of the disease, someone who doesn't even know they have it yet. Best to stay clear of the others until the cholera runs itself out."

"Well," Bree said thoughtfully, and frowned. "I want Lucy out of there. She's done a fair share, I'd say. Would you go on over to the line and make her come back? I swear, *you* can persuade her better than I can! She'll listen to you."

"Yeah, sure, I'll go." Jemson nodded sharply and rose to leave. "I left some breakfast warming on the coals. Don't force it but eat what you can."

"Yes sir, Jemson, sir! I declare, you're gettin' as bossy as Lucy!" Bree saluted playfully.

"I'll be back toward noon," Jemson muttered, refusing to let himself fall in with Bree's light banter. His thoughts as he walked away were focused on the promises he's made himself the night before. To deliver Bree safely— and untouched—into the arms of her husband. She was safe from the disease and she would be safe from his need of her. But damn, she made it tough. Sitting there with the sun bouncing off her red curls, making her hair look like a crown of burnished gold. Emerald eyes shining teasingly, maybe even invitingly. The memory of how smooth her skin was—the soft rise and fall of her breasts as she slept. The taste of her full, eager lips. How could he be expected to keep firm the resolutions he'd made when every movement, every glance sent out the message he'd been waiting for?

Damn, but she made it rough!

CHAPTER EIGHT

It was hours before Jemson could fulfill his promise to persuade Lucy to return from the quarantine camp. Bree searched frantically for chores to keep her hands busy— cleaning dishes, starting the evening meal, scrubbing clothes—anything to still the persistent thoughts that invaded her mind. Finally, with nothing left to do, she sat quietly in her rocker by the fire and gave in to the staggering scope of her emotions.

Nothing was as it had been. The safe, snug world she was accustomed to lay shattered and broken at her feet. Absently poking at the fire with a stick, Bree was suddenly aware of its uncomfortable heat and nudged her chair away.

If only it was that easy to back off from what she was feeling, she mused dejectedly. If she could only go back and start again. But somehow, Crosshaven and the life she'd always known seemed like a fairy tale remembered from a childhood story. Not even Phillip seemed real any more. As hard as she tried, Bree couldn't summon up the image of his face, the way his hand felt when it grazed her arm.

Nothing was alive and tangible except the events that had brought her to this lonely reverie. Jemson was real— she could still feel the aching sweetness of his mouth brushing across her lips. Death was real—the void Netta left in her passing throbbed painfully in Bree's chest. Work was real.

It was all so confusing! One day even these realities would seem a dream. She would soon be reunited with Phillip Alexander, her husband, the man she had once thought she would love forever. Life would slowly evolve back to luxury and Crosshaven; the sharp, clear images of the past weeks would eventually fade into obscurity. *That* was the irrevocable truth. She was daughter of Liam McCarty, wife to Phillip Alexander. Wanting anything else would only cause her the pain of loss and ill-content existence.

But, Bree's stubborn heart pounded, just once to feel the breathless, consuming passion of Jemson's body.

She gasped and grew flushed, anxiously looking about to see if anyone was near, afraid she had said the words aloud. She swallowed and shook her head, a black, rolling mass of unshed tears gathering her throat. Jemson had shown her with his eyes, his touch, a single kiss, what Phillip would never be capable of giving her. Passion. She had made her choice of a husband without knowing, never guessing, and now she must live her life without the warm glow of desire. The realization was devastating. Before Jemson Tyler, she had felt just a tinge of discomfort, a nagging sense of unfulfillment, but now she would forever know the wrenching lack of passion in her life with Phillip.

Still, it *was* possible that Phillip had never exhibited the desire she'd felt emanating from Jemson because he, like Bree, had only a dim knowledge of its existence. Wasn't it? Not likely, but there was a remote chance. Perhaps together . . .

Bree shook her head despairingly, knowing the thought was foolish. She'd been married to Phillip long enough, shared the frighteningly brutal ritual of his bed enough times to be aware of his idea of lovemaking.

"Missy, you still lookin' peaked, chile." Lucy's voice jarred Bree's daydreaming.

She leaped from the rocker and threw her arms around Lucy. "I'm just fine, you ole thing! But I thought you were never comin' back. La, you got a nerve sayin' *I'm* peaked!'' Bree stepped back and eyed Lucy closely. ''Looks like you could use a few days' sleep, yourself. How long since you ate proper?''

Lucy's answering laugh lacked its usual volume and warmth. ''There's lotsa things I needs, honey. Vittles ain't at the top of my list. But you is right about the sleepin'.''

''Well then, get yourself up in that wagon.'' Bree whisked Lucy away and climbed up in the wagon after her. ''Gimme that dress you're wearin', Lucy. I'll scrub it for you while you sleep.''

Lucy stripped to her petticoats and sank listlessly into the softness of quilts and blankets. ''You takin' mighty good care of things, honey. I's proud of you. Just keep an eye to Mister Jemson. That man been drivin' hisself hard, too hard.'' Lucy mumbled sleepily and turned her face away. ''Everbody wantin' somethin' from him, sappin' his strength, pullin' him down. Take care . . .'' Lucy fell into sleep before finishing her instructions. Bree frowned and bent to kiss Lucy's forehead.

I wonder, she mused sadly, do you know what *I* want from Jemson? I'm the worst of a bad lot. Wantin' everything but not willin' to give enough in return.

Bree sighed and climbed down from the wagon. The sun was at its highest point and its warm rays hit her full in the face. Unconsciously, Bree's hand reached up to touch her face. She had forgotten her bonnet again. A light spray of freckles had begun to show across her nose, marring a perfect milky complexion. She looked at Lucy's dress, tucked under her arm, and decided she would wash it before getting her bonnet.

An hour later, her task completed and the noon meal bubbling enticingly over the fire, Bree heaved a sigh of relief and looked up to see Jemson returning with Abel Dunsfield.

''We can't wait no longer,'' Dunsfield was saying urgently. ''Supplies are low and we have to restock at Fort Lyon. The longer we stay around the quarantine area the worse our chances are of having more people come down with the cholera.''

"I agree, Abel," Jemson answered heavily, his blue eyes unnaturally bright. "But I still think I ought to stay behind and guide the survivors to Fort Lyon when the disease has run its course. There haven't been any new cases today. We shouldn't be but a few days behind."

"Dammit, Jem, there's only one trail to the Fort. A ten-year-old kid could find his way in a dust storm! Vanmire and Scott are stayin' behind with their wives. We'll wait a week at the fort—that'll give them plenty of time to catch up."

"All right, Abel, stop shouting." Jemson gave in more easily than was his normal practice. "We'll break camp and be ready to move out in an hour."

Dunsfield tipped his hat to Bree and walked off to alert the other travelers of his plans. The wagons of those stricken with cholera would stay behind while the others pushed on to Fort Lyon.

Jemson whipped off his hat and ran the top of his hand over his forehead. Squinting as though the sun's brightness was painful to his eyes, he turned and found Bree watching him, concern etched on her face.

She whispered hoarsely, sudden dread and fear entering her voice. "Scott? Wasn't he one of the men helpin' you bury the dead?"

"Yeah. His wife took sick last night. Come on, Bryna, we haven't got time to talk right now. Lucy back yet? Good." He nodded when Bree pointed wordlessly toward Lucy's wagon. "Shame to wake her. I guess we can pack up ourselves." He turned away and bent to scoop dirt into the campfire.

They worked quickly and efficiently, their routine broken only when Robb Andrews rushed breathlessly into camp.

"Miss Bree," he shouted, overjoyed at the news. "Have you heard? We're movin' on."

Bree replied as politely as she could. "Yes Robb, I

know." Then, barely able to keep the contempt from her voice, she asked, "Where have you been, Robb? We haven't seen you in days."

"Why in my wagon, of course," he answered unshaken. "Ah'm not fool enough to wander around beggin' some filthy farmah to infect me, Ah assure you."

The sound of his jubilant announcement had awakened Lucy, and she poked her head through the flap in the wagon, scowling dangerously.

Bree was about to let loose a string of insults when, out of the corner of her eye, she saw Jemson crash to his knees, hands clutching his belly as spasms of pain ripped through him. Instead, she quickly forgot Robb, a scream of alarm tearing from her throat. Rushing to Jemson's side, Bree gathered his crumbling body in her arms. The heat of his fever almost glowed off his skin.

"Help me, Robb. Help me get him into the wagon." Bree looked up to see Robb backing away, his mouth slack with terror.

Then Lucy was beside her, and together they lifted Jemson's bulk and dragged him toward the wagon. Lucy crawled in first and pulled Jemson in after her. It took the last of her strength to manage the feat, and she stumbled and nearly fell trying to lay him on her own bed. In that split second of time, Bree made a decision.

"Stand away, Lucy." She spoke clearly, softly. "I want you to take the supply wagon on to Fort Lyon. Pull in after Mr. Andrews. Go on, you need your rest. We'll be along when Jemson is feelin' better."

"There ain't many what gits better, Missy, you know that?"

"Reverend Bruce's son has broken his fever; so did Constance Feeney. Jemson will too. Now, get movin'."

Lucy bit back a protesting plea. She knew the familiar stiffness of Bree's back, the deadly seriousness of her tone. Nothing would dissuade her. It was just like the time when she decided to marry Phillip Alexander. There wasn't a thing on God's earth that could have swayed her once her mind was set. The decision brought her brief. But, instead of voicing her qualms, Lucy kept her tongue and patted Bree's shoulder before turning to leave.

"Bryna," Jemson groaned weakly, his eyes clouded with fever and pain, "go with Lucy. Please go with Lucy."

"You hush now, Jemson, I'm stayin' right here and you aren't in any condition to argue. Save your strength." Bree placed her cool hand on his forehead and grimaced. "Just lie still while I start the fire again."

Jemson's objections were lost to a low, agonizing groan. His eyes shut and his head rolled from side to side. Bree left the wagon, started the fire, and grabbed Jemson's bedroll before returning with a basin of fresh water. She searched through her trunk and found a clean petticoat to tear into strips. Then she struggled to remove Jemson's dirt-encrusted boots. The fleeting thought—if only he had hidden in the wagon like Robb—was dismissed as quickly as it entered her mind. Jemson wasn't the sort of man who could hide from anything. It was the reason other men valued him so highly and why she had grown to feel respect.

His pants and shirt came off easily. Bree hesitated, but only for a moment, before removing the long underwear. Now was no time to get the vapors like a proper Southern lady. All of his clothes would have to be burned and replaced. Besides, any feelings of desire she may have had were eclipsed by the single purpose of keeping Jemson alive. Working quickly, Bree washed Jemson's body and covered him with a light blanket, leaving him naked underneath. His fever was so intense, and climbing steadily, that she feared the extra piling of clothes would smother him completely and snuff out the last of his life.

When she was done and he lay restlessly sleeping next to her, Bree paused to wonder what quirk of fate kept Lucy and her free from the disease and felled this strong giant of a man. Why should Robb Andrews be spared and this man—a man who, without complaint or concern for his own safety, buried the dead and comforted the victim's family—be stricken? There were no answers, but what did it really matter? He was ill and there was nothing to be done but see him through it. If . . . no, *when* he was better they would continue on to Fort Lyon and, ultimately, Colorado.

In the quiet of the wagon, with only the weak sound of Jemson's moans to intrude on the swiftly descending night, Bree bathed his face and neck with cold water to reduce the fever. She waited. Her eyes began to droop with fatigue but she fought it off and waited. Then he seemed to relax and drift into sleep, so Bree took the opportunity to doze along with him.

She was awakened before sunrise by muttered, incoherent ravings. Jemson's body jerked and rattled under the skin as if trying to shake its way out. His jaw was locked tightly and purple cords swelled along his neck.

"Sorry, Papa—Matthew and me, we need more. Can't stay locked in this town, have to go beyond. She's a beauty, Matthew. All fire and ice. Not for me. Simon married her but she died. Not for me. Matthew, get the hell out of that mine! Papa would skin you if he knew. I'm leaving, Matthew—can't stay. Just a boy, Matt. You don't know what you want. Fire and ice, Matthew. God, she's fine! Ask Simon, he knows. All right, Matthew, come along. We'll look for it together."

All through the morning Jemson ranted, speaking mostly to Matthew, who Bree assumed was his younger brother. She hardly had a moment's free time to ponder the meaning of his obviously admiring deliriums regarding the dead bride of Simon—another brother?—but it gnawed at her to think that Jemson had once, almost certainly, loved her. Fire and ice, indeed!

It was late afternoon before the doctor found his way to Bree's wagon. He was a small, frail man, hardly the image of the city doctor he had once been. His skin was gray with weariness and his brown eyes, behind spectacles, betrayed the horror and death that had surrounded him the past six days.

Sixteen dead, he told Bree, and ten new cases since yesterday. Mr. Scott was still ill, but Vanmire was on his feet and burying the dead quicker than the doctor could shroud them in blankets. Seven wagons were filled with twenty-seven patients. Five people, two of them children, had recovered completely and escaped the ravages of the disease.

Bree shuddered as he left and stared at Jemson angrily, as if the force of her rage and the strength of her will might somehow fill the wagon with a blazing, ominous quality that would prevent death from entering. The doctor had said that if Jemson could breach the pitch of his fever, he might survive.

You will live, Bree commanded as she applied cold compresses to his face and neck again. Grabbing the basin, she sloshed the remaining water over his naked torso and rubbed his legs and arms vigorously, hoping to bring the fever to an ebb. Jemson thrashed helplessly and tried to pull away from the biting sting of cold water on his burning skin, but Bree held him fast. When she was through, she folded the blanket back over his body and watched sleepily as he calmed and fell into deep coma.

Don't fall asleep, she demanded of herself. Not now! Netta had slipped away because Bree had fallen asleep at a crucial time, but it wouldn't happen again. Not to Jemson.

He moaned and Bree instinctively moved closer, one arm slipping under his neck until his head came to rest on her breast. With her other hand, Bree grasped his shoulder and drew him tightly into an embrace.

She wondered and marveled at the desperation that whirled around inside her and held her heart in a firm grip. Jemson Tyler wasn't a man she could truly love, not really. Not a man she could stay with forever. He had none of the grace and manners she'd been raised to want in life. Why, he couldn't hold a candle to Phillip at a cotillion or one of the picnics Crosshaven had been host to. Bree smiled faintly to think of what a ridiculous picture Jemson would make with his massive shoulders stuffed into a silk waistcoat and his callused hands encased in soft kid gloves. No, he wouldn't fit into her world and she was loath to stay in his any longer than was absolutely necessary. Even so, he had an odd sort of mildness in his strength and usual grace for a man his size. And, though his hands were leathered by the sun and hard work, he had a soft, gentle touch when he set his mind to it. He could bellow, and it was like thunder rolling over the Peachtree Valley or, as on the night of the party, his whisper could be like the tender, caressing rain that followed.

The seeds of Bree's discontent had been sown long before meeting Jemson Tyler, but he had the strange power and insight to pluck the budding harvest and hold it in open hands, taunting Bree, making her face the truth of what she had reaped.

He was a danger to the future. Any happiness she might hope to find or build with Phillip was thwarted by Jemson's persistent, tantalizing image in her brain. It would be so easy, so convenient to let him go now. Let him slip away quietly into death and out of her life, her heart, forever. All Bree had to do, she was sure, was to remove her arms and go out by the campfire. In the time it would take to warm some coffee, he would be dead and the fitful, obsessive yearning would die with him. All she had to do was remove her arms, the protective embrace that stayed the grim reaper.

No, she sobbed aloud, I *can't* let you go! I can never let you go. It doesn't matter if you live or die, if you're near me or a thousand miles away. Only my own death can set me free. It's wicked and wrong but it's true.

Bree tightened her hold on Jemson and clung to him throughout the night.

CHAPTER NINE

Through sheer determination of purpose, Bree was still awake in the morning. Her eyes were heavy, only half open, and her head throbbed with fatigue. Jemson slept peacefully in her arms, the sweat of his broken fever soaking the front of her dress. Every few minutes Bree had to shake her head vigorously against the temptation to sleep.

"I feel as though a herd of buffalo has camped in my mouth." The latest jerk of Bree's body woke Jemson, and he whispered, his voice cracked and dry. He was weak, terribly drained, as he squinted at her through bloodshot eyes. "God, woman, you look worse than I do! Just give me a sip of water and stretch out here beside me."

Bree nodded mutely, and raised a cup to Jemson's fever-cracked lips. The blackness behind her eyelids whirled like an out-of-control weathervane forcing her into a dizzying spin as she sank and burrowed snugly next to him.

Her sleep was dark and dreamless, and when she woke six hours later the inside of the wagon was oppressive with the heat of the noon sun. Jemson stirred restlessly when Bree raised herself to her feet and moved away.

Check the team, she thought mechanically, unable to resist the urge to groan and stretch her arm over her head. The bones in her neck cracked. Gather wood, start a fire, make coffee. Forage food supplies and make something nourishing for Jemson when he wakes.

But first, first get out of this sticky, smelly dress and

wash the sweat and grim away! Bree grabbed a blanket and some loose pieces of the mutilated petticoat she had used to sponge Jemson's body. Feeling stiff and years beyond her age, Bree set herself down from the wagon and hobbled toward the water barrel strapped to the side of the wagon. She pulled the cork in one barrel and watched greedily as the clear, fresh water gushed into the wash tub she sat beneath it. The events of the last few days had robbed her of the final grace of her birth—modesty. Even without the blanket clutched between her teeth and draped carelessly down the front of her body, Bree would have eagerly stripped naked in her hurry to bathe. Her bathes at Crosshaven had been heavily scented with oil of jasmine and honeysuckle but never had they been as refreshing as the plain water she now splashed and rubbed over her tired body. When she was through, Bree wrapped the blanket under her arms and around her torso before going back into the wagon for a clean change of clothes. Her movements were slow and quiet so as not to wake Jemson. The lid of her trunk squeaked rebelliously as Bree lifted it. She turned her head and glanced worriedly at Jemson, but he hadn't moved. Satisfied, Bree returned to the task at hand and selected her clothing quickly. She stood and allowed the blanket to drop to the rough wooden floor of the wagon before stepping gingerly into her drawers and pulling a chemise up over her arms. The job of fastening the ribbon ties across her bodice was time-consuming and exasperating.

How much easier to be a man, she thought with irritation. A pair of pants, a shirt, some boots, and they're ready to go. Women, by tradition, are forced to bury themselves under layers of petticoats, silk and lace chemises, an underskirt, an over skirt . . . Absurd!

She slipped a blue cotton dress over her head and, as she buttoned the front, turned around toward Jemson. Now you. What am I goin' to do about you? He was still too weak to wash himself, but Bree didn't warm to the idea of doing it for him, not with Jemson conscious, his fever broken, with his grinning at her in that devilish way he had. No, she would put fresh water and clothes beside the bed before going about her chores and hope that when he woke he'd be able to manage it himself. If he couldn't, *then* she would swallow her embarrassment and do what needed doing. After all, there was a pronounced difference between bathing down an unconscious, desperately sick man and washing a man when he's well enough to snicker.

It was turning night, the time Bree liked best on the plains. The vibrant oranges and pinks of the sunset had faded into blue-black, and the stars were just beginning to sparkle and make their presence known. She sat in her rocker and tipped back and forth lazily, thinking about the day's outcome. After watering down the team and tending to the campsite, Bree had walked over to the other wagons, anxious to check on the conditions there. The pall of death hung heavily in the expressions of the survivors, and those who had stayed behind to nurse loved ones back to health or tenderly commit them to the earth. A total of forty-one travelers had died; eight, including Jemson, had been stricken but had somehow had a deeper reserve of strength and beaten off the greedy hands of death. And the doctor's report was encouraging. None of those still on their feet evidenced any sign of the disease and, barring some new disaster, they would give themselves two or three more days to recoup before journeying on to Fort Lyon.

As Bree rocked she felt a wave of self-indulgent vanity wash over her. She had faced the crisis boldly and emerged victorious. She was alive and she had kept Jemson alive. He had been moving around inside the wagon for almost an hour. Bree would allow herself a few more minutes of congratulatory pampering before going in to see to his needs. But, for now, she was lost to an all-consuming feeling of power. There was nothing beyond her reach. If she could endure and survive the last week, if her will was strong enough to pull Jemson back from the brink of death, she could accomplish anything!

Bree reached out and touched the cane-back chair she had brought over from another wagon for Jemson's use when he was able to leave his bed. Smiling confidently, she pictured Phillip sitting there next to her, his expression full of pride. The smile waivered and froze on her lips. Try as she might, the image of Phillip's face faded in and out, replaced by the warm, granite lines of Jemson Tyler's profile.

"You saving that chair for somebody special or can just anyone sit down?" He came up so quietly behind her that Bree nearly jumped out of her rocker. Guiltily, unable to trust her voice, she motioned for Jemson to sit. He moved with the uncertain hesitation of an invalid, all color drained from his face. A huge sigh of weariness escaped his lips as he lowered himself into the chair. The effort of washing and dressing himself had taken an incredible amount of stamina. Even his hair glistened with drops of water. A four-day growth of beard stood out from his jaw and he reached up to scratch at it in an unconscious gesture of discomfort.

"I can shave you if you like, Jemson," Bree offered, at last finding her voice.

"Thanks, but right now I'd rather have some of that stew and a pot of coffee." He smiled weakly, even his voice lacking the thunderous authority of a week earlier.

He ate scantily, his shrunken stomach refusing the large amount of food he'd hoped to fill it with. A man of power and strength, Jemson was irked to admit that his illness had left him with the appetite and resilience of a child.

"I'll take that shave now," he growled self-consciously. "My gear's in the bedroll. You ever shave a man before?"

"No, but I've done a lot of things lately I've never done before," Bree replied lightly. "I'll struggle through somehow."

When she returned with the mug of soap and the brush and straight razor, Bree stood behind Jemson's chair. Seated, he was about the same height as Bree. It gave her a good feeling—for once she wouldn't be craning her neck to meet his gaze. Rubbing the brush briskly into the soap, Bree worked up a lather and slapped the foamy stuff on Jemson's face with deliberate casualness. She came around in front of him and leaned back, viewing her handiwork with glee.

"*Very* nice," she said teasingly. "You look like a caricature of Saint Nicholas."

"Just get on with it!"

Bree's answer was a laugh, high and tinkling in its insistent badgering. She glided gracefully to stand behind him again. Her arms came around his shoulders, one hand holding the razor, the other poised underneath his chin. Drawing the razor slowly upward, Jemson's beard grated and cut away from his face. He grimaced and squirmed uncontrollably.

"Hold still, Jemson," Bree ordered, barely able to keep her hand steady against the giggling movement of her body. "You keep jerkin' around like that and I'll cut your throat for sure."

"Never mind!" Jemson pushed the hand holding the razor away from his face. "I'll do it myself. Christ, woman, you damn near lifted my hide with that last swipe."

"Hush, you big baby," Bree retorted, feigning indignant shock. "I've done this a hundred times for my papa. He says I've got the lightest touch that ever laid razor to face, so just sit still and enjoy it!"

Bree ignored the tenseness she felt in Jemson's rigid posture and proceeded to shave him neatly and cleanly without a single drop of blood shed.

"There! Now, don't you feel like a fool for squirmin' around like a frightened little boy? You better put a strap to that razor though. It's mighty dull, by the feel." Grinning, Bree gathered his shaving gear and returned it to the bedroll.

Jemson was sitting quietly, almost dozing, by the fire when she returned, his eyes nearly closed. "Thanks, Bree." He was roused by the sound of her nearness. "Feels real good."

It was the first time he had ever called her Bree—the first time the affectionate shortened version of her name had come easily to his lips. Jemson stood up and turned toward the wagon.

"Damn. I'm still weak as a colt. I better get some more sleep or you'll be doing all the fetch and carry until we get to Colorado." Jemson started walking, then burst out in laughter when Bree hurried to join him and offer her shoulder to assist him. "Are you joking, woman? If I leaned on you, you'd go through the ground like a tent stake! I can make it on my own steam. You get back to your rocker and do some resting for yourself. One of us has to stay on his feet and it doesn't look like I'm going to be much good for a while."

"Goodnight, Jemson," Bree whispered to his retreating figure, grateful that he had suggested she stay by the fire for the time being. She couldn't be sure if it was a gesture of consideration or not, but she intended to accept it as an act of decorum. After all, there *was* only one bed in the wagon and it wouldn't be seemly, even as weak as Jemson was, for the two of them to stroll off to the wagon together.

La, what a silly, stuffy thing to think about now, Bree scoffed and shook her head. All they'd been through, and she was worried about sleeping next to a man who was only one day short of the grave.

When she crawled in next to him a few minutes later, Jemson was fast alseep. Yet, even in the deep throes of unconsciousness, he felt the warmth of her nearness and his arm reached over to pull her closer. Bree lay still and compliant beside him, willing sleep to come but unable to quench the confusing torment that plagued her mind.

The feelings she nurtured about Jemson confused and shamed her. They were emotions she had never dealt with before. True, she had wanted the comfort of Phillip sharing her bed but now she realized that need grew out of a desperate desire to prove herself worthy of being his wife. The few times they'd made love had left her unsatisfied and humiliated. In Jemson, Bree sensed a bottomless reservoir of tenderness. Somehow, making love with Jemson would be different, finer, she was sure! His touch would be the culmination of what she suspected might be possible between a man and a woman. Yet, her yearning for Jemson would also be her destruction. She doubted she could ever look at Phillip again without guilt, without the knowledge that she had burdened herself with the ultimate betrayal.

You silly fool, Bree scolded angrily, an hour ago you were braggin' to yourself how you were strong enough to do anythin'. Anythin'! Well, here's a chance to really prove it. Save up all that yearnin' and give it to the man who really matters. Phillip!

Bree yawned, sinking into oblivion, the courage of her conviction marred only by the slight frown creasing her brow and the way she snuggled closer to Jemson for comfort.

Jemson's quick recovery astounded both Bree and the doctor. Either his strength had returned with amazing speed or he was pushing himself beyond the limits of a normal man. Bree believed the later.

Fool man! Him and his stupid pride. He'll probably keel over any minute. Still, he didn't show any sign of weakening or slowing down. Each day, he contributed more and more. Seeing to the teams, gathering firewood, mending the canvas of the wagons. On the third day he even rode out to hunt and had returned with enough rabbit to make a delicious stew for everyone. They would be pushing on to Fort Lyon in the morning, and the stew served as a kind of celebration dinner.

Bree had managed to stay out of Jemson's way, for the most part. Even though, for once, there was no anger between them, few words had been spoken. Preparing sixteen travelers and seven wagons had kept them both so busy there was little time for anything other than work and blessed, much needed sleep.

Now, with all in readiness for the next morning's departure and the dinner dishes cleaned and set away, they sat before the fire with nightfall just upon them.

"I never thanked you proper for staying with me, Bree." Jemson shifted uneasily. His chair was tilted back on two legs, anchored by his boots dug into the dirt in front of him. "What I mean is I'm grateful. Anything I can do to repay you, you've got it."

"Well, there *are* two things, if you really mean it." Bree stopped rocking and leaned forward anxiously. "First, I want that marriage certificate. You've teased me with it long enough."

"Can't oblige you with that," Jemson lied smoothly. "I hid it in Lucy's wagon and she went off with it to Fort Lyon. But I'll give it over as soon as we see her. That suit you? What else is on your mind?"

"Ah, well, it's silly but . . . when you were sick," Bree began nervously, "delirious, you know? You did a lot of ramblin' on and, well, a woman's just naturally a curious creature."

"Come on, woman, spit it out!" Jemson laughed good-naturedly. "Just what did I say that has you so piqued?"

Bree gasped, exasperated, and turned an icy stare to Jemson. "I swear, don't you know anythin' about polite conversation? Must you always jump, feet first, into everythin' you do?"

"You really love the social amenities, don't you? All right, Bree, I'll go along with it, but just this once, by God, because I'm showing you how grateful I can be. Now, you were at the part where I was delirious and you were gripped by female curiosity, right?"

"Just tell me about Simon and his wife, damn you!" Bree spat, resenting him for putting her off balance once again. She'd forgotten Jemson's talent for making her feel like a foolish, stammering Southern belle.

"Simon? He's my brother, older by three years. And his wife, Emma, is a dull-witted, sharp-tongued shrew. Can't stand the woman!"

"You liar!" Bree stormed, rising from her rocker to confront him, jealousy and rage suddenly flaring, her eyes large orbs of emerald flames. "If you can't stand her, why were you mutterin' all night about her? Fire and ice?" She stood with her hands on hips and mimicked, "Simon married her, he knows, fire and ice. Are you ever goin' tell me the truth or just keep on lyin' every chance you get?"

"Hold on, I wasn't lying." Jemson raised his arms to cover his face in mock terror. When he dropped them he was smiling. "When you said Simon's wife, I just naturally thought you meant Emma. But she's Simon's second wife. Molly Sullivan was his first wife. She was daughter to one of the miners that work in the family business, sweating his life away. Christ, my pa damn near had a stroke! Simon was only nineteen then. When he brought Molly home, my mother fainted dead away. They never did accept the marriage." Jemson chuckled, as if the image was as clear as yesterday. "But, Lord, she was a beauty. Black Irish, with a temper to match. Molly just said the hell with them and she and Simon set up house in the town. I was sixteen and Matthew, my youngest brother— hell, we were crazy for her. Used to sneak down and visit her whenever we could get away. She made Simon happy too. Damn, they were always laughing about something— either that or she'd sit herself down in his lap and they'd start kissing and fondling each other. In that case, Matt and me got thrown out and sent home. I spent a lot of sweaty nights thinking about Molly, I can tell you." Jemson laughed at the memory and then sobered abruptly. "But she died after they'd been married a little over a year, giving Simon a son. My folks started pressuring him and finally Simon caved in and brought the boy to the main house. A marriage to Emma was arranged—a proper, socially and financially acceptable marriage. Shit! From the day he married that she-wolf, I never saw Simon smile, let alone laugh. A woman like Emma can kill a man in a hundred little ways and he won't even realize it until he's been gutted and left to the buzzards. She got her hold on Molly Sullivan's boy and raised him so he's not worth

113

the dynamite it would take to blow him up. He was ten years old when Matt and I left Pennsylvania, a cruel little bastard always picking on younger children, lying and cheating. Jesus, I hope I never seen them again! When I went back for Matt's and my share of the trust, I couldn't even make myself go to the house. Just stayed at the hotel in Monaca and had my Pa's lawyers handle the details.''

"But your parents, why blame them?'' Bree protested. "Simon made the decision to marry Emma. It isn't right to turn your back on your parents just because Simon was weak and disappointed you.''

"My folks married for convenience, not love. I never saw a touch pass between them. How they managed to have four boys, I can't reckon. But I know they haven't shared a bed in twenty years and I couldn't walk through Monaca without seeing my pa's face on half the bastards in town. They pushed Simon into marriage with Emma when he was still bleeding so bad over Molly he didn't know day from night. Sacrificed him for profit, another stinking mine. Matt was still a boy when I decided to leave home, but he was smart enough to know they'd bury him too, so I took him with me. Daniel, he's two years older than Matt, was set to marry the next year and, besides, he liked the money and position of being a mine owner. We've done all right, Matt and me. The money from the trust is going to help us develop one of the richest gold veins in Colorado.'' Jemson looked up at Bree and smiled. "You might end up being sorry you're not really married to me.'' He tried to say it in a teasing manner, but the words came out quiet and sad.

CHAPTER TEN

"It seems I've been monopolizing our talks every night, Bree," Jemson ventured four days later. They would reach Fort Lyon late the next afternoon. "Why don't you tell me about Crosshaven and your husband, that paragon of virtue and grace."

"Oh, you don't really want to hear about Phillip." Bree dried off the last of the dinner dishes and turned away to hide the flush that was creeping to her cheeks.

"Sure I do. You've spent most of the trip comparing the obvious differences between us. I want to know all about the man you married." He said it with more venom than he'd intended. It didn't really matter what she said. Jemson hated and envied Phillip Alexander for possessing the one thing Jemson wanted—Bree. "I insist. Here I've poured out my heart and given you my life story. Come sit down and tell me about him."

Bree's shoulders sagged, but she turned and walked reluctantly to the fire. Jemson reached out and pulled her rocker closer to his chair. Her look was pleasing as she sat down.

"Honestly, there's not all that much to tell," she stammered, knowing if she began the truth would pour from her in uncontrollable gusts. "We weren't married very long before he went west. Jemson, really, I don't want to talk about Phillip. I . . ."

"Are you afraid to see him again?" Jemson asked kindly, compassion and hope gripping at his heart.

"Don't be absurd!" She shot back much too quickly. "It's just that it's late and I'm tired, too tired to try and tell you all the things Phillip is in a few sentences. We really should get some sleep. See," she added with a sweep of her arm toward the other wagons, "everyone else has had the good sense to get the rest we'll all need for tomorrow." It was true. Theirs was the only lantern still burning. Each night it had been the same. The sleeping arrangements had reverted back to the way they had been before Jemson's illness. And Bree missed the warm security of knowing he was close enough to touch. So instead, she kept him talking long past the time they should have gone to their separate beds. But now Jemson was suggesting she allow the painful realities of Phillip intrude upon her growing enjoyment of just listening to the deep, rumbling sound of his voice as he told her about his childhood and the wondrous things he had seen since leaving Pennsylvania. It was more than she could bear.

Bree stumbled to her feet, grabbing Jemson's shoulder for support.

"Goodnight, Jemson," she whispered, fighting back the tears that gathered like a storm behind her dark lashes.

"Good Lord, woman!" Jemson's hands shot out and encircled her waist. She was so tiny, his fingers touched at her back. "Has the bastard hurt you so much you can't even talk about him? Or," he growled, fear and anger growing as an ugly notion crept into his brain, "does it offend your sensitive nature to soil his name by speaking of him in my presence?" Unconsciously, Jemson's grip tightened, nearly crushing Bree's ribs. She moaned slightly but made no move to pull away. Instead, her hand rose and gently stroked his cheek. For a moment he seemed paralyzed by the tenderness and longing in her expression. There was a kind of innocence in her desire that shamed him and made him release her and turn his face away. As much as he might want to, Jemson couldn't bring himself to take advantage of the momentary weakness she was displaying. They had been through hell together, and the pain and terror of the past weeks had brought them closer. He was convinced she didn't turn to him out of love. Rather, she was driven by the yearning to seek assurance in the face of so much death and despair. He was the closest at hand. She probably saw him as something more than he was.

"You're right, Bree," he muttered, afraid to meet her gaze. "Tomorrow's going to be a long day." But, he thought to himself, not nearly as long as this night. "I think I'll turn in."

Still standing above him, Bree choked back her embarrassment and turned to flee the mocking silence that fell between them. The cool darkness of the night outside their campfire enveloped her like a protective cloak. She ran blindly until the breath tore raggedly from her throat, ran until the light from the lantern was just a speck of yellow in the distance. Panting, she dropped to her knees and covered her face with her hands.

God, what a fool she'd made of herself! Offering her body like a common tramp, letting Jemson see the desire she felt. It was true, then. The awful thing that had made Phillip turn away. Something deep within Bree made a man turn to stone. Some horrible part of her cooled a man's lust as readily as a bucket full of spring water. She had been sure, absolutely certain, that Jemson felt the same passion as she but he, like Phillip, had pulled back from her touch.

Then suddenly Bree felt herself lifted to her feet and strong arms encased her trembling body. Jemson's head bent toward her, blocking out the sky. His lips took possession of her uplifted mouth, kissing her long and deep, his tongue searching and finding hers. Bree responded with an almost agonizing intensity. Her arms wrapped around his neck and tightened. Dizzy, she was caught at the knees and carried back toward camp.

"I thought you didn't want me," she whimpered brokenly against Jemson's mouth.

He stopped and stared at her incredulously. "Want you?

117

Lord, woman, are you really as naive as you let on? Want you? I ache for you, like nothing else in my life.''

Bree buried her face in his neck, clinging desperately as he walked her back to the wagon. Her mind reeled wildly with desire, mingled with the heady scent of earth and grass that the evening breeze carried with it.

Once inside the wagon, reclining against the blankets and quilts on her bed, the doubts Bree had struggled with began to surface and plague her. Jemson had extinguished the lantern, and only the outline of his body was visible in the dark, cool confinement of their quarters. He stood over her, huge, demanding, wanting. And, with a certainty that crystallized and tore at her heart, Bree knew she would fail him. Fail Jemson as surely as she had failed Phillip. Miserably, her eyes growing accustomed to the dark, Bree watched as Jemson began to unbutton his shirt. If she was going to do anything, now was the time. Before it was too late, she could send him away, exile the both of them to another restless, sleepless night.

Jemson sank to his knees next to her, his mouth once again seeking, exploring, and tracing a burning path along her cheek to her neck. He gathered Bree hungrily in his arms. Any reservations she felt disappeared as quickly as they had materialized. She sighed contentedly and Jemson stood and started to unclasp the buttons of his trousers. Preparing herself, Bree reached under her skirts and hurriedly removed the lacy drawers that had suddenly become so oppressive, thankful the darkness hid her furtive movements. Then she gathered the hem of her dress up around her waist, turned her face away and waited.

''What the hell are you doing?'' Jemson's voice was soft, controlled.

''I, ah, I thought you wanted . . .'' Bree cringed visibly, confused. ''Oh Jem, I'm not very good at this, am I?''

''Hush darlin','' Jemson reached and clasped her hands, pulling her up off the bed and to a standing position. She felt dazzled and faint by the closeness of his naked maleness.

"Just forget everything you think you learned about making love. You and me, darlin', we'll start new and fresh." Leaning forward, Jemson kissed her lightly, his tongue moving slowly across Bree's mouth, enticingly bringing her own tongue out of hiding. He chuckled and whispered, "Remember? You used to kiss like a ten-year-old. See how fast you learn? Come heart, sweetheart. It's a lot more fun without your clothes on."

Bree tried to pull away, protesting. "I can't! No, Jem, it's indecent! No!" She squirmed half-heartedly, resisting Jemson's attempts to loosen the buttons of her bodice. Still, she eagerly met his kiss, losing reason and control under the onslaught of his passion. Before she even knew it, her gown had slipped off her shoulders and fallen in a heap at her feet. Jemson's hand fumbled with the ribbons of her chemise and it, too, fell away. Shivering against the feel of the night air on her bare skin, Bree moaned as her petticoat, a last defense, was tugged down over her hips. The symphony of ragged, gasping breath filled the silence of the wagon. Jemson stepped back, his eyes devouring the shadowed contours of Bree's body. She closed her eyes, unsure of what to do, ashamed of her inadequacy. Then, gently, his hands touched her shoulders and slid slowly to her neck and down, softly trembling to her breasts. His fingers teased and caressed Bree's nipples until they were rigid and she was gasping. One hand slipped slowly lower, trailing to her hips until his fingers sought and found the moist, honeyed softness between her legs. She moved closer as Jemson worked his magic, her thighs trembling.

"Jemson, please," Bree moaned helplessly, "I can't stand up any longer. My legs are turnin' to butter."

He laughed agreeably, knowingly, and nudged Bree back toward the bed. She lay back and offered her arms up invitingly, anxious to continue. Waves of sensuous, throbbing pleasure washed over her. Jemson lowered himself over her body, one leg thrown over Bree's hips, one arm sliding under her back, the other crossing over and grasping her shoulder, locking her in his embrace. She could feel the proof of his readiness, hard and pulsating against her leg. It was both a frightening and exhilarating experience. She was timid and proud of the reaction she'd aroused.

"Your husband, sweetheart, is a horse's ass!" Jemson reflected, astounded by the conflict of emotion he could feel coursing through the woman in his arms. "Did he really let this magnificent body go unappreciated?" The moment he asked it, Jemson was sorry. Bree stiffened and he could sense a slacking in her ardor. Damn! The very mention of her husband's name filled Bree with a sickening apprehension. She just wasn't the kind of woman who took the act of infidelity lightly, not the kind of woman he was accustomed to using and then leaving behind. He'd been a clumsy fool to use the bedside patter that had proved successful with easier, less important prey.

"Forgive me, darlin'," he murmured, gently nuzzling the soft pulse of her neck. "I don't mean to shame you or remind you of something you'd like to forget, at least for a while. I'll leave if . . ."

He didn't get to finish his offer. Bree locked her arms around him and forced his face to hers, mouth parted and inviting. She melted eagerly against him and basked in the feel of Jemson's hands as they started their gentle assault on breasts, hips, thighs. Once again her breasts grew taut and swelled under the tender, artful persuasions as Jemson's tongue slid across and around the nipples, teasing and nibbling.

Blindly, in a frenzy, Bree wanted nothing more than to touch and hold Jemson, to give him as much pleasure as she was receiving. Her hand reached down until her fingers brushed against the pulsating, velvety smoothness of Jemson's erection. Timorously, Bree traced the length, surprised that the organ was not the cold, hideous weapon she had so often envisioned but a warm, enticing extension of the heat and passion that were building to a feverish pitch.

"Bree. Darlin'." The words sounded like a moan and she thrilled at the need in his voice. Jemson's hand was between her thighs, his fingers stroking the wet, hot inner skin. Bree trembled and uttered a strangled, incoherent cry. Her hips arched and weaved with the movement and swing of Jemson's hand. She wanted to scream and laugh, curse and pray. Spasms rocked her body, shooting up the base of her spine, setting every nerve on edge.

Jemson raised himself above her, a hand parting Bree's legs. He stopped, poised, and bent to kiss her eyes, cheek, mouth—started to say something and then thought better of it. Eyes fused, their gazes locked in mutual ecstasy, Jemson penetrated Bree slowly, deliciously slipping into the heated, welcoming sweetness. He had said she would learn quickly and she did. Bree matched his pace, the quickened movements and rhythms, with ease. She luxuriated in the urgency of his thrusts, wildly responding until all thought of past or future was eradicated from her mind and heart. Nothing existed but the driving, throbbing climb to heights she would never have known without Jemson's sensual ministrations.

Later, as she lay exhausted, curled in the protective curve of Jemson's arms, his breath warm and satisfied on her cheek, Bree thought she had never felt so contented, had never experienced such peace. His gift, this marvelous sharing, had given her something no amount of parental pampering, wealth, and position had allowed—a sense of her own being, of womanhood.

Nothing before or that would come after could ever be as wondrous. She stifled a yawn and shivered as the moisture of sweat, the glorious evidence of the task they had performed, met with the night chill. Jemson felt the involuntary movement and pulled a quilt over their nude bodies.

He kissed her forehead and murmured sleepily, "Can't have you getting sick, sweetheart. There's a lot of long, dark nights between here and Denver and we've got some catching up to do."

Bree sighed her agreement and nestled closer, not really sure of what he had said, responding merely to the deep, resonant sound of Jemson's voice. At this moment she could think of nothing else but the strength and warmth of the man who had brought her to life, the man who had awakened all the dormant needs and emotions, the man who would somehow always give her shelter and protection.

CHAPTER ELEVEN

Bree woke with a start, her eyes wide open. A moment of panic seized her. Something she couldn't quite remember, something buried just beneath the surface of her consciousness filled her with a crushing sense of dread. The morning sun delicately pierced the heavy canvas of the wagon and the air was alive with particles of dust and dancing sunlight. Bree's eyes felt heavy and swollen, as though she had just awakened from the deepest sleep she'd ever experienced. Cautiously, still worrying the nagging fear, Bree moved slowly and stretched. The quilt that covered her shifted and rolled along her naked body like a gentle touch and she remembered. It flooded through her memory, vivid and teasing, the images crystal clear, taunting and accusing. Bree's hand flew to her mouth to smother the scream that gathered deep within her throat. She fought to recall the exact events of the previous night and blushed to think of them.

It was true. Not a dream or a secret desire. She had betrayed Phillip, willfully going against everything she knew to be right and decent. Mindless, directionless guilt and rage surged in her heart. She was consumed by the swirling, liquid heat of regret. Choking back the bile that threatened to explode behind clenched teeth, Bree thought of Jemson, and the flow of her anger rushed easily and eagerly toward him and settled there.

Jemson. *He* had taken advantage of her emotions, had manipulated her in such a way that she couldn't possibly be held responsible for her own actions. Jemson had seen with the instinctive eye of a low-life womanizer. He had felt her insecurities and played upon them, each day luring Bree closer and closer to what had passed between them last night. Somewhere deep inside her mind another voice spoke, reminding Bree of her willingness, even eagerness, to be lead, of her passionate response, but she pushed that voice aside and listened only to the voice of recrimination. How much easier it was to let someone else bear the full burden of blame. Knowing she could never face Phillip again and look him squarely in the eyes unless the heavy weight of her own desire was diminished, Bree again turned angry thoughts to Jemson.

He had known she was married, promised for a lifetime to someone else, and still he sought to tempt and entrap her. Plying her with what seemed to be grudging compliments, slapping her down and then, oh! so slowly, lifting her back up, confusing her, beguiling her. Making her care about the opinion he held of her. It was all part of the insidious game he played. What was that he had whispered—"we have a lot of long, lonely nights to make up for." His intentions were so obvious that it was pathetic. He had picked the wrong woman to use as a diversion against a cold bed on the seemingly endless journey to Colorado.

He values you, makes you feel like a woman, the small voice protested. He's not the one playing childish games. No! Bree overpowered the voice of reason. She could not live with the implications that followed in its wake. She liked to think of herself as a strong person, a woman who could handle any situation, but, deep in her heart, she knew she was too weak to give up the security and luxury of her life with Phillip, the life of genteel elegance at Crosshaven. The idea of the unknown terrified her and she suppressed it. Feeling stronger, Bree told herself that if she ignored the realities of last night, pretended it never happened, then everything would be all right. Mentally, she would go back in time to the day *before* yesterday. That way she could protect herself, and the feelings of those whose lives she could so easily shatter—Phillip and her father. Jemson was the strongest man she had ever known, both physically and emotionally. He would survive while all others fell by the road.

Fortified by her decision, Bree rose shakily and began to pick up her discarded clothing. A furious blush sprang to her cheeks as the unwanted memory of how they came to be in a pile on the floor returned, but she pressed it out of her mind and doggedly attacked the task. Only then did she notice the sound of Jemson outside the wagon. He was humming a nonsensical tune under his breath and moving around the campsite. Fully dressed and without bothering to brush her hair or to apply the precious skin-saving cream to her face, Bree sucked in her breath and opened the rear flap.

He was kneeling by the fire, his back to her, as she stepped from the wagon. He was so lost in thought that he didn't notice her until he heard the sound of splashing water as she lifted it in handfuls to bathe her face. He turned quickly then and the warmth of his smile and the mellow caress of sky-blue eyes washed over her. Just for a moment, Bree felt her knees go weak and she lost herself to the intensity of his gaze. Then, in a physical movement of shaking off the cloak of intimacy he wove around her, Bree returned his stare with all the coolness and disdain she could muster.

"You shouldn't have let me oversleep," she observed casually, looking around their clean campsite. "I should have helped you pack up." Fighting the nervous urge to busy her hands, Bree looked away helplessly.

Jemson laughed good-naturedly and motioned toward her rocking chair. "I thought you could use the sleep after last night. I even made milady's breakfast, such as it is." In a great sweeping gesture, Jemson indicated the bacon and biscuits that rested over the fire.

"Last night?" Bree repeated lightly. "Last night I slept soundly, thank you. And, as for breakfast, I don't require any. I'm anxious to move out for Fort Lyon. It puts me," she smiled prettily, "all the closer to my husband." Bree turned away quickly and rushed over to the other wagons, ostensibly to check their readiness and the health and strength of the other travelers. Her heart was pounding and the saliva in her mouth had turned to dust. She hadn't turned quickly enough to miss the clouded look of pain that had flickered across Jemson's face. Instantly, her resolve weakened. She steeled herself against the impulse to throw herself into his arms, to cover his face with kisses and tell him that she would follow him wherever he led, do whatever had to be done, turn away from everyone else she loved—anything, just to remain by his side.

Fool! The accusation rang loudly in her head as she made her way to the doctor's wagon. And when it's over and he's grown tired of you, what is left? Where will you go then? Who will you turn to? Will you throw away your whole life in exchange for a moment's pleasure?

When Bree had been assured that the recovering patients and their loyal companions were strong enough to pull out and, indeed, were anxious to be reunited with the rest of the wagon train, she returned reluctantly to her own wagon. The site had been totally cleared away and Jemson sat perched high atop the wagon, waiting. He wore a guarded, moody expression and pointedly avoided her cold, blatant stare. Her icy behavior nearly melted when she hiked herself up the side of the wagon and sat down next to him on the bench. The enticing, male scent of him filled her nostrils and made her dizzy. But her mind persisted and she thought only of Phillip, of Crosshaven. She sat quietly beside him, her back rigid and unyielding.

"There's biscuits wrapped in that kerchief beside you if you change your mind." Jemson's rumbling voice broke through the silence, the muscles in his jaw moving stiffly, painfully.

"I won't change my mind." Bree answered, icy with resolution. The words broke in her throat and she repeated. "I *won't* change my mind."

•   •   •

Late that afternoon the stragglers reached Fort Lyon, only to learn that the main body of the train had left the day before, headed for Bent's Fort on the north side of the Arkansas River. Disappointed, Bree spent the night slipped between cool sheets on a real bed inside the walls of Fort Lyon. As much as she tried to appreciate the comfort, her dreams were filled with disquieting images and wild yearnings. In the morning, her eyes were swollen and heavy from lack of sleep. She nodded sharply to Jemson and climbed atop the wagon without a word. Not one syllable had passed her lips since the previous morning and she was determined to keep it that way. Still, it rankled that Jemson seemed to accept her rejection with such a nonchalant ease. It was almost as if he didn't care one way or another. She could be loving and warm, cold and distant; it was all the same to him. He appeared to be completely comfortable with the long stretches of silence, the hurried meals. And he had the audacity to leave her and mingle among the other passengers. Truly, an unfeeling oaf!

Two days later they limped into Bent's Fort amid much cheering and back-slapping. Jemson was immediately surrounded by Abel Dunsfield and his cronies, pulled from the wagon, and passed a shot of whiskey. No one seemed to be paying much attention to Bree until Lucy materialized out of the crowd and rushed forward to hug her.

"Praise be, chile, the Lord done seen fit to deliver you and Mr. Jemson." Lucy shook her head, tears coursing down her face.

"The Lord," Bree snapped peevishly, "had nothin' to do with it! *I* nursed Jemson back to health. I'm the one who stayed up all those nights with him." The minute she spoke, Bree was ashamed of herself. First off, I'm takin' out my anger on poor Lucy. I really must get a grip on myself.

Still, she was hard put to apologize outright, so she just hugged Lucy and smiled. It was a small gesture but all she could bring herself to do.

"So, tell me, Lucy, how you been spendin' your time

without me to take care of?'' Bree giggled and took Lucy's arm. ''I'll wager you haven't moved from your bed in a week.''

''Lawd, no, Miss Bree. I been tendin' Mr. George's children. They's a handful, I swear! But they's awful dear, too.'' Lucy looked back at Jemson and grinned wickedly. ''Mr. Jemson, he lookin' mighty fine. I's proud of you, Missy. Seems you took real good care of that man.''

''I did what I had to do, Lucy, nothin' more.'' Bree pulled Lucy back, anxious to change the subject and begin exploring the fort. ''I give him over to you now. My, this is a big place.'' Bree waved her hand and indicated the solid adobe walls of the fort.

The walls were at least four feet thick and stood fourteen feet high. Guarding the tunnel entrance was a square watchtower armored with swivel cannons. On either side of the ponderous sheet-iron doors protecting the tunnel, windows were situated to allow Indians to trade with the fort without actually entering. Passing through the entrance, large enough for a prairie schooner, Bree walked toward a courtyard that was so enormous it housed a caravan of wagons she recognized as Abel Dunsfield's, Robb Andrews's, and her own supply wagon, among others. Running the perimeter of the huge structure were rows of living quarters and other rooms used for kitchens, arsenals, workshops, and storage rooms. Peeking inside one of the rooms, Bree noticed the dirt floors had been sprinkled with water to prevent dust clouds.

A person could feel really safe here, she was about to comment to Lucy. Just then a familiar voice called her name and she turned to see Robb Andrews rushing toward her, an expression of joy and relief on his face. In that split instant Bree made another decision. Nothing would be more distasteful to Jemson than for her to take up with Robb Andrews or at least to give the appearance of such an alliance. She would be protected from any further problems with Jemson by just the hint of interest in Robb. Jemson's pride and his dislike for Robb were too intense for him to take it lightly. Eliciting Jemson's anger would help her retain her own. Robb might misinterpret her interest as something more than it was, but anything would be easier than trying to handle the attraction she still felt for Jemson. And she had to admit that it was getting harder and harder to remain aloof from him. She was nearly overcome with the urge to explain why she had felt it best to remove herself from the closeness that had sprang up between them. The danger in that was that he might have some very good arguments as to why they should let their relationship take its natural course, and she knew she would be unable to fight once he set his mind to breaking down her resistance. No, if she continued to keep him at a distance, she would be safe. And Robb Andrews was the best insurance for her safety at hand.

"Robb!" Bree returned his smile with more happiness than she actually felt. "It's so wonderful to see you again. I swear I thought we'd never get here." The last of her words came out in a gasp as Robb lifted her off her feet and swung her around.

He set her down again without releasing his hands from around her waist. Bree's nose wrinkled at the flowery, sweet smell of him. She had forgotten he used perfume, as did Phillip and her father.

"Oh, Bree, Ah've been worried sick about you, wonderin' if Ah'd evah see you again. I swear I was ready to take mount and go back for you, truly."

Bree smiled endearingly, all the time thinking that he didn't have the courage to come out of his wagon during the cholera epidemic, let alone travel unescorted through Indian territory.

"I'll admit there were times when I wondered if we'd make it. But, I'm here with you again and that's all that really matters." Lucy's shocked gasp of indignation stopped Bree for a moment, but then she rushed on. "I've been just dyin' for some intelligent conversation. Why don't you come with me right now and I'll make us dinner. Oh yes, I do have a favor to ask, Robb." Bree lowered her eyes as though even the mention of his name was more than a woman of refinement could bare. "Jemson was rather tiresome this past week. I would so appreciate ridin' with you until we reach Denver."

"Has he harmed you or done . . ." Robb's face reddened, his fists clenching impotently.

"No, no, nothin' like that," Bree hurried to reassure him. "But, you know," she said, laughing airily, "the company of shopkeepers and pig farmers gets a little wearin' after a while, you understand. Lucy can drive the supply wagon and Jemson can handle the other without help from me."

Robb responded to her fluttering lashes and pouting mouth exactly as Bree had intended he would. The next morning, when they pulled out on the last leg of their journey, Bree sat beside him on his wagon. Strangely, Jemson had little to say about the new system Bree had maneuvered. He nodded sharply when Bree explained that she would be riding during the day with Robb, then looked away from her as though the sight of her was unpleasant.

In truth, he was at a loss as to what she wanted from him. But then, it was his own damn fault. He had known from the beginning that she wasn't like any of the women he had known before. He had even warned himself against the parlor games she played so brilliantly. Still, he wanted her like no other woman and he got what he wanted. Only trouble was, he wanted more of her, all of her, all the time. He was so blind with wanting her he had, after the night they spent in her wagon, begun to plan ways to free her from the husband she thought of as the perfect gentleman. Jemson hadn't mentioned it to her, but he'd had occasion to meet the object of her fascination. Last year, before returning to Pennsylvania, he had stopped in Black Hawk Point on his way down the mountain. Sitting in on a poker game in the back room of one of the saloons there, he'd watched with growing scorn as a well-dressed, soft-spoken man lost hand after hand and got steadily drunker and more obscene. Phillip Alexander. He had juggled that glass of whiskey in one hand and fondled a saloon girl so easily with the other that Jemson had been sure he was a professional gambler. The man's manners had gotten so offensive that the table had broken up.

And this was the man Jemson was thinking about the morning Bree had so shocked him with her indifference. He could still picture her as she lay sleeping in the crook of his arm, her mouth parted softly and her breath coming out in sighs. He'd kissed the tender brow and slipped quietly from under the covers, dressing hurriedly and leaving to ready the campsite so that he would have more time with her before they pulled out with the others. Occupying his mind with ways of getting Bree free from Phillip Alexander before she found out what he really was. And then . . . nothing. She had appeared and looked right through him, acting as if nothing had passed between them. But he had waited for her to come around, waited for Bree to come to terms with whatever was troubling her. And now, this. Playing the coquette with Robb Andrews. Doing anything she could to push Jemson further away. He wanted to tell her that it wasn't necessary that she lower herself to wallow in the muck that was Robb Andrews. He wouldn't pressure her or force her to do anything. But the look she leveled at him whenever she wasn't careful to completely avoid his gaze was so hard, so void of feeling that he was speechless, knowing that anything he might say would fall on deaf ears. She was no longer open to him, would no longer listen to anything he might say. Whatever had been his, if only for a few hours on a warm, summer night, was gone and he knew the woman he'd awakened would never venture toward him again.

BOOK TWO

CHAPTER TWELVE

Colorado's rolling plains edged steadily upward before giving way to the plateau upon which Denver, its largest and most important city, had been built. City, Bree observed sourly, was far too generous a word to give what lay before them as the wagon train pulled in after fourteen long, agonizing weeks on the trail. Nightmare, disaster, staggering disappointment—to Bree's way of thinking, only those words applied. Settled at the base of towering mountains of breathless beauty, Denver was nothing more than crudely built log cabins cluttered along dusty streets devoid of sidewalks and trees. Every green, living thing had been leveled and carted away to make room for the ugly, barren structures used for living quarters and businesses. The town's population, it seemed, surged out to meet them—shabby miners, Indians, merchants hawking their wares, gamblers looking over the crowd with a practiced eye. Strolling from a massive tent structure and smiling fetchingly, saloon girls waved and called explicit invitations.

Already the train was breaking up. Small groups of wagons moved from the main body. Six hours of daylight remained, and they were anxious to continue the short jaunts it would take to get them to Cripple Creek, Golden, and Russell Gulch. Bree felt the same urge. Knowing Black Hawk Point was less than a day's ride in the huge mountains that lay to the west of Denver, she hoped that there would be some respite from the dust and emptiness. Convincing Robb and Will George to move out immediately proved to be no problem. They were as eager to leave behind the dissolute, charmless Denver as she was. Will and Lucy hurried to stand in line at the general store in the hopes of purchasing items that they feared might not be available to them when they reached the more remote Black Hawk Point.

Bree steeled herself and went to seek out Jemson Tyler. There was still one matter of unfinished business between them, and she wanted to resolve it before departing. As usual, it wasn't hard to spot him even in a crowd as large as the one that surrounded her. He stood almost a head taller than anyone else, leaning easily against Abel Dunsfield's wagon. She hesitated approaching him there and then went on. She should have been used to the looks of disgust and the lack of respect by now. For a week, since leaving Bent's Fort, the men had looked on her as a woman fallen from grace, a woman not as worthy as the others. Because Jemson was their friend, the men, notably Abel Dunsfield, had not voiced the unspoken questions the whole train had been buzzing about. They had too much respect for the man to embarrass him with questions about why his wife was traveling in another man's company. Oh, she slept with her slave at night in their supply wagon, but why did she choose Robb Andrews's company during the daylight hours? And why didn't Jemson take a length of branch and lay it to her backside? Why did he allow his wife to shame him?

He spotted her approach and stepped outside the circle of men to meet her, his face as dark and stormy as any thundercloud she'd ever seen.

"I believe I owe you some money, Jemson," Bree whispered, her eyes darting unconsciously about to make sure no one could overhear her. "And, I also believe you have somethin' in your possession that by rights belongs to me."

"Ah, the marriage certificate." His mouth turned cruelly into a smile with little mirth behind it. "I think I'll just hold on to that myself. Just call it a sentimental gesture, something to remember you by.'' Jemson was making no attempt to keep their conversation private. His raised voice was attracting attention. "Now, about the fifty dollars. Under favorable circumstances, a gentlemen would tip his hat and say it's been a pleasure bein' of service and let it go. But nothing about you is all that favorable, lady, so I'll just say turn over the money you promised me to impersonate your husband and we'll have no more to say." He stood like a stone in front of her, his blue eyes flashing with bitterness, hard and brittle.

"Oh, here!" Bree muttered, flustered and embarrassed by the knowledge that Jemson's friends were listening intently to every word that passed between them. She reached into her bag and withdrew a fifty-dollar gold piece. Then, moving her position, Bree turned her back to the curious eavesdroppers and held out the coin. "We're leavin' in a moment, Jemson. Would you walk with me? I find I just can't go with you hatin' me as much as you do. I want to explain about that night, all the guilt and confusion I was feelin'. I . . ."

"What night?" Jemson hissed angrily, his voice suddenly low and menacing. "We got nothing to talk about, Mrs. Alexander, except maybe you've got change coming on your fifty dollars. Tell me, just how much do you ladies of refinement and breeding charge for an evening's diversion?"

Bree gasped and stumbled as though he had hit her. The gold piece dropped out of her hand and into the dust. She turned to leave, but Jemson grabbed her arm and yanked her brutally toward him. His head lowered and his breath was harsh and warm against her ear.

"On second thought," he whispered wrathfully, "I'm not being paid half enough for all the slaving and mooning around I did. I want more." His free arm shot out and closed around Bree's waist. As he drew her closer, she was keenly aware of the soft, worn material of his flannel shirt, the heat of his body burning through the shirt. Even as his mouth came down on hers, searching and demand-

137

ing, Bree greedily took in all the textures and hot, enticing odors that she would forever associate with Jemson. Just before her eyes closed and she lost herself to the engulfing need to return Jemson's kiss, Bree noticed how his hair lightened and reflected the afternoon sun. Then, dreamlike, her arms snaked around his neck and she held on desperately, knowing this would be the last chance, the only opportunity she would have to tell him—not with words but by her actions—that she loved him, that her desire was a great as his. All the things she could never say to Jemson were found there in her response. This was the last time he would ever hold her and to hell with what the crowd of snoopy busybodies thought. They were getting quite a show. Bree pressed herself tightly against Jemson's chest, her breasts rubbing ever so slightly, provocatively. Her tongue danced lightly in his mouth, evading and then touching his own. Hands trailed delicately along Jemson's neck and tangled in his hair.

It was he who first broke the embrace, breathless and astonished. Bree's intense reaction to what he had meant as a challenge and humiliation left him speechless. He fought to clear his head, assemble his thoughts, and failed.

"Goodbye, darlin'." Bree's trembling smile waivered. Bending, she picked up the coin from the dirt and pressed it into Jemson's hand. "It was worth every penny." Flashing a defiant gaze at the onlookers and lifting her chin, Bree turned and began to walk back to her wagon.

"But not worth everything—is that right, Bree?" Jemson found his voice and called after her.

She stopped dead in her tracks, afraid to turn around and face him. What use to try and explain to a man with no responsibilities the burden she carried, the duty she was entrusted to fulfill. And how could she tell him what she didn't really understand herself? The selfish clinging to a way of life she was afraid to lose. Staying with a man she now realized she could no longer love because it was her birthright, her obligation and intention to do so. Jemson would never understand her weakness, her fear.

She felt as though her feet were imbedded in the claylike dirt, terrified that if she turned around to face him all composure and determination would slip away like a discarded cloak. Back stiffened and shoulders squared, Bree took a deep, shuddering breath and forced herself to put one foot in front of the other until she was walking then running away.

"Did you see that, Lucy?" Will George's eyes widened with surprise as he watched Bree hurry away from Jemson. "I thought you said they weren't really married." He shifted the box of supplies he held in his arms and gave Lucy a penetrating stare. "What was *that* all about?"

"What that was all about ain't got nuthin' to do with who's married to who and who ain't!" Lucy chuckled knowingly. "They's like two bulls lockin' horns. They's ruttin' and kickin' up the dust but ain't neither of 'em gonna let go. Now, you get movin' and stop worryin'. I gotta see to Miss Bree." Lucy moved away in the direction she had seen Bree take. "An, mine you," she called over her shoulder, "give the chilluns them licorice whips for bein' so good stayin' in the wagon."

When she found Bree, Lucy's light, teasing mood turned quickly to concern. Never had she seen her Missy so miserable and forlorn. Bree sat on the bench of her wagon, her shoulders sagged in defeat. Lucy climbed up next to her and put a comforting arm around her.

"Time to go on, Missy," she chided kindly. "Don't you fret none. You ain't seen the last of that man."

Bree's eyes were lost and haunted when she turned her face to Lucy. "No, God, don't say that, Lucy. I *can't* ever see him again or I don't know what I'll do. I'll get through this somehow, knowin' I'll see Phillip and we'll be goin' home to Crosshaven soon. But I just know if I see Jemson Tyler again and he still wants me, I'll die if I have to turn away from him again." The tears were there, the need to cry out all her sorrow but, just then, she heard her name called. Bree swallowed the painful lump in her throat and looked around to the back of the wagon to see Robb Andrews approaching, a large, false smile plastered across his face. The hard glint in his eyes and the flushed look on his face betrayed his cheerfulness. He had already heard about the scene between Jemson and Bree at Abel Dunsfield's wagon. And although he preferred to ignore the implications, he couldn't shake the feeling that he had been used in Bree's attempt to discourage and deny the emotions that despicable Yankee brought out in her.

Patience, he told himself. Patience and persistence. Tyler was pulling out for Central City and *he* was escorting Bree to Black Hawk Point. Soon Jemson would be a vague, unpleasant memory and he, Robb Andrews, would be the one she turned to.

"You ladies all set?" he inquired innocently. "Will's got that passel of screamin' donkeys settled down and ready to go."

Lucy glared angrily at Robb's reference to the children, ready to spit back a retort, then felt Bree's hand cover hers in a gesture of restraint.

"We're ready." Bree smiled prettily, eager to throw herself into something, anything to take her mind off Jemson. "Lucy, get on over to the supply wagon. I'll follow behind Robb and you pull in after me." She cringed inwardly as Robb reached up and patted the folds of her skirt but forced a tight grin. She heard Lucy's disgusted snort and felt the easy, rocking movement as the bigger, heavier woman lowered herself from the wagon.

How long was Robb going to stand there grinning at her like a damned hyena? What was he waiting for?

"Well, go on, Mr. Andrews." Her jaws ached from keeping her smile in place. "Lead this small wagon train to safe harbor."

He reacted as she had intended he would. Robb's chest swelled with self-importance, but, more important, he hurried off to honor Bree's request. She watched him as he disappeared into his own wagon.

Soft, she thought with disgust, everything about Robb is

soft. Just like Phillip. They could have been made from the same mold.

At once Bree was ashamed of having thought so unkindly of her husband. There had been a time when that same soft-spoken, easy manner had appealed to her. When long, lazy days spent on the plantation house veranda fanning herself and watching Phillip do the same was the pinnacle of marital bliss. It surely wasn't Phillip's fault that she had changed her way of viewing a man's place in the world. It was her cross to bear without self-pity and regret. If she couldn't love Phillip as she had in the past, she would offer him her new awareness and her determination to help build a solid marriage. Bree had no intention of making Phillip suffer for her sins of thought and deed. If necessary, she would spend a lifetime making up for the truth that she loved another man so much it made her ache and fever from wanting. She would, by God, be the wife Phillip had tried to make her. Gentle and subdued, Bree would never give another thought to the wild, hot feeling of abandon she'd experienced in Jemson's arms.

CHAPTER THIRTEEN

Black Hawk Point, Colorado
September 1860

If it weren't for the flooding sense of dismay Bree might
have delighted in plodding slowly along the snakelike
street that wove lazily through the center of town. The
cool mountain breeze and soft, glowing sun were blessed
respite from the harshness of Denver. Nestled in a valley
between gently sloping mountains, Black Hawk Point occupied a two-mile stretch along North Clear Creek. Spruce,
fir, and cedar trees stood silent sentry around the town.
The air was thick and sweet with the smell of pine.
Children laughed and played in front of a two-story school-
house. Main Street boasted a blacksmith shop, three general stores, a dry goods store, one bank, a cobbler's shop,
and several saloons. Not one of the brightly and carefully
painted storefronts read Alexander Mercantile. Bree's sense
of panic heightened. She sat atop her wagon and watched
as a tall, gaunt man ran from Andrews Bros. General Store
and embraced Robb. Her breath was coming in short,
frightened gasps. Robb looked up and waved as his brother
clamped an arm over his shoulder and dragged him into
the store. Before looking away, Bree thought she saw a
strange, shining gleam move across Robb's face, but she
was in no humor to reflect on what the cause of his
triumph might be.

"Wait here, Lucy," Bree instructed, lowering herself
from the wagon. "I'll speak to someone in charge. Perhaps Phillip changed the name of our store without tellin'
me." Even as she said the words, Bree doubted they were

true. She sucked in a breath and set out to find the sheriff.

The building housing the official law for Black Hawk Point was small and unimpressive. The legend *Jail* had been burned into a piece of raw pine and hung over the door. Inside, a man of enormous girth sprawled in a swivel chair that threatened to collapse under the burden of his weight. His half-closed eyes flew open in surprise when Bree entered like a gust of howling wind and slammed the door behind her.

"The Alexander Mercantile," Bree demanded, ignoring politeness. "Where is it?"

"Wha—who the hell are you?" The man staggered to his feet, mustering what dignity he could after having been found napping.

"I am *Mrs*. Phillip Alexander," Bree stated with more pride than she felt. "Come all the way from Georgia to meet my husband. We have a mercantile store in Black Hawk Point. This *is* Black Hawk Point, isn't it?" Her voice was laced with sarcasm, a ploy to hide the fear that lay like a icy layer over her skin.

"Yeah, this is Black Hawk Point, Missus." The Sheriff squinted meanly, fully recovered and irritated by the woman's high-handed ways. "But there ain't no Alexander anything here."

"What does that mean? Can you read?" Bree babbled uncontrollably. "I have his letters right here in my purse."

The Sheriff softened visibly, becoming aware of what his duties were. He was still slightly agitated—the damn woman woke him up just when he was getting his hands on Matty, down to the Golden Bull Saloon—and he was less kind than he normally might have been.

"Look, ah, sit down, Mrs. Alexander." He indicated a small wooden chair on the other side of his desk. "You didn't come all the way across country for what I got to tell you, but sit down; it's gotta be done."

Without feeling any movement, Bree glided to the chair and sat down lightly, her hand reaching unconsciously to her neck. Her eyes widened into stark, depthless green pools as she waited for the small wooden structure to come crashing down over her head.

"I knew your husband, Mrs. Alexander, but I gotta admit, he never said he had no wife. Your turning up like this is a big surprise, kind of a complication, you might say. I just don't know where to begin."

"You can begin, Sheriff, by tellin' me where I can find my husband," Bree encouraged stiffly, without anger.

"Dory Hill, ma'am. The, ah, cemetery. Your husband died last winter." He cleared his throat and waited for the news to sink in before continuing. "Like I said, he never mentioned no kin so we just buried him. If I'd known about you, I'd of let you know the whys and hows but I did my duty as far as I could see it."

Suddenly the Sheriff wished he had been more gentle. The woman seemed so small and defenseless sitting there with her head bowed. Damn job! He'd have never taken it on if he'd known there was more to it than jailing a couple of Saturday night drunks once in a while.

"What about the store my husband owned, the inventory? Surely you didn't just divide it all up among the townspeople?" When she lifted her head, Bree's eyes were tearless and blank. She could hear her own voice and it sounded like the faint echo of a scream filtered through a tunnel. Her head was pounding so badly the image of the Sheriff swam drunkenly in front of her.

"I'm real sorry, ma'am, but it seems like I got nothing but bad news to tell you. Your husband lost his store and inventory, legal and proper, in a card game a few weeks before he died. He put it up to cover Lyle Andrews's bet and lost with three jacks." The Sheriff coughed nervously, remembering the night well. "I was there and saw the whole thing. The Golden Bull, it was. Lyle had an ace high flush, all diamonds. That one hand cleaned your husband out, but good. Matter of fact, I remember now he was coughing real bad that night. Fluid in his lungs, the doc said."

"I see." Bree stood up and extended her hand, fighting

the tremor that shook beneath her skin. "Thank you, Sheriff, I appreciate your time and candor." She lifted her chin and turned to go. "By the way, if Phillip lost everything in the card game, how did he live after that?" Bree gazed searchingly, sensing the Sheriff's growing discomfort, something unsaid.

"Shit, lady, you just aren't gonna let me do this nice at all, are you?" The Sheriff reddened. "He'd been carrying on with an Indian saloon girl for about a year. She took him in and worked the bar to support him. When he died, she took one of them pearl-handled derringers he had in a box and shot herself. That's all. You satisfied now?"

Bree gagged and nodded mutely, the insane urge to laugh and cry at the same time catching painfully in her throat. Walking stiffly to the door, she felt her knees waiver like mush. Grabbing the door for support, she waited until she was ready again to straighten her back and leave the jail.

When the late afternoon sun hit her face, she shivered and hugged herself. So many things to think about, and all that whirled around in her head was Robb. He knew all along and had said nothing. He must have known and he let her come ahead. Hatred welled up inside her, and the heat of it warmed the icy shock that made her tremble. A dead calm descended over Bree as she made her way back to the wagon and Lucy.

One look and Lucy knew something was dreadfully wrong, but instinct told her to hold off questions and wait until Bree had fully gained her composure. She nodded briefly when Bree instructed her to secure lodgings in one of the two hotels in town, to put up the wagons at the blacksmith's shop overnight. Lucy scrambled from the wagon, alarmed by the flushed, angry expression on Bree's face, and watched as the woman she had loved and raised walked slowly, purposely, toward the Andrews Bros. General Store.

Outside the store, Bree noticed that the newly painted sign was of a different kind of wood from the rest of the building, obviously added after Phillip had lost the store to Lyle Andrews. She passed through the door and entered the dimly lit room. A small group of men turned to eye her appraisingly. Robb separated himself and came to her cautiously. He had known this moment would come but had put off deciding how to handle it. He was unprepared for the dark, penetrating glare of Bree's eyes. Nervously, he pulled her aside, out of earshot of the others.

"Ah meant to tell you, ah swear it," he began clumsily, his voice pleading, whining. "Ah was afraid you'd turn back and ah'd nevah see you again."

"Filthy liar!" Bree accused, shaking herself free of his grasp.

"It's true, Bree, ah swear it! Ah love you, Ah mean to take care of you." He was sweating, his eyes wild and glazed, licking his lips feverishly. "Ah want you to be mah wife. Phillip Alexander was a gambler, a womanizer. You deserve bettah, much bettah. Ah just wanted to give you time to know me before Ah told you the truth about him, but then there nevah seemed to be a right moment."

"Did you think I'd be so stupid to take a fool and a coward to replace my no-good husband?" Bree demanded cruelly. "No, Robb, I didn't come here to throw myself at your feet and ask for mercy and protection. I know I'm stranded here until after the winter thaw but I did want to get one thing straight with you, since we'll be livin' in the same town until I can get back to Crosshaven. If you speak to me, I'll accuse you of whispereing filthy suggestions. If you touch me, I'll tear my clothes and scratch my face and accuse you of tryin' to attack me. If you ever come sneakin' around when I'm alone, I'll find a way to kill you."

With that, Bree turned on her heel and stomped out of the store, leaving Robb stunned by the fierceness of her rage. He stood open-mouthed, shaking his head like a man waking from a drugged sleep.

Later that night, Bree told Lucy of the seriousness and desperation they faced. Giving Jemson Tyler the bulk of her cash funds and expecting to be taken care of by Phillip and a thriving business had left them practically destitute. All they had were a few dollars and the contents of the supply wagon they'd hauled all the way from Missouri.

"I read over Phillip's letter and there's only one thing we can do." Bree sighed and began to pace the room. "If nothin' else, he *did* leave me a good piece of advice." She picked up the letter and scanned it with her finger until she found the passage she was looking for. "Black Hawk Point can't really be called a minin' town," she quoted, pausing over each word as if to let the significance sink it. "More than anything else, it offers a much needed service to better areas like Gregory, Quartz, and Mammoth Hills. Almost everything the miners could want or have a yen for can be purchased in Black Hawk Point. We are building a great industrial town here. Even a refinery, so the ore doesn't have to be sent to Wales and—oh, never mind about that, Lucy, this is the important part—the miners never seem to get enough sweets. They're like little children cravin' candies and pies. If the needed supplies were better available and less expensive, I'd send to Denver and open up a small bakery in the back of the store." Bree finished reading and sat down on the bed, a happy, self-satisfied look on her face. "There! That's what we'll do with the supplies we brought with us." Seeing the puzzled look on Lucy's face, Bree hurried on enthusiastically. "Don't you see, Lucy, we'll bake for the miners. I know we don't have enough flour and canned peaches to get us through the winter if we make pies, but we can make small tarts, just enough to satisfy a sweet tooth and keep them comin' back for more. We'll charge a dollar each—you don't have to look at me like that. I know that's a lot but the miners are willin' to pay it—and we can pay our livin' expenses until next spring and save enough money to join a wagon train out of this godforsaken place."

"And just who's gonna be doin' all that bakin', Missy?" Lucy grumbled, already knowing the answer.

"Why, you and me, of course." Bree bounced up and

hugged Lucy. "You'll teach me what I need to know, won't you? I know what you're thinkin'. You're sayin' to yourself I won't be a lick of help, but you're wrong. We'll work together and we'll get out of here together." Lucy laughed, believing Bree and trusting her determination.

"There's another way, Missy." Lucy grinned slyly. "All's you has to do is send word to Mr. Jemson and he'll come swoopin' down the mountain for you."

"*No!* You have to promise me you won't ever do anything like that, Lucy. Promise me now." All the girlish laughter drained out of Bree and she turned deadly serious. "Jemson Tyler and I were nothin' more than a mild diversion for each other when the trip here got borin'. Nothin' important happened between us." Bree lied smoothly, hoping she sounded convincing. "A little flirtation doesn't bind us for life, you know."

But when the gaslight had been extinguished and Bree lay sleeplessly beside Lucy and listened to the soft, rhythmic sound of her breathing, it proved impossible to think about the events of the day without thoughts of Jemson creeping in to torment her. It was easy to think of Phillip. He was more like a stranger who had died, nothing to do with Bree. The gambling, whore-chasing Phillip Alexander was unknown to her. She could barely remember his face and was ashamed at the relief she felt at not having to live with him again. Robb Andrews was easier still. He was nothing, an insignificant problem to be mulled over and promptly forgotten. After the warning she had given him, meant wholeheartedly, Bree doubted that she would ever be bothered by him again. And she wasn't really worried about the prospect of staying alive in this foreign country. Lucy was strong enough to carry them through. The months of winter would pass swiftly with the two of them keeping busy, and soon they would be on their way home. Bree congratulated herself on the brilliance of her plan to supply the miners with a much-desired delicacy.

The idea had come to her in a flash and she had known instantly that it was the right thing.

It was Jemson, Jemson who filled her mind with troubled thoughts and kept her awake. There was a time, after the night they had spent together, when Bree had been certain that all she had to do was indicate her agreement and Jemson would have asked her to go with him. But she had been too frightened, too panicked by the prospect of losing the things she had grown to take for granted, and the words had never been said between them. She had not allowed it. Bree had cheated herself out of something and she resented Jemson all the more for the feeling of loss she suffered. Her body was flaming with unquenched needs, desires Jemson had awakened and walked away from. She hated him. In less than three months he had called her lazy and spoiled, then turned around and complimented her on some small, meaningless task, told her she was behaving like a whore and then treated her with respect, even reverence, said she did not appeal to him and then pursued her. He had made love to her, been on the verge—she was certain—of committing himself and then let her leave without so much as a word, even a gesture, that might persuade her to stay. Why, it was really his fault she found herself in this mess. So much easier to blame Jemson, to inflame the hard, bitter emotions against him than admit her own failings. So much easier to hate him than to loosen the tight rein she held on her feelings, swallow her damnable pride, and crawl up the mountain to him.

CHAPTER FOURTEEN

The weeks sped by quickly, filled with the tasks of finding a deserted cabin, setting up shop, and making the place livable. They had to settle on a drafty, delapidated wood structure on Chase Gulch, situated amid rows of other wood boxes housing the miners and their families. From the crack of dawn to the last light of day the air buzzed with the sounds of children playing and screaming, dogs barking, mothers and wives yelling and calling gossip from house to house. The noise was deafening and Bree found herself irritable and jumpy.

Lucy proved a tough taskmaster, and if there was one thing Bree learned about baking it was that she hated it with a passion. Her hands were too small and delicate to handle the sticky dough with the ease and dexterity Lucy showed. A thin, powdery layer of flour rested everywhere, making it almost impossible to keep their working and living areas clean. At first light, they began the arduous process of mixing the ingredients for crust, kneading and rolling, then doctoring up the canned peaches with added spices—sugar, cinnamon, and salt—before putting them all together in tin and glass cups and bowls for baking. It was the actual baking that was so time-consuming. There were only so many dishes that could be crammed into the wood-burning stove at a time. Still, the enterprise had proven wildly successful, far beyond what Bree had hoped.

"Child, you gonna wear them coins down you don't stop fingerin' and countin' 'em all the time." Lucy chuckled and slapped her flour-encrusted hands on her apron. "Quit that jinglin' and smirkin' and tell me how much we got."

"Lucy, darlin', you just won't believe it! Why, I never knew it was so easy to make money." Bree giggled and lifted the coins again, smiling triumphantly as they slipped through her fingers and clanked back into the jar. "Seventy-four dollars, that's what! Our food is stocked in for the winter, we've paid that Tennessee man to cut and pile the wood, and we've still got seventy-four dollars! Oh yes, I near forgot . . . that bolt of lavender gingham for the dresses you're going to make us . . . that's counted in the before figure too. Seventy-four dollars and the winter yet to come!" As if to agree, a cold burst of wind slipped through the gapping cracks of the cabin and rushed over Bree's shoulders. She shivered and pulled her shawl tighter, hugging herself. "Remind me to ask Will if he can find the time to repair this old shack. The kind of luck he's been havin' at the creek, I'm sure he could use the extra money." Bree bent to check the progress of the last batch of tarts for the day, then reached for a cloth to protect her hands as she pulled them from the stove and set them on the table to cool. "Fool men!" she continued. "There's better ways of livin' than grovelin' in the ground for a few ounces of gold, I can tell you!" Bree sniffed and tossed her flame-red curls. "I thought Will George was a lot smarter than that. Why, in all the time we've been here, a few ounces is all any one of those men have to show for paddin' around knee-deep in water all day."

"Ain't no man gonna strike it rich workin' the creek, Missy. Takes money to stake out a hunk of the mountain . . . look for a vein, a blossom rock. Creek pannin', that ole placer gold, just good for a stake to search out a lode." Lucy crossed over to the pies, checked them, and nodded her approval, then went to the basin and began to clean up.

"My, my, don't you know just everythin' there is to know about placers and lodes and the like." Bree smiled teasingly. "All right Miss Smarty, just when was the last

151

time you heard about any of these stupid miners findin'
anythin' worth braggin' about?'' Bree turned without waiting for an answer and began the ritual of washing off the
morning's accumulation of flour and sticky syrup.

"Come to remember." Lucy grinned slyly, watching
Bree's face. "I did hear tell of a big lode just today, down
to the store when I was fetchin' the thread for that gingham." Lucy paused for effect, vexed that Bree evidenced
little interest. She edged closer to Bree. "Up to Central
City . . . the biggest mother lode yet, they say. Heard
some men talkin' 'bout how luck just naturally seems to
fall in Jemson Tyler's lap." At the mention of his name,
Lucy was rewarded by a slight, shuddering movement
from Bree. "Calls that old mine the 'Southern Belle,'
now why do you suppose?"

"I'm sure I have no idea, or interest, for that matter,"
Bree answered stiffly. Her curiosity was piqued, but she
was loath to give Lucy the satisfaction of knowing she was
anxious for word of Jemson. Instead, Bree finished washing her face and hands, then took a brush and began to
beat the flour mist out of her hair. Conversation stopped
altogether while the two women pan-bathed and changed
their clothes.

It had become a habit, over the past weeks, to set aside
three or four nights to spend in the company of Will
George and his children. They made the mile hike to his
cabin on the creek, loaded down with supplies for the
nutritious dinner they decided the children needed. Bree
welcomed the diversion. She played and instructed the
girls in needlepoint, the boys in reading, until she was so
exhausted she barely made it home again. Then it was only
a matter of a few minutes before her head hit the pillow
and she sank into dreamless sleep. On the nights she and
Lucy spent at home, there was no reprieve, no escape from
the taunting, painful memory of Jemson. It was the loneliness, the silence that hurt most of all. Lucy worked harder
than Bree, and she had little time for talk before crawling
into her bed. Bree was left with hours of listening to the

winter wind howl through the cabin, counting off the beats of her own heart. There were times when the depression was so great she thought her heart would stop under the burden of its grief.

She looked for excuses to busy herself. The cabin across the way was inhabited by five New York boys, regular customers and none of them older than Bree. She had taken to playing penny poker with them and was amazed at the proficiency she'd shown. They had a regular game on Tuesday and Friday nights that lasted until the early hours of the morning. Bree had to admit that it was the devil to get up the next morning, but the long games kept her mind occupied for long stretches at a time. The luck and the bluffing of the game intrigued Bree. Just the night before she had taken a chance and drawn to an inside straight and caught. She raised the opening player's bet and won the hand. The next time she drew only one card, Bree raised the bet again and the other players folded their hands, electing not to call the bet and see her cards. She didn't even have a pair.

Lucy tapped on Bree's shoulder just as she was smiling at the memory of the men's faces when she turned her cards over and showed them nothing. It wasn't something she had to do. She just delighted in letting them know she had fooled them.

"You thinkin' 'bout Mr. Jemson, chile?" Lucy asked kindly, sorry now she had even brought up his name.

"As a matter of fact, *no*, I *wasn't* thinkin' about Jemson Tyler," Bree snapped peevishly. "I was thinkin' that most men are plain fools. They go around underestimating women, thinkin' they're so much stronger and smarter. Bah! A woman with any brains in her head can outwit a man ten times over!"

"I don't rightly know what you said, Missy, but that kinda hard figurin's gonna bring you trouble, just like it did with Mr. Jemson."

"Whatever are you babblin' about, Lucy? No, don't tell me! I don't want to discuss Jemson Tyler with anyone, least of all you. Why can't you just accept the truth of it? Jemson was a man we met on our way to Colorado. He had his amusin' moments but that's the whole of it. We're never gonna see him again and that's fine with me. Now, will you just drop the subject, once and for all?''

"I can drop it easy, honey. I ain't the one runnin' around like a crazy woman tryin' to forget him.'' Lucy mumbled, her voice dropping so Bree had to strain to hear the last of her words. She whirled around and held the door open to Bree, an innocent smile on her face. "You ready, honey?''

Bree sighed, exasperation etched across her face, and then stomped out the door ahead of Lucy. Dry, biting wind hit her face and she pulled the hood of her cape closer for protection. Harsh snow would soon be upon them, a new element Bree looked forward to and yet dreaded. The last few days had been colder than anything she had ever known. It seemed as though she was chilled down to her bones and it would only get worse.

As they walked the sun began to disappear behind the treetops. Each time they made the trip to the George cabin, it seemed to get dark earlier. Even so, Bree was not made uncomfortable by walking as darkness descended. Lucy's size and strength were formidable, and she let it be known that she kept a ten-inch Bowie knife strapped to her calf. Still, this night, Bree found it impossible to shake the feeling that they were being watched. Other times she had sensed the same, flesh-crawling feeling, but tonight it was stronger, as though the dangerous presence had somehow moved stealthily closer. A branch crushed under a footfall, the rustling of a mountain maple off to the side of the path, a spatter of rock slipping down the ravine.

Bree shuddered and looked at Lucy. If she heard the same noises, she either chose to ignore them or felt they were just the sounds of the terrain, magnified by the ominous curtain of night. Still, Lucy was unusually quiet, as if alert to the presence of unknown danger. Bree walked quietly beside her, her heart thumping uncontrollably. She kept her head lowered against the wind and her feet moving in time with Lucy's.

Lucy slowed suddenly and when Bree looked up, Will George's cabin stood ahead of them. A warm, yellow-orange glow filtered through the windows. The children must have been watching for them, because in seconds they were surrounded, clung to and hugged. Amy George, the youngest at three years old, grabbed Bree's skirt and pulled her into the cabin. Lucy followed, surrounded by the boys, Ben and Andy, and the oldest girl, Christine. She plopped the basket of food on a sparsely set table and turned to stare seriously at Will.

"I'm takin' you up on that offer, Will." Lucy lowered her voice so as not to alarm the children. "Missy and me'd be pleasured to have you walk with us from now on."

"Were you followed again?" Will advanced and put his hand on Lucy's shoulder. She cocked her head and looked him square in the eye, nodding sharply. "Ben, you get the books out for the youngsters and sit by the fire," Will instructed, sending the children off to the far side of the room. He whispered, his grip on Lucy's shoulder tightening. "I *told* you it wasn't safe for two good-looking women to go traipsing around by themselves. It's time you let me help take care of you."

Bree's mouth dropped slightly, stunned by the obvious display of affection. Her mind didn't register the differences in the color of Lucy's and Will's skin. For the moment, she was astonished by the sight of Lucy with a man, any man. It amazed Bree that she had never considered Lucy in that way, that Lucy had the same needs and desires, the same dreams. She was chastised and ashamed. It was one thing to take your surroundings, your home and its furnishings, for granted and quite another to realize Lucy had fallen into the category of possessions. She was so caught up in her own emotions that she had never stopped to consider that Lucy might have some of her own.

Bree tried to busy herself with the children's lessons but

155

found that her eyes glided time and time again to the sight of Lucy and Will getting supper ready. Was it just her imagination, or did Will seem to touch Lucy each time he walked by her? And the look on Lucy's face . . . there was none of the guile and coyness Bree thought so useful in entrapping a man's attention. Lucy looked at Will openly, lustfully, a slight constant smile playing around her mouth.

Once again, Bree felt guilt, certain that if it wasn't for her dependence and uselessness Lucy would be here with Will all the time instead of working for passage back to Georgia. Lucy was a free woman. Only her love and concern, a lifetime habit, bound her to Bree. For a moment, a fleeting moment, the old Bryna McCarty Alexander of Crosshaven plantation surfaced and whispered through Bree's head.

Why should Lucy be happy and bask in the glow of love from her man if she, Bree, was miserable and alone?

Bree blushed, her shoulders sagging. New maturity, acquired on the long trail from Missouri, surfaced and swept aside the selfish, spiteful thoughts. Lucy deserved a chance at a life of her own, a home to set her things about, a man to love and honor her.

At least one of us will have gotten something good and true from all the misery, Bree mused thoughtfully. Knowing it was only a matter of finding the right moment, Bree decided to discuss with Lucy the possibility of going home without her. It would be Lucy's decision to go or stay. There would be problems, so great they boggled Bree's mind, if Lucy chose to stay with Will. But at least she would have the opportunity to make a choice knowing Bree would not stand in her path.

When they were all seated at the table, Bree watched with envy the secret looks that passed between Lucy and Will. She found it hard to speak for fear she might cry with the anguish of her own situation. Her emotions bounced back and forth like a ball tossed from hand to hand. One moment she ached for wanting to see Jemson again, to hold his large face in her small fingers and feel the power of his mouth against her lips. The next, she loathed him for the pain of her need, remembering him as an uncouth hayseed, a Yankee who could never possibly find a place in her world. Crosshaven, the world she was returning to as quickly as possible. Crosshaven. It loomed like a palace, shrouded in mist, just beyond her reach. She could almost conjure up the smell of magnolia and the feel of lying amid the azaleas and white dogwood in the groves just beyond the big house. She would return to the bosom of her family, a bereaved widow, and, after a respectable time, rejoin the social life that, even now, assaulted her memory with images of Chinese lanterns burning softly on a warm summer's night, of beautifully dressed partners at elegantly staged cotillions.

If all else vanished—old friends and lovers gone by the wayside—Crosshaven would always stand like a beacon, beckoning her home.

CHAPTER FIFTEEN

Bree sighed happily and sank blissfully into the rocker that had been with her all the way from Missouri. Not a stick of work to do all day, not a blessed thing to worry about except taking a real tub bath, washing and scrubbing her head, maybe even trying her hand at putting on the finishing touches to the lavender gingham dresses Lucy had sewn. She rocked contentedly, pausing occasionally to poke at the raging fire she had build to ward off the freezing cold wind that blustered and forced its way through the crevices in the cabin. Will had promised to repair the walls as soon as he and Lucy returned from Central City, but until then there was nothing to do but bundle up and keep an eye on the fire that cracked and blazed in the hearth.

The two lovebirds, as Bree secretly called them because Lucy hadn't yet opened up to her, had gone up the mountain to Central City to buy much needed spices and supplies before the hard winter set in and made traveling impossible. By the feel of the wind and the clear, bright cloudless sky, Bree guessed it wouldn't be long before she woke to find a blanket of snow covering everything for as far as the eye could see.

The black cast-iron pot hanging over the fire began to steam, and she poked her finger tentatively into the heated water. It would take at least five such pots of water to fill the tub and it would no doubt be rather cool by the time she was ready but, oh, the luxury of a full bath. Besides, she had a whole day of privacy. Lucy and Will wouldn't be back with the children until nightfall.

Thinking of nightfall brought on an added chill. Will's concern and Lucy's readiness to have him escort them to and from his home had only made her conviction that they were being watched stronger. It didn't matter if the person behind the ever-watchful eyes was a danger to her or not. It was the feeling of being violated, her privacy meaningless, the walls of her shabby home vulnerable to intrusion. Involuntarily, Bree's eyes slid to the table where Lucy had left her knife. It was done without a word between them, but the meaning was clear. Her gaze shifting, Bree checked the latch on the front door and seeing that it was firmly in place, she relaxed and forced her mind on more pleasant diversions. Remembering to wrap a thick cloth around the handle to protect her hands, Bree lifted the heavy pot, her face reddening and neck muscles straining as she lugged it over to the wooden tub by the side of the hearth. It was amazing the lengths a person would go for a good bath.

Humming, carrying the empty pot, Bree unlatched the front door, walked around to the side of the cabin, and refilled the pot from the water barrel. Her arms felt nearly pulled from the sockets by the weight of the water, but she swung it back and forth, the force of the momentum propelling her back toward the door. Once inside, she relatched the door, hung the pot over the fire and covered the tub with a heavy blanket, hoping to keep the water hot. She returned to her rocker and picked up a newspaper brought all the way from Denver and passed from miner to miner until it had finally fallen into her hands. This was the first chance she'd had to read the two-week-old paper, but she was hungry for any news at all. The print was torn and smudged, and its poor condition seemed to illustrate the disastrous news that filled the front page. *War*, the headlines read. War between the northern and southern states. Secession was inevitable. Abraham Lincoln called the nation "a house divided." Whole states were mobilizing for the prospect of war. Bree devoured the entire article, devastated by its implications. She had, of course, heard the rumblings of discontent all her life—the South wanted to be left alone, to govern and have sovereign state's rights, to keep their slaves for the sake of the economy—but when the serious talk started, her men retired to the study and the ladies gathered around petit point and the piano. Never had she been a participant in a political conversation; her womenfolk never spoke of it. Bree had no idea there could actually be a war fought between citizens of the same country. A civil war, the newspaper called it.

The paper slipped to her lap from shaking hands. Lord, she prayed fervently, if there has to be a war please let me make it home to my family before it starts.

She sat, stunned, so lost in thought the pot began to hiss and steam without her knowledge. The water spilled over the rim, dousing the fire below. Bree scrambled from her rocker and snatched the pot from its hanger and poured it into the tub. Her movements were almost mechanical as she went outside again to refill the pot and go to the woodpile for more wood to rebuild the fire. Inside, once again, she stoked the fire until it was raging under the pot, all the time thinking of her father and her younger brother, Kirk. If there was a war, her father would almost certainly be called to duty, but if it was over as quickly as the reporter predicted, Kirk would be safe.

Bree was chilled to her bones, fear heightening the cold, so she pushed closer to the fire. Its flame and heat soothed and lulled her. She felt engulfed in a cocoon of warmth, her eyelids growing heavy, her head a burden of weight she couldn't carry. Unconsciously, she sank deeper into the rocker and lifted her feet, tucking them under the protection of her skirt. The dancing flames hypnotized her and she felt herself slipping away.

The dream took her back to Crosshaven, to the time she had flirted and danced with Georgia's most eligible bachelors. She was wearing her most beautiful ballgown, the one she had been forced to leave behind. A pale yellow silk with four rows of flounces accentuating the skirt, worn over the stiffest of crinolines. A deep, plunging, off-the-shoulders collar was edged with a festoon of deeper yellow honeysuckle flowers. She wore the same flowers in her hair, pinned all along the back and sides of her chignon, a hairstyle she had never been particularly happy with but which was, nonetheless, striking against her small face. Surrounded by a circle of admirers, Bree bypassed Phillip to focus her attention on a strange, silent young man. She had never seen him before. Indeed, his face was half-hidden in the shadows of the garden but she was drawn to him. His touch was gentle as he took her in his arms and began to whirl lightly in circles. He was large and graceful and reminded her of Jemson Tyler. He *was* Jemson and yet not Jemson. This strange man spoke in the soft dialect of her people, had the charming manners of a Southern gentleman. She allowed him to lead her away from the others and into the darkness beneath a trellis covered with primroses. Sighing as he put a searching hand on her shoulder, Bree felt herself pressing, lifting toward him. And then she was struggling to resist the hands. They were everywhere, pawing, grabbing, pulling her closer.

Bree woke screaming, still fighting off the demanding grip. A cold hand clamped down over her mouth and she looked, dazed and confused, into Robb Andrews's eyes.

"You forgot to latch the door that last time, Bree," he whispered, dragging her from the rocker, his hand still pressed painfully against her mouth, another hand locked around her neck. "Mighty careless, girl, you nevah know who's lurkin about just waitin' for a chance like that." He smiled with false benevolence. "Now, I'm gonna take mah hand away but I don't want you screamin' or misbehavin', hear? I just want to talk. You promise?" He waited until Bree nodded, then dropped his hand slowly, ready to spring again should she try to deceive him.

"I had a feelin' it was *you* lurkin' around in the bushes

all this time, Robb," Bree spat contemptuously. "I don't know anybody else could sneak and spy like that."

Robb waved a warning hand, silencing her. "No more insults, honey. Ah don't have to take that kinda talk from a slut who crosses the country with a man pretendin' to be her husband. I came here to do you a favah. Figurin' you'd be lonely by now, not havin' a man to share your bed."

"You, Robb? A man? Why, you snivelin' little bastard, get out of here at once, before Will gets back and thrashes you proper!" Bree pointed a dramatic finger toward the door, speaking with more bravado than she felt. "I said get out! *Now!*"

Robb's face flamed and his eyes glazed with anger. A silly thought, something Lucy was always telling her, flashed through Bree's mind the second before Robb grabbed her.

That poison tongue of yours, chile, gonna get you in a passel of trouble one of these days. You'd best think before your mouth takes off.

Robb's fingers clutched at the bodice of Bree's dress and in one vicious movement it was torn down the front, her undergarments with it, and she was exposed to the waist. His eyes fed greedily while she made an effort to cover herself with her hands. Moving more quickly than she would have thought possible for him, Robb grabbed her around the waist and pressed against her.

"You think you're too good for me?" he rasped, shaking with rage. "You're trash, Bryna Alexander, just like the girls down to Mad Lorrie's whorehouse. You make a man nothin' and get pleasure from doin' it. Ah cain't work . . . my brothah's about set to send me back to Georgia. Ah cain't sleep. All for a tramp!" His arms clamped tightly around her waist, Robb lifted Bree easily and carried her toward the bed and then laid her roughly, spread-eagled across it. His hands were already busy trying to lift the skirt of her torn dress, his fists pulling frantically at her pantalets. "Don't play the virgin with me, bitch," he hissed vehemently. "Ah've watched you with Tyler and now with Will George. Well, jus relax and Ah'm gonna give you somethin' you're gonna like even bettah."

Bree knew it was useless to fight. Robb was bigger and stronger and the chances of eluding him were almost impossible. She lay like a stone beneath him, her skin crawling, trying to focus her mind on the most distasteful thing she could. The image that popped into her mind almost made her laugh out loud but she forced herself to remain quiet and passive. Kneading dough. She despised kneading dough. Picturing herself picking up the sticky white stuff in both hands and plopping it down on a flour-dusted cloth, punching and rolling until her arms ached, Bree wasn't even aware that her pantalets had been yanked down around her ankles, her legs forced apart. Punching with one fist and then another, flipping the dough over and starting again—she whimpered as Robb plunged into that dry, closed part of her—rolling and squeezing, pinching the dough to test its readiness—he drove into her with the wildness of a madman, pumping and thrusting—rolling the dough into a tight snakelike rope and folding it over, punching and pulling—he shuddered and fell heavily on top of her, his breath ragged and panting against her ear.

Bree turned her face to the wall and waited. Would he get up and leave without speaking? She prayed he would. The brief thought that he might kill her entered her mind, but she dismissed it immediately. He was too much of a coward. If only he wouldn't speak. She was only working the dough, a job she truly hated. If only he left without saying anything.

Robb got up silently and straightened his clothing, looking down at Bree witha a puzzled, suspicious frown. She moved her head and stared blankly at the ceiling, almost as though she wasn't aware of his presence. Confused, he waited for her to scream, to cry, to curse him. Nothing. She lay there rigidly, her skirts bunched up around her waist, the bodice flapping open unnoticed. Robb backed up slowly toward the door, not certain what to make of her. Her quiet unnerved him. Anything would have been better than the unearthly silence. He cleared his throat and glanced at her nervously, finally deciding that the silence was her way of telling him she really hadn't minded, that he had been right about her.

"We'll get together again soon, honey. Just stop by the store and let me know when the nigra woman is gonna be gone." He grinned confidently, knowingly, but only for a moment.

At the sound of his voice, Bree sprang from the bed. A high, thin, animal-like wail erupted from her throat. He stood dumbfounded, frozen, as she flew to the hearth and grabbed the pot with her bare hands. The handle burned ribbons of iron-hot fire on her hands but not until she swung it with all her might toward the door. The pot missed Robb but hit the floor with a terrible force near him, and its bubbling, boiling contents flew upward and splashed across his chest, seeping under his coat and down his chest, biting at his neck and the right side of his face. He howled, clutching at his burned flesh, flapping wildly and moving toward her. But Bree was too quick for him. She ran to the table and picked up Lucy's knife, waving it menacingly.

"You take another step and I'll cut your heart out!" she shrieked, out of control, advancing unafraid. "Get out! Get out before I kill you." She jabbed the knife at him threateningly, prepared to use it.

Moaning and clutching at the burns on his neck and face, Robb retreated, murmuring and cursing. Just as he opened the door, Bree rushed forward and shoved him the rest of the way out. She latched the door and collapsed against it, panting. The knife dropped out of her hand and she looked at the burning paths across both palms. The pain was only just now beginning to spread up over her wrists and along her arms. She held her wounded hands in front of her and rushed to the tub, then plunged her hands in the water. It had cooled considerably and gave her momentary relief. Still, she knew it wasn't enough. Searching through Lucy's things, she came upon the salve that had been used to treat the blisters she'd acquired along the trail. Jerking with each touch, Bree applied the cooling salve and then wrapped strips of clean cloth around her hands. Staggering, she crossed again to the tub and stripped off what remained of her dress and undergarments. A vicious flick of her wrist sent the tattered remnants into the fire. It was cold inside the cabin, but she ignored it as she lowered herself into the tub and began to wash off the evidence of Robb's lust. She shuddered, feeling she would somehow never be as clean as she had once been. At that moment she made a decision. She would never tell what had happened. No matter what the men of Black Hawk Point did to Robb, she knew that she would always be marked as a raped woman. No, his punishment wasn't worth the burden she would have to carry. Lucy would believe her when she said she burned her hands picking up the pot, having forgotten to use a protective cloth. Lucy would chuckle and shake her head. Whatever am I gonna do with you, chile, she would say, you just wasn't meant to be anythin' but a doll sittin' in some man's china case.

Bree choked, swallowing her tears. She scrubbed her body until her skin throbbed and her hands were soaking, aching. Lifting herself from the tub, she was surprised at how heavy her body felt. Her hands had to be treated and rebandaged, and when that was done, Bree struggled into a gown and crawled into her bed, pulling the covers up over her head.

The fire flickered and waned, dying from neglect.

CHAPTER SIXTEEN

Lucy watched Bree with growing concern. The burns she'd gotten while Lucy was with Will in Central City, ugly burns that stretched across her palms, had blistered, broken, scabbed, and were now almost fully healed. Yet she seemed to sink further into depression every day. She was jumpy, skittish, and no longer joked with the miners who dropped by each day to buy their small peach pies. Even the twice weekly poker games had been dropped. And the nightmares—Bree would wake in a cold sweat and wander silently around the cabin like a phantom.

Lucy thought to cheer her up with bits of gossip she'd picked up at the general store. Levi Dingham's wife was seen in the company of his partner once too often and old Levi had taken a bullwhip to the both of them. That young Quaker boy, Nathaniel, had taken it into his mind to marry one of the whores down to Mad Lorrie's and was jumping into fights with any man who even dared snicker. And, oh yes, did Bree know Robb Andrews was down with a bad case of the grippe—sweatin' and shakin' it out for these past weeks and no one even seein' so much as his shadow.

Nothing worked; no amount of teasing or cajoling brought a smile to Bree's face. The only time she left the cabin was when Will walked over to escort them both back to his cabin. She was still patient and loving with the children but, even with them, she just couldn't seem to relax and be herself again. Whatever was on her mind, whatever it was that was eating away at her, Bree hadn't chosen to share it with Lucy, and all she could do was watch and wait—and, in the meantime, think up small ways of bringing her out of the sorrow.

"Honey, you gonna have to make a run down to the store for me." Lucy one day addressed herself to Bree's quiet form. "I's up to mah elbows in flour so you jist go on down there and pick me up five pounds sugar for to make the chillun a taffy pull. Plenty of daylight left so you jist take it on over to Will's place and I'll meet you there."

Bree threw a heavy cloak over her shoulders and stepped outside the cabin into the winter day. She walked slowly, the snow crunching beneath her feet, steeling herself—knowing that if she ran into Robb at the store she would have to somehow find the strength to pretend nothing had ever happened between them. It was difficult. All she had been able to think about over the past weeks was the casualness of his brutality, the indignity of his rough hands on her flesh. The fear and hatred were like a cancer growing in her heart, turning everything else in her life sour. She found she couldn't even look at another man without suspicion, could barely leave the cabin without her heart pounding wildly in her chest. Every shadow, behind each tree, lurked the unseen danger. For she knew with certainty Robb would come back for her, come back to hurt and humiliate her. Her only defense was staying close to Lucy, never allowing herself to be out alone in a dark, lonely place.

A light snowfall began as she rounded the bend and headed down the main street to the general store. Bree pulled the cloak tighter around her body and bent slightly, in an unconscious gesture, to feel the reassurance of the knife she had hidden in the deep pocket of her skirt. Fifty feet away from the store she stopped cold and swung away. Hands flying to her mouth to capture a scream of surprise, Bree bolted blindly. Jemson Tyler! Standing there bold as brass, his unmistakable height looming over the group of men that had gathered to congratulate and question him. What was he doing here? Had he seen her? No, she doubted it. He was too busy basking in the glory the other miners were so anxious to heap upon him.

Still, she was shaking as she fled across the ravine and over to the path that led to Will George's cabin. She was too preoccupied to notice the menacing black clouds that swirled around the sun and blocked out its warmth and light. She was shaking too hard to feel the added blast of freezing wind that danced and lifted her cloak.

The path moved upward and her feet slipped on the fresh snow. Still, Bree half ran, putting as much distance between herself and the general store as she could manage.

In a matter of minutes it was upon her, a storm of wind-driven snow that enveloped and beat against her. She lifted a mittened hand to shield her face, puzzled by the ferocity of the white mass that bit at her. The wind forced her against a boulder of granite and pinned her there. Bree gasped, fear clouding her reflexes. She could see nothing but the madly dancing snow. Drifts began to build at her feet, soaking the hem of her skirt. She was so cold, so vulnerable. The storm howled in her ears and forced its way into her mouth, sucking the breath from her throat. Vaguely, as though it was happening to someone else, Bree noted that the drifts were up around her knees now. The wind kept up its assault, pushing her further against the rocks until she felt the dull pain of it on her back. Bree strained to pull away, move against the force, but she wasn't strong enough. The effort sapped her resilience. She opened her mouth to cry and only a dry, cracked moan came out. She was gasping with the effort to breathe.

From nowhere, hands grabbed her and yanked her away from the rock. It was impossible to make out the figure, but as soon as she felt herself hugged to his chest, she knew it was Jemson.

He bent his head and bellowed over the storm. "Get down! Grab on to my belt and don't let go."

Bree dropped to her knees and slipped her fingers through his belt, crawling after him as he led her across the path.

Jemson stopped and began a flurry of movement Bree was unable to make out. Then she felt his hand search and find hers and she was dragged forward into a hole he had dug in the drifted snow. She was small enough to curl into a ball but Jemson's hips and legs stuck out of the hole. Bree groaned with relief. Her face and body found relief from the lacerating wind. She snuggled against the familiar feel and scent of his body and closed her eyes.

"Hey, wake up!" Jemson nudged Bree as he began to back out of the protective hole. "Jesus, woman, you're the only one I know could fall asleep in the middle of a snowstorm!" Bending down to grab Bree at the waist, Jemson hauled her out of the snow and set her on her feet. She groaned, stretching her neck and shoulders, trying to work out the kinks. Dazed, she looked up at the sky and was greeted by a radiant sun, innocently shining as though nothing had gone amiss. Off to the east, beyond Black Hawk Point, the vicious black clouds drifted to devastate some other part of the mountain.

Bree suddenly choked, realizing whe was expected to say something, to thank Jemson for his assistance. No words would come out. She was too happy, too frightened, too confused.

As was his habit, Jemson sensed her turmoil and took pity. "Come on, I'll take you home." He put his arm casually about Bree's shoulder and lead her back down the path.

All the way back to the cabin, Bree drank in the sight of him behind guarded, expressionless eyes. The winter clothes he wore made him look bigger, bulkier, more formidable. A close-cropped beard edged its way around his jaw, shining with auburn highlights. His face was a bit thinner— hard work had taken its toll there—but his eyes had never shone as clearly, as blue.

When they reached the shack they found Lucy trying to force open the door from the inside. A drift of snow fifteen inches high held it fast. She squealed and hooted at the sound of Jemson's voice, and when he had moved the snow away Lucy gathered him in her arms and gave him a loud kiss on the cheek before leading them inside, insisting they shed their wet clothes. Bree followed sullenly, jealous and resentful at the outpouring of affection Jemson was always about to command.

He went over to the fire and slipped off his boots and heavy sheepskin jacket, hung them near the flame, and turned to look at Bree. "Looks like you seen the worst of it, darlin'." He grinned impishly. "Want me to help you out of those soaked clothes?"

"Thanks, no! Lucy and I can manage just fine," Bree snapped. "Just be gentleman enough to turn your face to the wall."

"You're a hard woman," Jemson observed dryly, anger beginning to surface. "Not even a words of thanks, huh? When are you gonna learn that you're not so special, that things don't just come naturally as your due?" He turned with a shake of his head toward the wall. "Shit, Bree, I just saved your miserable little life out there."

"I was gettin' around to thankin' you, Jemson," Bree hissed, struggling with Lucy's help out of her clothes. "Why do *you* always have to rush everythin'?"

"Well," he mumbled in exasperation, "I guess that's as close as I'll ever get to a thanks, so I'll just accept your kind gratitude."

Knowing she was behaving poorly added to Bree's resistance. She sputtered as Lucy brought her dress roughly around her head and down over her shoulders. "Just *why* are you here, Jemson? Surely you didn't make that treacherous trip down the mountain anticipatin' an opportunity to save me and prove your superior strength and cunnin'!" Bree wiggled away from Lucy's hands. "You can turn around now."

"I came, darlin', to take you home before the snows get too bad for traveling."

"I *am* home, thank you."

"I mean my home, Bree, our home. In Central City."

Jemson said it casually, bracing himself for another storm to break.

"What the hell do you mean, Jemson Tyler? You think I'd be willin' to go up that mountain and live in sin with you?" Bree practically shrieked. "What right have you got to think so low of me?"

"You got it all wrong, darlin'." Jemson began to walk toward Bree. "It's simple, honey, I'm just claiming my conjugal rights. Lucy and Will were kind enough to stop by when they made their trip to Central City. And what they had to tell me proved very interesting. I've already checked it out with a lawyer, so it won't do you any good to fight me on it. Phillip Alexander," Jemson smiled mischievously, "well, he was already dead when you and I went through that ceremony in Missouri and that makes our marriage binding and valid. So you just pack up your things. We're going home."

"Wait a minute! You just wait a minute!" Bree backed away, her hands spread in front of her. "I'm not goin' anywhere with you, Jemson Tyler, and you can't just come bargin' in here tryin' to force me. Lucy, go run and get the sheriff."

"Sure, Lucy, go and get the sheriff." Jemson chuckled gaily. "Look, baby, you got two choices. You can send for the sheriff and have a gay old time explaining how you entered into a bigamous marriage with me or you can save yourself a lot of trouble and shame and come home with me without any fuss." He stood in front of Bree, eyes shining with victory.

Bree shot a pleading look to Lucy and found no comfort there. Lucy shrugged as if to say, Don't ask me; I'm not mixin' in this.

"But, I can't," Bree almost whined, her voice laced with panic. "Lucy and I have been workin', savin', to get back to Crosshaven. I *can't* go with you!"

"That's easy." Jemson cocked his head jauntily, fully enjoying Bree's desperate confusion. "You just turn over that money you've been saving to Lucy. She and Will are

171

going to need a grubstake anyway. I've got more than enough money for us. And, if you're good, maybe I'll even take you back to Crosshaven myself next spring if the country can manage to avoid a war that long.''

''You've got this all figured out, don't you, Jemson?'' Bree stormed breathlessly, not knowing how to curb the flow of events that were sweeping her into Jemson's clutches. ''All right! I'll go with you and you can tell everyone I'm your legal wife, but that's all you'll get from me. You can even force me to wash your clothes and cook your meals. But you'll *never* have any part of me, you understand?'' Bree rushed angrily to the bed and knelt, her arms thrashing wildly underneath it for her carpet bags. Furious, she threw them on top of the bed and spun to face Lucy. ''Well, just don't stand there! You and Will are the reason I'm in this mess. You think you can stop grinnin' long enough to help me get my things together?''

Jemson watched with amusement while Bree and Lucy stuffed clothes and personal articles into the two bags. Every now and then Lucy looked up to wink and smirk. Even though Bree was fighting like a wildcat against the idea, Lucy was sure it was what she needed, even secretly wanted.

Finally, when the task was completed, Bree marched angrily to Jemson and threw her bags at his feet, her head raised proudly.

''I'll make you sorry you ever bullied me into this, Jemson Tyler, I swear it!'' She glared at him coldly, her jaw tight.

''Darlin'.'' He spoke softly, unruffled. ''I've been sorry from the first day I met you. But it didn't stop me then and it's not gonna stop me now.''

CHAPTER SEVENTEEN

The snow had already made it impossible to make the trip between Black Hawk Point and Central City by horse or wagon so they traveled on foot. Bree's legs ached and rebelled from the added bulky weight of the snowshoes that Jemson had insisted on buying for her. The hem of her skirts and pantalets hung heavily with the moisture of wet snow. Under layers and layers of wool clothes and a fur-lined cloak, rivers of sweat ran between her breasts and down her legs. Jemson held her hand, seemingly undaunted by the uphill climb, and dragged her along behind him. Hours passed and she held her tongue, unwilling to give him the satisfaction of hearing her whine and complain.

Past Central City, the path narrowed and grew even more treacherous. A steep-sided ravine, seventy feet deep, edged along the left side as their bodies hugged the mountain. The path was only wide enough to walk single file.

An hour out of Central City they passed under a crudely carved sign bearing the legend "Southern Belle." Jemson seemed to have timed it perfectly, as though their passing through that portal was a signal for the sun to drop unceremoniously out of the sky. Darkness, a peculiar shade of liquid lavender, swirled in front of Bree's tired eyes. She felt as lifeless as the last rose of summer.

Ahead, she made out the outline of two cabins, smoke billowing out of the one with a lantern perched in its window. Jemson hooted and the door flew open. A younger, slightly smaller version of Jemson Tyler came bearing down on them, his face open and friendly, etched with relief.

"Well, brother, that's certainly cutting it close." The young man laughed and pounded Jemson on the back. "I worried you might be spending the night under a pine tree." He eyed a bedraggled Bree with compassion. "Introduce me to your lady, brother, and come on in. I've got supper on and you two look as though you could use a good, stiff drink."

"Bree, this is my brother, Matthew." The introduction was short and not very sweet. Jemson watched Bree moodily for her response.

She clamped her lips together and nodded abruptly, refusing to mellow in the slightest. The boy's exuberance was hard to ignore, his friendliness difficult to set aside, but she was unwilling to let go of her anger and resentment.

"You'll have to excuse my wife's rudeness, Matt," Jemson drawled sarcastically. "She's just so excited and anxious to set up her own house that it looks as though she's forgot her manners. Thanks for the offer of supper, but Bree's just dying to try her hand at being domestic so she'll fix up something for us." Jemson grabbed Bree's arm roughly and began to propel her away from the warm, brightly lit cabin to the darkened one fifty feet to the right. "I will take you up on the offer of that jug, however. Just let me show Bree her new home and I'll be over for it."

Matt watched as the two of them trudged off through the snow, aware of the tension and bitterness. He shrugged and turned away.

Jemson's grip almost cut off what little circulation Bree felt in her mittened hand. None of the gentleness she had spent reluctant nights remembering was present as he pulled her toward the inhospitable little house. At the bottom step of the porch he untied the length of rope that held her bags securely tied under his arm and let them drop with a weary thud. Then he bent and untied the leather straps of his snowshoes and slipped out of them. Bree cringed when he lifted the hem of her skirt to repeat the task on her.

Looking down at his head, bowed in front of her as his near-frozen fingers struggled with the ties, Bree wished fervently for the feel of something heavy and lethal in her hands—something she could use to club him senseless, to beat out of him all the domineering smugness, the meanness. But her moment of opportunity passed when he straightened up and overpowered her again with his size and strength.

Jemson opened the cabin door and left Bree on the porch as he fumbled through the darkness and lit a lantern. Mutely, she trailed in after him, not even bothering to inspect her surroundings. The place smelled of freshly cut pine and cedar. Jemson bent over the hearth and began to pile on the wood from a box next to it. After a few silent minutes, he lit a match and set it under the wood; the fire leaped to life. Bree stood in the middle of the floor, shivering, her lips nearly blue with the cold. Jemson turned to her, his eyes raking her in a single, sweeping glance.

"Best bring in your bags from the porch and get out of those wet clothes while I talk to Matt." He stood up to leave and crossed the room, turning again at the door. "By the way, there'll be no servants here to wait on you. If you want to eat, there's some bacon and biscuits in the fodder. Start coffee. I'll be back in about an hour."

Bree waited until he'd left and then picked up her bags from the porch and brought them in. She stumbled as she approached the hearth, dropped the bags, and fell in a heap in front of the fire. Comfort. There was so much to do to obtain even the smallest degree of comfort that she didn't know where to start. Her legs trembled and throbbed. She was wet and dirty to the bone. Her stomach grumbled with the delicacy of a freight train.

Fingers numb from the cold, Bree peeled off her mittens and tugged at the tie around her neck; the heavy cloak fell away. The fire in the hearth had begun to take the chill off the cabin and it was too warm to move. Bree arched her back cautiously and rolled her head from side to side, feeling her muscles and bones strain and pop. It felt good.

Suddenly she was struck again by the new smell of the cabin. Still seated in front of the fire, Bree moved her body slightly and began to really look at the things that sat, shiny and clean, around her. The beams on the ceiling were still white-wooded, and sap glistened on the fibers. A large, round table—newly oiled—with four matching chairs dominated the center of the room. The style and craftsmanship were reminiscent of New England's finest furniture makers. The top of the table was decorated by a intricately crocheted lace doily and a basket of dried wildflowers. The light from the fire cast a delightful golden glow over freshly starched window curtains. In one corner, shelves of canned goods lined the walls and a white porcelain basin and copper hand pump shined brightly. In another, an oversized bed had been built into the wall and was covered with a multi-colored quilt and soft down pillows. Next to the bed stood a huge maple wardrobe.

Her curiosity piqued, Bree stood up and walked slowly over to the small cooking area of the room. She opened a cabinet and checked its contents. New dishes—white with delicate red roses, heavy steel pots and pans without a mark on them, a gleaming copper tea kettle. Everything new, bright and new.

It warmed Bree's heart to know Jemson had built and furnished this place especially for her. That he had gone to great time and expense to bring in shiny new things to make the cabin more attractive. It warmed her heart and gave her a heady sense of ultimate power, because she also knew she would never, by word or action, acknowledge the loveliness he had worked so hard to achieve. She would never show the slightest appreciation. As far as Bree was concerned, she might as well be in the darkest, dankest pit, the filthiest jail or prison; it was all the same to her.

Bree's fingers trailed over the surface of the table, an absentminded gesture. If he thought to entrap her body and win her affection with new curtains and fancy knickknacks, he was in for a surprise. He seemed to have forgotten that she was a woman born to privilege—she had grown up surrounded by the finest English lace and china, the best of French craftsmanship. Why, this pathetic little cabin was no more than the servants at Crosshaven occupied. And, Bree told herself maliciously, she would let Jemson know that in a hundred different small ways.

Bree yawned, the sight of the massive bed reminding her just how exhausted she was. She eyed it for a moment and then reached out, her hand patting the quilt. It was soft, and as much as she would have wanted to be standing on her feet defiantly when Jemson returned, she couldn't resist. Her plan to stuff herself with the biscuits from the fodder before Jemson got back and then refuse to cook something for him vanished. She forgot hunger, anger, everything. The bed beckoned her. She would lie down for just a few minutes, get rid of the nauseating, swirling feeling that was consuming her—then it would be easier to force the cold, hard biscuits down her throat. When she heard Jemson coming, she would rush back to the fire and be waiting for him proudly, fiercely—no coffee on the fire, no bacon cooking—when he walked in the door.

It was a nuisance, a bother to be tugged at and pulled in every direction. Bree swatted groggily at the offending presence and woke with a start to find Jemson towering over her, his brows knit with frustration.

"Damn fool woman!" he muttered while pulling off her dress. "I didn't haul you halfway up this mountain for you to catch pneumonia and die on me." He held her nightgown, clenched and knotted in his hands. "Here! Put this on before you freeze to death." Flinging it at her, he stomped off in a rage to check the fire.

Bree watched him suspiciously, expecting him to turn at any moment and pounce on her unwilling body. With just a trace of disappointment she realized quickly he had no intention of doing any such thing. Jemson kept his back discreetly turned while she struggled out of her clothes and hurriedly pulled the nightgown down over her head.

He used a poker to spread the wood and embers of the fire in the hearth. When he finally did turn around, Bree was beneath the heavy quilt. He walked over to the edge of the bed and looked down at her before stripping off his clothes. With amusement, he gazed deeply into her frightened eyes. She looked like a cornered rabbit—desperately wanting to bolt but uncertain of which way to run.

"There's only one bed in this cabin, Bree," Jemson observed wryly. "If you don't want to sleep on the floor, move over and make room." Smiling as though to a dim-witted child, he made a flicking motion with his hand. "Move it over, darlin', or I'll get in on top of you."

"If you think . . ." Bree sputtered, her cheeks and neck growing hot. "If you try to . . ."

"Right now," he cut her short, "I'm tired. I'd like to oblige you but what I really want is a good night's sleep. Now, move your shapely little ass over to the wall and be quiet or I just might forget how tired I am!"

Bree moved quickly, enraged by the laughter in his voice. She pressed against the wall, her heart hammering, her mind whirling and trying to find something she could do or say that might help her save face, might let him know in no uncertain terms that he could never totally dominate and possess her.

"Aren't you goin' to have something to eat before you go to sleep?" she purred with false sweetness. "I was just *too* tired to cook so I had some of those biscuits you told me about." Bree lied smoothly, hoping her point was being made. She was not a woman to be ordered about and made to play the obedient servant. "I know you were hopin' for more but that's about the best this humble house has to offer."

"That's all right." Jemson yawned and settled down deep in the bed. "I figured you for that, so I ate supper with Matthew. Best damn stew he ever made. Hot biscuits too, dripping with butter. He even made a pie, in honor of our homecoming." He yawned again, his voice dropping off.

Bree clenched her jaw, furious at the smug, casual way

Jemson had of squelching her, putting her in the place he thought she belonged. He had a positive talent for remaining one up on her. As if in agreement, her stomach growled noisily and her tongue felt numb from hunger.

Bree waited until she heard the heavy, even sounds of Jemson's breathing in sleep before crawling out of the bed and making her way to the storage bin near the water pump. The light from the fire had dimmed considerably and she was afraid she might bump into something and awaken Jemson. She would die of mortification if he caught her scrounging around for food. Greedily, she extracted several hard biscuits from the bin and then went to the shelves and took down a jar of honey. Sitting by the fire, Bree used its waning light to tilt the jar and pour some of the amber liquid over the biscuits. Warm, they might have been good, but cold, they tasted like dust. Bree grimaced and forced herself to eat every last crumb.

In the morning, when she woke, she lay in the bed silently, listening to the sounds around her—Jemson moving about, a bird outside the window singing happily, the fire crackling in the hearth. Bree was playing possum, making plans, deciding which course of action would reap the most benefit. It was getting increasingly harder to concentrate, though. The sound of Jemson's low-pitched singing intruded on her thoughts, irritating, grating. What in heaven's name did he have to be so good-spirited about? Hadn't she made it clear that she intended to be more a burden than a helpmate?

"Get up, sleepy." Jemson was standing over her, making it impossible to pretend any more. He touched her shoulder gently. "Come on, Bree, no more lazing around. You've got two hungry men to feed."

She was off the bed in a second, her hands placed defiantly on her hips, her eyes blazing. "What do you mean *two* men? Isn't it enough that you expect me to slave and cook for you? Now you expect me to do the same for Matthew?"

"You sure do wake up with a roar, honey." Jemson chuckled and backed away, his hands held up in surrender. "Come on, Bree, be fair. It's no more trouble to cook for three than for two and it just doesn't seem right having Matt sitting all alone in his cabin."

Bree glared at him, but the conviction had gone out of her anger. Without knowing it, Jemson had hit upon the right words to cool her rage. She had spent so much of her adult life feeling alone, even in a group of people, that she couldn't bear the thought of anyone else suffering the same loneliness.

"Very well," she agreed sharply, "I'll cook enough for the three of us, but I will not tend his cleanin' and washin'. You managed that fine without me and he can go on the same way. It's bad enough I'm forced to play wife for you and I'm not goin' to let you push everything off on me."

"Lord, woman, you sure got the nagging part of being a wife down fine even if you are bucking against all the rest." Jemson laughed. Nothing seemed to bother him. "How about I give you a hand until you've got the cooking down pat too?"

Bree stiffened, suddenly aware of the ridiculous sight she made standing there in her nightgown, reading Jemson the new rules of the house. "I don't need your help, thank you. I'll manage just fine on my own." She pointed loftily toward the wood pile, grabbing at an excuse to get Jemson out of the cabin while she dressed. "You can bring in more wood, though. The stock is low. Or do you expect me to do that, too?"

"No, honey, I don't expect you to fetch and carry." Jemson started for the door and then turned around to face her. "I didn't bring you here to work you like a pack mule, Bree. I wanted . . ."

Bree held up her small hand to silence him. "I'm aware of what you want, Jemson Tyler," she spat, anger building again. "But I'm not prepared to give it." She swallowed the bile and forced herself to lower her voice and add, with a hint of promise, "At least not now."

Jemson shook his head and turned back to the door as if he were resigning himself to the lack of communication between them. What he had started to say, before Bree interrupted him, was that he had brought her here because he loved her, couldn't stop thinking about her, and he wanted them to have time together before deciding whether to tear up the marriage certificate or not. That he had no intention of forcing himself upon her. As a matter of fact, the cabin had originally been intended for her use alone. He had planned to bunk in with Matthew. But when he'd returned to say goodnight, Bree had been so spoiled and spiteful it had got him riled, so he had stayed to try and knock some of the wind out of her sails. But now wasn't the time to go into all that. Matthew would be knocking on the door in a few minutes, expecting breakfast and a contented family scene. No point in starting a fight with Bree. And that's what it would turn in to if he tried to reason with her now. What it always seemed to turn to between them. Wanting and needing so much more but always dissolving into harsh words and cold, empty looks.

When Jemson went out the door, Bree scrambled to her bags and pulled out her clothes and shoes. She had never dressed so quickly in her life. She was covered, head to toe, when he returned with an armful of wood from the shed in back of the cabin. Without a word Bree set about making breakfast. Her expertise in cooking was limited, and with breakfast it was even more so. She had helped Lucy on the trail but mostly with the afternoon meal and supper.

Matthew's knock sent a shiver of fear up her spine. Now not only Jemson but his brother too would know what a helpless, useless piece of fluff she was. Matt greeted her warmly, as though he had known her for a long time and held her in high regard. His kindness only made Bree feel worse, knowing she was about to make a horrible mess out of their breakfast meal. The two brothers sat around the table and talked in the easy, light banter of men who were secure and comfortable with each other.

Bree tried desperately to remember all she had seen Lucy do and to reproduce the same results. The bacon burned, the gravy had lumps the size of walnuts floating conspicuously on top, and the biscuits had a ball of chewy, white dough in the center of each of them.

Jemson ate heartily, not uttering a word of criticism, even taking seconds. Bree felt the first small burst in the icy disdain she wanted above all else to feel. She had seen Matthew blanch slightly before eating, but Jemson hadn't even flinched. Why did he not take this excellent opportunity to rebuke her, to shame her?

When they were finished and the dishes stacked for washing in the basin, Jemson and Matthew put on their heavy coats and prepared to leave. Matthew mumbled something about the breakfast and kept his eyes averted. He walked out the door first, leaving Jemson a few minutes alone with Bree.

"Fine breakfast, darlin'." He reached out unexpectedly and kissed her lightly on the forehead. "There's a skinned rabbit, ready for the pot, out in a box buried in the snow in the back of the cabin. Look in Matt's cabin for any canned things you'll need for a stew. We'll come up out of the mine about late afternoon and we'll be starving again. By the way, there's a light snow falling, so don't try to wander off. You could never find your way to Central City alone. Don't do anything stupid. I promise, if you still want to leave, I'll take you there myself at the first thaw." The words were hard to say and he almost choked over them.

"I'm not goin' anywhere, Jemson," Bree whispered breathlessly. Unable to resist the impulse, she pressed against Jemson, her face buried in his shirt. She didn't want to be kissed, just held in the protective curve of his arm for a moment. She was confused, dizzy with the small show of kindness he had given her. Her arms wrapped around his waist and she tightened her embrace, breathing in the scent and the heat of him. Then, abruptly, remembering the importance of what she had decided was her course of action, Bree backed away, turning her face as he turned and walked through the door.

She ignored the dirty dishes and sat beside the fire. Fool! She scolded herself mercilessly. You're behavin' like some mangy dog that just got a pat on the head. Remember, he's good at that. Makin' people feel good about themselves, confusin' and beguilin' until they don't know what they want.

But Bree knew what she wanted. She wanted Crosshaven and all it stood for. And what she didn't want was to be buried alive in this wilderness with a man she could neither trust nor care deeply about. Not that she didn't feel a certain attraction, a kind of yearning that left her gasping and made her angry one minute, tender and soft the next. Still, there was only one thing she had to concentrate on—getting the marriage certificate so she would be free to go home. Home to Crosshaven.

She had already decided that she would do anything, play any part necessary, in order to obtain the coveted document. It wouldn't hurt her or scar her permanently to feign the loving wife, if that's what it took. Four months with Jemson or anyone else, for that matter, were nothing if she found her feet planted firmly on the path back to Crosshaven.

CHAPTER EIGHTEEN

Late that afternoon Bree pulled a chair over by the window and sat like a sentinel, watching, waiting. The air outside was crystal clear and, as the sun began its descent, the snow on the ground glittered like diamonds laid out on a white blanket. There was no sound except for the crackling of the fire and the thumping of her own heart.

Then, through the trees at the right of Matthew's cabin, Bree watched as the brothers trudged wearily home, ankle deep in the powder snow. She got up so quickly the chair dropped out from underneath her. She scrambled to retrieve it and return it to its place beside the table. Wrapping a cloth around the handle of a cast-iron pot that hung over the fire, Bree lifted and carried it over to a basin bowl that sat empty on the washstand beside the bed. She tipped it carefully and grinned smugly as the steaming water began to fill the bowl.

Jemson's footsteps on the porch could be heard just as she returned the pot to the fire. Bree quickly perched on the stool next to the hearth, spread her skirt prettily, patted her hair and pinched her cheeks to heighten an alluring pink color.

When Jemson came through the door, Bree's mouth dropped slightly. It had never occurred to her he might be covered, head to foot, with so much filth. Dirt clods, wet and slimy, hung from his jacket. The grime was dried and cracked over his face. He noticed her dismay and smiled humorlessly.

"The clothes will dry by the fire, darlin'." He began to strip off his jacket first, and then gloves, hat, and pants. "I'll take them out on the porch later and pound the dirt out." Clad only in his long underwear, Jemson piled the discarded clothing in front of the hearth. "Matthew'll be along directly. He's cleaning up."

"That," Bree noted primly, "is an excellent idea. There's hot water on the washstand if *you've* a mind to follow your brother's example." Bree lifted a delicate hand and made a brushing movement, waving Jemson away. He turned but not before she noticed the surprised look on his face, surprised that she had been thoughtful enough to anticipate his needs.

In front of the basin, Jemson unhooked the buttons of his underwear down to his waist and shrugged out of them. He bent over the washstand and started to splash water over his shoulders and neck. Then, scooping water in both hands, he lifted it to his face.

Bree turned away to check on the stew, willing herself not to notice the fine, strong muscles working along Jemson's arms and back. She gulped, flushed and shaken, berating herself for reacting to a simple little thing like seeing a man's bare torso.

Forcing her thoughts elsewhere, Bree lifted the cover to the stew pot and smiled with satisfaction. Why, it smelled nearly as good as one of Lucy's delicious concoctions. And to think it was achieved with what she had pulled out of the "keepin' " box at the back of the cabin. When she had first opened it and pulled from it a scrawny, grayish-pink lump of rabbit, she'd almost screamed and thrown it back in the box. But, steeling herself, Bree held it gingerly with two fingers, at arm's length, and carried it back into the cabin. It took an hour of poking and prodding before she finally figured out how to separate the meat from the bone. But, once she got the hang of it, it was only a matter of minutes before the rabbit was in the stew pot, along with the onions and herbs she had taken from Matthew's cabin. Then she was able to wash her hands and turn her attention to a less gruesome detail. The rest of the day had passed quickly, with a measure of grudging enjoyment, as she pressed out and hung her few dresses in the wardrobe. And, upon closer inspection, she took a restrained delight in all the new things that surrounded her. However odious the circumstances, it was the first time she had been mistress of the home, the first time neither her mother nor Lucy had been close at hand to oversee and instruct.

So deep was her concentration that Bree didn't notice when Jemson took the water from the basin and transferred it into the pitcher that stood nearby, but she was jarred from her reverie as he bent over the basin and poured the water over his entire head. He shuddered, made a loud exclamation, and shook his head back and forth ferociously, drops of water flying everywhere, before he reached for a towel and began to rub his hair and beard.

"Darlin'," Jemson groaned, his eyes clenched tight, sputtering and grimacing like a little boy, "hand me a clean shirt and pants, will you?" His arm shot out, hand groping the empty space. He seemed almost panic-stricken. "God, I hate the feel of water on my face."

Bree crossed the room quickly and grabbed the clothes he had requested from inside the wardrobe. She shoved them wordlessly into his searching hands, concern creasing her forehead. Against her will, she felt a rush of sympathy, a softening.

Then the towel fell away from his face and he seemed instantly to have regained his composure. He caught a glimpse of Bree's unguarded feelings. They watched each other like wary animals. Bree broke the locked glance first, turning away angrily. She stomped back toward the hearth, furious at herself for allowing him to see the vulnerability she had felt in that instant, the impulse that had almost dictated she put her arms around him and comfort his distress.

Irritated and peevish, Bree rushed to the cupboard and started to take down the dishes for the table. Jemson pulled on the clean shirt and pants and then wandered over to the fireplace and lit a cheroot. He leaned casually up against the stone and lifted the lid to the stew pot. Nostrils flaring, inhaling the aroma, he smiled appreciatively.

"Smells real good, Bree. Good enough to make even Matthew sit up and take notice," he commented to Bree's stiff, unyielding back.

She ignored the compliment and went about setting the table, slamming the dishes and flatware with uncontrolled anger, directed more at herself for the weakness she had shown than at Jemson. One of the plates hit the edge of the table at an odd angle and broke, the pieces falling to the floor at her feet. Bree glared at the ruined plate as though it had betrayed her.

"Well," Jemson observed lazily, "can't say as to why you're so het up but I guess I should be grateful you didn't smash that plate along the side of my head."

Bree smirked contemptuously and bent to pick up the pieces of the plate. Her sulking silence was broken only by the sound of Matthew knocking on the door. She really hadn't paid too much attention to him the night before or at the morning meal but, as she served up the stew and biscuits, Bree examined the young man who bore, even for a brother, an uncanny likeness to Jemson.

Matthew was a smaller likeness, to be sure. Jemson was three inches taller and outweighed his younger brother by at least thirty pounds. But the color of the hair, the sky-blue eyes, the strong jaw, and proud, aquiline nose—they were the same. And there the resemblance ended. While Jemson was strong-willed and sure of himself in any situation, Matthew seemed shy and hesitant. Making an impulsive judgment, Bree decided Matthew would never come into his own until he was out from under the protective wing of his older brother.

Why, even now he came to the supper table with his hair slicked down close to his head, smelling vaguely of lavender toilet water. He was stiff and uncomfortable, in contrast to Jemson's casual air of authority.

Well, it was too much! How was she expected to

nurture and fan the flames of her rage when Matthew sat there looking at her with silent, admiring cow eyes and Jemson was observing the whole scene with the satisfaction of an overindulgent father?

Sighing with exasperation, knowing her anger was slipping away with each minute, Bree sat down at the table and nodded her permission to begin the meal. She reached for a biscuit and noted, with dismay, that although the centers were not little knots of sticky dough the bottoms were burned to a crisp. She glanced defiantly toward Jemson and watched as he cut off the blackened bottoms and proceeded to devour the white, fluffy tops. Tentatively, Bree lifted her spoon to taste the stew. Well, at least there was no fault with that. It was spicy and hot. There seemed to be total agreement at the table, because all three of them ate heartily.

After supper, Jemson started to clear off the table and Matthew followed his lead. Bree observed them in silent surprise. At Crosshaven, her father would never have given a hand in woman's work. Instead of feeling superior, a model of polite etiquette, Bree felt merely grateful. Suddenly, with a full meal in her stomach, she felt very tired. Still, it was abominable the way that men always seemed to gauge her emotions with such accuracy.

He stooped over the fire and poured steaming coffee into a tin mug, then lifted a jug, uncorked it, and added a rich, golden liquid.

"It isn't a mint julep, darlin'," Jemson whispered in her ear as he handed her the mug, "but it'll warm your insides like nothing else."

Bree took a sip. The whiskey was bitter and stinging but, once again, Jemson was right. As the liquid passed through her throat, Bree felt a trail of warmth. Purring, she snuggled down in her chair and listened as Matthew took a mouth organ from his pocket and began to play softly, a gentle, haunting tune Bree couldn't identify. She finished the whiskey-laced coffee greedily and set the empty cup on the table. Her eyes felt heavy-lidded, and she struggled to keep them open. From behind her back, Bree could hear Jemson and Matthew move closer to the fire, Matthew's playing interrupted occasionally while they talked in low tones so as not to disturb her.

"How much you figure we brought out today, Jem?" Matthew took the harmonica from his mouth and batted it against his hand to clear the wood of saliva.

"Oh, I'd say about ten ounces by the scale. Why?" Jemson rubbed the back of his neck.

"Nothing. Well, I just thought that now . . . well, you've got Bree to consider now. Doesn't hardly seem fair, leaving her alone six days a week. I mean, what with the winter being so hard and all." Matthew was taking his sweet time getting to the point. "Well, we've got a lot of gold already, Jem. Don't you think we can afford to take it easy during the winter? You can spend more time with your wife, is what I mean. We're rich men, Jem, how much gold do we need?"

Jemson laughed softly, affectionately, reaching out to pat his brother's shoulder. "I appreciate the sentiment, Matt, but we work as always. A man can't ever have too much gold. And, as for my wife, well, I'll see to that. Bree's a woman used to fine things." Jemson glanced toward Bree and satisfied himself that she was asleep. "I want to leave this mountain with so much gold that I can buy her anything she desires and never have to work another day in my life. Just spend my time showing Bree the beauty of countries outside of Georgia. You know, she's got this idea that there's nothing outside of Crosshaven worth looking at. I've got to have enough money to show her the way of things."

The brothers talked for about an hour longer while Bree drifted in and out of restless sleep. When Matthew had said goodnight and left for his cabin, Jemson stood over her, gazing down at the peaceful, childlike radiance of her face in repose. Thinking to lift and carry her to the comfort of the bed, Jemson slipped his arm under her legs and started to move the other arm to grasp her shoulders.

Bree came to full consciousness with a start. The heat, dozing off, the feel of unexpected hands on her body—Robb! Robb was coming after her again! She gasped and wrenched away, nearly toppling herself and the chair. And then she was on her feet, confusing the horrible memory of Robb Andrews, seeing Jemson but not really seeing him at all.

"Don't touch me!" Bree cried out wildly, drawing back. "Stop pawin' me; I told you I don't want your hands on me!" She jumped up and started to run past him.

It was the last straw, the final indignity. Jemson felt he had put up with her shrewishness and bad temper long enough. As she pushed by him, he lunged for her, but Bree sidestepped him, putting the table between them. She was panting, glaring reproachfully. Jemson lifted his arm and swept the table off its legs, swatting it off-balance like an angry bear. In two strides he took hold of Bree, her hands locked behind her back. Squirming and kicking, she was pinned helpless. With his free hand, Jemson closed around the material at the neck of Bree's dress and ripped it open to the waist. He let go of her long enough to change the position of his arms and sweep her up into his embrace. Purposely, he crossed the floor to the bed and paused. Bree wiggled violently, trying to escape, but Jemson's arms closed tightly around her body. She quieted, defeated for the moment, and he held her silently.

Bree had been expecting this, but she had bargained on more time. Calmly, without surprise, she accepted his kiss, trying to remain detached as she had when Robb had violated her. Lips cool and unresponsive, Bree waited passively while Jemson's mouth moved slowly, lightly, his tongue playing gently against her teeth. Then the tip of his tongue touched hers and it was like igniting a bonfire. She felt a hot coil stir deep in the pit of her stomach. Bree willed it to recede, to sleep again, but it had a life of its own, winding and curling its way through her body. She whimpered helplessly, hopelessly, as the memories rushed back to her brain. The feel of his hands, his mouth. The tender, never-before-felt sensations. The yearning.

Bree felt as though she were physically melting and then lifted, floating, suspended in time and space. She hit the bed with a resounding thud. Sputtering and confused, it was a moment before she realized Jemson had tossed her there like a discarded sack of dirty laundry. His eyes were cold and passionless as he gazed at her disgustedly.

"You put too high a value on that precious body of yours, lady," Jemson snarled sarcastically. "I'm not willing to pay your price. I can buy what you're so afraid is gonna be taken by force for a dollar in Central City *and* get a kind word thrown in for the bargain."

Mouth open, so indignant she was unable to speak, Bree glared incredulously as Jemson turned on his heel and grabbed his jacket before slamming out of the cabin.

It was only after he had gone that Bree found her senses. Kind word, indeed, she thought huffily, removing the torn remnants of her dress. What would a brutish lout like Jemson Tyler know about the tender, caring emotions a woman stored in her heart—the good and sweet things she saved within herself to lavish on the man who didn't demand them roughly or think, selfishly, they were his right to command!

Why, she was full to overflowing with kind words— kind deeds, too, for that matter—but she'd allow that softness to wither and die before she allowed it torn from her like a ruined dress.

CHAPTER NINETEEN

She wasn't sure when it had happened, but sometime during the night Jemson had returned to his bed and crawled in beside her. Bree's mouth tightened and she crawled gingerly over his sleeping form. It was still dark outside and the fire had burned down to cinders. Rubbing her arms briskly against the bitter cold air that invaded the cabin, Bree pulled open the door to the wardrobe. Her teeth chattered noisily as she struggled with her underclothes and tried to pull them on under her nightgown. They felt like ice against her skin.

Two dresses, she fumed silently. Jemson's show of strength had left her with only two dresses and both were light cotton, totally unsuited to winter weather. She never thought she would be grateful that the dresses were so ill-fitting, but now it would be easy to put both dresses on over her underclothes. That might offer some measure of comfort and warmth. In one movement, Bree whipped her nightgown over her head and dove into the first dress. Her fingers were numb with the cold and the buttons seemed to fight her attempts to fasten them. The second gown slipped over her shoulders, its light-weight fabric giving none of the warmth she had hoped for. Exasperated, Bree bent to pull on her stockings and shoes. She grabbed the button hook angrily and began to work the tiny black knobs that ran along the outside of the shoes. The job finished, Bree exhaled quickly, her breath settling in the air in puffs of white fog. She turned toward the fire, anxious to bring it to a blaze, thinking that what she'd really like to do was stoke it to such a fury it might burn the whole cabin down.

"I'll tend the fire, Bree." Jemson pulled back the covers and got out of bed. "Here. Wrap yourself up in this." He yanked the quilt off the bed and offered it to her.

She watched him, feeling a moment of guilt, then shaking it off. He couldn't possibly have known what she was thinking. Besides, she hadn't thought to let the cabin burn with him in it, after all.

Jemson padded across the room, oblivious to the cold. Of course, Bree thought sulkily, it helped that he was wearing thick long johns and heavy woolen socks. She wrapped the quilt around her shoulders and tucked it in at her feet, still shivering as she slumped into the chair by the hearth.

"I should have thought to check your clothes when you were packing," Jemson muttered thoughtfully to himself. Then, realizing he had said the words out loud, he turned toward Bree. Raising a hand to silence her, Jemson shook his head and smiled mirthlessly. "I know, don't say it. *Lucy* would have taken care of seeing to it you were warm and comfortable." He got up and went back over to the wardrobe, retrieving a pair of his own worn denim pants. "Well, this is the best I can do." Jemson held them out for Bree's inspection. "There's needle and thread over there in that box on the shelf."

Bree eyed the pants greedily. It would have been an immense source of satisfaction if she'd been allowed the luxury of flinging the pants back in his face, but they looked so *warm*, so inviting—she could almsot feel the protection of the denim soothing her legs. Disregarding the false display of modesty she had been so intent on establishing between them, Bree snatched the pants from Jemson's hand and lifted her skirts. The quilt fell off her shoulders as she slipped first one leg and then another into the pants. Her dreams of ecompassing comfort were immediately dashed. *Two* Bree Alexanders could have fit snugly, with room to spare. The pants hung ludicrously around the

193

waist and hips, the legs flared out, and at least ten inches of denim gathered around her feet.

Jemson moved his head from side to side, inspecting the sight, and then began to snicker softly. Looking down at herself, Bree gathered the excess material on either leg and pulled it out like a skirt, dipping gracefully into a curtsy. Laughter bubbled from her lips. She had never looked more foolish and yet it was impossible not to laugh at herself.

Matthew knocked on the door, his brows gathered in confusion. Jemson was close-mouthed about his relationship with Bree, but he'd intimated that it was strained, not exactly an ideal marriage. And yet he could hear them in there laughing like a couple of village idiots.

Bree gaped at the sound of Matthew's knock, knowing he would wait only a moment before walking in. It was one thing to let Jemson see her this way—they had shared worse times—and quite another to allow his brother to witness the silliness.

Jemson saw the laughter turn to distress on Bree's face and yelled for Matthew to stay where he was as Bree scrambled toward the bed. She pulled at the pants as she went. Her foot caught in the roomy material just as she stepped out of the leg. The cabin tipped crazily, spinning as she fell. Bree felt something tear inside the ankle before she hit the floor. It was an odd, burning sensation. She wasn't in any real pain and yet she was breathless and sweat broke out on her forehead. Jemson was beside her, pulling the pants from her slim legs and calling for Matthew; then he was lifting her gently. Still, there was no pain, just the burning and the feeling that she was shaking apart inside.

"Hand me that button hook over there, Matt." Jemson laid Bree on the bed and pushed her skirt up to her knees. "I've got to get these shoes off before her ankle starts to swell."

"What the hell were you two doing in here?" Matt asked shakily, handing Jemson the button hook.

"Nothing to go to confession about, brother, I promise you." Jemson's large hands labored over the small hooks on Bree's shoes until they were free. He carefully slipped the shoe from her foot and touched the already swelling ankle. Cautiously moving her limb, Jemson satisfied himself that the foot was not broken.

"Why isn't she crying or something?" Matthew bent over Bree anxiously.

"Shock," Jemson answered slowly, reaching to feel Bree's forehead. She was so quiet and passive it worried him more than if she were screaming her head off. "Remember back home, Shamus Ryan? He lay in that stinking pit of a mine for more than forty hours with a beam crushing his chest before he died, talking and laughing, drinking whiskey with his mates. I asked Doc Gregg later how he could stand the pain while the crew was trying to dig him out and he said Shamus most likely didn't have any pain. The body can sometimes defend itself by shutting down the other senses. Look, she's asleep." Jemson caressed Bree's cheek gently. "With any luck at all, she'll sleep for most of the day. It's my guess she's torn some of the ligaments inside her ankle. It'll probably swell up soon, and when she wakes up there'll be plenty of misery." Jemson cursed softly and went to retrieve the quilt, covering Bree while she slept. "Look, Matt, I've got to try to hike into Central City. I want you to take care of Bree until I get back. When she wakes up, give her coffee with whiskey in it. I don't think that can hurt her, and it might ease the discomfort."

"Are you mad? You can't walk into Central City in the dead of winter, Jem. The snow drifts are eight feet high out there. You could walk off the side of the goddam mountain thinking you were on solid ground!"

"She needs warm clothes, medicine, something to occupy her hands while she's laid up," Jemson explained patiently, patting Matthew's shoulder. "She's my woman, Matthew, and I won't see her go without because I didn't try."

"Well if loving a woman makes a reckless fool of a man, I hope to God I never fall prey to the same affliction," Matthew shouted desperately, knowing his brother's mind was made up and there was nothing he could say to dissuade him.

Jemson shushed him, pointing toward Bree. He chuckled knowingly. "Don't ever wish that on yourself, little brother. There's a fine bliss in all the madness." Jemson grinned as he pulled on his clothes and reached for his jacket and snowshoes. "Don't start worrying about me until tomorrow night." He turned to go. "Smile, Matthew. Just last night you were lecturing me on spending more time with Bree, not working the mine this winter. It looks as though you just might have gotten your way. Take care of her, Matt. Stay close and don't let her wake up alone."

The day slipped by quietly, interrupted only by the sound of snowflakes gently tapping against the windows and the occasional restless thrashing and moaning from Bree. Matthew looked over at her nervously. Each new sign, every movement, seemed to pull her closer to consciousness and he dreaded the responsibility of taking care of her when she was fully awake. He was fine when it came to the cooking and cleaning—he'd made a repetition of last night's meal that was tastier and more aromatic than Bree could have hoped for—but the tending, the strength . . . well, that was left to Jemson. He was the one who could be depended on for knowing just the right thing to do and when to do it. Matthew had never had the responsibility of someone else's comfort, their well-being. He poured a cup of coffee and laced it heavily with the whiskey from the shelf, knowing it was only a matter of time before Bree awakened.

Bree stirred again fitfully and opened her eyes. It felt as though each lid weighed ten pounds. Her head was foggy and her tongue felt like wool. She tried to focus on the figure standing near the hearth and whispered Jemson's name.

"No, it's me, Matthew." He rushed forward with the mug in his hand, thrusting it into Bree's face. "Here, drink this."

"Why? What is it?" Bree slurred, pulling away from the strong-smelling liquid. Her foot dug into the bed as she moved and she yelped in pain. Her hand shot down her leg in an effort to feel where the pain was coming from.

"You fell and hurt your ankle," Matthew hastened to explain, not knowing if Bree remembered what had happened. "Jemson said you were to drink this when you woke up." Again, he pushed the mug toward Bree.

This time she accepted it. Her ankle throbbed, sending bursts of shooting pain up her leg. "Where is Jemson?" she asked between gulps.

"He went into Central City." Matthew took the empty mug from Bree's hand. "Do you want another cup of coffee?" Matthew turned and walked back to the hearth. "I don't expect he'll be back until tomorrow."

"Why did he pick this particular time to go traipsin' off to Central City?" Bree snipped, anger clearing her head. She accepted the fresh mug of coffee and whiskey Matthew held out to her. Visions of scantily dressed saloon girls danced with abandon through her brain. Animal. The man was an animal to go lustin' off after sluts when she was laid up in agony.

"He said you needed things, clothes and medicine and the like," Matthew offered simply, pulling up a chair to the side of the bed. "There was a bad snowfall after he left and night's coming on, so I don't think he'll try to make it back until tomorrow."

"Jemson told me it was dangerous to try to travel around the mountain in winter," Bree muttered accusingly, hoping Matthew would deny the warning Jemson had given her and lighten the burden of shame she felt for having thought Jemson would be callous enough to go off in the pursuit of pleasure while she was hurt, laying helpless in the cabin he had built for her.

"I told him not to go but he wouldn't listen." The

resentment was clear in Matthew's voice although he tried to mask it. "Are you hungry? The stew's ready any time you've a mind to eat."

For lack of a better way to a bridge the uncomfortable silence that had fallen between them, Bree agreed to eat, adding that she would appreciate another coffee.

She picked at the food, not really hungry, preferring instead to drink the coffee Matthew handed her. It was warm, soothing, and made her feel light-headed and content.

"What kind of a boy was Jemson?" Bree asked after the dishes had been cleared away from the bed and Matthew had taken his seat next to her again. "You know, he never really talks about himself much. Would you feel as though you were betrayin' him if you told me somethin' about him before he grew into the mountain of a man he is today?" Bree giggled uncontrollably. She waved her mug drunkenly. "Why don't you pour me another one of those delicious coffees and then tell me all about little Jemson Tyler." Bree giggled again when Matthew took the mug from her wobbly hand. Laughing himself, he carried the pot and the jug back to Bree's bedside and set them on the small table next to the bed. He mixed the inebriating brew and handed it to Bree.

"Well, let's see here." Matthew settled into the chair and smiled with the memories. "There were four of us boys. Simon's the oldest, then Jemson, then Daniel and me. Our Ma waited seven years between Jemson and Daniel—Jem says it's because it took her that long to get over the revulsion of letting Pa into her bed but, after she had Daniel, she figured what the hell and let the old man have one more try at it, the result being me. Jemson was always the hell-raiser. He got in more trouble than the rest of us put together. He was the one who went sneaking off to the mines, hanging around with the children from the village, exploring the woods, coming home dirty. It didn't matter how many times our Pa took the strap to him. No one could ever control him. And, by the time he was fourteen, he was bigger than Pa and told him never to lay a hand to him again. Simon and Daniel, well, they went the way our Pa had planned except for the time Simon married Molly Sullivan.''

"That I do know about,'' Bree interrupted excitedly. "Jemson told me all about Molly and how the two of you were secretly in love with her.''

"Ah, hell, I was only seven years old when Molly came into our lives. But Jem, he was sixteen.'' Matthew blushed self-consciously, visibly squirming. "Besides, he has good reason to think Molly was the finest girl ever set on the earth. She saved his life.''

"When? What do you mean?''

"Well, Simon and Molly lived in Irish town, away from the family. Simon working in the mines and Molly scrubbing the coal dust out of their little house and then watching it build back up again. It must have been pretty dismal, so every Sunday, after Mass, they'd go to the woods for a picnic and sometimes Jemson and I got to tag along. This one time we were all having a good time, laughing and carrying on, when some old friends of Simon's, the rich friends who wouldn't have anything to do with him after he'd married what they called scanty trash—anyway, they happened by and saw us. There were about ten of them, and they started hooting and calling Molly foul names, so Simon upped and began swinging and cursing and then Jemson jumped in, bigger and stronger than any one man there but not strong enough to handle the whole of them. We were out by the lake, and one of the men picked up a piece of dead tree limbs and smashed Jemson alongside the head. Then a couple of them picked him up and tossed him into the water. Simon was unconscious, all bloody and beaten. The men turned to Molly but they were frightened away by a carriage coming from the church. Molly pulled Jemson out of the lake and rolled him over, pounding on his back and all the water spurting out of his mouth. He was floating face down when Molly waded out to get him. The water went near up to her neck and she couldn't swim. We never went on a picnic again but Jem always said he owed Molly his life. He cried like Simon did when Molly died. But then Simon let Pa talk him into coming home and bringing the baby that was Molly's last gift to him.''

"Is that why you two left Pennsylvania?" Bree could see how distressed Matthew was at remembering Molly and tried to channel his thoughts in another direction.

"No. Hell, we didn't leave for another ten years. Jem tried to follow Simon's lead, tried to find some kind of happiness living off the sweat of others but he just wasn't made that way. He stayed as long as he could, trying to improve the working conditions in the mine, putting his own money into rebuilding the shacks the miners and their families lived in. Damn, Simon and Molly lived in one of those dark, dirty places but he forgot it all after he married Emma. Finally I suppose Jemson had enough of fighting a losing battle and he pulled up stakes.''

"And he took you with him?"

"Not without a great deal of begging and pleading on my part. But, yes, he took me with him.'' Matthew gazed curiously at Bree's eager, slightly flushed face. She was hauntingly beautiful—dark shadows contouring her small, lovely face and the firelight dancing across tousled red curls. He imagined wistfully that this is how Jemson must have felt every time he looked at Molly Sullivan. They were both women to be adored, idolized—knowing you could never have them for your own and being content to know they belonged to another you loved just as well.''

"Where did you go?" Bree repeated a second time, struggling to make the words come out slow and deliberate. It was getting harder and harder to talk, even to think coherently. The whiskey was dulling the pain but it was also dulling her senses.

"It might be easier to ask where we didn't go and what we didn't do.'' Matthew laughed fondly. "We went to New Orleans and worked on a plantation hauling tobacco; we even played cards on a riverboat. Then we made our way west through Texas and the New Mexico territory on a cattle drive. We had saddle sores and blisters for months, I can tell you. Finally, we ended up in Denver and Jemson sat down to play poker. He staked all our savings on a pair of aces, just had a hunch the other man was bluffing and that's how we got this mine. The miner *was* bluffing, took a one card draw to a straight and missed. We packed up what we needed and came up here. The miner, his name was Ottel, thought he'd gotten the best of us, that the mine was dry, but he just hadn't gone deep enough.''

"And,'' Bree added tipsily, "you needed more money so Jemson went back to Pennsylvania to claim your part of your father's estate, joined the Dunsfield wagon train on the return trip, and had the extreme bad fortune to have met me.'' The last of Bree's words trailed off in a yawn.

"You're tired.'' Matthew jumped up from the chair. "I guess I was rambling. Sorry, I'll let you get some sleep. I'll just go over and get my bedroll and set up in front of the fire.''

"You didn't ramble, Matthew. Really, I wanted to hear all about Jemson.'' Bree waved away his apologies with a drunken sweep of her hand. "You do whatever it is you're gonna do and I'll just close my eyes for a minute until you get back. Go on now, I'm fine.''

The stomping. The sound vibrated through her head, slicing through her brain like a knife. Bree pressed her fingers against throbbing temples and raised her head, squinting beyond the hazy sunlight that poured through the window. Jemson, having just pounded off the snow that clung to his boots, opened the door and entered the cabin. The noise had also awakened Matthew, who appeared embarrassed at having been caught sleeping.

"My head,'' Bree groaned and rolled over toward the wall. The movement jarred her ankle and she whimpered, feeling thoroughly sorry for herself.

"Let's take a look at that ankle, darlin'.'' Jemson walked

over and lifted the quilt to inspect her foot. "Matt, stoke up that fire and start some coffee."

Bree moaned again at the mention of coffee but turned back to face Jemson obediently. Grimacing, she noted how the crisp winter weather had heightened the color of Jemson's skin, how the exertion of hiking from Central City made his eyes sparkle. He was the picture of robust health and Bree was certain she appeared pasty and gray in comparison.

While Jemson poked and gently turned her ankle, Bree lifted herself up to take a first look at the wounded limb. What she saw made her cringe and gasp. The ankle was four times its normal size and a hideous bruise trailed from her toes halfway up her calf.

"Isn't that the prettiest shade of purple you ever saw?" Jemson observed lightly. He hefted a canvas bag, stuffed to capacity, off his back and let it slip to the floor before replacing the quilt.

"Don't fret, Bree. I've got some things in this bag that'll bring a smile back to your cheeks." Loosening the drawstring, Jemson smiled devilishly. "First off, some denims for my lady, a few flannel shirts, a personal pair of bright red woolen longjohns—all in the smallest size I could find. A pair of boy's boots—just slip them on, no more button hooks."

Despite herself, Bree couldn't help smiling with pleasure as Jemson pulled the articles of clothing out of the bag. Even Matthew stopped what he was doing to watch Jemson mug and carry on like a tinker with his wares.

"Now, this." Jemson extracted a bottle from the bag. "This is to rub on the ankle after the swelling has gone down. It's horse liniment, I admit, but the smithie assured me it will work just as well with humans. Now, to fill the idle hours of convalescence, I've included two books. One is the usual book of verse, the other a far more interesting selection—one *Uncle Tom's Cabin* by Harriet Beecher Stowe. It was written nine years ago by a woman who thought slavery was . . ."

"I *know* the subject of the book, thank you." Bree

lifted her chin defiantly and snatched the book from Jemson's hand. "I read it when I took my schoolin' in New York, so you can just stop sneakin' around tryin' to get your point across."

"No insult intended, my lady, I swear it." Jemson raised his arms in mock surrender. "Now, if I may continue, I have a few more articles for your inspection. Here's an interesting little box." He handed Bree a beautifully carved wooden box about twelve inches square, satisfied at her exclamation of pleasure. He had gone to no small amount of trouble having the clerk at the general store assemble the makings of a sewing basket. In addition to the needles and threads, Jemson had purchased heavy Irish linen that Bree could use to fashion anything that suited her fancy.

Delighted, Bree impulsively grasped Jemson's hand and pulled him closer to her on the bed. She sat up fully and wrapped her arms around his neck, burying her face in the warm spot there, murmuring her thanks.

The scent reached her nostrils almost immediately—the strong scent of cheap perfume that permeated his shirt and clung to the woolen fibers like the possessive stink of a skunk.

Jemson could feel her stiffen in his arms. Still, her small balled fist came as a surprise as it caught him under the ear. Bree squirmed away, careful not to move her ankle sharply, her green eyes flashing like emerald steel.

"I thank you for the gifts, Jemson." Muttering through clenched teeth, Bree lay back down in the bed and pulled the quilt high up over her shoulders as she turned her face to the wall.

Jemson sat for a moment, stunned at the ease from which she slipped from pleasure to irritation. He looked over at Matthew, who was at as much of a loss as he was, and shrugged defeatedly before rising to join him by the hearth. Jemson took the mug of coffee Matthew offered silently and shook his head.

"Forget what I said yesterday, brother, and if you find

it's a hard place living without a woman just remember
this morning and at least have brains enough to choose a
woman who's as plain as a mud fence. A gal with a fancy
face brings nothing but grief.''

CHAPTER TWENTY

It was more than a week before Bree decided to stop sulking, and that was only out of consuming boredom. At first it gave her immeasurable pleasure to have the upper hand with Jemson. If her demands were not met properly and without comment she lost no time in reminding him just who it was who had nursed him through the cholera and without a single grumble, mind you. Chastised, Jemson swallowed his anger and did the bidding of her slightest whim. Fluffing her pillows, (it was just too painful for Bree to turn on her ankle), reading aloud the books he had brought her from Central City (it was so tiring but she did so love the sound of the written word), crossing the room fifty times a day fetching coffee and spring water (being bedridden made her enormously thirsty), delivering and removing the bedpan (well, as private a matter as it was, she couldn't very well be expected to hop out of bed and perform the task herself).

It wasn't so much doing the chores and waiting on Bree hand and foot that Jemson minded. It was the attitude with which Bree expected the aid given. If she'd just once smile and say thank you. But no—her small back was rigid against the pillows, her green eyes steely, and her mouth never cracked except to issue an order or complain that something wasn't being done quickly enough to suit her.

The only pleasant company Jemson enjoyed was Matthew's, when he came over in the early afternoon to spend some time with them. It had been decided that since

Jemson was no longer able to work the mine, as long as Bree was laid up and needed his assistance, then Matthew, in all fairness, could not be expected to spend his days knee deep in muddy, melted snow. It was a decision Matthew relished. Still, he found something to do in the morning hours before knocking on their door, and he left immediately after the evening meal. He tried hard to give Jemson and Bree time alone together, time to work out whatever the trouble was between them. Yet he could clearly see that they weren't making progress. Bree chattered happily with him but never had a word or look for Jemson, who for his part merely sat silently in a chair by the fire and puffed lazily on a cheroot, never even bothering to enter into the conversation or venture near the bed. While it was true Jemson was a solitary kind of man and could never be accused of being a blabbermouth, his long periods of total silence were becoming absurd. Days passed and all Bree's demands were met with nothing more than a grunt and a brief nod of his head. Matthew felt as though he were caught in the vortex of a storm, a strange, disquieting calm before the tornado hit and flattened everything in its path. Also, Matthew was becoming increasingly suspicious of the tedious length of Bree's convalescence. A sickly yellow smear along her ankle gave proof to the fading bruise, but the limb had lost most of its swelling. Still, he was too fond of her to suspect she might be dragging out the advantage she'd found in bringing Jemson to tow the mark she'd set.

On the morning of the ninth day, Bree shifted uncomfortably in bed. Her backside was feeling increasingly numb from remaining in bed so long. Eyes slipping secretly to Jemson, deep in thought, Bree grimaced and decided her recuperation had gone on long enough.

"I'm goin' crazy cooped up in this cabin!" she announced with just a trace of a whine. "I think it's time I got up and started exercisin' my ankle." The tone of her voice left no doubt that she expected Jemson to jump to his feet and accommodate her graceless request.

"It's been time for more than three days," he grumbled harshly, not moving a muscle. "If you're ready to stop playing the grand dame, get dressed and I'll take you for a short walk outside the cabin."

"You're very obligin' this morning, Jemson. Now, if you'll just put some water on the fire so's I can bathe myself . . ." Bree raised her eyebrow and made a sweeping motion with her hand in a condescending gesture, urging Jemson to scurry to the task like a trained lackey. "And you can just wait outside, too. I'm not movin' from this bed while you're standing there leerin' at me." Instinctively, Bree pulled the quilt up around her neck, as if that were enough to fend Jemson off if he had a mind to approach her.

He turned away with a snort and plunged the dipper into the water by the hearth, transferring it by scoops to a cast-iron pot hanging over the fire. It seemed to Bree the job took longer than was necessary, as though Jemson were deliberately baiting her, but finally it was done and he straightened up and reached for his jacket.

When he had shut the door behind him Bree threw back the quilt and swung her legs off the bed. Applying weight to the injured ankle a little at a time, Bree found what she had suspected to be true. She felt very little discomfort. The ankle was weak but she found herself more than capable of walking as long as she favored it slightly.

Hobbling over to the wardrobe, Bree gathered together the new clothes Jemson had brought her and arranged them neatly over her arm. She picked up the boots and limped over to the fireplace. She sat in the chair by the fireplace and waited for the flames to take the chill off the water in the pot. When it was ready, Bree dunked a washrag into the lukewarm water and, after wringing it out, proceeded to wash her body the best way she could while still leaving her nightgown on. It was just too nippy to run around completely unclothed. Besides, she still didn't trust Jemson not to come barging in the door unannounced.

After washing and drying herself, Bree struggled out of

the arms of her nightgown and worked to pull on the long underwear while still confined in the gown. When the longjohns were buttoned up, she yanked off her nightgown and let it drop to the floor beside her. The denims came next, not a bad fit, and then the flannel shirt. Sitting back down in the chair, Bree bent to slip on the boots. Since they were a boy's size and wider than her own foot, they went on over the injured, still swollen ankle without any problem. Confident that she would never have to feel cold and miserable again, Bree stood up and scooped a dipper full of icy water into her mouth. She swished it around and spit it out in the fire, watching the flames sizzle and wane and then struggle back to life again.

When she was ready, Bree went out on the porch, only to find Jemson was not there. She waited a few minutes, growing impatient; just before she decided to shout angrily, demanding his attention, Jemson came out of Matthew's cabin and slauntered easily toward her.

He could see she was agitated and that made him grin all the more as he held out a bright red, woolen cap. "Here. You better wear this. It'll keep you warmer."

"I'm just fine, thanks." Bree eyed the cap disdainfully. It was red, the worst possible color against her copper curls.

"Suits me." Jemson shrugged and watched as Bree bent to strap on her snowshoes. "You won't be needing those. Haven't had a snowfall in days. Just be careful where you step. Some of it's a bit slippery." He offered his arm to Bree for support and sighed heavily when she snapped her head in refusal.

The air was brisk and clear with the scent of pine wafting heavily from the trees. The sun peeped through a mist of clouds and washed warmly over Bree's cheeks. Lord, it felt good to breathe in the tingling air.

She stepped carefully from the porch and looked up expectantly at Jemson.

"We'll take it easy today." He answered her look, reading her thoughts. "There's a point about a quarter of a mile downhill, before the mountain drops off to Central City—we'll walk there.''

Stubbornly refusing his assistance, Bree hobbled along beside Jemson. He cut his normally long strides to match her own small, hesitant steps. What might have taken them a few minutes stretched into fifteen, but they finally reached the point Jemson had spoken of. It was a ledge jutting from the side of the mountain defiantly, hanging suspended over the valley below. Bree gasped happily and clapped her hands like a child. Directly below her, she could see the smoke from pot-belly stoves billowing from the shacks and cabins of Central City. But, even better, a little further down and to her rght, Bree recognized Black Hawk Point in the distance. The valley was crusted with a blanket of pure white snow with deep-hued green treetops poking out and rivers of ice meandering in all directions. It was more beautiful than any picture she had ever seen.

Bree shifted her weight from her injured ankle and stared wordlessly at the panorama stretched out beneath her, feeling suddenly intimidated, overpowered by the immenseness.

The scene was breathtaking, but at that moment she had never felt so small and alone.

''There's space now,'' Jemson murmured almost reverently, so softly Bree could barely hear him. ''Freedom to move around, but it won't be that way for long.'' His voice hardened. ''When the winter thaws set in, this mountain will be crawling with farmers and shopkeepers, all of them looking to strike it rich and then light out again.''

''Isn't that why you came?'' Bree asked absently, not unkindly, forgetting for the moment that she was nurturing anger and resentment toward him.

''Yes, I came here to find gold but I also came to stay. Matthew and me, we figure to outwait the others, and when the gold's panned out and the mountains have been plundered, we'll stay on and watch her heal herself.''

Bree shuddered at the thought of spending a lifetime on the formidable, lonely mountain.

"There's not a whole lot to recommend her now," Jemson mused, "not for a city girl like you. No fancy houses and gala balls, no shopping for the latest Paris fashions, no grand restaurants. But in ten, maybe twenty years, she'll come into her own. But slow like, so a man can be a part of it, grow with it."

Bree reflected silently that he didn't include himself in the "city-bred" mold he had lumped her into. His family was as affluent as her own and yet he didn't consider himself a part of that. It was as though, in walking away from it, he had erased it from his mind. Well, she could never walk away from it! Never settle for less than what she had once had at Crosshaven. Why, her fingers were sore and full of pin pricks from embroidering the dish towels he had included in the sewing box from Central City. She felt in a constant state of near filth without someone to wash her hair and perfume her body. Cooking was detestable. She would never get it right—the biscuits would always be uneatable. She felt drab and unattractive without the trappings of silk ballgowns and velvet chokers. The one thought that kept her going was that the affliction was only temporary. Like a nightmare she would soon wake up from, Bree would someday soon return home to Crosshaven.

"We better start back." Jemson's deep voice echoed faintly through the trees. "Your ankle can't take much pressure the first time out." He took her arm to steer her away from the ledge and back to the cabin.

Bree hadn't walked more than ten feet when she felt the ankle pull sharply and seemingly turn to liquid under the skin. She pressed on a few more feet and then her step faltered, the limb gave out completely. She would have fallen except that Jemson was standing close by and noticed the slip. His hands shot out to steady her and, without a word, he swept her up into his arms to carry her the rest of the way.

Blindly, without thinking, Bree reacted defensively, wiggling and squirming frantically, ignoring Jemson's protest. All she could think of was that she was where she didn't want to be, where she was afraid to be—trapped and imprisoned in Jemson's embrace.

Her legs flayed wildly, her fists pounded fiercely at his chest, one of them clipping Jemson's temple just above the eye. He staggered for a moment, losing his balance, and they went down. The fall was cushioned by the snow. Jemson landed flat on his back with Bree sprawled out across him.

"Goddammit, Bree, do you have to fight me every inch of the way?" Jemson shouted, spitting the wet snow out of his mouth. "I was only trying to help you. If I wanted to make love to you, I'd sure as hell pick a more comfortable place."

"I'm aware of the places you'd chose, Jemson Tyler. *And* of the woman, too. Your jacket still reeks of her perfume. A rather cheap blend, I might add, no doubt befittin' the lady's occupation."

Jemson roared with laughter while Bree tried vainly to regain her balance, but he clamped his arm around her shoulders and kept her pressed tightly to his chest, oblivious to the wet, seeping snow that was soaking into the back of his jacket and pants.

"Is *that* what all this has been about? A little perfume? Well, darlin', there was nothing to it, I promise. You can stop acting like a jealous wife."

"I am *not* actin' like a wife, jealous or otherwise, Jemson Tyler!" Bree strained to escape the hold he had on her and finally sagged, giving up the effort.

"Doesn't sound that way to me," Jemson observed softly, his voice grown husky by the feel of Bree pressed along the length of his body.

He eased her up slowly until her face was over his and kissed her lightly. Bree head snapped backwards, out of his mouth's reach. Jemson's free hand, the one that wasn't being used at her back to hold her still, tangled itself in her hair and drew her face close again, immobilizing her head so that she couldn't move. Still, he had to apply pressure to force her mouth to his. Patiently, Jemson brushed her face with his lips, at the corner of Bree's eye, down her cheek, finally straying to her mouth. He hovered there, gently prying apart her lips with his tongue, waiting, knowing. Bree groaned hopelessly, eagerly. Her arms crept up and tightened, one around his neck, the other lightly caressing his forehead, her hand snaking through his hair.

He's so sure of me, Bree thought despairingly. So certain. He knows he has a power over me, somethin' that makes me want him, somethin' that makes me forget everyting else when he touches me.

She was dizzy, reeling under the heat of Jemson's mouth, drawn further and further into a mindless, frenzied void. Now, she cried inwardly, the last vestige of her resistance melting away under the relentless surge of Jemson's practiced lovemaking. She had to say something now, before it was too late.

"Is this the response you were aimin' for, Jemson, or should I put more into it?" Bree drew back slightly and whispered hoarsely, the cruel taunt registering instantly in Jemson's eyes. "Tell me, does the whore in Central City positively swoon when you touch her or does she give you a good run for your money?"

Bree's crudeness had the desired effect. Jemson pushed her away and jumped to his feet, then reached down and yanked Bree up off the ground. Stunned, glaring with anger, he took a long withering look at her and then, in one swift movement, hoisted her over his shoulder like a sack of flour. When she protested and began struggling, his hand slammed up across her backside, planting a resounding and silencing slap. She yelped in protest and then quieted.

What a conniving, scheming little bitch she could be, Jemson fumed angrily. The consummate liar. With her mouth, her words, her body, every gesture, every sigh. She could make a man believe anything she wanted him to believe and then draw out the satisfaction of laughing in his face. God, how many times did it take before he wasn't fool enough to walk into that trap?

He doubted now that she was even the slightest bit jealous of his activities in Central City. And he wasn't about to tell her that the night had consisted of nothing more than Mad Lorrie sitting on his lap while he downed a few whiskeys to take away the chill. It was true she had offered, as she had countless times before, the use of her private room for the night. But Jemson had refused, the image of Bree's small, lovely face intruding on his more lecherous thoughts.

Now, though, Bree's face was far from lovely. Her body bounced heavily up and down on Jemson's shoulder as he stomped toward the cabin. Her face was reddened, her breath coming in grunts, and her hair swirling in a tangled mass behind him.

When he reached the porch of the cabin, Jemson grabbed Bree by the collar of her jacket and dumped her uncermoniously. She landed on her good foot and hopped to keep her balance before applying weight to both feet. When she did, Bree's hands came up to her waist and she met his look with equal rage. Her stomach felt as though she had been hit with a tree stump and her ears were ringing from being lugged upside down. It was a moment before her head cleared. When it did, she lashed out harshly.

"I don't enjoy bein' tossed around, Jemson. Or yelled at *or* made to feel like an object, bought and paid for. But, if that's what it takes to get off this mountain and away from you, so be it! You want me. You want me in that big old bed inside the cabin." She paused confidently, smiling crookedly. "Well, you can have me but not until *I* have our marriage paper. Then I'll accommodate you as much as you like, until it's safe for me to leave this hellhole and go back where I belong."

"You sell yourself cheap, darlin'," Jemson answered sarcastically, a look she had never seen before crossing his face. "And you're stupid to boot! A smart doxie would stick around long enough to angle a share of the mine before leaving."

Bree's eyes broke the steadied, anguished look between them. She blushed, knowing she had sounded cheap and calculating, ashamed of the way she made herself look in his mind. She looked away and closed her eyes, hoping to block out the memory of what she had just done. She stiffened when she heard the sound of Jemson's footsteps coming toward her. The feel of his hands on her shoulders, his fingers biting into the flesh, made her wince. She opened her eyes again and looked quietly into Jemson's pained expression.

"If you're worried I'll take you by force," he said slowly, his voice thundering through her head, "don't be. I've done enough fighting with you to last me a lifetime and I'm through with it. I was an idiot for it but I thought I saw in you things that just aren't there. Wanting you to be the woman I thought you were isn't enough. I could force you into submission, take your body if that's all I wanted, but I can't bully you into being a woman of honor and gentleness. It's as though there's something missing in you that no one but you can find." Jemson shook his head as if to clear it, visibly bewildered and defeated. "I brought you here to give us a chance to get back the feelings that were so strong and good between us on the wagon train. I hoped you'd see the beauty in this land, this life, and choose to share it with me. Holding you and loving you was all a part of that but, I swear to God, that alone just isn't enough. Maybe I expected too much, more than you're capable of giving." With that, Jemson walked by her and went into the cabin.

Bree stood for a moment, letting the sun beat down on her face. The impulse to run after him, to explain, was so great she had to hold on to the railing to prevent herself from moving.

What good would it do? Telling Jemson that she longed for him, that she was torn between wanting the warmth and the security of staying forever tucked away in the protective curve of his arms, and knowing her true course was one that led her back to Crosshaven. That kind of admission would only cause them both the pain she had experienced since first meeting him. Jemson stood, strong and exciting on the one hand, and home, Crosshaven, beckoned her return on the other.

She, too, was sick at heart with the arguing and the suspicion, the constant bickering, offers, counter-offers, challenges, surrenders.

She wanted desperately to let Jemson see she *was* the woman he thought her to be. That there were depths of unexplored tenderness and feeling that had yet to be unearthed. But the danger there was in the discovery. Could she ever leave him if she allowed herself to be drawn in to the tight, possessive circle of his passion?

Bree shook her head frantically. No! It wasn't a chance she was willing to take. Still, she couldn't bear to have Jemson think so poorly of her. All she could do was set aside the problem, erase it from her mind, turn off her emotions at the core of their being, and concentrate solely on making life at least bearable between them. If she refused to be wife and lover and he refused anything less, perhaps they would somehow find a halfway place, a place to rest and enjoy some measure of peace and contentment. She would have to make the first step, of course. Jemson, as he had said, had been led down a seductive path before and had no more stomach for it. But if she could at least show him the consideration and care she might show a friend, perhaps they would find a way.

Shoulders squared, Bree took a deep, determined breath and walked through the cabin door after Jemson.

CHAPTER TWENTY-ONE

Once Bree had made up her mind that the only way she and Jemson would be able to make it through the months ahead without seriously wounding each other was to find a point at which they could inhabit the same house in a civil, even distantly friendly fashion, the days passed quickly. She threw herself into domestic duties with the same fervor and dedication she was channeling into getting back to Crosshaven. Jemson saw the changes in her attitude, the way she was striving to be pleasant and helpful. He softened toward her, showing signs of appreciation and respect, but he never went over the invisible line she had drawn between them. Bree made it clear that she was doing her part to make their life harmonious and he was to do his by keeping the accepted distance. She cooked all the meals and found that practice truly did make perfect. After several bad starts, her biscuits were light and airy and the gravy was as smooth as cream. Stews were seasoned to perfection, eliciting compliments from even Matthew, the culinary expert. To her surprise, Bree found that once she'd gotten the knack, meals were prepared with a minimum of fuss and bother. Clothes were scrubbed, dried, folded, and put away at a speed that astounded her. She even added Matthew's clothing to the sack to show her appreciation for his kindnesses. The cabin was small, and she had the cleaning of it down to a routine that took only an hour or so out of her mornings. Even the dreaded needle and thread had given up trying to draw blood, and she patched their clothing and spent many free hours embroidering doilies and finishing the kitchen towels. She'd made a pattern out of a discarded newspaper and was in the process of attempting to sew a dress. Its possible outcome was a source of teasing and laughter at the supper table.

Jemson and Matthew went hunting every few days after they had gone back to working in the mine. Those afternoons were particularly long for Bree, but there was always a freshly skinned rabbit or squirrel in the box buried beneath the snow at the back of the cabin. After dinner, the three of them had fallen into the habit of sitting at the table and playing card games they taught each other. Pinochle—which it seemed Bree could never lose or overbid, Red Dog—Matthew's particular favorite, and Gin Rummy, a game of memory Bree was sure Jemson had introduced because of his uncanny skill at remembering the cards that had been picked up and discarded. At times, Bree found herself foolishly thinking of spring in terms of having visitors, getting enough people to play a rousing game of poker. It was times like these that she had to remind herself that she wouldn't be sitting around the table, basking in the glow of the fire, come spring.

Even after Matthew left each evening for his own cabin, a routine had been established. Jemson turned his back while Bree got into her nightclothes and then stripped off his own clothes while she lay with her face toward the wall. Getting into bed beside her, an absentminded pat on the shoulder, a whispered goodnight, and then the long hours, laying stiff and still, until exhaustion overtook her and she was able to sleep. Jemson seemed to fall asleep immediately but she couldn't be sure. Was he as restless as she? As . . . what? She felt like a pin cushion, as though a thousand ants were crawling under her skin. Waves of hot and cold washed over her body, fantasies that made her blush to remember them plagued the silent hours. Jemson appeared oblivious to it all, but Bree found herself waiting, wanting him to turn to her in the night, pull her close, love her as he had in the dark privacy of her wagon. The more he seemed to accept the sexless state that existed like a siege of war between them, the more Bree found herself wanting to draw him closer, to ensnare him totally. His apparent lack of interest became Bree's obsession. The hot, torturous yearnings overflowed from nocturnal day-dreaming to invade her daylight hours. She found herself recalling each touch, each caress, dwelling on the memory of how it had felt to have Jemson deep inside her body, how he had seemed to fill up every empty space.

But the way things stood now, following the pattern Bree had laid for them to follow, Jemson wasn't likely to make the first move toward her until she gave him some kind of sign, an open invitation. And, even then, it was possible he might refuse, driven away by suspicion and doubt. And, of course, there was the problem of an emotional involvement Bree was not yet ready to face head on. She wanted him, yes, but only on her terms. She wanted him for the time being. She still had every intention of leaving in the spring and returning home, but what did one desire have to do with the other? And she steadfastly refused to face the realities of her own desires. It would be too frightening, too final. It was easier, as it had always been for Bree, selfish though she often was, to interpret the other person's needs. If Jemson imagined himself no longer in love with her, well, he was a man, wasn't he? If the women who chattered and gossiped in her mother's parlor were to be believed, Jemson had certain basic animal needs, didn't he? As to the intensity of her own longings, Bree closed the door on that question. It was much more convenient to ignore her confusion and pretend to concern herself only with Jemson. What little honesty she would allow told her that one thing followed the other. If she were to establish a closer relationship with Jemson, their life together would take on a new dimension. It was advantageous to both of them. As long as he understood that her need for him would disappear with the melting snow, that she still would expect him to hand over the

marriage paper and let her go back to Crosshaven, who would it hurt? Unable to bear the sleepless, tormented nights any longer, Bree began nervously to plan Jemson's seduction.

They had had a particularly bad day in the mine. Pick handles broke, a support beam cracked and gave way, and now the arrastra—a circular basin chipped out of stone and sided with wood, used to free the gold from hard chunks of quartz—had fallen victim to the constant battering of melted snow. Its wooden sides were warping and they were losing too much gold through the crevices. After supper, Jemson and Matthew left to repair the arrastra so they could continue work the following day. They were anxious to get in as much work as possible before the steadily building winter made mining impossible.

Bree used the time wisely. She filled the tub with hot water, then bathed and perfumed her body. Drying her hair by the fire, she heated more water and waited for Jemson to return.

When he did, he was dirty and tired. If he was surprised to find Bree walking around in her nightgown, he didn't mention it.

"I thought you could use a nice, relaxin' bath." Bree smiled bewitchingly and pointed to the full tub by the fire. "Everythin' all right with the arrastra?" She used her best concerned-wife voice.

Jemson nodded mutely, wondering at the new game. He knew Bree well enough to know that she hadn't given up that easily. She wasn't one to wave the white flag of surrender until every card had been played. But he was too weary to spend much time trying to figure her out. Instead, he walked heavily to the tub and looked. It sure was inviting. He peeled off the heavy coat and sat in a chair to remove his boots. He glanced up to see Bree watching him boldly and it made him hesitate. What *was* that woman up to now?

"Oh, Lord, Jemson, hurry up or it'll be midnight before

you get that dirt off." Bree laughed lightly and crossed the room to stand beside him. "Don't be so shy, darlin'," she continued brazenly, forcing herself to appear casual. "I've washed you before if you remember right." Steeling herself with a great, heaving gulp Bree started to undo the buttons on Jemson's shirt.

He stood passively, beginning to enjoy the new game, aware now of what she intended. Not the reason behind her actions certainly, but the intent. Shrugging, he decided to relax and enjoy it. When he was stripped down to his long underwear, Bree hesitated, her insides churning. She felt like a hussy, and the role was foreign to her. She concentrated on the image of Crosshaven, and it helped her to continue. She kept her eyes leveled at Jemson's face and was irritated by the amusement she saw there.

Once he was in the tub, it went a little easier. Bree rolled up the sleeves of her nightgown and reached for the soap and cloth. As she rubbed his shoulders and back, Bree felt the tight muscles give under her touch. He broke the water at his waist and as much as she tried, Bree couldn't get herself to wash him any lower. Jemson took pity on her and took the cloth out of her hands. She began to wash his hair, loving the feel of it. Her own hair was thick and slightly coarse. Jemson's was as soft as cornsilk. Raising the bucket of fresh water to rinse his head, Bree tried unsuccessfully to pull her eyes away from the sight of Jemson's smooth, muscular skin. She stood behind him and let the water trickle over his head and down his neck and chest. She had taken such great pains to plan her every movement and gesture but the next was spontaneous, impulsive. Bree locked her fingers in Jemson's wet curls and gently pulled his head back until his face was directly below hers. Slowly, breathlessly, she bent and softly brushed her lips across his mouth. Her tongue licked deliciously, teasingly. Jemson could feel the trembling in her hands. Still, he waited. Bree's breath was hot and sweet against his face. She might be a master at parlor games and intrigue, Jemson admitted, but in ways of love she was an amateur. The boldness at undressing him, the willingness to bathe him, the soft, seductive voice—that was probably all a sham. But this new rush of feeling, the yearning that made her face glow—this was something she had no control over, something that was beyond manipulation.

Bree pulled away, stunned by the ferocity of her emotions, not wanting to let them gain power over her will. She stood a foot away from Jemson, swaying, panicked. He rose from the tub and dried himself off, making no effort to shield himself from Bree's reluctantly greedy eyes.

He's so beautiful, she thought dreamily, unable to help herself. I'd forgotten, tried to push it from my mind. Dazed, like a sleepwalker, Bree reached up to unfasten the buttons that ran halfway down the front of her nightgown. She shrugged gracefully out of the gown and it fell around her feet. They stood watching each other in the soft, golden glow of the fire, unable to speak. Jemson took the first step but before he could reach her, Bree flew willingly into his arms and offered her mouth hungrily. She moaned, pressing closer, wanting more. Her stomach lurched crazily and she felt a ball of fire ignite and spread through her body. Had there ever really been any plan beyond this? She wasn't sure any more. Perhaps the formulation of a plan was the only way she could excuse herself for wanting Jemson with this wild, driving passion.

As Jemson's teeth bit tenderly into her bottom lip, she could feel him, hard and throbbing against her leg. In one movement, he swept her up into his arms and carried her to the bed. The cabin was chilly but he made no move to cover them with the quilt. Instead, he laid her on top of it and stretched out beside her. Raising up on one arm, he watched her responses adoringly. His fingers skipped gently over her skin, touching the curve of her neck, the swell of her taut, sensitive breasts. Her nipples hardened and raised under delicate strokes. Jemson's head bent to kiss one of the rosy peaks and Bree groaned with happiness. Her hand lifted to caress his neck and shoulders. She shifted her position so that she could face him, touch him. His eyes were glazed with desire and she knew he must be seeing the same thing in her eyes. Jemson rolled over on his back and pulled Bree with him. His hands lifted her, guilding her legs to either side of his hips. She knelt, poised and uncertain above him—not knowing what was expected of her, a little frightened of the unknown. Then, with the certainty that he would never do anything to harm her, Bree relaxed. She let Jemson lead her and then she felt the tip of his manhood kiss and part the tender, pulsating moisture between her legs. He filled her until she thought she would scream with pleasure. Jemson moaned and licked his lips, keeping a tight rein on his reactions. His hands slid up her hips, over her ribs, and cupped the full, tingling breasts. Urging her forward, his mouth claimed first one and then another. Bree shuddered and her breath came in pants. Bracing herself with her arms straightened near Jemson's shoulders, Bree moved her hips, swaying with an intuitive motion. His hands moved from her breasts and wound in her hair. Pulling her closer until the pointed, teasing tips of her breasts brushed his chest, Jemson whispered hoarsely, "I love you, Bree. My beloved, my wife." Bree sighed deeply, her face rubbing against Jemson's cheek. Her mouth, wet and burning, moved down his cheek and clung to his lips. She barely felt the movement as Jemson raised himself and pushed her over on her back, his mouth never leaving hers, their bodies locked in a single, unbroken rhythm. Bree's legs locked around his back and she lifted her hips, beckoning him deeper, closer. With each thrust, her breath sucked in raggedly and came out in a moan of delight. The moans turned to ecstatic little whimpers as they soared higher, faster. Bree felt her whole body explode in a kaleidoscope of light and colors, felt it melt and weld itself to Jemson.

When the moment of mutual gratification had passed and Jemson had pulled the quilt up over their nude bodies, Bree lay almost purring in the curve of his arm. His hands stroked her back and his mouth danced lightly over her face. She snuggled tighter against him. At that moment, if it were possible, she would have devoured him so as to never lose the warm, dreamy sensations she felt.

Bree woke with a violent start, the sound rumbling loud and threatening in her head. Above the bed, the roof shuddered and creaked, the wood groaned. She turned, wide-eyed and frightened, to Jemson and found him watching her, a smile across his lips.

"It's just the snow shifting on the roof." He sought to calm her. "I'll climb up tomorrow and shovel it off." He wrapped his arms around her and laughed to find that they were both shivering. "Right now, I think we'd best get some warm clothes on or Matthew will find two frozen blocks of ice in the morning." He got out of bed and padded across the floor to retrieve Bree's nightgown and his long johns. "How about a cup of coffee to warm you up, darlin'? I'll put the pot on the fire."

Bree nodded eagerly, murmuring her thanks. Jemson made a thick, bitter liquid but she was cold to the bone and would have settled for melted-down axle grease, as long as it was hot. She pulled the covers up under her nose and watched Jemson as he pulled on the long johns and bent to place the pot on the embers. Her heart was still pounding erratically.

What a desolate place this is, she thought grumpily. Primitive, hard, ungiving. A person worked and sweated, pouring his life's blood into the land just to make it livable, and it gave nothing in return. Suddenly, she longed for the feel of the hot Georgia sun on her face. Even the still, muggy days were preferable to this biting cold.

Jemson returned to bed and handed Bree her nightgown. She slipped it over her head and it was like putting on a sheet of ice. Gasping, she hopped out of bed and sprinted toward the fire. Jemson stood and chuckled, a kind of "you'll get used to it" laugh. He came up behind her and

223

slipped his arms around her shoulders, drawing her closer until her back rubbed up against his chest. His head bent and she felt his lips brush her ear.

"Don't fret so, darlin'," he whispered consolingly. "Come spring, we'll bring in some comforts, maybe even build a small barn for livestock so we can have fresh eggs and milk all the year."

Bree stiffened and broke away from him, turning her body until she faced him, head tilted and defiant. "Don't go to that trouble on my account, Jemson. I won't be here." She blushed, the flame spreading over her cheeks. "What happened last night doesn't change anything. You promised to give me the marriage paper and let me go back to Crosshaven in the spring. That is still my intention." She glared at Jemson questioningly. "You won't go back on your word, will you? You'll let me go?"

A flicker, just a glimmer of intense pain flitted through Jemson's deep blue eyes. In that instant, Bree could almost read the thoughts that lay behind the pain. No, she wanted to cry, I wasn't pretendin'. I've yearned for you, dreamed every night of being back in your arms. But I can't ever belong to this place, not the way you want me to be. I must go home to Crosshaven, the life I was bred to.

She knew instantly that saying the words would do no good. He wouldn't believe or understand. Jemson's face turned to granite, hardening her own resolve.

"Well, what did you expect?" she cried bitterly. "I'm human, I have the same needs you do!"

"You're wrong about that, Bree. Our needs are strangers to one another." Jemson's voice sounded hard and sad, distant. He lifted the coffee cup and poured two cups, handing her one. "You just go on being fair and decent with me—I don't mean in bed, that's up to you—but just stop scheming and playing games long enough to pass the winter and I'll keep my end of the bargain. You'll be off the mountain in the spring."

Accepting the mug of coffee as though it were a peacepipe

passed between them, Bree sighed and nodded her head in solemn agreement. It was a compromise of sorts, not what she had wanted to give him for the time they had left, but it would have to do.

CHAPTER TWENTY-TWO

The first two months of the new year brought to full impact the worst winter Colorado had seen. The snow piled so deep it was impossible to work in the mine and a path, five feet high on either side, took three days in the digging to clear a way from one cabin to the other. Even so, Matthew found himself spending more and more time in the solitude of his own cabin. It was embarrassing, the way those two carried on! He could almost pinpoint the exact time when things had changed between them. Bree's cheeks took on a radiance that nearly blinded him and she hummed and sang all the time; Jemson, well, he stopped taking offense at every little thing, stopped growling like an angry bear. And the touching! Damn, they couldn't walk within four feet of each other without reaching out, as if to assure themselves that the other one was really there. It sure put Matthew in a hell of a sticky position. He never knew from one minute to the next if he was welcome or wished away. In defense, he'd begun to spend mornings and afternoons in his own cabin, reading well-worn books and year-old newspapers. He might not be getting the attention Jemson was, but he sure was getting smart!

In March the snows started to melt. The ground turned to mush and birds appeared from out of nowhere to perch on the tree branches and add their music to the warming sun. It was possible now to go outside in the daytime hours without the protection of a heavy jacket and gloves.

Bree woke slowly and opened her eyes, taking in all the familiar morning things, embers in the fireplace, sunlight filtering through the windows, and Jemson sleeping peacefully beside her. She smiled, debating on whether or not to wake him up. Then she decided to hold greedily whatever time she had left with him. The conditions were favorable again but, she knew that he had postponed going back to work the mine, choosing instead to spend their days as though they were still snow-bound. Of course, he never said anything about it, but, then, he was an irritatingly close-mouthed man.

There hadn't been a harsh word between them since the night they had first come together. If Jemson ever thought about the time when she would be leaving him, he never mentioned it. Bree was certain she thought about it more than he. As a matter of fact, that single thought occupied most of the time she didn't spend in his arms. That and the desire she had to hear him say he loved her. But he never spoke of the spring and he never again repeated the tender words whispered in her ear on that first night of love. She was torn with wanting to hear the declaration anew and hoping he would remain mute, knowing that putting words to the feelings might only serve to weaken her resolve. Each day, each moment, every time Jemson took her into his strong arms pushed Crosshaven further from her mind.

And, she reminded herself, yawning and stretching out the morning aches, it doesn't do a bit of good to dwell on it now! Raising up on one elbow, Bree bent to trace a path of light, airy kisses along Jemson's rock-hard jaw. He stirred, edging away as though she were tickling him. Bree persisted, slipping her hand underneath the quilts to start a slow descent down his chest and along the side of his leg, giggling happily when he suddenly lurched out and grabbed her. Bree snuggled next to him, finding just that comfortable part of his body where she fit so perfectly.

"You're gettin' to be a real man of leisure, Jemson. Lollin' around in bed all day while the rest of the world is busy workin' to feed their starvin' families." Bree teased his ear with her tongue. "But, as long as you're here . . ."

"No time for such foolishness, darlin'." Jemson threw off the covers and heaved himself off the bed, dragging Bree with him. "I've got a surprise for you today. Something we both need."

"I was tryin' to tell you what *I* need!" Bree protested weakly.

"You need this more, trust me."

Jemson pulled the quilts off the bed and wrapped one around Bree's shoulders, then padded across the room to the wardrobe and took out two more blankets. "You and I, sweetheart, are going to take an honest-to-God, head-to-toe, dunking bath. Come on now; don't stand there with your mouth hanging open. Time's a-wastin'."

"I'm not movin' from this spot until you tell me just how . . ."

"The creek, my darlin', the creek! It's running like tinkling bells over the rocks, shoulder high, behind Matt's cabin."

"I don't care how it's runnin'! It's runnin' *cold*! You're talkin' like a crazy man, Jemson Tyler, if you think for one minute I'm goin' step foot in that freezin' water."

"Suit yourself." Jemson shrugged elaborately, scooping up the soap on the basin on his way out the door. "As for me, well, I'm feeling a mite stale and I intend to do something about it." He paused at the door, pulling the quilt tighter around his shoulders.

"Oh, all right!" Bree sputtered, joining him. "But if I turn to ice, you got nobody to blame but your own self!"

"Hold on! Better put on our boots or we'll be tracking mud from here to Sunday. And as for you're turning icy, I'll take my chances. If you remember, that state of your feelings isn't all that unknown to me." Jemson pulled on his boots and helped Bree with hers.

They made a ridiculous pair, stomping down through the slush to the creek, wrapped in quilts, their long underwear peeking over the tops of boots.

The flow of the creek was increased by all the melting snow above it. The sound, as it rushed over the rocks, filled the air with roaring. Bree stood uncertainly at the water's edge, eyeing Jemson warily as he stripped off his long johns under the quilt, dropped the extra blankets in a heap, stepped out of his boots, took a firm hold on the soap, and in one blurring movement threw his naked body into the creek. He was submerged for only a second and broke water sputtering and gasping. Bree panicked, knowing it was now or not at all. The temperature of the water would allow them only a few minutes, and if she didn't join him quickly, she would be left to bathe in the creek alone or miss the opportunity entirely. In that case, Jemson would come out smelling like fresh flowers and she would still have the peculiar odor of someone who hadn't taken a complete bath all winter.

Without allowing herself time to think about it, Bree stripped off her clothes and jumped in after Jemson. The shock almost made her faint. The water was so cold it actually hurt her skin. She could feel her fingers and feet begin to grow numb.

"Keep moving! Keep moving!" Jemson instructed, lifting his arms and hitting his body like a great flapping bird, whooping and yelling away the cold.

He rubbed up a lather on the soap and passed the bar to Bree. She took it eagerly and began to scrub, following Jemson's lead. Her hair, because it was so much longer, posed a problem, but Jemson jumped in and helped her. Then, wading to the side where the water was only waist deep, she scrubbed every niche of her body. Holding hands, the two of them went under the water again to rinse off the soap and came to the surface screaming. Jemson swooped Bree up in his arms and waded to the creek's edge, wrapping her up in a blanket before he grabbed one for himself. She was afraid to move, certain that if she did, her skin would break like glass. Shaking, Bree watched as Jemson toweled himself off, his skin glowing bright and

229

golden. When he was done, Jemson tucked the blanket around his body and under his arms, then looked at Bree and chuckled. She made a pathetic little figure, bundled from the top of her head on down in a huge blanket, nothing visible except wide, green, suffering eyes. Taking pity, Jemson rubbed her arms and legs vigorously on the outside of the quilt, patting her head to absorb some of the water from her hair. She whimpered, teeth chattering, lips blue while he worked. And finally, finally, she began to warm up a bit. Bree closed her eyes, wallowing in the growing feeling of contentment, only vaguely aware that Jemson had stopped drying her off and had gathered the rough, woolly material of the blanket at her throat and was pulling her toward him. She felt her feet move lightly over the ground, moving her closer. When Bree opened her eyes, Jemson loomed above her, blocking out the sky. She was momentarily stunned by the familiar look she saw on his face. Lips slightly parted, golden flecks moving and glowing behind intense blue eyes. She was at once ashamed and excited by the surge of passion and desire she returned. Breathlessly, Bree pried his hands loose and opened the blanket like a cloak, beckoning Jemson in. A brief thought—what would the ladies in our parlor think if they could see me now?—flashed through her brain, but she quickly forgot everything but the fluid heat that swirled slowly inside her body.

Jemson dropped to his knees, his arms clasped around Bree's waist as she closed the quilt around them. He pressed his face into the cool, pink flesh of her abdomen, feeling it warm under his touch. Mouth and tongue flicked slowly, exploring every part of her. He could hear her soft moans, feel her fingers work their way through his damp hair, sense the moment before her knees began to buckle. Pulling her down, Jemson smoothed out the blanket underneath Bree and used the one that was wrapped around his body to cover them. He stretched out over her, his eyes never leaving her face. Bree felt his hardness slide smoothly between her legs. She gasped breathlessly, straining to lift her hips, to hurry his entry. He was like a hot poker, warming her from inside. The heat spread quickly, wild-fire igniting every nerve, every part of her. She cried out, shuddering, her body rocking in rhythm with the soaring waves of ecstasy that washed over her. Clinging to Jemson, Bree panted erratically and then sagged and fell silent.

"Dammit, woman," Jemson breathed hoarsely, dipping to kiss the tip of her nose, "I love it when you play hard to get."

He carried her back to the cabin, striding along in bright red long underwear, the damp blankets piled in her lap. Once inside the cabin, although she'd worn boy's clothing all winter, Bree was struck with the urge to put on a dress. While Jemson threw on his denims and flannel shirt, Bree slipped a cotton dress over her long underwear and was dismayed to find the buttons strained, threatening to pop open.

"Why didn't you tell me I was puttin' on so much weight?" she scolded Jemson. "I don't understand; I haven't been eatin' all that much."

"You were too skinny anyway," Jemson scoffed. "And you eat like a starving coal miner. Lord, woman, you tuck away almost as much as I do! Must be you're getting fat and sassy like a contented cat."

Bree grumbled under her breath as she struggled to take off the offending garment. She was more comfortable in pants anyway. Still, irrationally, she secretly fretted that the ballgowns tucked away in ceder chests at Crosshaven would no longer fit, so she determined to watch more carefully the food she put into her mouth. Jemson was right about that, however; it seemed she was always ravenous, and a steady diet of starches and gravies wasn't doing her a bit of good.

Seeing that Jemson had taken a chair by the fire, Bree slipped on her denims and shirt and crossed the room to sit in his lap. He bent to strike a match on the stone fireplace and then lifted it to light a cheroot. He leaned back, contentedly sucking the light, billowing smoke into his lungs. His arm moved casually to encircle Bree and press her against his chest. She sat quietly, listening to the sound of his heart beating.

CHAPTER TWENTY-THREE

Laughing joyfully, Bree tapped on the window glass to attract the attention of a beautiful blue bird that perched in the branches of a blue spruce. It had stopped raining the day before and the sky was a blue as the pretty bird. The trees were beginning to show leaves again and the air was crisp and clean. In another month, the mountains would be alive with the blossoms of columbine flowers. The dogwood trees would be in bloom.

Bree left the window and put away the last of the breakfast dishes. She took pen and paper and sat at the round table, preparing to make a list of provisions. Matthew had left early that morning for Central City to assay and bank the gold they had brought out of the mine during the winter months. He was going to scout around and see what was available; then they would compare lists and strike off what couldn't be bought.

At the top of the list Bree wrote "cow" and "laying hens," fervently longing for the taste of fresh milk and cream and fried eggs to brighten up the monotonous breakfasts. Jemson's idea of housing their own livestock had been a good one. Jemson could build the structure they needed and teach her how to tend the animals. Pen working furiously, Bree added to the list. Needles, thread, a bolt of cloth she could use to make them all serviceable summer clothing. Provisions were drastically low. Sugar, flour, bacon, honey, and salt. Maybe even some fresh vegetables and canned fruit. Oh yes, and a clock for the mantle. She'd spent the last four months on a hit or miss basis. Jemson had a pocket watch, so when he said he'd be back by four o'clock, Bree could look up at the fireplace and know exactly when that meant.

Time. How it had slipped away, melting like the snow. With the spring and summer upon them, Jemson and Matthew would be spending more and more time in the mine. She would have less of Jemson than she'd grown accustomed to.

Bree sighed heavily, already missing the intimacy the winter had afforded them, knowing she would have to wait a full seven months before winter came again and she would have him all to herself.

They would, however, have to do something about Matthew. It just didn't seem fair to have him stuck off in his cabin all by himself. Matthew. Sweet Matthew. Bree had grown to love him as much as her own brother. He needed more than the occasional company of two people totally caught up in each other.

Bree made a mental note to ask Jemson if he thought it was a good idea to look around for a nice girl, worthy of being courted by Matthew. Bree smiled, remembering the look of envy that filled Matthew's face each night when he rose to leave their cabin and return to the emptiness of his own. Yes, it was time Matthew had a woman of his own.

Bree laughed out loud and hugged herself tightly, swaying back and forth in the chair. Thoughts of Matthew disappeared and she felt full to spilling over with love for Jemson. He was the real reason she found it hard to keep a straight face this day. Tonight, in the privacy and warmth of their bed, she was going to tell him. Sighing again, Bree thought back on the time she first realized she loved Jemson and had given up the idea of ever leaving him. He had told her the lovemaking part of their relationship was strictly up to her. And she had felt compelled to go to him each night, put her arms around him and draw him to her breast. Then, the realization that she might become pregnant. And the certain conviction that she wanted, would welcome Jemson's seed growing inside her body. At first she had wondered if it was the loneliness that made her wish for a child. But no, it was much more basic than that. Since their first night together, when Jemson had whispered words of love and then they had fought, he had been as silent as a stone. Oh, he took her in his arms when she came to him and his hands and his mouth told her of his feelings, but the words never came. And she longed to hear them again and to be able to say, "I love you too." A child, a child given in love, would ease Jemson's mind and tell him far better than words that she belonged to him forever. Bree could turn to him a thousand times and he would still be uncertain. Still remember those foolish words she had uttered. Instead of I love you and I need you, she had crushed him with "I have needs too." It was true. Her body craved his touch, his kiss. But, even more, she yearned for the soft sound of his voice, the gentle feel of his hand on her shoulder when they walked, the look of respect that came into his eyes when he say her working alongside him, the abundant gifts of comfort and sensation.

Bree hummed and looked around the clean, shiny room. Home. She hadn't thought of Crosshaven as home in weeks. Home was anywhere Jemson was. She would tell him that, too. As the winter thaws came, he had grown quiet and expectant; the question hung silently between them. Even his lovemaking was more restrained, as though he were holding back, waiting for the moment when Bree would say it was time to take her down the mountain, to let her go home.

The rest of the afternoon was spent preparing a delicious venison stew in celebration of Matthew's triumphant return from Central City. Grinning, Bree pictured an image in her mind. After Matthew had told them all his news and they had eaten the fine dinner she had made, Matthew would bid them goodnight and return to his own cabin. Jemson would help Bree with the dinner dishes and then pour himself a glass of whiskey, light a cheroot, and go to sit pensively by the fire. It was then that Bree would walk over to him, snuggle into his lap and press her lips to his ear.

About my goin' home, she would start casually. I've decided to wait ten or twelve years, if that's all right with you. Then, laughing to see the expression on his face, Bree might say, by that time we ought to have four or five grandchildren to present Papa. Jemson would be stunned, Bree giggling, hugging him.

She shivered with anticipation, wishing the day would go faster.

The months of solitude had given her great insight into Jemson's emotions. He said nothing about her leaving, made no overt attempt to keep her, refused to ask. But he loved Bree, of that she was sure.

The scenario Bree had imagined fell apart the moment Matthew walked in the door. He was panting, a wild, frightened look in his eyes.

"We're at war, Jem," he announced bluntly, breathlessly. "It's crazy, but the states are at war! Charleston harbor was attacked, and now the forces, Confederate and Union, are collecting in the Shenandoah Valley. President Lincoln has proclaimed a blockade of the South. What are we going to do, Jem? Should we go home and enlist?"

"Calm down, Matt! Don't lose your head and run off foolish," Jemson ordered firmly, his mind racing. "I want to think this out."

"You're right, I know you're right, but I can't help thinking about our brothers fighting for their lives." Matthew shook his head miserably. "Talk in town is that it'll all be over in a few weeks. The South isn't strong enough to take on the Union army."

Jemson reached out instinctively and drew Bree close. "Don't underestimate the Confederacy, Matt. They're a strong, proud people. Right, honey?" He hugged Bree, wanting to protect her from the pain that was clearly etched across her face. She nodded numbly, straining to

236

catch her breath, gasping with the fear of Matthew's news.

"I'm sorry, Bree. I didn't mean any disrespect to you. God, it's all so mixed up." Matthew staggered over to a chair and sank in it, his hands running nervously through his hair. "Central City's gone wild, Jem. The whole territory's divided in its sympathies, but it seemed to lean mostly toward the South, as far as I could see."

"That could be bad for us, being from the North," Jemson mused thoughtfully. "Well, I'm not going to decide anything on an empty stomach. Let's have supper and sleep on it. We'll go into town tomorrow and try and get a better perspective on things; then we'll decide—all of us."

The next morning Bree saw Jemson and Matthew off when they set out for Central City. They'd urged her to accompany them but she'd refused. She needed the time alone to think, and being next to Jemson had a way of obscuring the clarity of her mind. Having left everything unsaid, Bree wondered if there would ever be another time to tell Jemson all the things she had planned to say. Last night had passed without the endearments being voiced. After Matthew had left for the night, they had sadly gone to bed, but not with the fervor she'd imagined. She had fallen asleep in Jemson's arms, weeping for her father and the young men she knew would be called to fight a losing war. How could she tell Jemson of her love when the whole world was collapsing around them? If he chose to return to Pennsylvania and enlist in the Union army, what good would it do anyway? She wouldn't try to bind him to her with a declaration of undying passion. It seemed ludicrous in the light of neighbor fighting neighbor, north against south. The cold hand of fear tightened in her belly. Only if Jemson chose to stay in Colorado, and *if* the territory opted to support the Union, would they remain together. If he went home, she would have to go home. The horror of that prospect made her faint and nauseated. It could be years before she saw him again—if he lived through the fighting and if he came back for her.

The rest of the morning, Bree walked around in a daze. A week ago, she'd had a choice—to return to Crosshaven or stay with Jemson. Now, the decisions were being made on an obscure battlefield in South Carolina. Just yesterday, she had set aside all thought of seeing Crosshaven and her family for years. Now, she feared she might never seen any of them alive again if she didn't go home now.

Bree curled up on the bed, small and miserable, waiting. She dozed and was awakened by the sound of a footfall on the porch. Running, she flew to the door and threw it open. And then she screamed. Her scream echoed through the valley, careening off the high cliffs, and came back to her, faint and eerie.

"That's a reaction Ah expect Ah'll have to learn to live with," Robb Andrews touched his face self-consciously and sneered. "But, then Ah have you to thank, don't Ah?"

Bree stared, open-mouthed, her eyes riveted on his face. Scar tissue, wrinkled and puffed an angry crimson, pulled one side of his face in a grotesque mask. His mouth drooped downward and the eye socket was exposed.

"This is what scaldin' water does to a man's face, Bree," Robb growled and pushed by her. "Not very pretty, is it?"

Bree choked back the bile that had risen suddenly to her throat and raised her eyes to meet his stare. "What do you want here, Robb?" Her voice quavered slightly when she noticed the gun he had clenched in his hand.

"Ah 've been waitin', Bree. Been in Central City for five days now, just waitin'. Saw Jemson Tyler there this mornin' and knew it was time. He didn't even recognize me, ain't that somethin'?" Robb laughed without humor and advanced menacingly. "What Ah want, Bree, is you. Ah am takin' you back to Georgia with me. Yore responsible for what yore starin' at so we're gonna be companions in mah hell. You'll be mah lovin' wife, Bree, and every night you'll kiss this face and Ah'll live behind it." His arm shot out like a snake and grabbed her, pulling Bree's face within inches of his own. "No need to pack, mah love. We're leavin' now!"

Savagely, Robb pulled her from the house. She fought, trying to pull out of his grip, but it was like iron. Robb threw her to the ground and bent over her, the gun tucked neatly under her chin.

"If Ah have to, Ah'll kill you right here instead of a little at a time. Do you understand?" His eyes blazed with hatred and madness.

Bree nodded silently, trembling with revulsion and fear. She cringed as he grabbed her again to lift her up off the ground.

"Now, Ah'll put the gun back in the holster if you behave yoreself. Agreed?"

Again, Bree nodded mutely. Terrified, she thought of Jemson and Matthew returning home soon, unarmed, walking in to find a madman. First, she had to get Robb away from the house, as far away from Central City as possible. Then she would find a way to escape him. At this moment, all she had to worry about was staying alive and getting away quickly enough to make sure Jemson stayed alive too.

They hadn't gone more than twenty feet when the thing Bree feared most materialized out of the trees. Jemson and Matthew returning. She opened her mouth to warn them. Take cover. He's armed. Before she could utter a word, Robb's gun was out of the holster and leveled at Jemson.

"Stand aside, Tyler," Robb barked fiercely. "Ah'm takin' Bree away from this hell hole and ya'll can't stop us. Now, stand aside."

"This what you want, Bree?" Jemson asked her, his tone incredulous. Matthew stood open-mouthed at his side.

Bree hesitated a moment, the possibilities exploding in her brain. If she said yes, Jemson would step down and let them pass. If she said no—no, I don't ever want to be separated for you—Jemson would stand firm and most

239

probably be killed. First Jemson and then Matthew.

"Yes." A single word and she was destroying her whole life.

If she had hit him alongside the head with a stick, Jemson couldn't have looked more stunned, more uncomprehending. Still, he didn't move. Then Matthew lightly touched Jemson's hand and a signal seemed to pass between the two of them.

A split second later Matthew dove into the trees on one side of the path and Jemson into the other. Robb got off a wild shot, more in surprise than anything else. Uncertain, cowardly, he moved behind Bree and jumped at every sound—a rustling in the bush, the crack of a broken twig.

Bree saw the blurred movement before Robb did. She dropped to the ground, out of Jemson's way, as he charged the six-foot gap that separated them. Robb screamed shrilly and fired. The bullet tore through Jemson's arm, splattering blood and flesh into the air. And then Jemson was on him, his fists clasped tightly together like a powerful hammer, swinging down on the side of Robb's head. There was a sharp, breaking sound; the gun slipped from his hand and Robb fell to his knees and then his face sank into the mud. He lay there, unmoving, his shoulder resting on Bree's leg. She moaned and scrambled away from the dead man, gasping with revulsion.

Matthew came out of the trees and examined Robb's prone form and then crossed over to look at Jemson's arm. "It's only a flesh wound, brother. You'll be fit in a week. But that fella there . . . well, he's dead. His neck's all wobbly. I guess you broke it."

Jemson cursed under his breath and nudged Robb's body with his foot, as if to confirm the fact that he was beyond hope.

"What should we do, Jem?" Matthew looked to his brother for guidance. "Should we take him into town?"

Jemson muttered and ran his hand through his hair, his thoughts taking form. "I don't know as that would be such a good idea, Matt. Any other time, yes, but not just now. You saw how things are in town. Whole mobs banding together, fighting the issues of the civil war out in the streets. Looked to me like the Southerners outnumbered the North about six to one. And I don't relish the idea of turning myself over and getting hanged by a pack, crazy with blood fever." Jemson seemed to notice Bree suddenly. He looked confused, as if finding her there surprised him. Then his thoughts cleared, and he remembered the reason he had just killed a man and was now trying to figure a way to save himself. His voice turned hard and cold. "We'll bury him in the mine. Grab his legs, Matt."

"Then what are we going to do, Jem?" Matthew insisted as he bent to lift Robb's lifeless legs.

"It's not a matter of what *we're* going to do. It's what *I'm* going to do. And I'm leaving. Somehow I'll make it back to Pennsylvania and enlist. You stay here and run the mine as best you can until the war's over. One of us fighting is enough, don't you think?" Jemson sounded suddenly tired. He leveled his frightening gaze at Bree. "How long you and Andrews have this planned?"

"Planned?" Bree bristled defensively. "I had no idea he would be comin' here. We haven't seen another soul in months. Just how do you imagine I could get a message off to him?" As she spoke Bree got to her feet and gestured toward Robb, his body now cradled between the two brothers. She felt a stab of regret. For all he had done to her—the deceit, the assault—Bree had only wanted Robb out of her life, not dead. "When he came into the cabin, he said he was on his way back to Georgia. I think comin' for me was something that's been festering in his mind for a long time. But," she added bitterly, "if you're worried about anyone else knowin' what he intended to do, I don't think he'd tell even his brother."

"Why is that?" Jemson snarled sarcastically, suspicion ringing clear.

"Can we talk about it in private?" Bree glanced pointedly toward Matthew. "Do what you have to about Robb and then come to the cabin and I'll dress your wound before you leave."

Jemson snorted disgustedly, shaking his head in wonder. Forever the intrigue, the lies. Well, the time it took to bury the poor fool would give Bree the opportunity to come up with she would consider a reasonable explanation as to why she was strolling out of his life on Robb Andrews's arm. Although why she felt she had to bother was beyond Jemson's reasoning. Why talk it to death and make excuses? He had always known she would be leaving him in the spring.

An hour later, Bree heard the brothers' voices as they approached the cabin. She has used the time well. Jemson's clothes and belongings were neatly packed in bags that sat beside the door. When they had carried off Robb's body, his gun had been left behind. That, too, had been hidden away, under Bree's petticoats in the wardrobe.

When Jemson came in, he was alone. It might have been Matt's intention to allow them the time together for an emotional leavetaking. The look that still radiated from Jemson's eyes belied Matthew's consideration. He was granite, set against her, against anything she might have to say. It irritated her that he sat in judgment so readily, believed her guilty so easily. Her first thought had been to explain everything—Robb's obsession with her, his knowing about Phillip and not telling her, the day he had forced his way into her cabin and how she was responsible for scarring both his face and the inner recesses of his mind. But this hour had given her time for second thoughts and she was more than a little angry. Jemson was so quick to believe the worst of her. She could bare the shameful secrets she'd tried so desperately to forget and he would still doubt her. And who made it an irrevocable law that a woman had to share everything with her man? Would the bond between them tighten only if he knew the truths that made her heart ache?—the years she had spent with Phillip as a sexual slave to his perversions, the nauseating feel of Robb Andrews's rough hands defiling her flesh. If she sent him away with these lovely truths, what would it accomplish? Her first instincts about Jemson were right. They were totally incompatible, except in the privacy of their bed.

Let him think what he likes, Bree decided stubbornly. She lifted her eyes and met Jemson's cool stare proudly. "Your things are there, by the door." Gesturing casually, Bree willed her heart to stop pounding so erratically in her chest. "You'd best leave now if you want to take the afternoon stage to Denver."

"I thought you wanted to tell me something," Jemson growled, refusing to give even a little.

"I've got nothin' to explain," Bree answered stiffly. "I wasn't leavin' here of my own choice, but you obviously don't believe that." Noticing Jemson's hesitation, Bree rushed on. "You don't have to worry about me stayin' on and corruptin' Matthew. As soon as I know you've had time to get away, I'm leavin' for Crosshaven to see my family. It's clear I never should have left."

Jemson nodded his agreement, a sad, weary expression softening his features. He bent to pick up his bags.

All of Bree's rigid determination washed away with a single thought. She was never going to see him again, and their parting, the memory he would take with him, was bitter and impersonal. An anguished cry escaped her lips. Bree flew across the room and into Jemson's arms. Her hands tightened around his neck and she buried her face in his chest.

"I can't let you go without tellin' you." Sighing, Bree's voice was muffled against the cloth of his shirt. "I wish it had been different. Just yesterday, there were so many things I wanted to say. I . . ." Bree moaned and pulled herself up until her lips were lightly touching Jemson's mouth.

Not unkindly, Jemson pried Bree's hands loose and stepped back. His face was as dark as a storm, his eyes clouded with pain and regret. Picking up his bags, he moved toward the door and then turned around to face her before leaving, his hand slipping into the jacket he wore and pulling out a folded piece of parchment. Silently, he held it in his outstretched hand. When Bree made no move toward him, Jemson leaned and dropped the marriage certificate on the table. His voice was so low she could barely make out the words.

"But it wasn't different, was it?"

BOOK THREE

CHAPTER TWENTY-FOUR

Crosshaven
May 1864

Bree's fingernails were cracked and bleeding from digging up the dirt floor of the smokehouse to get at its bounty of salt that years of hanging meat had hidden beneath the surface. She paused a moment in her work, wiping the sweat from her brow with the hem of her gown. Ears keen to any unfamiliar sound, she still could not hear any evidence of the Union advance. In her mind, Bree knew they were still too far away but still could not shake the cold fear that the main house might suddenly explode under a barrage of enemy cannon fire. Her knees ached from kneeling at her task, and a continuous, rumbling growl echoed through her stomach. It was pointless to give in to the hunger, foolish to think of the elaborate spreads of smoked meats and fish, juicy fruits and fresh vegetables that once graced the family's table. Even the long, polished table was gone now—chopped into the kindling that had warmed them last winter. One sparse meal a day was all they could hope for, and that was more than some Southerners could count on. Sugar was almost nonexistent; beef cost nearly five dollars a pound, potatoes and corn even more. Once Crosshaven had yielded plentiful bushels of fruit and vegetables, grown their own livestock and milk cows. But the Confederacy had confiscated everything and most of what little they were still able to grow went to feed the Southern troops. Sacrifice. The South gave up her life's blood to keep the war effort alive and, like the grasping tentacles of an octopus, Union forces reached out and encompassed large areas of her heartland. Bloody battles saw the rebels stagger and fall under the better-equipped, heavier-manned Yankees in Kentucky and half of Tennessee, Shiloh, Vicksburg, and Chattanooga. With the occupation of Vicksburg, General Grant's army controlled the Mississippi River between Memphis and New Orleans. That occupation brought blockades and the railroads were almost totally crippled—supplies to the Confederate army cut off. The Rebs were starving, inadequately clothed, and poorly armed.

How different it had been when Bree had first returned home to the bosom of her family two and a half years earlier. The fighting had only just begun in isolated areas in Virginia and South Carolina. Optimism swept through the South. Gala balls were held at every plantation to see off, in grand style, the men who laughingly promised to be back home again in a matter of months.

"You seem a mite unhappy for a lass just returned home to those who would love and protect her." Liam McCarty took his daughter's hand reassuringly. He'd followed her out to the veranda, where Bree had gone to escape the near-frantic gaiety of the party going on inside the house. "Your poor hands are shakin' that much. Come now, give your old Da a hug. You've had a bad time of it, my dear, but it's in the past, girl, you have to let it go." Liam's soft Irish brogue and twenty-five years of living in the South mingled to make a style of speech uniquely his own. "It's a sad thing to lose the one you love, but Phillip's been in his grave for almost two years and it's time, girl, time to put aside your mournin'."

"It's not Phillip makes me sad this night, Papa." Bree sighed and disengaged herself from her father's arms, turning away to lean against the railing of the veranda. "I just can't bear to watch all those young men in their brightly colored uniforms and fancy regalia, the orchestra playing 'Dixie' and 'Bonnie Blue Flag' and their ladies pretendin' they're not dyin' inside from fear."

"What would you have them do, girl? Spend the evening weepin' and bawlin' for something that's not in their power to change? I swear, I don't believe even half of them have any idea what really is ahead. We've harsh days comin', Bree, time enough to weep, I can promise you that. *Now* is the moment for a smile and a dance. Make the best of what we have while it's still in our hand." Liam grasped Bree's shoulders and turned her around to face him. He studied her face carefully, lovingly, and his heart grew heavy at what he saw there. "It's more than the party, more than the war comin' and the young men marchin' away, isn't it? You're not the same lass you were when I tried my damnedest to stop you from goin' off after Phillip. Aye, you were a lass then but you've the look of age to you now. The twinkle's gone out of your eye and the rose from your cheek. Tell me, girl, what is it made you so unhappy?"

A small cry tore from Bree's lips as she buried her face in Liam's shoulder. She longed to tell him about Jemson, yearned to share the burden of her grief.

The sound of someone softly clearing his throat made Bree's head snap in the direction of the intrusion. Standing with his back to the lights of the party stood a man whose identity she struggled to remember.

"Neal!" Liam called out happily, moving away from Bree to clasp the man's hand in a friendly welcome. "Lass, you remember Neal, don't you? Grayson Petrie's boy?" Liam beckoned Bree closer with a wave of his hand. "Well, no longer a boy, is it? Had your schoolin' in England and returned to us a man, full grown."

Despite the desolation she had felt only moments before, Bree allowed herself a tinkling giggle. The sound erupted into laughter as Neal bent over her hand to kiss it. Neal Petrie. She hadn't recognized him, but the name conjured up visions of a silent, gangly twelve-year-old boy watching an equally sullen ten-year-old girl and then reaching out to touch the girl's thick red curls gently before pushing her to the ground.

"Are you daft, girl?" Liam asked increduously, stunned by Bree's bad manners. "Is this any way to welcome a guest to our home."

"It's all right, Mr. McCarty." Neal hastened to calm him. "Miss Bree has a good memory after all."

"Well! I won't pretend to understand the workin's of the young mind, so, if you'll both give me leave, I'll see to my other guests." Liam excused himself and left the veranda, a satisfied smile on his face. It was the first real laughter he had heard from Bree, good to see her eyes glow again.

"I'm sorry, Mr. Petrie." Bree swallowed her laughter, the sound of it trailing off with Liam's exit. "My father's quite right. My manners are atrocious. Forgive me."

"There's nothing to forgive, Miss Bree, I assure you." Neal lifted Bree's hand to his lips again. "I shudder to think of the picture I must have made all those years ago. My only excuse for actin' the bully was that I was hopelessly smitten. Truly, when I was a boy I loved your ten-year-old grace. So it follows, naturally, that I strove to pick on you at every opportunity."

"My mother didn't see it quite that way, Mr. Petrie." Bree remembered, smiling. "She was always complainin' that whenever the Petrie boy came to visit with his father my dresses were either torn or stained so badly with mud they had to be thrown away. She thought you the very worst of ruffians."

"And right she was!" Neal laughed and offered Bree his arm. "But, if you and she will both forgive my past antics, I promise to behave myself in the future if you'll honor me with this dance." Without waiting for an answer, Neal led Bree from the veranda and through the open doors of the ballroom, guiding her smoothly into the center of the dancers.

He was no longer a shy, skinny boy, Bree thought as she flowed in Neal's arms to the strains of a waltz. A man, full grown, hadn't her father said? And he was . . . tall and well shouldered, sure of himself, confident. He knew as well as she that the dance card tied to her wrist with a delicate blue ribbon was filled with the names of other men and yet he gave no thought to it. It pleased Bree that no one tapped him on the shoulder, reminding Neal that he had taken the wrong dance. That meant either they liked and respected him too much to bring the social blunder to his attention or they recognized him as a man who was capable of taking what he wanted without tolerating the interference of other men. And, whatever the reason, Bree admired the deference he commanded.

Watching Neal covertly through lowered lashes, Bree saw even more to admire. His hair, black as a moonless nightfall, curled casually at his neck, and his eyes, a curious dark violet, twinkled mischievously under thick, black lashes. He was very handsome and dashing and she was aware that the eyes of the other dancers were on them, admiring them, thinking them a well-matched couple on the floor. Throughout the dance, Neal kept up a soft-spoken litany, his mouth moving breathlessly near Bree's ear. She was exquisite, a gorgeous creature whose child-like face had followed him throughout his adult life, a memory he had never been able to set aside.

When the dance was over and Neal had led her out to the darkness of the veranda once again, kissing her mouth hungrily, breathless with excitement, Bree found herself responding passionately out of some vague need to be the object of his happiness. She saw herself through Neal's eyes, a woman to be desired again, and her heart swelled with tenderness and gratitude.

"What damn luck!" Neal sighed bitterly, his arms tightening, his lips moving lightly over Bree's upturned face. "I only just heard you had returned. I broke all records getting here, if only to catch a brief glimpse of the girl who has haunted my dreams. I am blessed beyond my wildest dreams to hold her here in my arms only to lose her again."

"When do you leave?" Bree whispered, knowing he referred to going off to war.

His face was grave. "Two weeks, my dear, two short weeks!"

"My father says we must take what joy we can, for the time we have left." Bree heard herself repeating Liam's words with new-felt urgency. "Two weeks? We have fourteen days and nights to call our own." Bree smiled tenderly, marveling at the affection she felt for a man she had not seen in over ten years. She reached up to caress Neal's face, momentarily stunned and then pushing away the thought of how like Jemson this man smelled—clean, manly, and fresh, not heavily perfumed like the other men of her acquaintance.

The next two weeks were a whirlwind of excitement and activity. If they were not out during the day riding in a carriage, Bree and Neal joined the other young couples at their favorite pastime, viewing the pageantry as marching bands played accompaniment to the state militia, who drilled every afternoon in the town square, the sound of drums and bugles blaring in their ears. The evenings were a long, continuous party; they were seen everywhere together. And, toward the end of Neal's leave, in the same dark shadows where she had once promised herself to Phillip Alexander, Bree repeated the pledge.

It was the first time she had allowed herself to think of Jemson Tyler. Legally, she was still married to him, but when he had handed over the marriage certificate and walked out of her life all emotional bonds had been severed. She was not prepared to confide the truth of what had happened to her in Colorado to her parents and then face the shame and humiliation of a public divorce. Instead, Bree pushed that part of her life away from conscious thought. She promised to marry Neal when the war ended and tried to convince herself that his need and enduring love would be enough to make both of them happy.

Later, Bree could never really be sure when her dreams had all begun to fall apart. It all happened so fast. Only weeks after he left, Neal was shipped home, after the battle of Pea Ridge, Arkansas, to die of his mortal wounds.

Liam left Crosshaven to join the command of his old friend, General Albert Johnston. Their remains were never brought back from Shiloh, named for a church that stood silent witness to the slaughter.

It was then that Bree retreated permanently to Crosshaven, shunning the balls and parties, the senseless parades. She stayed home, turning a deaf ear to her mother's bitter ravings, keeping a tight rein on her younger brother, Kirk—fearful he would take it into his mind to run off and join the army. Bree sealed off her pain, welcoming the numbness, and turned her energy to overseeing what was left of Crosshaven. Most of the plantation's Negroes were freemen and chose to run for the North or join the Union forces. Those who didn't have their papers Bree insisted her mother free; then they were given the same choices. A handful elected to stay. Crosshaven withered from lack of care. The fruit trees—apple, peach, and lemon—thrived on their own, but the crops—wheat, vegetables, and cotton—diminished quickly. Cattle, sheep, and hogs were taken and slaughtered to feed the Confederate troops. The flour mill and ginning machine fell silent. The oak and long-leaf pine that bordered the road leading to Crosshaven grew wild and unpruned; weeds overtook Crosshaven's famous gardens. Dust gathered over mahogany heirlooms and settled into crystal chandeliers. Wallpaper was stripped off the walls for use as newsprint. Curtains were pulled from the windows, carpets from the floor, to turn into clothing. Half of the main house was closed off and took on a damp, stale smell. It took every ounce of strength just to fend off illness and keep the body going.

Bree was often amazed at how resourceful she had become. Salt was to be found at the floor of the smokehouse, wooden combs were shaped and filed and polished, soap was made from animal fat and ashes, chickory and okra seed were found to be a passable substitute for coffee. Each week Bree sent someone in to Atlanta for the latest war news and each week it was more disheartening. For every battle won, ten were lost. Month after month, the bright hope of victory dimmed. Bree took to hiding money—the small amount they still had—and jewels, for her mother would most surely turn them over to the army and they might someday mean the difference between life and death.

Bree sighed heavily and got to her feet. The moist, cool dirt clung to her gown but she made no effort to brush it away. She was in a hurry. Len would be back from Atlanta soon with the latest report on the advancing Union army. Picking up a small tin of salt she had managed to collect in four hours' time, Bree pushed open the smokehouse door and walked into the bright, afternoon sun. She squinted and rubbed her eyes, thinking briefly how nice it would be to cream the rough skin from her face and hands, to feel clean and safe again.

News of the war was worse than even Bree could have imagined. The Confederate army had been beaten back from Rocky Face Ridge, Snake Creek, and Dalton as the Union forces advanced one hundred thousand strong from Chattanooga. All able-bodied men from the ages of sixteen to sixty were instructed to report to the City Hall in Atlanta. There they would be equipped and armed for local defense. The city's surgeons had been ordered to the front lines. Three thousand wounded poured into Atlanta's poorly supplied hospitals.

At Cassville, the rebels retreated again, then south to Etowah, Allatoona Pass, and, each retreat bringing General Sherman's Union troops closer to Atlanta.

Doireann, Bree's mother, collapsed with the news, her face a tapestry of hatred and despair. Kirk shouted stubbornly that nothing Bree could say would deter him from defending his father's land. He might have left at that moment except for the rain that had begun to batter the house and turn the roads to mush. Bree's assurances that the fighting would lull during the storm was the only reasoning the boy would hear. But how long would the armies be paralyzed, bogged down in a quagmire of mud?

"When the rain stops, I'm leavin'. Don't try to stop me!" Kirk faced her grimly and spoke with the passion of his fourteen years. "Our soldiers are at Lost Mountain near the base of Kenesaw. I'll join them there." He looked so much like her father in that moment that Bree felt the repressed anguish pull at her heart. This, she mused sadly, is how Liam must have looked, so intense and determined, when he made the decision to leave his beloved Ireland. They were people of small stature, made bolder by the scope of their feeling and dedication. Kirk lacked none of his father's gifts. He had the same shock of unruly flame-colored hair, burning green eyes, the quick flush of reddish stain on his cheeks when angered or upset. At all costs, Bree cried silently, this boy will not be sacrificed. Not Kirk, she thought, reaching blindly for him.

"Let him alone, Bree." Doireann rose from her stupor and interjected, eyes bright and shining. "He's a man now and he has a right to protect his family."

"A man?" Bree shrieked uncontrollably. "A man? Kirk is a *boy*, mother, fourteen years old and filled with your hatred and your anger. Does he have to die before you'll see how senseless it all is? You're always remindin' him how Papa died but I wonder just how much truth you've really told him." She watched Kirk's eyes shift from her mother and then back to herself. He was confused, uncertain. "Kirk, do you know why Papa joined the army and went off to Shiloh? The real reason?"

Doireann crossed the room and put her arm around her son's shoulders protectively, encouragingly. "Kirk knows very well why the Confederacy is fighting this war, my dear. He needs no history lesson."

"Papa didn't leave us because he believed in the ideology Mama's been spoon-feedin' you since he died. He fought to protect Crosshaven property, nothin' more. He didn't care a fig for the issues of slavery and state independence. All he ever cared about was Crosshaven. You know he thought slavery was wrong. That's why our Negroes were freemen. Can't you see how useless it is to try and avenge him? You're not goin' to fight for the same things he died to protect." Even as she spoke, Bree could see she had lost. Kirk's young mind was closed, warped by his mother's incessant lecturing. In a last attempt, she stood to block them as they tried to leave the room. "Crosshaven was lost the moment the war started." She lifted her chin and glared at her mother. "The land is dead, Kirk, and we can't ever bring it back. There won't be enough time and money in your lifetime to restore it. All we have is stayin' together, livin' through the war, waitin'." Bree sagged in the face of his scorn and contempt and backed away to let her mother and brother pass. When they had walked by her and started up the stairs, Bree turned her face to the wall helplessly, her fist pounding rhythmically against its drying, parched wood.

It poured rain for five days and, on the sixth, Kirk was noticeably absent from the house. Nothing was said between Bree and her mother, but the triumph in Doireann's eyes made Bree sick to her stomach. The days passed and moved slowly into weeks as the armies of both sides regrouped and prepared for battle. Then it began, the distant, echoing boom of cannon from the fields beneath Lost Mountain. Atlanta, alert to the ominous artillery rattling through the air, rapidly filled with military supplies and personnel ready to serve under General Joseph Johnston. Ten thousand men were quickly drafted into service, drilling daily in the city park, awaiting action.

In late June, the morning dawned warm and clear. Union guns hurled rounds off solid shot and shrapnel into Confederate troops, anxious to take the mountain that stood between them and total victory, the claiming of Atlanta. At noon, Sherman's troops advanced slowly in the blistering sun. Rebel sharpshooters and snipers picked them off easily and Confederate artillery tore through the lines. Still, the Yankees advanced in waves until they were looking down the throats of Johnston's troops. Hand-to-hand combat broke out at the summit of Little Kenesaw. It was a slaughter for both sides. Men fought and died with bowie knifes, rifle butts, and bayonets. Then shells exploding in the meadow set it to flames, the fire spreading quickly up the side of the mountain. The fighting forgotten, Yankee and Reb raced to save whomever they could. A truce was called and those killed were buried in a common grave. The Union army had suffered a terrible loss of life. They retreated to Marietta, and Johnston set up camp eight miles away at Smyrna. The wounded and dying flowed into Atlanta, doubling its population and need for proper food and comforts.

Kirk settled into the underbrush, his face white and sweat-lined with soot. Burying his face in his hands, he wept at the carnage, the blood, the burned bodies he had seen. He looked out over the Peach Tree Valley and thought wistfully of home. His sense of honor was too strong to allow him to desert but, more than anything, he longed to walk away from the fighting and death.

The mood of the rebels was depressed even more when General Johnston was replaced in his command by another, less-liked, general. Sam Hood took the command reluctantly, knowing Atlanta was lost and his doubts were echoed by the men on the line.

Kirk McCarty took his position along the Peach Tree Creek, a wide and muddy tributary five and a half miles from Atlanta. He crouched behind a breastwork and waited. Union troops were advancing across the creek and it was only a matter of time before he and his comrades were ferreted out and killed. He was dizzy with fatigue and hunger, black spots dancing in front of his eyes.

CHAPTER TWENTY-FIVE

"Wake up, boy." Kirk felt himself prodded from sleep by a blunt instrument applied not so lightly to his side. He rubbed his eyes and peered at the figure standing over him. It hadn't all been a terrible nightmare! The man looming over him wore a mud-splattered blue uniform. He was holding a rifle in one hand and a ledger in the other.

"Give me your name, boy. It'll go on a list so's your family will know you're alive and being shipped off to the prison camps."

"Kirk McCarty," Kirk stammered, his face dissolving in fear. He'd heard the horror stories of the prison camps, both Union and Confederate. Some said it was better to die quick and clean on the battlefield rather than rot away slowly in the camps.

"How old are you, Kirk McCarty?" Another man's voice thundered from behind the soldier with the ledger.

"Fourteen."

"And your rank?" The disembodied voice asked.

"I have none, suh. I, I, uh, just joined the fightin' because . . ."

"Well, you'll be treated just like any other Johnny Reb," the soldier with the gun snarled and then turned toward the other man. "Christ, Captain! This is the fifth one I've run across today. This war goes on any longer and them stinking Rebs'll be sending their womenfolk in for the fight!" He looked toward Kirk and spat on the ground beside him. "These little beggars think all they have to do is start crying they're not regular army and we'll send them home with a slap on the wrist. Well, boy," he directed his stony gaze at Kirk, "you got into the thick of it, maybe even killed yourself a few Yankee blues before you got caught, huh?"

"How far are you away from home, son?" the other man, the Captain asked, his voice not nearly as harsh and spiteful as the soldier with the ledger.

"Not far," Kirk answered shortly, suspicious of the officer's intent. Was the Captain speaking softly, even kindly, in an effort to pry information about Confederate movements out of him?

The Captain seemed to sense Kirk's sudden hostility. He nodded briefly to the Sergeant in charge of taking down the prisoner's names and walked on.

In the week that had passed since the battle at Peach Tree Creek, Bree had heard nothing of Kirk's fate. Forty-five thousand Rebels had met the might of one hundred thousand Yankees; the list of casualties was still not completed. Atlanta was occupied by Union forces but Bree had yet to see a blue uniform on Crosshaven property. News of General Sherman's erratic behavior trickled in from neighbors who had been to the city checking on the well-being of loved ones, but there was no news of Kirk.

Bree held back a sob and continued scrubbing the hearth. The homemade soap was harsh and smelled terrible, but she ignored the stench and the red soreness of her hands, throwing all her effort into the work. Still, the thoughts and fears crept through—dark, angry thoughts. She hadn't spoken to her mother since the day Kirk had run away to the fighting. Doireann's obsessive drive for vengeance was responsible if Kirk lay dead in some forgotten trench, and Bree would never forgive her. All the same, though, the agonizing look of guilt on Doireann's face was plain to see as she passed through the crumbling mansion like a phantom. She had taken to her bedroom of late, rarely leaving her bed, disinterested in sharing the meager table Bree set each midday.

Just as Bree was thinking of her, Doireann's scream vibrated through the rooms, a high-pitched wail of fear. Bree was up on her feet and running without a second thought. She took the stairs two at a time and rushed, panting, through her mother's bedroom door. Doireann stood poised at the window, her hand pressed tautly against its glass. Her chest heaved rapidly, changing the scream into a low, monotone keening. Bree approached cautiously, afraid her mother's mind had snapped and not knowing what to expect from her. Looking past Doireann's shoulder and out through the window, Bree saw what it was that had caused such a violent reaction.

Five Union soldiers were riding steadily for the house, the sun to their backs, brass buttons reflecting like pieces of gold. Around the waist of the one officer who rode slightly ahead of the others, Bree could make out an outline of two skinny arms locked tightly. She held her breath, afraid to hope. Then she turned away from the window and lead her mother to her bed, instructing Doireann to stay in her room until Bree returned to her. Doireann allowed herself to be lead like a child.

Hurrying back down the stairs, Bree's heart hammered in her chest. She raced to the front veranda and grabbed hold of a column, chipped and peeling, for support. The riders passed under an overhanging weeping willow. The tree shielded their faces from the sun, allowing her to make out their features as they reined back. Bree's racing heart nearly stopped. Her brother's name froze on her lips.

"Are you Mrs. Alexander?" Jemson tipped his hat and spoke as though he had never seen her before.

Bree nodded slowly, unable to speak, unwilling to take her eyes from the face she had thought she'd never see again.

"Well, ma'am, the Union army doesn't take young boys like this as prisoner," he drawled lightly, reaching around to his back and pulling Kirk unceremoniously from the saddle, dumping him into the dust on the ground.

For the first time, Bree removed her gaze from Jemson's face. She closed her eyes and swayed precariously. Then, lifting the hem of her stained and wrinkled gown with as much dignity as she could manage, Bree descended the steps and bent to help her brother.

"I appreciate your kindness, ah, Captain." Bree spoke strongly, impersonally. "You're quite right, of course. My brother is only fourteen, too young to join the army of the Confederacy, but filled with boyish enthusiasm and mischief. I thank you for returnin' him to his family and I can promise you, you'll have no more trouble with him." Bree's eyes swept the other Union soldiers, including them in her gratitude. They appeared uneasy, anxious to take their leave and, in that instant, she knew Jemson must have overstepped his bounds of authority by bringing Kirk back to his home.

Her heart fluttered rapidly and she longed to touch him, to throw her arms around his neck and kiss the familiar mouth. Instead, she inclined her head graciously toward Jemson and his men, then turned and ushered her tired, dirty brother into the house. She didn't even bother to look back. If Jemson had taken this action on his own, she would be seeing him again. Minutes later, when she heard the sounds of the soldiers' horses leaving the house, Bree gently guided her brother upstairs—all the time thinking of the pale yellow gown she had locked away in the chest at the foot of her bed.

They boiled huge cauldrons of water and filled the tub repeatedly, refusing to leave the room while Kirk bathed two weeks of filth and grime from his body. Doireann couldn't stop touching him, as though the feel of his skin was needed to constantly remind her that his return was not a dream.

"Are you ready to tell us what happened?" Bree leaned forward eagerly in her chair. "Why did that Union Captain bring you home?"

Kirk looked away and blushed, seemingly reluctant.

Then he heaved a great sigh and turned a face toward her that looked older than his years. "It was awful, Bree, just like you said it would be. There was nothin' glorious and brave, just a lot of dyin' and screamin' in the darkness." He paused, his voice haggard, eyes slipping accusingly toward his mother. "We were dug in at Peach Tree Creek, hopin' to hold the Yankees back, keep 'em out of Atlanta. But we hadn't had anything to eat in three days. I don't remember much of what happened. I could hear the sounds of cannon and rifles all around me, gettin' closer and closer." The faint flush crept up his neck again. "Truth is, I must of fainted dead away 'cause I heard all that fire explodin' in my head and when I came to I was layin' on the ground with a lot of others and the Yankees were everywhere, standin' guard. They separated us—the dying in one spot, the wounded in another. Then the doctors looked us over. A bullet must of nicked my head so the doctor put something on it and sent me back with the able-bodied men. That Captain, the one I was riding behind, was in charge of the prisoners. They were makin' a list of names and when he came to me, he seemed kind of surprised when I gave him my name. He asked me where my home was and then went on to the next man." He looked at Bree a little defiantly as he said the word "man," challenging her to take exception. She didn't, merely smiled encouragingly and nodded so he went on. "Then two nights later, a sentry took me to his tent and he started asking a lot of questions. Like, what was the name of my home and where was my father, things like that. Then he gave me some coffee and biscuits and sent me back. But this mornin', they came to get me again and brought me home."

Bree grinned, the first real happiness she had felt in over two years. Rising from the chair, she stroked her brother's tousled head, kissed her mother's cheek, and went to her own room to get out the yellow gown and hang it in her wardrobe until the wrinkles fell out.

• • •

262

The wait was longer than Bree had expected. Three days passed before Jemson came to her. Each morning she got up before anyone else and washed her body and her hair, taking special care with the clothes she wore to work around the plantation. She was determined that he would not catch her looking as pitiful and wretched as he had the day he'd brought Kirk home.

She was working the corn field when a young, red-faced enlisted man rode up to tell her that Captain Tyler requested the honor of calling upon her at her home later that evening. Bree felt the joy swell in her throat. She accepted the Captain's kind invitation demurely and watched as the young man rode back toward camp. Then she let out a cry of happiness and raced toward the house. It wasn't until she had bathed and used a small amount of scent that Bree stopped to realized the effect Jemson's visit might have on the rest of her family. The thought of what she was doing, looking forward to so eagerly, momentarily staggered her. All she could hope for was that Jemson had the good sense to wait until after dark before letting his presence be known.

Both Doireann and Kirk had retired to their rooms and still Jemson had not come. Bree slipped into her yellow gown and brushed her hair until it shone like copper-gold in the moonlight. She tiptoed slowly through the hall and down the stairs, praying the heavy oak door leading from the house wouldn't squeak as she opened it. Waiting on the veranda, Bree was suddenly nervous and tense. Three years had passed and she had successfully thought little of Jemson. Seeing him again had brought back a rush of painful and delightful memories. She trembled with excitement and anticipation. Would it be the same for Jemson?

He stepped out of the shadows and stood like a mountain before her. He had come up so quietly that it startled Bree, and she opened her mouth to scream. Jemson moved abruptly, clamping his powerful hand over her mouth. The pressure wasn't meant to hurt her but when Bree looked up into his face, she felt a stab of pain ripple through her

263

body. The features were familiar, strong and angular, but the eyes—sharp blue and enticing—had a cold glint of steel about them. His full mouth seemed harder, somehow.

When he saw she recognized who it was stepping out of the darkness, Jemson released Bree immediately, as though he was loath to prolong physical contact. Stepping back, his eyes raked her mercilessly.

"You're more beautiful than I remembered," he observed passively, reluctantly. "Somehow, it doesn't surprise me to find you untouched by the miseries of this war. You always did have a talent for making the best of a bad situation."

The soft smile turned sour on Bree's mouth and her twinkling green eyes glazed over with rage. Why did he seek her out if only to humiliate and insult her?

"I manage quite well, thank you," she lied smoothly. "Of course, I have friends, many friends, who help out from time to time." She laughed coyly and lifted a dainty hand to pluck a wayward curl from her face.

"Tell me something, Bree," Jemson demanded harshly. "Do these men friends of yours know you're a married woman?"

"Married? Me?" She raised her brows innocently. "Why, I'm a grievin' widow, Captain Tyler, everyone knows that."

"I'm not talking about Phillip, goddammit!" Jemson exploded and grabbed Bree's arm, pulling her to him. "You're married to me. You're *my* wife."

"What a ridiculous charge, Captain. Can you prove it?"

"That's what I thought," Jemson muttered disgustedly and shook her away. "How long did you wait before destroying that marriage paper I gave you in Colorado?"

Bree raised her head and glared defiantly, a small, taunting smile playing across her mouth. "Why, Jemson, I could still hear your footsteps on the porch when I threw that paper into the fire. What did you expect? Did you think I'd keep it to my heart and come back to Georgia just pinin' away for my Yankee lover?"

"No. I expect you did anything you had to do to survive. That's why I'm here."

"What do you mean?" Bree whispered slowly, suspiciously.

"Well, your friends aren't in a position to protect you now. They're all prisoners of the Union occupation and we're going to be here for a while."

"Are you offerin' me *your* protection?" Bree was stunned. Did he really think so little of her? How could he have forgotten the times of passion and tenderness that had passed between them? Her heart turned to stone, aching with despair and disappointment. "All right, Captain, we bargain. You're in a position to offer me decent food and clothing, protection against Crosshaven bein' looted, and other comforts an occupied city would be hard put to supply. I, on the other hand, can give you only one thing. But then, you did say that was why you came here, didn't you?" She reached out and took Jemson's hand with her fingertips, grateful that the moonlight softened their redness and chafing. "There's a couch in my father's study. It's a little dusty but, in these times, we have to make do. It's on the first floor, so there's little chance of wakin' my family. You just follow me and walk softly."

The study was dark and musty and smelled like the family crypts Bree had visited in New Orleans. There was no kerosene in the gaslights because it was too precious to let sit in rooms that were no longer occupied. Bree watched as Jemson walked to the double French doors leading off to the veranda. When he parted the heavy drapes to allow the moonlight to stream in and lighten the room, dust lifted and floated through the beams. Then he turned, silent, without preamble and began to remove his jacket. His eyes never left her face. There was a trace of cruel enjoyment at her discomfort on his lips. Raising a quizzical, challenging eye, Jemson paused. Bree swallowed deeply and took the cue. She reached up with her hands and began to unfasten the buttons at the back of her dress. She was in misery, had never felt so unclean. Her eyes begged for pity, some sign from Jemson that the charade would soon end and they would start again. He gave her none.

His kiss was harsh and demanding, his mouth raping her tongue and moving hotly down her neck and shoulders. He lifted her in his arms and pressed her tightly to his chest, crushing the breath out of Bree's throat. Carrying her to the brocade-covered sofa she had once sat on listening to the low, droning voice of her father, Jemson laid her back upon it and entered her quickly, brutally. She was dry, unready for the maniac thrusts. Shame rippled in waves through her body. Pain burst like fireworks in her groin.

With strength she hadn't known she possessed, Bree pushed at Jemson's chest with her hands and forearms. Her fist doubled up and she rammed it into his neck, not hard enough to really hurt him but with enough power to shock him from movement.

"If this is all you wanted," she gasped uncontrollably, "get out of here and try Decatur Street in Atlanta. The whores started linin' the streets when they heard our armies had been defeated. But *I'm* not defeated, Jemson. You haven't conquered *me*!"

He was poised over her while she spoke, still and unmoving. His eyes closed slowly and a shudder erupted from his throat. Gently, so as not to hurt her any more, Jemson withdrew himself from between Bree's cramped legs. His arms slipped around her and he pulled her close, breathing in the fresh, clean scent of her hair and the light jasmine perfume.

"I don't want this," he whispered, musing almost to himself. She had brought him to his senses, stopped him from doing something he would have looked back on in shame. "I wanted everything from you. Every part, every thought, but not like this." Fingers tangled in her hair, Jemson bent to kiss the soft pulse at Bree's forehead and then dropped his arms and began to move away from the sofa.

Bree's hand shot out with a will of its own and caught him. She pulled him back and wrapped her arms around

266

his neck, her lips moving lightly over the spot she had bruised. "Don't go." She murmured so breathlessly he barely heard her. "Stay here with me, at least for this one night. We'll hold each other and be good to each other. I don't want the clothes or the food or even the protection. Just stay with me tonight and make love to me. Help me, Jemson. Help me forget!"

CHAPTER TWENTY-SIX

"Ah nearly died of shame!" Doireann McCarty stormed, pacing the foyer angrily, her pale blue eyes clouded with rage. Tearing off her bonnet, she threw it to the floor. The wheat-colored hair she still insisted upon torturing into tight curls bobbed frantically as she shook her head. "Bryna, what were you thinkin' of, behavin' in such a shameless manner? It was bad enough when you allowed that Yankee into our home, into your bed. But to publically display yourself, it's unforgivable." Doireann moaned, flushed, fat tears squeezing out the corners of each eye. "Mah daughter, paradin' through town like a brazen hussy. Ah cain't show mah face in public."

"I see, Mama. It's perfectly all right for me to carry on with a Yankee as long as I'm discreet," Bree observed drily. "My sin isn't in beddin' Jemson Tyler, it's in gettin' caught."

"Don't you get uppity with me, Missy." Doireann shook her fist dangerously close to Bree's face. "I told your father sendin' you to New York for schoolin' was a mistake, but, oh no, he wouldn't listen! You came back here with your high-tone ideas, thinkin' you're bettah than us, thinkin' you can have everythin' your own way."

"Mama, please, this isn't doing either of us any good." Bree raised her hand to her face and sighed heavily.

"Do you know what our friends are callin' you on the streets for all the town to hear? The Captain's whore, that's what!"

"I'm not Jemson Tyler's whore, Mama, no matter what your so-called friends might think." Bree stiffened in the face of her mother's accusation, bristling with indignation. "I'm his . . ."

"Ah *know* what you are!" Doireann interrupted, her delicate face twisted with sudden, violent hatred. "You're a harlot. A hussy who wasn't satisfied with drivin' her own sweet husband outta this house and into the wilderness, where he died. A whore, heapin' disgrace on her dead father's name and pushin' her mother into an early grave." Doireann turned on her heel and started for the staircase. She paused, looking back at Bree and fixing her with a cold, heartless stare. "Ah can also tell you what you're not, Missy. You're not mah daughter, not any more. I cain't evah hope to live down the shame you've brought on me but, until you end this scandalous affair, you're not mah daughter. Until you come to me on your knees and tell me you're no longer the Captain's whore, I'll keep to mah rooms. Until that time, Bryna, Ah don't want to see you or hear you. Am Ah makin' myself clear?"

Bree nodded helplessly, knowing it was useless to argue with Doireann when she had managed to work herself into one of her legendary rages. She remembered the months of stony silence that had followed just such bouts between Doireann and Liam. Her father had finally had to humble himself, beg forgiveness for some minor infraction, in order to restore peace to the house.

How quickly Doireann forgot the boxes of food and clothing that came with each of Jemson's visits. She hadn't been too outraged to wear the dresses and devour the meals the food provided until busybody friends had put a filthy name to her daughter's personal life.

The only thing that prevented Bree from charging up the stairs after her mother, grabbing her by the shoulders and shouting hypocrite into her hard, unyielding face was the sight of Kirk standing further up on the stairs as Doireann brushed by. He had hard the whole ugly name-calling

269

tantrum and his eyes were glazed with confusion. And behind that—what?—some glimmer of understanding.

Kirk, unlike his mother, tried to take the realities of his sister's affair with the flexibility of youth. But it was like learning a difficult game. You had to understand the rules first. The way Bree played was easy. She gave and received in kind. But Doireann made up the rules as she went along. It was all right to accept the Captain's generosity, the food, the money and clothing. It was acceptable to turn your eyes when he entered the house and went with Bree into the privacy of her bedroom but it was not good manners to ride in an open carriage or go off to a party with him.

It was true enough—Jemson Tyler was an enemy officer, a member of the occupation army, a blight on the South. But, now this was the confusing part, he was also the man who had saved Kirk from the prison camps and sent the other boys home on the same day. He was the man who took Kirk riding several times a week and taught him how to load and fire a hand gun with precision, the man who hunted and moved through the woods with the grace and ease of an animal. And, too, he made Bree happy. She had never been more content and beautiful. He tried to make their lives easier, without expecting sniveling gratitude and fawning attention. All he really seemed to want from them was the pleasure of Bree's company. He was the enemy, but he had won Kirk's grudging respect and admiration.

As with Doireann, the price was high. His childhood friends were unceasingly cruel with their comments. He'd had to sneak into the house to nurse a bloody nose more than once. But Kirk was more able to shrug off the dirty talk and innuendos. No one had time any more for the childish games. The carefree times he had spent passing his days in the pursuit of frogs at the edge of the swamp were gone. It was a consuming struggle just to keep the crops alive and food in their mouths. The Captain's generosity helped, but it wasn't enough to feed them all. No, his friends were no longer his friends but he didn't have time for them anyway.

Mama's problem was different, Kirk thought as he watched Bree regain her composure. From his vantage point at the top of the stairs, she looked very small and doll-like. Mama really shouldn't have been so hard on her. It was clear to Kirk that Bree loved her Captain. And, anyway, he thought, cringing at the disloyal thought, if Mama spent as much time helping out as Bree in the management of Crosshaven, she wouldn't have to worry about what her friends thought. She'd be too busy to go visiting and gossiping, as though there weren't a war on and men weren't getting killed.

Bree stooped to pick up her mother's bonnet and hang it up on the hall tree. Her eyes met with Kirk's once more and they smiled gently at each other. Then she turned and opened the front door. Watching her walk out onto the veranda, Kirk promised himself to speak to his mother and try to get her to be a little more understanding, a bit more tolerant. He wondered briefly what kind of a mood he would find her in when he knocked on her bedroom door, and then decided it didn't matter because, bad temper or no, they were going to have a talk.

Once out on the porch, Bree felt the cold breeze of dusk touch her shoulders. She wished she had thought to take a shawl on her way out. Debating on whether or not to go back in the house, Bree realized she would rather brave the chill. The feeling had been growing of late, a distaste for the confinement and the sense of decay about the house.

That overpowering feeling was almost surely the reason she had allowed Jemson to lure her from the privacy they shared when confined inside the halls of Crosshaven. Lure? That word wasn't really fair. Telling herself she couldn't deny Jemson his smallest whim, Bree had stepped into the carriage that morning, but the truth was she had wanted out. Out of the responsibility, out of the stench of things that had been left to rot, away from the death and destruction that hovered over her homeland like an ominous cloud of doom.

Stepping into that open carriage was like throwing off shackles. It wasn't until they had ridden around the countryside in full view of friends and neighbors and Bree had seen the curious faces etched with hatred and sense of betrayal that she realized the full import of the blunder. She did not share the common beliefs in the South but, still, she was a Southern woman consorting with an enemy officer, a traitor. She was, in their eyes, a whore.

The sound of Jemson's carriage approaching snapped Bree from her reverie. It was just as well. This line of thought always brought Bree to ask herself a question she had no answer for. Had Jemson temped her deliberately? Had he known better than she how much the carriage ride would cost her? Had he wanted to brand and humiliate her? Did he hate her that much? Certainly, he no longer loved her as he once had. Jemson was kind, kinder than Bree knew she had a right to expect, but kind at a strange, held-back distance. He'd never been a man to shower a woman with flowery prose and sugary phrases of undying love and devotion, but this new Jemson was even more reticent than the Jemson she had known and loved in Colorado.

"You don't look much like a woman going to a fancy party with her beau, darlin'," Jemson called from the carriage before stepping down. His uniform was brushed, the buttons polished, his boots glistening.

"Good evenin', Captain." Bree gestured solemnly.

"Evening, ma'am."

"Now, what's all this about a party?" Bree smiled as she came down the porch stairs toward Jemson.

In place of an answer, Jemson gathered her into his arms. Bree clung to him, eager to kiss away the sadness. Their lips were chilled by the cool night air but quickly warmed under their tender mutual assault. Jemson pulled away first.

"Whoa! Enough of that, madam. I have to keep a clear head about me tonight. My presence has been requested—that's a polite way of saying I'm ordered—at the Carlyle Hotel this evening to celebrate the continued aging process of one of my senior officers, a Colonel Lembert." Jemson laughed, teasing Bree. "I invited a dozen other ladies but they all turned me down so I thought I'd take a chance you had no other plans for the evening."

"Well, you can just turn that carriage around, Captain, because I'm turnin' you down too!" Bree retorted bitterly. "I've been on display quite enough, thank you."

"Just what is *that* supposed to mean?"

"It means, Jemson Tyler, that I'm not content to go snivelin' after you in public while you flaunt me as your own genuine, personal Southern hothouse whore!" Bree stomped her foot angrily, eliciting only a chuckle from Jemson. "Don't you dare laugh at me! The whole country's callin' me a whore, the Captain's whore!"

The twinkle drained out of Jemson's eyes immediately, replaced by cold, hard anger. He grasped Bree's shoulders and pulled her toward him, bending at the waist so he could look her straight in the eye.

"Forgive me, darlin'. I had hoped you'd never hear that kind of talk but, as long as you have, I guess we better discuss it."

"Let me go! What do you care?" Bree struggled to get away.

"Don't be a child, Bree. Come on, darlin', just sit down here on the porch with me."

Bree shrugged petulantly but allowed herself to be seated beside Jemson on the wooden rung of the porch step. Still angry, she stiffened when Jemson put the arm of his cloak over her shoulders. She was so miserable, so caught up in the harshness of her mother's accusations and the anguish of her own uncertainties that tears stung behind her eyelids.

"Listen to me, darlin'," Jemson said slowly, as if to clarify his actions in his own mind too. "I never meant to cause you pain or see your name dragged through the mud.

But I got so sick and tired of lurking around in the dark just to see you, be with you. I felt like the house was closing in on us, trapping us, as though what we were doing was something to be hidden from the light of day. And it isn't. I didn't feel that way. I'm proud of you, Bree, proud you're with me. At the time, it seemed like hiding in the shadows wasn't the honorable thing to do.''

"You were right, Jem," Bree whispered fiercely, burying her face in the warmth of Jemson's chest. "I'm overreactin', takin' it out on you because my mother lit into me when she got back from town today. The situation's a poor one, at best, but I reckon I'd feel a lot worse if you settled for sneakin' in and out of the house." Bree leaned up and kissed the tip of Jemson's chin. "Now, you did mention somethin' about a party, didn't you? Well, you can come up with me and help me scrub some of this dirt off my back but, mind you, no rovin' hands or we'll never make it to Atlanta in time for a grand entrance.''

All around her there was the sound of laughter, the deep, resonant chuckle of men and the tinkling bell-like quality of the woman. For a few hours, it was as though the war had been locked outside the doors of the Carlyle Hotel. Bree noted, with no small amount of relief and satisfaction, that she was not the minority of one she had feared herself to be. At least a dozen other genteel Southern ladies clung warmly to the arms of their Yankee lovers. Each had a slightly haunted, brittle look for the other. They were a ladies' club of traitors, some caring more than others. Glad to be alive and happy and ashamed of it, too. Basking in the warm glow of Union victory, clawing to escape the total devastation that surrounded them every day.

What will become of us, Bree mused wearily, looking across the room to catch Jemson's eye, pleading that he return to her side at once and rescue her from the boring chatter of the Major from Indiana. He was a rather portly man who smoked the fattest cigars Bree had ever seen, hacking and coughing absent-mindedly after each puff.

Jemson extricated himself from the company of officers and wandered nonchalantly in Bree's direction, nodding here, smiling there. In what seemed to take far too long a time for Bree's tastes, Jemson finally arrived, nodding smartly to the Major and taking her arm to lead her in a leisurely stroll around the room.

"You're looking particularly beautiful tonight, darlin'," Jemson told her gallantly.

"Well now, I have you to thank for that, don't I, Captain?" Bree grinned wickedly, batting her eyes shamelessly.

Jemson almost choked, grimacing when reminded of how much Bree's finery had cost him in cold, hard Yankee dollars. The gown, a little fluff of imported white lace, had set him back three hundred dollars, the satin shoes another hundred. Damn occupation inflation! Still, he was a rich man, and would be richer still when the war was over and he could return to Colorado and join Matthew. And he could think of no better object to adorn than the woman who walked sedately by his side, drawing glances of admiration from the men and sidelong looks of envy from the other women. The other women. Jemson hated the idea that Bree was lumped into their category. Not one of them had the grace and beauty she wore like a mantle from head to toe. Not one of them had the courage and strength to hold their heads high in the face of adversity and scorn, not like his Bree. Despite the anger and hostility he had felt toward her when they'd first started up again, Jemson staunchly refused to sully her name by discussing her with his fellow officers. Most of the women gathered in the room tonight were shopgirls, the daughters of plantation overseers. None of them retained the air of mystery that made Jemson's heart thump with pride. Regardless of what her Southern neighbors said about her, Bree was a lady, an aristocrat in the finest tradition. Her small hand was, at that moment, resting lightly on his arm as he guided her steps. Jemson tried hard not to think of the men who had come after him, after Bree had left

Colorado and returned home, although the images had cost him several sleepless nights. Not wanting to hear it and yet strangely driven to know, Jemson had tried, earlier on, to gather as much information as he could. Sly, seemingly meaningless questions just popped out of his mouth with a will of their own and Bree, never rising to the bait, coyly brushed his questions aside with a wave of her hand or an arched eyebrow. She was evasive, tantalizing, changing her stories from one day to the next. Yes, she had gentlemen friends helping her. No, did Crosshaven appear to be that prosperous? Yes, she had a very gay time after leaving Colorado. No, the young men had been called to action almost as soon as she had returned home; there had been no time for gala balls and long walks in the moonlight.

Jemson's head hurt with the pressure of never knowing if she was sincere or playing one of the games he had come to expect of her. She was elusive, impossible to pin down. It made her at once exciting and exasperating. He supposed, grimly, it was the reason he came back, again and again, for more.

"Are you going to answer me or just walk around with your head swimmin' in the clouds?" Bree inquired teasingly, tapping Jemson on the arm with the flat of her fan. "I said, how soon can we get out here? I feel like I'm fallin' asleep on my feet. There are those of us, you know, who have to work to keep body and soul together. Those of us who are not as fortunate as some I'll not mention, them bein' the ones who spend the day leanin' over a desk plannin' battle moves and shoutin' out important orders and the like."

"God, woman, how you do go on." Jemson chuckled, shaking his head in disbelief. Five hours ago, Bree was desolate, stinging with the shame of being called the Captain's whore. Now, there she stood, her head cocked to one side, a jaunty smile lighting up her face, suggesting she had more in mind that just sleeping. It was a look Jemson recognized, one that sent his blood pulsing. "Now, darlin'. We're leaving now!"

CHAPTER TWENTY-SEVEN

"What do your superiors really think about you consortin' with the enemy, Jem?" Bree asked him casually one night several months later. She lay on the bed in her room at Crosshaven toying with the delicate lace of a shocking red chemise Jemson had just given her.

"They think I'm an incredibly lucky man," he answered lazily, reaching out to pull her back on the pillow next to him. "Why do you ask at this late date?"

"Just curious, I suppose. I know there's an official mandate sayin' you're not to give aid and comfort to us poor, dangerous women but, everywhere we go, the men are knee deep in Southern hospitality and the Union army doesn't do a thing about it. I was just wonderin' if maybe General Sherman has a lady friend hidden away somewhere and that's why he goes so easy on the rest of you."

"Sherman doesn't have any friends, lady or otherwise," Jemson snorted, verging on anger. "If the army had to see to it that each and every one of Sherman's regulations were observed, there wouldn't be enough men out of the stockade to . . ." He paused, alert to the sound outside the door and then relaxed. It was Doireann. She passed loudly by the door every time he was there, letting them know, without words, that she knew they were in the room, knew what they were doing and damned them to eternal hell for the impropriety. If Bree was unhappy about the estrangement she suffered from her mother, she said nothing about it. Jemson knew she hadn't seen or spoken to her mother in months, that Doireann was waited on, hand and foot, and never left her rooms except for this habitual display of defiance. The footsteps faded as Doireann gave up the pace and returned to slam the door of her bedroom behind her. Snickering like a guilty child, Jemson realized they had both been holding their breath until she passed by and the marching stopped. In another moment, the intrusion was entirely forgotten.

"What would you like to do tonight?" Jemson murmured idly, opening Bree's bodice to playfully kiss the pale pink nipples of her breasts. "You have a choice, darlin'. The night is still young and we can either go to a rather boring party one of the junior officers is hosting or we can attend an equally boring play put together by a troop of ragged Shakesperean actors. What's it to be?"

"Ah, love, I have another choice, don't I?" Bree sighed contentedly, nudging herself closer to Jemson's exploring mouth. "It's really much too cold to be ridin' about in a carriage."

"Cold? Woman, have you gone soft on me. Cold? Perhaps you don't remember the winter nights in Colorado?" Jemson raised his head, feigning shock and disbelief.

"I remember *everything* about Colorado." Bree shrugged uneasily and got up off the bed, closing the bodice of her chemise as she walked toward the mist-covered window. "But I'm surprised you'd be fool enough to bring up the subject when you were gettin' ready to seduce me."

"Uh-oh, I think I hear a note of anger in the lady's tone." Jemson raised himself on his elbow and watched as Bree paced nervously back and forth in front of the window. "But this talk we're obviously going to have promises to be more interesting than the activities *I* mentioned and you seem to have plunged out of the mood for what *you* mentioned so, all right, I'll ask. Why am I being a fool to talk about about Colorado?" He sighed dramatically and waited for her answer, still not fully aware that he had struck a chord, a memory that had turned Bree away from him.

"I suppose you remember draggin' me up to that drafty, snow-bound cabin of yours? And how we fought and then I hurt myself and you went into Central City? And how I learned to cook and clean for you and how we found a way to live together to pass the winter peacefully? Knowin' you for the randy bull you are, I suppose you remember best the amount of time we spent in that big, old bed you built." Bree gritted her teeth when Jemson nodded his agreement happily, blissfully blind to the wound that had been festering inside of Bree, the unspoken questions that were exploding to the surface. "Do you also remember the way you looked at me on the trail that day you came home and found me with Robb Andrews?" There! It was out and she gasped as the bitterness spewed from her mouth. Jemson was no longer smiling. He had a stunned look on his face, and then a dark cloud passed over his eyes, his face flushed with an anger of his own. "Did you really think I was leavin' with Robb because I chose to? Did you really think me so great a cheat, so fine an actress, that I could pretend for months to be happy with you and then skip off with the first man who came along? Why were you so prepared to think that small of me?" Once she started, Bree couldn't control the anguish she felt. Shaking, she advanced toward Jemson, her fists tightened into tiny balls as if to thrash the answers from him if he refused to give her the satisfaction of an answer. "What did I ever do to deserve such scorn?"

"Does that matter now?" Jemson hedged, choosing not to fan Bree's rage with accusations of his own.

"Yes, damn you!" Bree leaned forward challengingly. "On the trail that day you looked at me as though I were the foulest thing you'd ever seen, believin' the worst. You wouldn't even give me a chance to explain. Your mind was set like a rock against me. You left me and went away. Two long years pass, and when you stroll back into my life, you treat me like somethin' cheap. Don't ever think I've forgotten that first night in Papa's study. Oh, you're gentle enough, concerned about the well-bein' of my family, buyin' me pretty clothes and bringin' gifts every time you come to visit. But what does that make me in your eyes? What kind of a woman do you hold me to be?''

Jemson scowled, as though weighing his words carefully. There was a time when he had been sure that all he wanted was Bree—good, bad or indifferent—he wanted Bree. He'd tried a hundred ways to win her, to please her, and just when he thought the prize was his, she'd managed to thwart him, to escape him. Now, he wasn't as sure that the anguish loving such a volatile woman brought him wasn't worse than being without her. He wanted to be truthful, but he still wasn't certain what that truth was and, in her present frame of mind, she was as explosive as a case of dynamite. ''Let's just say I believe you play the odds very well.''

''Now just what is *that* supposed to mean?''

''It means, my darling, that I don't believe you sent for Robb, but I know you wanted to get away from me and he was handy so you took him up on the offer.'' He frowned again, wanting desperately to change the subject before the discussion escalated into a battle.

''And you *didn't* take advantage, I suppose.'' Bree's face flamed with deep-rooted anger. ''You wanted me to warm your bed and cook and clean but, at the first test of faith, you lit out like a jack rabbit!'' Hands on hips, she crossed over the bed and stood over Jemson's reclining body. She glowered, waiting for a retort.

''Well, honey, you sure didn't give me much to go on in the way of faith, now did you?'' Jemson raised up on his elbow, his own anger beginning to flare. ''As I recall it, lady, it was *you* hired me on as a surrogate husband; I didn't search you out. Then we danced around each other for weeks—you batting those big eyes and me stomping around like a rutting bull—and when we finally did get together, it was you again acted like it was nothing more than a handshake. Do I have to remind you who it was high-tailed her shapely little fanny off to Black Hawk

Point, leaving me behind with my tongue-hanging out?''
He got up off the bed and stood in front of Bree, putting
an end to her incessant pacing. He wanted to hold her but
her rigid stance put an end to that idea.

"I should have gone with you then." Bree hung her
head and whispered.

"What did you just say?" Incredulous, Jemson used his
fingers to tip her face upward. "What was that you just
said?"

Bree snapped her head away petulantly. "I *said*, I wished
I had never gone to Black Hawk Point. I wanted to stay
with you then but I was stupid and afraid. There! See,
that's what I mean!" She pointed an accusing finger at
Jemson. "It's written all over your face! You don't know
whether or not to believe me, do you?" Bree circled him,
cocky and defiant. "Well, I'll tell you somethin' else
that'll really start you wonderin'! I loved you then, I ached
for you. When you came to take me up the mountain with
you that winter, I screamed and complained but, in my
heart it was what I wanted. I loved you then, too. I never
had any intention of leavin' you, ever. And, I love you
now, more than before. Now, am I tellin' you all this
because I want a new dress or some more supplies? Do I
want you to believe I love you because I've heard the
rumors that Sherman plans to burn and loot his way out of
Atlanta when you move on south and I'm makin' a last
ditch effort to save Crosshaven? Tell me, Jemson, do you
think I'm tellin' the truth?"

Unexpectedly, he laughed and drew her into the circle
of his arms, stroking her like a cat to soothe her squirming
body. "Sweetheart, to tell *you* the truth, I don't give a
damn if you're lying or not." His mouth came down
gently and brushed teasingly along her cheek, then sought
and claimed her soft lips with exquisite delicacy. She
moaned urgently and pressed closer as he caught her knees
and lifted her body, carrying her toward the bed.

"Will you be comin' back tomorrow night?" Bree yawned

sleepily. They were lying spoon fashion, and she rubbed enticingly against him, inviting his response.

"No, honey, I can't. We've got a staff meeting and they tend to stretch into long hours." Jemson ran his hand down the length of Bree's leg and then pushed himself out of bed and began to dress. "I'll come the night after next. Is there anything I can bring you?"

Just yourself, Bree wanted to say but she refrained. Although their lovemaking had been tender and sweet, Jemson had made no effort to declare his own feelings. And, without the words, Bree was reluctant to press the issue. Perhaps the aloofness he showed her was not merely a facade behind which he hide his emotions. It *was* possible he had ceased to love her. Even as the thoughts formulated in her head, Bree knew it wasn't so. The man might not completely trust her, he might even try to tell himself different, but Bree was certain he loved and needed her. It was just a matter of getting him to face it.

"No, there's nothing particular I want." Bree shrugged casually and flopped over on her stomach. Her head turned as she heard Jemson moving around in the darkness searching for the door. "I'll be waitin', darlin'."

As it turned out, Bree waited four days without sight or word from Jemson. She was nearly frantic with worry, sure that he had been wounded—even killed—by sniper fire. Just when she had decided that the only course of action open to her was marching boldly into Union headquarters, the same smooth-faced soldier who had heralded Jemson's first visit returned with a note from him. Bree hurried into the house and up the stairs, seeking the sanctuary of her bedroom before ripping open the folded letter. It was short and painfully, hopelessly, to the point and obviously written in haste.

We leave in three days' time for parts south. A list has been compiled of homes and industries to be set afire. Crosshaven is on the list. Save what you can and use the enclosed monies to stay you until the war ends. What God has joined together.

JT

The money, two hundred dollars drawn on a bank in Denver, fell to the floor unheeded. Bree read the note several times, stopping again and again at the last line. What new riddle was this? What message was he trying to convey without actually putting words to it?

It wasn't until hours later that the scope of what was about to happen sunk in. Crosshaven had been selected as one of the homes to be put to the torch. She was puzzled at the lack of passionate resistence she felt. Crosshaven was her childhood home. Shouldn't she feel a greater sense of loss?

Remembering with a clarity borne out of sorrow, Bree now knew she had mourned the leaving of that small, one-room cabin in Colorado more than she would miss Crosshaven. She finally realized that a home was more than wood and glass, rugs on the floors and curtains hanging in the windows. It was the memories tied up in a house that measured its importance.

Doireann would likely be devastated when she learned Crosshaven was to be reduced to ash; she had spent most of her adult life inside its boundries, loved her husband and borne his children within its walls.

But the best moments of Bree's life had been spent in the cabin in Colorado. Her happiness was tied to that place, not this one. When she thought of all the months she had yearned for Crosshaven, seeing it as some kind of mystical oasis rising, beckoning, out of a desert of loneliness and fear, Bree could have cried for all that wasted time.

But she wasn't going to spend time lamenting what might have happened or what she could have had. There were too many things to attend to. First, her mother would have to see her long enough to be given the news and they would go on from there.

When the troops came, they rode in single file, heavily armed to prevent resistance. Many of them, carrying unlit torches, were only a few years older than Kirk. They kept their eyes averted as though ashamed of what they were about to do, but when the time came they followed orders and Crosshaven ignited in a ball of flame that exploded in the foyer and danced merrily up the solid oak staircase. Even in the courtyard below, Bree could hear the sound of bursting glass when the heat rolled over the chandelier her father had imported from Europe. When the soldiers were satisfied that there was no possible way to save the house, they mounted and continued on their way.

To her credit, Doireann remained straight-backed and dry-eyed. Tears would come later when the enemy was denied the sight of them. A wagon, hidden behind the slave quarters, which the soldiers had left untouched, contained all the worldly possessions Bree had thought of saving. Their food supplies were stored inside the tiny, unoccupied cabins.

All through the day Crosshaven burned, the air thick with black smoke. By nightfall, the house Bree's father had built for the future generations of his family was nothing more than glowing embers.

"Mama." Bree bent anxiously over her mother's crouched figure. "You must take some nourishment. Kirk, make Mama drink this broth."

"You . . . you brought this on us." Doireann's eyes blazed accusingly as she spoke for the first time that day. "Playing whore to that Union Captain, that's why we were burned out."

Bree stiffened and handed the cup to Kirk. She grabbed her mother by both shoulders and forced her to meet her stare. "Once and for all, Mama, understand this! I'm not Jemson Tyler's whore. I'm his wife. It's too complicated to go into now, but we were married after Phillip died. I'm Jemson's wife, Mama, and if there's any way to find him again after the war is over, I'll do it."

"I'd rather see you dead then married to the Yankee bastard."

"I'd rather *be* dead than never see him again."

Doireann shook herself free of Bree's grip. "You've

brought shame to your father's name, Bryna. I thank God he's dead and can't be witness to your sins." Refusing to offer even the smallest shred of understanding, Doireann lifted her head disdainfully. "From the moment you took that Yankee to your bed, I had no daughter." With that she turned and walked away. Defeated, Bree watched her go, but Kirk loped off after her, having appointed himself as chief peacemaker between the two women. Shaking her head sadly, Bree knew it was a hopeless task.

Were the positions reversed, Bree might have reacted in the same manner. Had she a daughter who chipped away and tore down all that Jemson had spent his life's blood to build, Bree might have turned cold against her and disavowed her existence.

No, her heart cried, never. Three years ago, she might have been capable of such an act but she was not the same woman who had left the spoiled and pampered society of Crosshaven. She remembered the protected, useless hothouse flower she had once been and now thought her silly and petty. They were strangers to each other.

Bree slumped to the floor of the dank little cabin and heaved a sigh of relief, happy amid all the devastation, knowing that no matter what happened she would survive. Jemson had been right about her. She was a scratcher, a fighter. She would survive.

"Mama's stayin' in Lucy's old cabin," Kirk announced glumly when he returned. "She says she doesn't want to see either of us again. You, because of what you did and me, because I won't take her side."

"You don't hate me then?"

"Nah. I don't see as you did anything all that terrible." Kirk shifted uncomfortably, all angles and bones. "I kinda liked Captain Tyler, some of the other Yanks, too. I don't guess the enemy is only evil men."

Bree laughed at how clearly his fourteen-year-old eyes saw the simplicity of hatred and prejudice. She patted the dirt beside her and beckoned him join her. "When the war is over, brother, I don't see how I can stay here. It's best I leave first chance. So I'm goin' back to Colorado, the best way I can. If you want, you can come with me." She smiled, eyes shining. "There's lots of room to grow in Colorado, Kirk; I think you'd like the freedom there. Men start out the same and live by their wits and their strength."

"Seems I'd likely favor that, Bree. Thanks, I'll think on it."

Bree fell silent, pondering what her next actions would be. So Doireann had exiled herself from the both of them. It was a pity; she had turned her back on two exceptional human beings. But Bree wasn't going to dwell on her mother's choices, only on her own.

Their first priority was food. Shelter had been taken care of, but without adequate nourishment, there was too great a chance they might fall ill, too weak to make the journey away from Crosshaven's abyss of destruction and despair. The paper money Jemson had left her was virtually useless at this point. It was to be saved and used on the journey to Colorado, during which they would travel through states more partial to Yankee currency. The territory of Colorado had, in fact, after much debate opted to follow the North.

Instructing Kirk to go out behind the cabin and bring in her trunk, Bree waited for him to return and then opened it, pulling out the fading yellow gown she had saved to wear for Jemson. Tearing at the tightly sewn hem with her teeth, Bree grinned impishly as four small pieces of jewelry twinkled and fell into her lap.

"Here, take these." She held out her hand to Kirk. "There's still confusion enough to where you might be able to bargain for flour and sugar, maybe even a milk cow. I don't dare show my face, but I think you can without worry of harm. Jemson said he didn't think the war could last much longer than another six months and we'll need provisions for at least that long. You think you can do it?"

"Sure." Kirk shrugged cockily. "I may be gone a few days, so don't begin to worry." He scooped the jewels out of Bree's hand and turned to leave. Then he whipped around again and bent impulsively to plant a noisy kiss on her cheek.

When he was gone, Bree leaned back and hugged herself confidently. She wasn't able to spend too much time congratulating herself, however. There were still too many things to attend to. Venturing out in the waning light, she steered clear of Lucy's cabin but foraged in all the others for abandoned washtubs, cooking pans and utensils, even firewood. It was hours before her last trip was made. She fell exhausted into a pile of ragged clothes and slept.

Two days later, Kirk returned leading a scrawny cow behind him. Bree shrieked with delight and immediately set it to pasture. Kirk had proved quite the fancy talker. The sacks Bree pulled off the cow before setting her out to feed were filled with all the essentials they would need to sustain life. And he was still able to return one small emerald-encrusted ring. Bree gasped when she saw it and remembered where it had come from. A birthday present from her father. Without that reminder, the day might have slipped away and she wouldn't have heralded its passing. November 19, 1864. It was her twenty-sixth birthday. And, without knowing it, her brother had just presented her with the greatest gift of all. The means of survival.

"Give one third of everything to Len and Madra—they're tendin' to Mama. We'll take out only what we need for a few days at a time and bury the rest in the smokehouse, just in case we get raided." Bree hugged her brother happily, knowing together they would make it.

EPILOGUE

Crosshaven
May 1865

General Sherman's march to Savannah successfully laid
waste to everything that might have helped the South
continue its struggle. Six months after Sherman began—
taking Savannah and then sweeping through North and
South Carolina—General Robert E. Lee of the Confederate
army formally surrendered at the obscure Appomattox Court
House in Virginia. News of the collapse spread slowly
through the South.

The moment Bree heard it, she thanked God there was
an end to the waste and killing and began to pack. Even
without a goal in mind, she would have left Crosshaven
blindly. The past months had been worse than she'd imagined. Catcalls in the night, little straw figures left hanging
in doorways—herself burned in effigy, their cow let loose
innumerable times and then finally stolen altogether.

Kirk walked through the door, his head hung dejectedly.
"I've just been to see Mama. She won't go with us. Says
her family is dead and she's going' to New York to join
her people. Bree, we just can't leave her like that!"

"Well, we sure can't stay," Bree reminded him gently.
"How long do you think it'll take our good neighbors
before the absence of Union soldiers makes them braver
than they've already been? So far, it's just been a series of
annoyin' pranks. I'm not waitin' around for what they'll
think up next." She reached in her pocket and withdrew
the small emerald ring. "Here, give this to Lem. It will
bring a high enough price to see Mama on her way to New

291

York. Don't you find that kind of amusin', Kirk? Mama going north to be with her kin?"

After Kirk had left to complete his final task and say goodbye to Doireann, Bree checked the ties on the wagon and hung a feed sack around the neck of their remaining mule. She patted his neck encouragingly, telling him to eat hearty because they had a long journey ahead of them. Then she climbed to the bench of the wagon and lightly flicked the mule's rump with a switch, urging him forward. Kirk came running from Doireann's cabin and jumped up beside her. Without looking back, Bree left behind the remains of Crosshaven.

Through fertile river valleys and long stretches of short grass, the journey was slow and arduous. Kirk's finger never left the trigger of the rifle he tucked in at his side. He was fiercely protective of Bree, especially in the warm evenings when they camped beside meandering streams, even going so far as not to allow her to fetch the water without escort. And when he had fallen into deep sleep, Bree lay close beside him and had the space and time to think about her future. It had taken months, but she'd finally remembered the meaning of the last line written in Jemson's note. *What God has joined together.* Their own marriage ceremony had been simple and swift but, in the more formal ceremony with Phillip, Bree recalled the words the minister had spoken. *What God has joined together, let no man set asunder.* She hoped fervently it was Jemson's way of telling her that he would be waiting for her in Colorado, waiting to begin again.

As always, when she thought of Jemson, a cold fear gripped and pulled at her heart. There were months unaccounted for—months during which he might have been killed, buried in a common grave where she could never find him.

Still, if she had learned one thing it was to never set her sights too stubbornly on one object. There were too many other avenues open to her. *If* Jemson had made it through

292

the war and *if* he still wanted her—too many ifs. There might not be a place for Bree and her brother in Colorado. Perhaps they would move on farther west. No matter, they would find a place to call home, a place to build a life and memories.

She cashed the first bank draft in southern Illinois. With the money she bought a new mule and more supplies; she outfitted Kirk and herself with the first store-bought clothes they'd had in over two years. Impulsively, she also purchased a saucy straw sunbonnet, more mindful now of the way the sun had of bringing out the freckles buried beneath her skin. And, although it was frivolous, they checked into a hotel and each of them soaked in steaming tubs for an hour before going down to eat a supper prepared by someone else.

They made better time from St. Louis to Kansas City, traveling unmolested most of the way. A few times they had been approached by army stragglers looking for an easy mark, but Kirk's rifle and his ferocious manner had been more than enough to discourage plunder.

By the time they reached Kansas City, eager to join the wagon train that would take them on the final leg of their journey, the supplies Bree had purchased in Illinois had dwindled considerably. She left Kirk to guard the wagon and walked a familiar path to Harald and Sons General Mercantile. Kansas City had changed greatly in the five years since she had first seen it. Whole new streets, hotels, and shops had been erected, but the Mercantile was instantly recognizable. It seemed to Bree that the same dusty black pots were hanging over the doorway. Pausing beside a horse trough, Bree dipped her handkerchief into the cool water and wiped the sweat and dirt from her face. The remaining gold coins from the draft she'd cashed in Illinois jingled loosely in her purse. The other one hundred dollar draft lay buried at the bottom of a trunk in the wagon, saved for the expenses she and Kirk would incur on the wagon train.

Taking a deep breath, Bree entered the store where she

had first met Jemson Tyler and walked up to the counter. She almost burst into laughter. The same clerk stood behind the counter but with a different, more secure attitude. She had an odd feeling that events were repeating themselves much too closely for comfort. A fleeting sign of recognition passed over the clerk's eyes but then he dismissed the notion. His gaze settled on her face and an admiring, almost lecherous smile crossed his face. Then suddenly his glance slid to something behind Bree, something that made him raise his head, neck straining.

Even before she turned, Bree knew what it was that had averted the clerk's eyes. Trembling, she swung around and saw Jemson leaning casually against the far wall. He grinned and started walking slowly toward her.

"Took you longer than I figured, darlin'," he drawled lazily. "I been holed up here for almost six weeks, waiting on you. Lord, you wouldn't believe the temptations this town tries to force on a man. Gambling, women, sinning— it's been a real struggle."

Now he was standing in front of Bree and she was dizzy and faint with the sight of him. Thinking she would have to be the one to seek him out, she never expected to find him waiting here. The shock of it left her speechless.

"You planning on joining the wagon train to Colorado, lady?" His hand reached up and touched Bree's shoulder, sending shivers of delight through her body. Something uncontrollable pulled her forward and she rested her cheek against the rough texture of his shirt, knowing she was making a public spectacle of herself and not caring. A silence fell over the other customers in the store as they boldly watched and listened to the drama that was unfolding.

"Yes, I'm traveling to Colorado." Bree finally found her voice, although it was weak and muffled. "Would you care to join me?"

"Oh, sorry, ma'am. Rules are an unaccompanied male can't travel on the train without the protection of a strong, capable female." Jemson grinned wickedly, happily changing the wording of Dunsfield's rules to suit his own purpose. "Now, if I had a wife . . ."

Bree had regained her composure and was cheerfully going along with the game. "And just how do you suppose you can get a wife, suh? You can't just tack a note on that board over there advertisin' for one, you know."

"I guess you're right. Too bad, though. I've had the Justice of the Peace waiting a long time." Jemson sighed dramatically. "I don't suppose you could suggest some fancy-free female eager to hook up with a man who's got more gold than he knows what to do with? I was thinking about someone on the line of kinda small but soft, you know. Someone willing to face a few hardships along the way to helping me build a home. I don't guess you'd know a woman fits that description?"

"No, I'm terribly sorry." Bree backed away and shook her head in mock sadness. "I myself am a married woman, off to Colorado to chase down a no-account husband." She reached deep into the pocket of her full skirt and brought up a folded piece of parchment. "This is my marriage paper. I plan to run him to ground and force him to honor it." She waved the paper teasingly in front of Jemson's face.

His mouth dropped open, the game forgotten. "You told me you threw that in the fire." Growling, not really angry, his large hands closed over her shoulders.

Bree grinned impishly. After all, hadn't he said he couldn't ever really trust her, could never know if she was telling the truth or not. Well, at least they would would never be bored.

"I lied."

Laughing, Bree threw herself into Jemson's astonished embrace. Her lips parted eagerly against his mouth, and she knew she had come home again.

Chasing Rainbows

A novel of love, enduring courage and soaring triumph!

BY
ESTHER SAGER

They grew up on a lush estate in Virginia—Winna, the selfish blonde beauty, and Libby, the lovable auburn-haired lass. Then, at ten, an accident left Libby to face life against towering odds. Yet Libby is a survivor, and it is she who captures the heart of sophisticated Adam Bainbridge.

Suddenly Winna invades their perfect world—with malice and betrayal in her heart. Libby and Adam must learn that love is, like a rainbow, so very hard to catch and keep.

_____ 05849-1 CHASING RAINBOWS $2.95